Dancing Prince

By Glynn Young

Permission to quote in critical reviews with citation:

Dancing Prince

By Glynn Young

Print ISBN 978-1-949718-06-5

www.dunrobin.us

Dedicated to my brothers and sisters-in-law,
Jim & Terri and Lee & Sandra

We may live in different places,
but our hearts are always New Orleans

Cast of Characters

The Royal Family and Friends

Michael Kent-Hughes – King since the previous royal family and his half-brother Henry Kent were killed during The Violence.

Sarah Kent-Hughes – Queen. She and Michael met at the University of Edinburgh.

Jason Kent-Hughes – Adopted son of Michael and Sarah, married to Jane Barry and father to Paul and Timothy Kent-Hughes.

Jim Kent-Hughes – Adopted son of Michael and Sarah; became Michael's ward in San Francisco after the death of his mother Jenny.

Henry Kent-Hughes – Firstborn child of Michael and Sarah who becomes the Prince of Wales.

Sophie Kent-Hughes and Helen Kent-Hughes – Fraternal twin daughters of Michael and Sarah.

Thomas Kent-Hughes – The youngest child of Michael and Sarah.

Iris McLaren – With Ian McLaren, guardians for Michael from age 6.

David Hughes – Sarah's twin brother and a professor of history at the University of St. Andrews.

Betsy Hughes – David's wife.

Gavin and Eleanor Hughes – The children of David and Betsy.

Tommy McFarland – Michael's best friend since childhood.

Ellen McFarland – Tommy's wife and mother of Emily McFarland.

The Palace Staff

Brent Epworth – Master of the House.

Ryan Mitchell – Head of Palace security.

Paula Abbott – Assistant head of Palace security.

Josh Gittings – Chief of Staff.

Jay Lanham – Head of Palace communications.

Simon Fredericks – Palace security officer.

Noah Bennington – Palace security officer.

Trevor Barry – Palace legal counsel, father of Jane Kent-Hughes.

Davey Malone – Palace chef.

Mrs. Richards – The Royal Family's housekeeper.

International Christian School

Mary Penniman – Widow whose husband was killed in the Mideast War.

Mark Penniman – Mary's son and friend of Thomas McLaren.

Amanda Gill – Mary's mother.

William and Ciara Gill – Mary's brother and sister-in-law, the owners of the guest house at Fort William, Scotland.

Staff and Students working on the Broughby Project

Dr. Farley MacNeill – University of St. Andrews.

Dr. Evan Elliott – University of Cumbria.

Angus McLin – Boyhood friend of Thomas Kent-Hughes.

Erica Larsson – Student at Cambridge University, daughter of Jenner and Billie Larrson.

Julia Heaton – Student at Newcastle University.

Alan Bishop – Student at University of Rochester.

Norah Bixby – Cook.

Elijah McCrae – Broughby doctor.

Others

Billie Larsson – Erica's mother.

Jenner Larsson – Erica's father.

Nan – Erica's grandmother.

Sarah

She must have left the door ajar.

She was always careful to close the door to her studio. Well away from the rest of the family rooms, a closed studio door translated into "Do not disturb; Mom is painting." She valued and needed her privacy to paint in uninterrupted silence. Michael, the children, and the personal staff all knew not to disturb her.

At some point, Sarah sensed a presence. She looked away from the canvas in front of her and at first saw only the room. She turned again; 4-year-old Thomas was sitting silently behind her, watching. His eyebrows went up in mild alarm when he saw she'd seen him.

"And what are you doing here, my son?"

Thomas, or Tommy as he was known inside the family, was their youngest. His brother Hank was 10 and twins Sophie and Helen were 8. Of all her children, it was Tommy to whom she felt closest. At six months, she'd nearly miscarried; the doctors required bed rest for the next 10 weeks, disrupting the family's and the palace's daily schedule of activities. He'd been born three weeks early and was the smallest of her babies, including the twins individually, at just under five pounds. He spent two days in newborn ICU, under lamps for jaundice and wired with monitors. The nurses had allowed her access, but not Mike; he was just getting over a cold.

Perhaps it was those weeks in bed that brought the closeness. She couldn't paint or do anything else involving physical activity. The children had been in school each day, and Michael had been growing increasingly occupied with the ongoing crisis with Government. Three national elections and governments in less than a year had brought

1

Parliament perilously close to collapse. And then a trade bill destroyed the then-governing coalition and brought the fourth government down.

Michael had come to her while she was on bed rest and told her that it was highly likely that Parliament would declare a government emergency and name him emergency executive, vesting all power in the person of the king for however long Michael deemed it necessary. British parliamentary democracy had exhausted itself, with no political will left to continue. The emergency executive plan had worked for London when its government had collapsed, the reasoning went, so why not for the country at large? It would likely last for no more than six months.

Four years had passed. Michael was still emergency executive.

When he first told her, she'd known that Michael, and her and the family by extension, were caught. Refuse Parliament's action, and government could cease to exist. The London Stock Exchange was in freefall, and the value of the currency was plummeting. The only thing that had stopped a run on the banks had been a statement by Michael expressing confidence in Britain's banking system to weather the crisis. Michael had initially objected to making the statement; for the monarch to directly interfere in political or economic issues was simply not done. But the prime minister said only Michael had the public trust to stop the run on the banks.

She knew what the emergency would mean for the family. She knew she'd have to hold the family together for however long the emergency lasted.

What she hadn't anticipated was the impact on her marriage.

While on bedrest, she'd read, and for some unknown reason, she'd started reading aloud. Michael had brought her books she asked for and some she didn't. Children's books. The Pooh stories. Beatrix Potter. And then Chaucer. The miller and the reeve in *Canterbury Tales* caused her to laugh so hard that the baby within her jumped, seeming to laugh with her. And she read Tolkien's *The Hobbit* and *The Ring Trilogy* aloud, wondering what the baby might think. She'd been in the middle of *The Two Towers* when Parliament declared the emergency, named Michael as executive, and dissolved itself.

By the time she went into labor, Michael was fully caught up in being Government. He missed Tommy's birth, having to deal with a Mideast crisis that nearly expanded the ongoing regional war into something larger. There was always a good reason now for Michael to miss something involving the family, even as she soon tired of hearing what that good reason was.

Perhaps it was Tommy's sensitivity to her painting that brought the closeness. Even at 18 months, she'd find him in her studio, staring at her canvases. He'd look at a painting, and then at her. And smile.

Looking directly at her, Tommy clenched his little fists. "I'm just watching. I didn't make a sound."

"This is my private time."

He nodded. "I'm sorry, Mummy, but the door was open."

Sarah smiled. Tommy sounded the most British of her four children, and the only one who called her by the traditional British "Mummy." To complete the oddity, he looked the most American. His brother Hank, who would one day become the Prince of Wales, sounded the most American, like his American mother and his two older adopted brothers, with a thin British overlay. The twins had some kind of cross between American and British accents but sounded more British. Tommy, the baby, sounded as British as anyone in the kingdom. Upper-class British. It was all distinctly odd.

Then she noticed the sheets of paper at his feet. "What's this?"

"I was drawing, too."

It was rough but also more than a child's crude drawing. Far more. She could see Tommy had drawn a surprisingly good likeness of her sitting at the easel.

"Tommy, you did this yourself?"

The boy nodded.

"Well, it's quite good. May I keep it?"

He nodded again, staring at her with those beautiful sky-blue eyes of his father. His eyes were his father's; his fair complexion and blond hair came from her side of the family. He looked so much like her twin brother David Hughes that the boy could easily be mistaken for David's child. Tommy looked more like David than his own son Gavin did.

A month before, David, his wife Betsy, and their two children had left the palace. David had moved the family to London from Edinburgh for him to complete research at the London Library and the British Library for what promised to be a paradigm-shattering work in Scottish history. He'd taken an extended sabbatical from St. Andrews University, and their stay in London lasted almost two years. Sarah and Michael had insisted the Hughes family stay at the palace, within walking distance of the London Library in Piccadilly and a short 15-minute tube ride to the British Library near the King's Cross and St.

Pancras train stations. Michael had also authorized David to have full access to the royal family archives at Windsor Castle. Gavin and Eleanor had enrolled at International Christian School in Notting Hill, along with their royal cousins.

Sarah also had an ulterior motive. With Michael sucked into Government and usually absent from the palace, David had assumed a large role in the lives of her own children. Her brother was a rock for all of them; it had been David who had held the family together when their grandmother Helen Hughes had died in California from what she'd insisted was nothing more than a bad cold but turned out to be pneumonia. Six months later, their father Seth Hughes had a fatal heart attack while playing golf in Beverly Hills. David had been the one to fly early to California both times to arrange the funerals and burials.

Both estates had been divided equally between Sarah, David, and their older brother Scott, a surgeon in San Francisco. Because of the vast wealth of the royal family, Sarah had declined her share, allowing the inheritances to be split between Scott and David.

Tommy adored his uncle. Sarah knew that, with Michael's extended absences, David had become Tommy's surrogate father.

David had played a critical role with Tommy when Michael's legal guardian, Ian McLaren, had died from a stroke just three months before. It had been Tommy's turn to spend a week with Ian and his wife Iris at McLarens outside Edinburgh, where Ian had a longstanding equine veterinary practice. Coincidentally, David had been at St. Andrews for a faculty conference and to work out final plans for his return to teaching; he and Tommy had traveled to Edinburgh together.

At 74, Ian was mostly retired, the practice having been taken over by Roger Pitts, Michael's Olympic cycling colleague who'd been ostracized at the Olympics and had come, at Michael's suggestion, to live with the McLarens as Ian's vet assistant. Roger had studied veterinary medicine and become Ian's junior partner, gradually taking over a larger and larger share of the practice. Roger and his wife and children had a farmstead and stables not far from McLarens, and Ian now only looked after an occasional racehorse with a leg aggravation or a prize mare preparing to foal.

Tommy had been with Ian in the barn. Ian was describing the pregnant mare when he looked straight at the boy, started to call his name, and then sank to his knees, collapsing against the side of the stall. Tommy had run screaming for Iris. She and Tommy accompanied Ian in the ambulance to the hospital, and it was there that David found them. He took immediate charge of the boy. Michael and Sarah were in flight to Edinburgh with Jason and Jane, Hank, and the twins when they received word that Ian had died. David, Iris, and Tommy had been in the room with him, and Ian's last act was to squeeze Tommy's hand, right after whispering to his wife. Only a few weeks later did Tommy find the studio door ajar and go inside to watch Sarah paint.

Tommy's shy smile told Sarah how pleased he was that she wanted to keep the drawing. Each of their children were so different, she thought. Hank, or Henry, the oldest and the heir to the throne, was outgoing, funny, engaging, and bright, almost a stereotype of what people thought a Prince of Wales should be. His sense of humor masked an extraordinarily analytical and perceptive mind. He looked like a younger replica of his father, with the exception of Michael's black hair; Hank's was more a dark brown.

Sophie, the oldest of the twins by two minutes, was studious, intelligent, friendly, and demonstrating a wisdom surprising for her years. She, too, resembled her father, including his black hair. Helen, who looked like her mother, was the family handful, privately referred to by Michael and Sarah as the Kent-Hughes drama queen.

And then Tommy, shy and, she knew, incredibly intelligent. He'd begun to speak and read much earlier than the other children. Sarah knew he grasped far more than most four-year-olds would, yet he rarely let on. He was a quiet, private child, with none of the boisterousness of his brother or his sisters. He kept his own counsel well.

All four of the children had Michael's eye color, apparently a family genetic trait. Michael's half-brother Henry and the previous royal family, killed during The Violence of 10 years before, all had the trademark sky-blue or ice-blue eyes. More than 2,000 people had died in an attempt by radical Muslim groups to bring jihad to Great Britain. The Kent-Hughes family had been living in San Francisco, and they'd learned that the hand of the jihadists reached even to California, with Michael shot and nearly dying and Sarah herself, very pregnant with Hank, the target of a murder attempt. A bodyguard had stepped into the path of the bullet meant for her, while Jason and Jim, their two adopted sons, took down and disarmed the assailant, a young German woman.

Jason was now 26, seven years younger than Sarah herself. He was the only member of the family other than Sarah with a serious interest in art. After military service and marriage to Jane Barry, the daughter of Michael's chief legal counselor and close friend Trevor Barry, Jason had attended the Slade School of Art. He was now an assistant curator at the Tate Modern. Their San Francisco street child had metamorphized into a serious artist with a gift for curation and art administration. And Trevor Barry likely saw more of Michael now than Sarah did; after his leadership in handling the reformation of the Church of England and bringing the church out of a broad and devastating child abuse scandal, Trevor had been pulled into government service when Michael had become czar.

She didn't mean to think that. "Czar" was the wrong word, if the accurate one. Sarah reminded herself not to allow the word out of her mouth, publicly or privately.

Sarah sat next to Tommy on the small sofa in the studio. "Let's take a close look at your drawing, shall we?" She leaned over and kissed his head. And she knew of all the reasons she felt close to this child, the most important was that he was the most like his father, the Michael she had fallen in love with and married. And the Michael who had changed, becoming more remote, more distant, his attention always away from her and the children.

The close look at her son's drawing soon developed into a series of lessons. On the mornings she painted, Tommy followed her into the studio, and she'd give him simple assignments while she painted. The boy would sit and draw. Sometimes he followed her instructions exactly, and sometimes he went off on his own in a different and, she had to admit, more interesting direction. Sarah began to see that her youngest child had the soul of an artist. She also knew that Tommy's presence was partially filling the emptiness of Michael's absence.

The lessons went on for several months, an unspoken confidence shared between mother and son, until the day Michael came home unexpectedly early.

Sarah's concern about saying the word "czar" aloud recognized how Michael reacted whenever anyone used the word. He wouldn't accept it. He was the king, and temporarily he was the emergency executive. He insisted he was not a czar; anyone using that expression drew a sharp rebuke.

And yet Britain's Parliament hadn't met in more than four years. After years of political chaos, the country seemed to have lost interest in elections and parliamentary government. Even Michael's ongoing coaxing in speeches, articles, and meetings for the country to renew its commitment to parliamentary democracy was received politely but largely ignored. The absolute rule of Britain by Michael I had brought stability and governmental effectiveness rarely, if ever, seen in Britain's history. No one wanted to return to the chaos and breakdown of parliamentary government.

"What the country has," Michael told his ministers, "is a benevolent dictatorship with the lingering exhaust fumes of democracy. No citizen rights have been lost or changed. And they think this is how it will always be, when we all know how quickly benevolence can turn to evil and corruption. They should read the histories in the Old Testament."

Michael had cut short a budget meeting in Whitehall and returned to the palace. He was tired, feeling more and more tired as each day passed. Good people worked for him, with several doing double duty for palace and government. But the wear and tear of being an absolute ruler was affecting Michael's health and, he knew, his marriage. He often slept in a bedroom maintained in one of the ministry buildings, particularly when a crisis was afoot. And a crisis always seemed afoot. Days might pass between the times he saw Sarah and the children. His rich, wavy black hair was already showing streaks of gray, and he was only 35.

The family compound at Buckingham Palace had, from the beginning, been called "the loft." It was the old palace nursery plus some additional rooms, with walls knocked down and reconfigured, a considerably larger version of the loft condominium they'd occupied in San Francisco.

When Michael arrived, he expected to find Sarah's studio door closed and Tommy under the watchful eye of the housekeeper, Mrs. Richards. Instead, the loft seemed empty and neither Tommy nor Mrs. Richards were in sight. The boy's room was empty. Wondering if Sarah and Tommy might've gone somewhere, he walked toward Sarah's studio and noticed the door slightly open. He could hear voices inside.

"What's this? Someone's in the studio while Mummy's painting?"

"You're home early. Did something happen?"

Michael shook his head. "Something's always happening, but nothing out of the ordinary. I just decided I wanted to come home." He pointed at Tommy. "I thought no one was allowed in here while you're working."

Sarah smiled, not sure why the statement irritated her. "He's just drawing."

Michael was feeling playful, but it was playfulness with a slight edge. "I thought there was only one official rule of the loft: no one's allowed in the studio when you're painting."

"Michael, he's only four." She realized she'd deflected his statement.

"You've never allowed anyone in here while you paint. How long has Tommy had a special dispensation? Where's Mrs. Richards?"

Sarah wasn't sure if Michael was playing or not. She sensed a rise in the temperature of his voice. Something must've happened in Whitehall to put him in an irritable mood.

"What does it matter? I give him some assignments, Tommy works quietly on his own, and he doesn't bother me in the least. It's actually been rather fun."

"Can I see your work in progress?" Michael pointed toward her canvas.

"No! It's not ready to be seen."

Michael didn't respond. He looked at Tommy, who was staring at his father. The boy was sitting where he had a clear view of Sarah's canvas.

She followed Michael's gaze to Tommy. "He understands what I'm doing. Michael, don't spoil this."

Michael turned red in the face. He opened his mouth to respond but stopped. He turned and walked out.

Sarah quickly followed him. "We never see you anymore. I never see you anymore. You show up unexpectedly and begin an inquisition. This isn't fair to me or to Tommy. You don't know what we've been doing or even why. You're never here, Michael. Hank and the twins never see you, either."

"You know what I'm doing."

"Of course, I know. I have to read the newspapers to find out. But you come in here and start acting like a jealous boyfriend over a four-year-old drawing pictures. Other than Jason, Tommy's the only one in the family who understands my work."

"And I don't?" He was nearly shouting. "I was there almost at the beginning, when you drew my calf for your assignment at school. I was at the San Francisco exhibition. I'm the one who told Tommy McFarland to include a studio when he redesigned this space." McFarland had been their college friend and architect. "And now you're telling me a four-year-old understands your work better than I do?"

From there, the argument became so heated that neither Sarah nor Michael realized they had an audience. Tommy had followed them into the living area.

Tommy interrupted them, his voice breaking into sobs. "Please don't fight. Please."

Tensions had remained high until Sarah and Michael talked through the argument late that night. Michael apologized for his words, Sarah for her defensiveness.

After Michael had left for Whitehall the next morning, she went to find Tommy for what they called "our session" and discovered him lying on the floor of his room, drawing.

"Are you ready?" She hoped he could hear the anticipation and cheerfulness in her voice.

Tommy shook his head.

"What's wrong?"

"Dad doesn't like it. It makes him cross."

She sat next to him. "Oh, Tommy, it's okay. Dad was upset with something that had happened at Government and we didn't talk to each other very nicely. But it's fine. And it's not your fault. Dad and I talked through the whole thing last night and it's fine. We're fine."

He shook his head again. "I made him angry. I can't sit with you anymore."

The resolute look on his face told Sarah that even if she convinced him to sit in the studio as before, it would never be the same. They'd lost something.

What none of them understood was how the incident in the studio would reverberate for the next 20 years.

A few weeks later, Michael asked Sarah to resume as many of her public duties as she could.

"We need to have a royal family presence," he said. "I can't do it myself and Government as well. Our public family presence has pretty much disappeared, except for what Jason and Jane can do, and they have their hands full with Jason's job and the children. This emergency won't last forever, and we need to move toward resuming our public appearances. I need you to do this, Sarah."

At first, she didn't respond. She wanted to push back at his insistent tone. "Our agreement, Mike, when you became emergency

13

executive, was that I'd manage the family and the palace and continue doing military visits." Until Michael successfully negotiated a ceasefire in the Mideast, Sarah had been a patron of military hospitals all over Britain, visiting soldiers recovering from wounds and attending the funerals of soldiers who were killed in combat or died from their injuries later. She'd had considerable other public duties, most of which had been set aside when Michael became executive so she could focus on the family. But she still visited military hospitals.

"I know, my love, but I need help. The council believes the country is moving back toward parliamentary democracy, perhaps even within just a few months. We're considering a call for elections and a revival of Parliament. Tommy will be starting at ICS in the fall and you won't have as many responsibilities here."

What Sarah really wanted to do was paint. She wanted to spend six months in Florence, absorbing the art they had seen briefly years before when she'd been pregnant with Hank. She wanted to wander ruins in Greece and travel to the Holy Land. And then she looked at her husband's graying hair and the circles under his eyes.

"You really think the country wants Parliament back?"

"I do. I think we're almost there. I've called the hereditary peers back to the House of Lords, to begin meeting as an advisory group and undertake various studies and steps to get us back to having a Parliament. I'm hopeful that soon we can return to being king and queen."

She heard the plea in his voice and saw the tiredness in his eyes. She knew they'd grown apart, but she didn't know quite how they might regain their former closeness. Even when Michael was with the family, he was tired and often cranky. And he was never out of reach from his cabinet. He'd quelled a national emergency, become Government, and run it well. And their marriage was suffocating.

She also knew that resuming public duties on the scale Michael wanted would mean the end of most if not all of her time for painting.

"All right. I'll start easing back in. But I won't have a hectic schedule filled from dawn to night. I'll do what's needed from 9 to 3, but when the children come home from school, I'll be home."

Michael beamed. "Thank you. This will work out. In a few months, this will all be over."

What neither Michael nor Sarah then knew was that it would be almost two years, and it would take an event that changed their family forever.

Michael

Two years later

Michael had surprised his cabinet at their Saturday meeting when he said he and Sarah would be spending two weeks in Italy. And he wouldn't be reachable by phone.

"If anything needs attention," he said, "Josh Gittings and Trevor Barry are authorized to make the decision. That includes any proposal to remove me as executive and let me return to the palace permanently."

They'd laughed, but they all knew the words had a serious undertone. Josh Gittings had originally been Michael's chief of staff at Buckingham Palace. Trevor Barry had been his legal advisor and the overseer of the reformation of the Church of England. Josh, Trevor, and Michael's communications director, Jay Lanham, all sat in Michael's cabinet as full-fledged voting members, along with some 12 heads of ministries.

"We haven't had a vacation longer than a three- or four-day weekend in almost six years," he said. "Sarah's been extraordinarily tired with all the royal duties and needs a rest. And I keep hoping someone will have a plan to get the British people back into the voting booth to elect a new Parliament. Perhaps we should start doing our jobs really, really badly."

A second, more serious reason for the holiday was Michael and Sarah's marriage. It was in danger of falling apart. Sarah had been doing her six hours of public duty, but she absolutely refused to do anything in the evenings, including state dinners. People had noticed.

Small notices had appeared in newspaper and online gossip columns. Hank and the twins had stopped even mentioning school activities to Michael; Sarah shouldered the responsibility alone.

Something had to change.

He and Sarah had rented a villa outside Florence. They'd spend time resting and visiting art treasures. The itinerary included two days near Assisi with the family of Michael's deceased mother. They could leave palace, Government, and family responsibilities behind. Jason and Jane were moving temporarily into the palace to chaperone the family, and they'd be bringing their two young sons, Paul Trevor and Timothy Michael, with them.

From the meeting in Whitehall, Michael was driven back to the palace. He smiled the whole way. Another week, and they'd be sitting on a terrace, watching the Tuscan sunset as they sipped Chianti. Things would get better. He could barely wait.

As the car pulled into the portico entrance of the interior courtyard, Michael was met by Ryan Mitchell, chief of security for the palace, and Brent Epworth, the palace's Master of the House.

Michael smiled. "A welcoming committee! I trust everything is well here at the palace?"

For a moment, neither man answered. Then Epworth spoke. "Yes, sir, everything is fine with operations. Her Majesty asked if you might join her in the woods behind the garden. She's painting, and she said she needed you for some final touches on the work."

Michael laughed. "There has to be a better subject than me. She's painted me enough times as it is. But I will follow Her Majesty's command." He walked through the reception area and toward the rear of the building.

Mitchell shook his head. "I'm going to lose it right here. I'm right on the verge of breaking down. Thank you for stepping into the breach. I could've never managed it on my own."

Tears began to spill from Epworth's eyes. "He doesn't know what he's walking into. He thinks they're going to Italy."

Whistling, Michael walked from the terrace, moving along the white gravel path that led toward the exit on Grosvenor Place but from which side paths led into the heavily treed area of the palace around the lake. At first, he couldn't see Sarah, but then he spotted the canvas and easel as he rounded his way through the trees.

She was so intent on the canvas in front of her that she didn't see him, although Tom Matson, her security guard seated on a portable chair off to the side, saw the king and stood. Michael put his finger to his lips, and then stood watching his wife work at the canvas.

Even with the strain of the past few years, he knew he loved her deeply and profoundly. From the moment he'd seen her in a university class on medieval church art, he'd known she was the woman God had created for him and him for her. Despite the trials in their relationship, he'd never wavered in his belief that they'd marry.

And here they were, 15 years and two adopted and four natural children later, still as deeply in love with each other as they'd been as newlyweds. Or so he told himself. They'd survived their attempted murders during The Violence; they'd faced the challenges of occupying the British throne and all that ensued. And they still loved each other, despite the estrangement. He hoped.

Sarah had noticed Matson's movement. "So, is my beautiful husband standing there watching me?"

Michael laughed and walked to her. "It is your humble servant, indeed, your majesty."

"I need you to sit, Mike, so I can get the eye color exactly right." Sarah was the only person he ever allowed to use the nickname.

He dutifully sat in the chair in front of her. "Can I talk, or do I need to be quiet?"

She surprised him. "I need to talk, Mike." She usually never spoke while she was drawing or painting. "And I need you to listen and not speak until I'm finished. And I'm almost done." She was working the canvas now. "I need to hold the moment, Mike, for as long as I possibly can. Because it's my one connection to before."

Michael frowned. "Sarah?"

"I need you to listen, Mike," she said, cutting him off.

Officer Matson knew what was coming, and he quietly stepped away from the royal couple.

For several minutes, Sarah said nothing as she painted. Michael held himself perfectly still, but he could feel turmoil within. *Something's off, badly off. Is it one of the children? Does she not want to go to Italy after all? Or is it just that painting causing her problems? Is she giving up on the marriage?*

"Mike, I've gotten the results of my physical. And I've seen several specialists. The short of it is, I'm sick. The tiredness, the lack of energy, the unexplained bruising and pain are all symptoms. I'm sick."

"How sick, Sarah?"

"Hold the moment, Mike. Please don't speak. I can barely say this. The doctors have confirmed it twice over. I haven't said anything because I wanted to be certain. What I have is called acute myeloid leukemia. It's sometimes treatable with chemotherapy and radiation, but mine has come on too fast and it's too far advanced. Even if it wasn't, and even if they could get it into remission, it comes back 70 percent of the time. I was terrified that I might've passed it to the children, but the doctors all say that's highly unlikely. But the children will need to have yearly blood tests as a precaution."

Michael felt her words with the force of a stunning blow. He was too shocked to respond. He was trying to get his head around the words. *Leukemia. Too fast. Too far advanced. Blood tests.*

From 30 feet away, Matson couldn't hear the conversation, only the murmuring of the queen's voice, but he could both see in the way the king was sitting that he'd just been told what he and his boss Ryan Mitchell already knew. Matson had accompanied Sarah to the doctor's offices, and he knew what the word oncology meant. Sarah had asked both Matson and Mitchell to say nothing until she had confirmation and could tell the king.

"The prognosis is not good." She stopped painting and laid her brush aside. "In fact, it's pretty grim. I might have as long as two months, more likely four to six weeks, and possibly less. They wanted me in the hospital yesterday, but I wanted one last weekend with you and the children. But I'm to be admitted tomorrow night." She gave a small smile. "I didn't know how to tell you. And I wanted more than anything to go to Italy. I know this seems overly dramatic, but I received the confirmation this morning and I had to finish this painting. And I need your help in telling the children."

Michael reached towards her. Sarah burst into tears.

Their arms around each other's waist, Michael and Sarah walked inside, followed by Matson holding the queen's easel and canvas, until they reached the elevator to take them to the loft. No one spoke. Michael hadn't even looked to see what she'd been painting.

In the elevator, Sarah clung to her husband. "I don't know how to tell the children. I don't know how to explain this, Mike, without getting hysterical. I want to put on a brave front, and all I am is terrified. And I'm angry. I'm angry at God and you and life and everything."

"We'll tell them together. I'll call Jason and Jane first and have them come over. I'll phone Jim in Basra later. I wish I could be with him when I tell him, but Basra is a bit far for that." Their adopted son Jim, 21, was stationed with his Royal Air Force unit in Iraq and was scheduled to return home permanently in January.

The elevator door opened, and they walked down the south wing toward the loft. One end of the loft faced the gardens in the rear of the palace.

Inside, they first saw 6-year-old Tommy, standing quietly as if waiting for them. "I saw from the window you were coming," he said. The only window he could've seen them from was the one in Sarah's studio. Michael felt a twinge of anger at the boy's words. Sarah, painting, and the studio were still unsafe topics between him and his youngest son.

Officer Matson carried the painting and easel to the studio and then left.

"I'm going to make myself presentable." Sarah walked toward their bedroom.

Tommy looked at his father. "I know, Dad."

Michael watched her walk away, and then turned to Tommy. "Son, what do you know? You have a look on your face that says you know more than I think you do."

"Mummy's sick. I heard her on the phone. She has leukemia. I didn't know what it was, so I googled it. It's cancer."

The boy's words hit Michael like a hammer blow. "Have you told anyone?"

Tommy shook his head. "You're going to make her better. I know you will."

"Tommy, there are things I can't do. I can't cure disease."

"But you will. I know it."

Sarah returned. "Hey, sir, do you know where your sisters and brother are?"

Tommy turned toward his mother. "Hank's in his room, and I think Helen and Sophie are downstairs in the library." He paused. "I know, Mummy, I heard you on the phone. But it will be OK." He looked at his father.

Sarah looked at Michael, a slightly panicked expression on her face.

Michael took charge. "Well, stay put for now. We're going to have a family confab in a bit."

He pulled his mobile from his suit pocket and called Jason, who answered on the first ring. "Dad! Jane and I were just talking about you."

"Jas, I know this is short notice, but I need you and Jane to come to the palace."

"Is something wrong? We were just getting ready to take the boys to the zoo."

Michael hesitated. "Yes, something's wrong. I need to have you here, Jason, if you can. We have to have a family discussion."

"Dad, what's the problem?"

Michael couldn't speak, as if saying it would make it real.

"Dad?"

"I'm sorry, Jas. I, uh, I'm struggling for words here." He paused. "Sarah's sick, and I need you here."

Jason wanted to ask his father at least a dozen questions, but he knew Michael was struggling with something, and from the sound of it, it was something awful.

"OK, Dad, we'll be right there. Give us 15 minutes. I have to round up Paul and Tim."

Michael took a deep breath. "Thank you, Jas. Thank you."

Thirty minutes later, the family was seated into the living area, Hank from his room and the girls from the library. In two months, Hank would turn 13, sharing his birthday with the start of The Violence.

Sophie and Helen were 10, twins born a little less than two years after Hank. Sarah's brother David and his wife Betsy's daughter, Eleanor, was the same age as Helen and Sophie. Their son Gavin was a year older than Hank.

The two grandsons, Paul Trevor and Timothy Michael, were 4 and 2, respectively. Jane set them up with trucks and coloring books adjacent to the seating area in the living room.

Michael, seated on the arm of the overstuffed chair next to Sarah, held her hand. "I'm sorry we had to do this all of a sudden, but we've had a bit of unsettling news. Your mom will need to go into the hospital for tests and treatments, and she'll be going in tomorrow night."

Helen looked from Michael to Sarah. "What's wrong?"

Michael felt Sarah tighten her grip on his hand. "She's had some tests done, because she'd been feeling tired and run down, and she had a bruise or two for no obvious reason. It turns out that she has a form of leukemia, which is a cancer of the blood."

He saw Jason and Jane both pale as they looked at Sarah. She gave them a small smile. Hank and his sisters looked concerned but didn't appear to understand the import of what Michael was saying.

Hank spoke next. "So, when do you come home, Mom?"

Sarah looked at her firstborn and shook her head.

Michael answered. "We don't know, son. It could be a long time."

"Dad will fix it." Tommy sounded completely sure. "He'll make her better."

"Tommy, that is my greatest prayer right now, but it's something that the doctors and God will have to attend to."

Jason chose his words carefully. "How long do the doctors think she'll be there?"

"Probably four to eight weeks," Michael said. "Maybe longer, maybe less."

Jason looked at his father and understood exactly what Michael was saying. Michael saw him clench his fists.

Jane looked at Sarah. "This may be a bad time to bring this up, but Jason and I have been talking about having a general overhaul done of our house, wallpaper and painting and some of the rooms that need fixing up. And it's going to be a mess for a while, at least the next two or three months. We were going to be here for when you went to Italy anyway. And we were wondering if we could stay here during the process, if it's not too much of a bother. In fact, we could move in tomorrow night." Jason, at first surprised, looked at his parents and nodded.

Michael and Sarah both knew their daughter-in-law was offering to care for the family. With tears in his eyes, Michael smiled. "That's a grand idea, Jane. We've plenty of room, and I think we're going to need you both a lot. And I love being around those two rascals over there."

As if on cue, the two rascals, bored with the coloring books and trucks, walked into the seating area, Timothy following his brother. Paul walked to Sarah and took her hand. "I'll take care of you, Gran."

Sarah pulled Paul to her and held him tightly.

An hour later, Michael sent a text to Jim's mobile in Basra. He knew he'd have to wait before Jim could call him back.

At 9 p.m., with the children watching television with Sarah, Michael went to the loft's small study and called Josh Gittings, Jay Lanham, and Trevor Barry. "I need to let you know we've had a bit of a curve thrown at us that we have to deal with. Sarah is sick and will be going into hospital tomorrow night."

"Michael, what's wrong?" said Josh.

"She has leukemia. It was confirmed in a second opinion. The prognosis is not good. She'll be in the hospital anywhere from four to eight weeks," and here he hesitated, "and then we'll have to see."

The three men on the phone were too stunned to reply immediately.

"I know this is something of a shock. We've told the children, although I'm still waiting on a call back from Jim. I'm going to need your help with telling the staff as well as what public things might be required. And while this is short notice, do you think you might meet me at the palace tomorrow morning about 9, so we can begin to see what needs to be done?"

"Absolutely, sir," said Jay. "It's no problem."

"We'll be there, Michael," said Trevor.

"And Josh, I'll likely take some kind of leave of absence from Government. I have to focus on Sarah and the family. We'll talk tomorrow. Trevor, can you check the emergency declaration law and see what options I might have?"

Jason and Jane had stayed through dinner, Jane calling the palace kitchen for pizza and salad. Of all the children, Tommy had been the quietest throughout the meal. He'd kept looking at his mother and then at Michael. Hank, usually irrepressible, began to follow his younger brother's lead.

After Jason and Jane left, Michael sat with Hank on the side of his bed in his room. Michael smiled to himself to see how the football posters and biking posters were vying for dominance on the walls.

"I need to make sure you know how serious this is with your mother, and to see if you had any questions I might answer."

Hank nodded. "I think I know, Dad. Tommy knows, too. He wasn't surprised. He always knows everything before the rest of us, or maybe he just understands it better. It's like he's older than the rest of us. I think what you're saying is that she's not going to come home." The boy looked down, then up at his father. "I think you're saying she, she won't come home." He bit his lip. Michael put his arms around his son.

"That's what I'm saying, Hank, but I always have to hope. Without hope, there's only despair. We have to keep hoping and praying."

Hank started to cry. "Can we pray now, Dad?"
Father and son both knelt on the floor and began to pray.

Michael talked with the twins, both of whom were subdued. And then he went to look for Tommy, who wasn't in his room. Where he found his youngest was in Sarah's studio. The boy was awake, curled up on the small sofa.

"This is a favorite place?"

Tommy nodded.

"I'm sorry you found out the way you did. It must have been hard to hear."

Tommy nodded again. "When I heard Mummy talking with the doctor, I looked it up. There are different kinds of leukemia. She has a bad one."

"Tommy, I said it earlier, but I need you to understand that I can't heal a disease, no matter how much I want to. I don't have that power or ability."

"But you and God won't let her die, will you? I know you won't."

"Tommy, I can't say that. I don't know what God has planned. If I did, there wouldn't be much need for faith, would there? We'd just know. And God may choose to heal your mother, or he may have something else in mind. I don't know. And I'll tell you I'm scared. I want to be brave for your mother and you and your brothers and sisters, and I'm scared."

"You can't be scared, Dad. You have to heal her. God can do it. I know He can. You talk all the time about how much He loves us."

"But loving us, Tommy, doesn't mean He answers every prayer the way we want Him to."

"I know He'll do it. He has to. It's Mummy."

Michael and Sarah got ready for bed. Sarah spent time reading her Bible, as Michael sat next to her, watching. When she put the book on her night table, he spoke.

"I feel helpless. I want to do anything and everything, but I don't know what to do. I don't know how to help our children understand. I don't know how to help myself understand."

She snuggled against him, and he put his arm around her.

"There's one thing you can do, Mike."

"Yes?"

"You can hold me, Mike. Just hold me like you used to."

Sarah waited until she was certain Michael was asleep. She quietly got up, put on her robe, and left their bedroom. Making her way to Tommy's room, she entered to find him asleep, his night light on.

"Tommy? It's Mummy. I need you to wake up."

Rubbing his eyes, the boy sat up. "Mummy?"

"I need you to help me," she said, whispering. "Can you stay awake and come with me for a few minutes?"

He nodded.

"We must be very quiet, so we don't wake anyone up." She took him by the hand, and they walked out of the room.

She led him to the studio. Once inside, she turned on the light, and found the painting left by Officer Matson. She turned it around so Tommy could see it.

"Do you like it?"

He smiled. "Yes, Mummy. It's beautiful."

"Tommy, it's my gift to you. But I need you to do something with it. We're going to wrap it, and then you need to help me find a good place to store it. It's yours, but we don't want anyone to see it for a time, perhaps a few weeks or months. Can you remember that, and remember where we put it?"

"Yes, Mummy. We could put it with the old toys downstairs, behind the boxes. No one goes there except to put something away."

"That's perfect, Tommy."

Sarah checked to see that the painting was completely dry. She then sat at the studio's small desk and wrote on a sheet of paper, dated and signed it, and then slipped it in an envelope with Tommy's full name on it. Taping it to the back, she wrapped the painting in brown paper.

"I think I need your help to carry the canvas." They each took a side and maneuvered the painting from the studio to the hallway outside the loft. Reaching the elevator, they descended to the basement floor and soon had the painting secured behind boxes in the toy storeroom.

"That was a brilliant suggestion to hide it here, Tommy. Now we both need to get back to bed. And remember, we need to wait a few months before we tell anyone, and then only if someone specifically asks. Can you remember that?"

He nodded. "Why do you want to hide it, Mummy?"

She smiled. "It's about the future, Tommy. It's about your future, in fact, but also everyone else's. And sometimes people aren't ready to consider the future." She paused. "And every time you see it, I want you to remember the good times we had painting together."

"Will it make Dad angry?"

She caught her breath. Sometimes she found Tommy's insight and understanding to be beyond shocking.

"It might, but eventually it won't. Which is why we're putting it out of sight for a time. Now, let's get back to bed."

Back upstairs, as she tucked him under the covers, she squeezed his hand. "This is for you, Tommy. You can go in there whenever you like, and you can remember how much fun we had."

Into his hand she pressed her key to the studio.

"Won't you need it, Mummy?"

She stroked his forehead. "If I do, I'll come ask you, okay?"

He smiled and nodded. "Thank you."

The next morning, Michael was in his office when Jay, Josh, and Trevor arrived. He smiled and nodded at them, and they sat in front of his desk.

"Thank you," he said. "I'm going to need your help tremendously. I've been sitting here making a list of what I think I have to do."

Josh spoke first. "Michael, how's Sarah? And the children?"

"Sarah is struggling. Jason and Jane understand what's happening, and they're moving in here tonight to care for the family. I've talked with Jim, and he's arranging for compassionate leave. He'll probably be here in 10 days, if not sooner. The girls haven't fully comprehended it yet. Hank knows how serious it is." He paused. "Tommy knows, too, and he thinks I can heal her. He heard her on the phone Friday and looked it up. He's been carrying it by himself."

Michael's voice broke. He looked down at the sheet of paper in front of him. "I'll need to rearrange my schedule to the fullest extent possible, for at least the next two months. There are several state visits

I'm supposed to participate in, and I'll need to postpone or reschedule or cancel them outright. There's one with the U.S. and French presidents that I may have to do, but it's in about three weeks and it might or might not be manageable. What I really need help with right at this moment is the public statement. Jay, what do we do?"

"Sir, we'll be as simple and straightforward as possible. I'll issue an announcement tomorrow, explaining the situation and asking for the public's prayers. The three of us talked last night after you called, and we'll begin some communications today."

"Michael," said Trevor, "I'll talk with your pastor at St. Edward's, Archbishop Nkane, and other church officials. Josh will get hold of the key cabinet and advisory people. I've got a list here of the people we need to speak with before the public announcement. That includes Dr. Owens at the school. The children will be there when we announce tomorrow."

Michael nodded. "Thank you."

"As you asked, I also looked at the emergency declaration law. And no surprise, it's silent on succession or even anything temporary. Parliament did not pass the law with due deliberation and knowledge aforethought."

"They likely passed it before they read what was in it," Jay said, "if they read it all."

Josh leaned forward. "Michael, who on the staff knows right now?"

"Ryan Mitchell and Paula Abbott in Security, and Sarah's personal security officer Tom Matson. He accompanied her to the various doctors' offices, so he had a fair idea of what was happening before any of us, other than Sarah. And Brent Epworth knows."

"Sir," said Jay, "have you talked with the extended family? I'm thinking of your mother, the queen's brothers, Mr. McFarland, and other close friends."

Michael shook his head. "I haven't thought that far."

Jay handed Michael a list. "You'll need to add any I've missed, but you should be the one to call them. As difficult as it will be, sir, particularly having to repeat yourself several times, you should be the one to talk with them. I've also listed the key staff people here, like Mr. Malone. They'll need to know before we announce publicly."

Michael nodded. "You're right. And thank you for this." He smiled. "You've even put their phone numbers down here." He looked at the three men who had been with him since they came to the palace 13 years before. "I won't be able to thank you enough for what I know you're going to do for us."

"Michael," said Josh, "we're here for you and Sarah and the family. Always." Trevor and Jay nodded.

The first call Michael made was to his mother, Iris McLaren, at the family farm outside Edinburgh. She immediately offered to come to London.

"Not yet, Ma, although I appreciate it. Jason and Jane have volunteered to move in and care for the family while Sarah's in hospital. But soon, I'm going to need my mother."

"Michael, what can I do?"

"Pray, Ma. Please pray for Sarah."

When he'd rung off, Iris walked into the rear garden and stared up at the hills. She remembered the Christmas that Michael had first introduced her and Ian to the young woman he was so in love with, there with her brother to stay with them for the holiday. *And now, and now what, Father God? Now what?*

Michael next called David Hughes and his wife Betsy. David was stunned.

"Michael, what's the prognosis? Will she do radiation and chemo?"

Michael at first couldn't respond. *I can't say this, Lord, I can't say this out loud. Help me.*

"Michael? Are you there?"

"I'm here, David. No, the doctors do not plan chemo or radiation."

"But why not? Isn't that standard? There's a colleague here at St. Andrew's who had leukemia, and that's what they did. And he's fine now, in complete remission."

"David, it's too far advanced. It wouldn't do any good." At that, Michael broke down. And then, a shocked moment later, David did as well. Michael could hear Betsy in the background, asking what was wrong.

Michael called Tommy McFarland on his mobile.

"Michael! I was going to be calling you this weekend. How are you? And Sarah and the children?"

"Tommy, Sarah's sick." He recited the facts, surprised at how the story did not get easier with each telling. "She'll go into hospital tonight. What were you going to be calling about? Are Ellen and Emily okay?"

Tommy hesitated. "No, they're fine, Michael. I was just going to call to hear your voice and catch up on things. What can I do?"

"Pray, Tommy, please pray. It doesn't look good. Ask Ellen to pray as well."

After ringing off, Tommy stared out of the window. *I'd ask her, Michael, if I thought she might talk to me. I was calling you to say we're separated. I was stupid, Michael, I've had an affair with a woman from work and I'm living with her now. Ellen's filed for divorce. But maybe she'll listen to me for this, as awful as it is. She still loves you and Sarah.* Tommy slowly punched in the numbers to call Ellen.

A few hours later, while Barb was still getting ready for church, Scott Hughes finished his call with Michael. He felt devastated, but he knew it was nothing compared to what Michael and Sarah were dealing with. Scott told Michael he would call contacts at M.D. Anderson Hospital in Houston, which had some of the best cancer specialists in the world.

He walked to their bedroom to tell his wife, and then to call their sons Scottie and Hondo. And he'd volunteered to tell the people there in San Francisco whom Michael still had close connections with – people from St. Anselm's Church and the old Frisco Flash cycling team.

At 3 p.m., Sarah hugged their children and grandsons and made them promise to listen to Jason and Jane and come see her in a couple of days. Tommy hugged her last and longest. She and Michael then left for Kensington East Hospital.

They checked Sarah in; a wristband was placed on her arm. They asked her to sit in a wheelchair while they took her to her room, but she refused. "I can walk," she said. The nurse and the admissions officer explained that this was standard procedure for all patients. She stared at them, looked at Michael and then, nodding, sat in the wheelchair.

Once brought to her private room, she changed into a hospital gown. As she changed, Michael could see she had lost weight. She looked frail.

"The last time I was here, Mike, it was to have Tommy." He and the twins had been born in the hospital.

"I remember. I missed his birth. Some stupid Mideast crisis just like the previous Mideast crisis and the next Mideast crisis."

Four weeks passed. London's leaves began to take a turn from green to reds and yellows. It was four weeks of tests, blood samples, IVs, medicines, and talks with doctors. A few experimental therapies were tried but resulted in no change in Sarah's condition except to make her violently sick. The doctors suggested they try chemotherapy, although they gave it little chance to be effective and doubted whether Sarah, in her increasingly weakened condition, could survive the treatments.

Michael wanted to consider it, but Sarah said no.

The statement issued by Jay Lanham at the palace had shocked Britain and well beyond. Trevor and Josh effectively took over government responsibilities from Michael. Jay met collectively with the editors of BBC, Sky News, *The Times*, *The Guardian*, *The Telegraph*, *The Scotsman*, and several other newspapers, and said the time had long passed for Britain to once again become a parliamentary democracy.

Jay was brutal in the discussions. "This country and all of its major institutions have used Michael Kent-Hughes like a drug. He fixed the chaos. He got government working again. He stopped the dysfunction. We want to keep using him like a drug because we're addicted to him making all the decisions we used to take responsibility for. And it's killing him. It's time for Britain to step up and be a parliamentary nation again, and let the king be the king and take care of his family. And you can quote me."

The news of Sarah's illness seemed to send a fog over Britain. In London's West End, theatre tickets went begging, and several theatres accepted what was happening and temporarily closed. Night life began to disappear. The social season simply didn't start; parties, balls, and events were postponed or cancelled. Similar effects were experienced in all the country's major cities.

The hospital in Kensington became the country's focus. People from all over Britain streamed their way to Kensington. The churches in South Kensington set up food tents and rest spaces to accommodate them.

What was most noticeable was that London had become a city of silence. Traffic, except in Kensington, became less congested. Street noise diminished. The City of Westminster set up news screens in Trafalgar Square for people to see the latest medical reports. Churches were packed, even for weekday services.

And then the news reports and editorials began, first with *The Times of London*: "It's time we give Michael Kent-Hughes back to his family and the palace."

Michael sat on the bed, holding Sarah's hand and stroking her arm. "It's quite a quiver we've produced, my beautiful bride."

Sarah smiled. "It is, indeed, my love. We've gotten six of the 12 you wanted."

"There's still time for the others."

The smile didn't disappear from Sarah's face, but it became smaller. "Mike, there's no time left."

"Sarah—"

She stopped him. "Mike, you've been carrying both of us. I've hung on because I don't want to let go of you, not until everything is settled between us. But I hurt. Everything hurts. I need to go home. I want to go home."

He rocked softly back and forth, still stroking her arm, looking at her hand. "And home's not the palace."

"It's not the palace, Mike." She paused. "I have to say some things, and I need to know you're listening."

He nodded, unable to speak without choking up.

"First, Jason. Mike, he's strong, stronger than you might think. You can lean on him, and you're going to need to lean on someone. Jason and Jane can help. So can Trevor and Josh. And Jay. And you need to love those two grandsons. They're already all over you whenever they're around you."

Michael gave a slight nod of acknowledgement.

"Jim's more fragile with all of this, Mike. I'll be the second mother he's lost, and he's only 21, and he's had me longer than his own mother. Let Jason and Jane help, but he'll need some of you, too. He may seem like he's all right, but he won't be. Make sure he takes that full month of leave and stays around family.

"And Tommy. He's our artist, Mike, and he has so many talents it's almost frightening. He's got his Dad's gift for faith and love. But he's only 6, and he thinks only you and God are perfect. He's going to be angry. You'll have to give him some space to be mad, but you'll need to hold him inside your love, too. And it'll be hard because he may blame you at first, and I know you still feel distance from him. He thinks you can make me well."

A single tear fell down Michael's cheek. He brushed it away. "I know. He told me that the first night we all found out."

"Of all of our children, he's the one I'm most worried about. He understands too much, grasps too much, and knows too much. He should be too young to fully process what's happening, but somehow, he does. You're going to have your hands full, and I've asked David to help. Tommy trusts him, so let David help. But Mike, Tommy loves you. And he thinks you're still angry with him about the painting and the studio."

"He may be right. I keep thinking I'm past that, and then something happens to remind me that I'm not."

"For his sake, Mike, and yours, you have to get past it. It was two years ago. It wasn't his fault. If you need to be mad at someone, be mad at me. Not him. He's a little boy, a sensitive little boy who's going to be overwhelmed by what's happening." She paused to catch her breath.

"Sophie's a different problem. She's got her dad's sweet spirit. She's going to want to take care of everyone, you included. She spent nine months inside me trying to keep Helen out of trouble."

Michael smiled. "That's probably exactly right."

"You'll need to encourage her, Mike. You'll need to make her test her wings and discover herself as a person. And she'll end up surprising everyone. But you're the only one who can do that with her.

"Helen." Sarah closed her eyes for a moment. "Helen is Helen, our drama queen. Every family should have one. She's 10 years old and thinks she commands the world. She reminds me so much of me at that age, it's scary. You have to draw boundaries for her and hold her accountable. She flourishes when she knows the boundaries. Mike, she'll listen to you, and probably no one else. That's what she does now."

Sarah suddenly shuddered.

"Sarah? Are you okay? Should I get the doctor?"

"No, it's just a pain, Mike, and it's passing." He watched her as she seemed to gather what little strength she had left.

"We have to talk about Hank," she said finally. "Mike, I need you to listen hard. You cast a long shadow, and he stands inside it. It doesn't help that he could pass for your identical twin, and the media love to film and photograph the two of you together.

"But Mike, Hank is his own person, and God's going to have him do great things. And so will Sophie, Helen, and Tommy. I'm not saying this because I'm their mother. It's a conviction that's been growing on me as I've watched them grow.

"But you need to help Hank. He adores you. He wants to be everything you are. You have to help him step outside of your shadow and be his own man. He can't be you. He has to be Hank. He's trying so hard to be like you with his bicycling and you and I both know that's not where his heart is."

"His passion is football."

"And you have to encourage him. You have to guide him to where his strengths are. And it's not just football. Mike, no one can encourage like you can. You need to spend a lot of time with him, talking with him, and letting him talk to you. You need to let him make some mistakes, but he won't make many. And he's Britain's future, but I need to be clear here. I don't mean Britain's future because of the throne."

She paused. "Mike, you have to give all of our children the room they need to be the people God created them to be, but especially Hank. You have to give them a choice about being royals. You have to give them as much space as possible to be independent people. We came to it as young adults, and it still almost suffocated us. They need the space to breathe. Hank needs more space than the throne."

"If not Hank, then whom?"

She pulled his hand to her face. "This will make you angry, Mike, but please don't be. I see Tommy. I know it doesn't make sense; he's only six with three siblings in line ahead of him. But I see Tommy. It's one of the reasons I let him paint with me in the studio. We talk. Or we did, before all this happened. Mike, I see him on the throne because he's the most like you. And you have to spend time with him. You have to teach him, Mike. Don't push him away because you're mad at me."

She stopped, exhausted. The conversation had drained what little energy she had left.

"I have one more thing to say, my beautiful husband, and one thing to ask."

He cocked his head at her, in the way she loved. She smiled.

"The thing I want to say is that I want you to remarry."

"Sarah, don't ask me that."

"Mike, listen to me. You are filled with so much love and passion that it would be criminal to lock it away. You're 37. I want you to remarry. I want you to promise me."

Michael was crying. He shook his head. "I can't promise that."

She looked at him. "Then can you promise me that if God brings love into your life, you won't push it away? That you'll accept it as the gift and blessing it's meant to be? Will you promise me that?"

He raised her hand to his cheek. "I will promise that, my love. But I could love no one like I love you."

"But you can love someone else just as much." She paused. "Now the thing I want to ask. Will you lie next to me and hold me? Hold me in your arms? Let me lean against your chest. Let me fall asleep in your arms, like we used to. Can you help me feel your chest and your heart?"

"There's been no time to fix things, fix us, make us right again."

"It's okay, Mike. Just left me feel your heart."

Michael unbuttoned his shirt, and moving her gently, lay next to her, folding her into him. He could feel how light she'd become. *Father God, she's disappearing in front of me.*

He placed her hand on his chest. She was too weak to lift it by herself.

"This is perfect, Mike," she said. "I've always loved your manly chest."

He smiled as he stroked her hair. He closed his eyes.

He felt himself trembling. It was fear and the beginning of grief, but it was also something else. It was anger, anger at God but also anger at his wife, his beautiful wife who was dying in his arms. She simply couldn't be right about Hank and Tommy. Hank was the firstborn and meant for the throne. She was wrong. She had to be wrong. No matter how many times they'd talked about it, her relationship with Tommy was like a constant jab in his side. Or in his heart.

Michael forced himself to relax. He saw the life they'd lived together. Seeing her for the first time in class. The famous tango at MedFest. Her touching his calf for her drawing. Their first Christmas together at McLarens. And letting her go at the airport.

He saw her standing on the steps on St. Anselm's, and her accepting his proposal. Their wedding, and that night when they physically and emotionally and spiritually became one. He saw her in Italy, looking with him for his family, and convincing him that Jason needed to be part of their family. He saw her sitting there when he woke in the hospital, and her placing Hank in his arms.

The family meeting on whether or not to accept the crown. Their first days in the palace, when he fired the security director and the chief of staff for how they'd treated her. The ivory dress she wore at the small dinner for Josh and the prime minister. The walking hand-in-hand in simple clothes for the coronation in Westminster Abbey. The school dance at the palace. And wandering through the crowd in front of the palace.

And being with her for the delivery of the twins and him showing up two hours late for Tommy's arrival. He mourned what they'd lost, he mourned what they wouldn't have, and he mourned it was ending before they'd restored their marriage.

She stirred slightly in his arms. He looked at her and smiled. *You've given me 15 years of life with her, Father God. And even this, as painful as it is, is more of that same blessing.*

At some point, he must've dozed off. What happened next had to be a dream, he'd think later.

He looked up, and he thought he saw her walking away. Then, turning towards him, she smiled, holding her fingers to her lips. She seemed almost illuminated.

Behind her stood Ian McLaren. He reached for her hand, and then guided her into the light. He turned and looked at Michael, smiling with a quick nod of his head. And then they were gone.

Michael opened his eyes and looked down at Sarah in his arms. She was still.

"Sarah?"

In the waiting room down the hall, Iris was talking softly with Jason, Jane, and Jim, while Helen and Sophie sat near their grandmother. Tommy was sitting next to David, and David had his arm around the boy. Hank, Emily and Gavin were talking among themselves, while Ellen kept trying to call Tommy McFarland on her mobile to find out where he was, but without success. Betsy was next to David, a sleeping Eleanor leaning against her mother. David had said little since arriving at the hospital three days earlier, the most recent of several visits. He'd been shocked at the sight of his twin sister lying so ill in the hospital bed. Scott and Barb Hughes stood nearby, talking with Josh and Zena Gittings.

Jay Lanham stood at the window, watching thousands of candles lit by the people standing vigil in front of the hospital, remembering the stories of thousands standing vigil at the hospital in San Francisco after Michael was shot and had nearly died all those years ago. *It's as if there is some mystical, spiritual bond between them and the people. I feel it, too. We all do.*

They were all startled by the sound of shouting and the sight of two nurses and a doctor running toward Sarah's room. The adults stood, frozen. Jason finally stepped forward and quickly walked after them to her room.

The doctor and nurses were at the bed. Michael, his shirt still unbuttoned, was standing nearby, staring at the bed.

He looked at Jason. "She's gone, Jas. She died in my arms. She's gone." And then he broke down. Jason threw his arms around Michael and held him. They stood there, Michael sobbing, Jason crying as he felt Michael clutching him desperately.

Jason buttoned Michael's shirt. Slowly they walked out of the room and toward the waiting area.

Iris saw them, Jason half-carrying his dad. "Oh, no," she said. "Oh, no."

Tommy looked at his father, his lip trembling as the tears started. "No!" he shouted. "No! You let her die." And he threw himself at Michael, pounding his fists at Michael's chest while Jason moved to hold him off.

"It's okay, Jas," Michael said, and in seemingly one move, he touched Jason lightly to pull him back from the crying boy and folded his arms around Tommy as he continued pounding at Michael's chest. As he pulled Tommy closer, the boy pushed Michael away and ran to his uncle, sobbing wildly.

Grief engulfed the family, as they clung to each other.

Finally, Jay, tears in his eyes, cleared his throat to get Michael's attention. "Sir, we'll need to make a statement. Do you want me to do it?"

Michael shook his head. "It needs to be family. But I can't do it. I just can't."

"I'll do it, Dad," Jason said. "I'll do it."

Michael stared at Jason for a moment, and then nodded. "Thank you." He reached and touched Jason's face. "You'll need to say what's happened. And thank the people for their prayers and support. Tell them for me that they've made an unbearable burden bearable."

"I'll stand with him, Dad," Jim said. And Jane nodded.

Jay led Jason, Jane, and Jim into the hospital cafeteria. The assembled news media, more than 200 strong, silently watched the four walk to the microphones. Rumors had been circulating for the last 15 minutes that the queen had died, and television and radio news were already citing unconfirmed reports.

Jason looked at the reporters and spoke into the microphone. "We have a short statement from our dad and the family."

"About 30 minutes ago," he said, "our Mom, Queen Sarah, went home to Jesus." He paused, almost succeeding at controlling his emotions. "She died like she wanted to die, in our dad's arms." He smiled. "Now she's in a better place, a place where there's no more pain and suffering. She's in Jesus' arms now."

Jane and Jim, standing behind Jason, began to cry softly.

"My Dad asked me to thank you," Jason said. "He asked me to thank you for your prayers, your cards and letters, and for all of the flowers. My mom loved the flowers." He looked around the room. "My dad said," and here Jason's voice faltered a bit, "my dad said that your love for us has made an unbearable burden bearable."

He looked around the room. "My dad is a great man. Not because he's the king, or because of the things he's done. My dad loves God, and he loves my mom, and he loves me and my brothers and sisters, and he loves his people." Jason could no longer contain his tears, and they rolled down his cheeks. "And he's hurting right now. My dad's really hurting. Please pray for my dad."

Going home for the night, the family split in different directions. Ellen, Emily and Jim rode with Jason and Jane to the house in Mayfair, where Liz and Trevor Barry had been watching their grandsons while Jason and Jane were at the hospital. Ellen was getting angrier by the minute as she tried to reach Tommy McFarland; they might be in the midst of a divorce, but Michael needed him now. David, Betsy, Gavin, and Eleanor, along with Scott and Barb, went to Betsy's grandparents' house, where they were staying. Iris traveled with Michael and the four children back to the palace. No one spoke while the security officers drove them home.

They slowed as they approached the palace. Thousands of people were standing, sitting and singing hymns in front of the palace. The mountain of flowers that had been there that morning when they left for the hospital had grown to several mountains. The four children watched the thousands of candles, torches and lights that blazed their way to the entry gate. Television news crews filmed the caravan entering the palace grounds.

The service staff was waiting inside, lining the way to the main stairs. Michael could see that some were crying, while still others bore the marks of crying. He nodded as they passed, stopping only to hug Davy Malone, the palace's executive chef and the staff member closest to Sarah. Davy broke down.

When they reached the loft, Tommy ran to his room and slammed the door. Hank and the girls looked at their father.

"Do you want me to go after him?" Hank said.

Michael shook his head. "Let him be, Hank." While the three watched with Iris, Michael walked to Tommy's door.

"Tommy, it's Dad." He paused. "I want you to know that I love you, son." He leaned his head against the door. "And if you get cold tonight, you can come to my room. I'll leave the door unlocked."

He turned to the others. "We need to try to get some sleep. We'll have a lot to do in the next several days." The girls nodded, and Michael reached and hugged them both. They walked to their rooms, Iris leading as she went to hers.

Michael looked at Hank. "Get some sleep. We have some long days ahead of us." He kissed the top of Hank's head.

He knew Sarah had been wrong. Hank had all the marks of a future king.

In their bedroom, Michael saw how much of Sarah surrounded him. The pictures on the walls, including the one she'd drawn of him sleeping during their honeymoon; the bedspread she'd picked out; the pile of books on her nightstand. He still had her Bible in his hand, making sure he brought it home from the hospital. Her terrycloth bathrobe was hanging on the peg behind the bathroom door. *What do I do with her clothes? Her jewelry? All of her paints and canvases?*

Their bedroom had become enormous. And empty.

He changed into his pajamas, and brushing his teeth, stared into the mirror. His reflection showed a man who still looked younger than his age, but the eyes betrayed deep and profound pain. The gray in his black hair had markedly increased in the last four weeks.

On her vanity next to his, he saw her perfume bottle. He stared at it. He hadn't remembered seeing it until tonight. As he stared at it, a sob broke from his chest. He slipped to the floor, holding himself as the sobs broke one after the other.

Through the tears, he heard a noise and opened his eyes. Tommy, in his pajamas, was standing at the open bathroom door, staring at his father.

Michael opened his arms. Tommy rushed to him.

"I know you want her back, son," Michael said, crying with him. "I want her back, too. You asked me if God could save her. He could've, Tommy, but He had a different plan. He knows how much this hurts. He knows we want her back. But He'd a different plan. And He wants us to let Him hold us. He knows we hurt."

Tommy didn't say a word. He clung to Michael as he cried.

Michael finally stood, and carrying Tommy in his arms, walked into the bedroom.

"You can sleep in here, tonight, son. He set the boy gently on the bed. Michael got into bed himself, and Tommy leaned against him as they sat there.

The door opened again. Michael looked up and saw Hank, standing in his pajamas.

"I got cold," Hank said.

Michael nodded at him to join them in the bed, and Hank dashed to them, scooting in on the opposite side of Michael and snuggling up next to him.

The door opened again. It was Helen and Sophie.

Sophie spoke first. "We got cold, Dad." And Helen nodded.

He beckoned them towards him. "It's a bit crowded here but we still have some room." The two girls ran and climbed on the bed.

For a few moments, they were all quiet.

"What happens next, Dad?" Hank said.

"Well, tomorrow I'll meet with Josh, Jay, and Trevor, and they'll help us plan the funeral. It won't be for several days yet, probably on Wednesday or Thursday. A lot of arrangements have to be made."

Helen was twisting the ring on her finger. "Where will she be buried, Dad?"

"She wanted Edinburgh, so Edinburgh it will be. She said at first that she wanted to be buried at McLarens, because it was her favorite place in the world. But she thought about it and said it wouldn't be good for Ma. There will be a lot of people who would want to see where she's buried and the farm might be overrun, and she didn't want to see that happen to the place she loved the most. So, she decided Holyrood Palace. But we have to plan the service and the funeral. We have to notify a lot of people and give them time to come to London."

"She gave us each instructions," Sophie said, and the others nodded.

"Why does that not surprise me? I got my instructions, too."

"She told me to open my eyes at the world and not worry so much," Sophie said. "Isn't that strange? And she told me and Helen both that we couldn't marry just anyone, that when we married, we had to marry someone whom we could love as much as she loved you."

"She told me to listen to you," Helen said. "She said I needed to listen to you even when I didn't want to."

"She told me to play football," Hank said. "And she said I had to be my own man. What did she mean?"

"It's a long story, for each of you."

"She said something else," Hank said. "She said that you needed to remarry, and we should encourage you to do that. Will you remarry?"

Alone of the four, Tommy said nothing. His mother had given him instructions as well, telling him to keep drawing and painting and to love his father, even when he felt afraid or didn't understand, even when his father was unlovable.

"Somehow, I think she knew we'd be having this conversation. And I just realized that because of the four of you, I'll always have her, because she's part of each of you." He paused. "She asked me to promise her that I would remarry someday. I told her I couldn't promise that. So, she asked that if God brought love into my life again, that I wouldn't push it away, that I'd accept it as the gift it's meant to be. And I told her I could promise her that." He looked at the girls, and then Hank and Tommy. "But you need to know there's no one I could love like I love your mother. Perhaps in a different way, but not like I loved your mother."

"Can we sleep in here tonight?" Helen said. "Sophie and I could share the sofa." Her sister nodded.

"I think we can do that for tonight. Run and get your blankets and pillows."

What Michael didn't notice immediately was that Tommy hadn't said a word. Two weeks later, he'd learn that his son hadn't said a word since his mother's death. He'd lost his voice.

When Michael awoke the next morning, Tommy was curled up next to him, still soundly asleep, as were Helen and Sophie on the sofa. Hank was gone.

Pulling on gym pants and a sweatshirt in the bathroom, Michael quietly slipped out of the bedroom and found Iris in the kitchen, sipping her tea and her Bible open in front of her.

"I've made some coffee, Michael."

"It smells good, Ma, thank you. Have you seen Hank?"

"He's in the gardens, practicing with his bicycle, I think. If you look out that window in the studio, I think you can see him."

Holding his coffee mug, Michael walked to the window and saw Hank practicing starts and stops on his bicycle. A security officer stood nearby. Iris stood next to Michael and watched as well. It was a beautifully sunny day.

"Last night at the hospital, I saw Sarah walking away from me, and Da take her hand. He looked at me and nodded, and then they walked into the light. That's when I knew she was gone. I didn't imagine it, Ma, but I might've been dreaming."

She watched Hank for a moment before she spoke. "I'm not one for mystical stuff, Michael, but I will say it sounds like something your father would do, letting you know she'd be okay."

"Does it get any better?"

She considered her words before she spoke. "There's not a day goes by, Michael, that I don't think of your Da. Not a day that I don't miss him. It's an ache. I thought it might lessen with time, and I suppose it has, but something will happen, or I'll see something or hear someone laugh like Ian, and the ache becomes a sharp stab.

"What helps is that I've a son who frets over his mother. I've a grandson who calls me every Sunday night and has those two little great-grandsons babble to me over the phone. And I've another grandson who writes me once a week and sends a few emails in between, letting me know what's going on with him. And I have four other grandchildren who love me so much that I want to hold them forever."

She paused for a moment, then went on. "It's funny, Michael. I always wanted a large family. I grew up in one and loved everything about a big family. But your Da and I just couldn't seem to have children. I prayed and prayed, but I finally realized that God had another plan. Then you showed up on our doorstep, and I gradually learned what that other plan was. While I had to wait a few years, I got that large family I'd so hungered for. I've been more blessed than I could've dreamed on my own. And God will do that for you, too, son, as awful as you feel right now. It will get better, but you'll have days when you miss Sarah so much you could draw the hurt like she drew on her canvasses. But Michael, the measure of that hurt is the measure of the love you had for her, the measure of the blessing she was in your life. You hold on to that, and you hold on to those incredible children you have. They need their dad, right now more than they've ever needed him before."

Still watching Hank down below in the garden, Michael smiled. "You and Da loved me more than I ever could've hoped. And you still do. I think right now I'm going to go see my son there. Can you keep an eye on the others if they wake, and maybe send them along to the garden?"

A few minutes later, Iris, still watching from the window, saw Michael, followed by a security officer, walk into the palace gardens and call to Hank. Michael was carrying a football. They talked for a few moments, and then she saw Hank lay the bike on its side and he and Michael begin to run on the grass, kicking the ball back and forth.

She watched them until she was startled by a voice.

"Is he going to be okay, Ma?" Sophie was standing next to her at the window.

"You startled me, Sophie Anna. I didn't know you were awake. And, yes, Hank's going to be okay."

"I didn't mean Hank, Ma. I know he'll be okay. I'm talking about Dad."

Iris noticed that Helen and Tommy were standing right behind them. She faced the three of them.

"You know the stories. When your Dad was 6, his parents died in the car crash, and he was tossed out of his home the same day. That's how he came to live with me and Da."

The children nodded.

"He had to be there for Jim when Jim's mother was killed. And when your Dad's brother was killed when The Violence started, he nearly was as well. And he survived a surgery that no one thought he could. Good thing, too, because I wouldn't be looking at the three of your faces right now.

"And he outlasted the church officials fighting him, and he's carried Government on his shoulders these six years, has he not?"

The children nodded again.

"Your Dad's made of strong stuff. And he's going to be okay because he knows he has to be there for you. And he will be. You can count on him. Now, why don't the three of you scuttle downstairs and go kick that ball with your Dad and Hank while I get us some breakfast together?"

The three raced to the door. Tommy stopped and came back, taking Iris's hand in his and kissing it. Then he was gone like a shot after the others.

Iris watched from the window as the three of them, with two security officers trailing after them, ran on to the grass of the garden.

At 11, Josh, Jay, and Trevor entered Michael's main office on the ground floor.

"Ready for some company?" Josh said.

Michael smiled and nodded, waving them in. "I owe you all an apology. I wouldn't hear of planning the funeral, and now I have us in a box. I've been sitting here trying to figure it all out, but it's not coming together. I can't concentrate."

"Michael, we disobeyed you to the extent we could," Josh said, "And we've been working quietly on some things. Last night, after we got home, we talked with the palace communications staff and Archbishop Nkane by conference call."

Michael looked down at his folded hands on the desk, and then at the three men who had done so much for him and with him. "Thanks to you all for disobeying and serving your king, in spite of his best efforts to stop you. I couldn't bear the idea of planning her funeral. It would've meant me giving up hope." Michael took a deep breath. "And thanks for being with us last night, and Trevor, for taking care of the grandsons. So, what do we have?"

Jay handed him several sheets of paper. "The details are here, sir, but essentially it's this. Beginning late on Monday and continuing Tuesday and Wednesday, the queen will lie in state at Westminster Abbey. You, the children and the family will visit first, on Monday evening. You'll be by yourselves, with just immediate family, but it will be televised. You'll be followed by the senior government people, the palace staff, and the diplomatic corps. Then we allow the public to view the casket. You haven't seen the papers, sir. The country's in massive grief right now. The queen was deeply loved and admired, and not only because of her words that stopped The Violence. Because the reaction's so broad and deep, we'll begin the visitation hours at 10 p.m. on Monday and continue without a break until Wednesday at midnight. Even then, it's going to be difficult to accommodate the people we expect.

"As soon as the public observance ends at the Abbey, we'll set up the seating for the service. That morning at 9, there will be a reception for the family and all of the dignitaries that have gathered, and we'll do that here at the palace. The guests will leave at 10 for the abbey, followed by the family at 11. The service begins at noon. The archbishop will officiate, assisted by your pastor from St. Edmund's.

We contacted both last night and told them we needed final approval, but we believed it's what you'd want."

Michael nodded. "Yes, that works."

"There will be two speakers, sir, other than the Archbishop and Father Ward. And that's Jason and Jim. We talked with David Hughes, but he said he didn't think he could do it. Jason and Jim both said they would."

"Sarah and David, being twins, have always been close." Michael made a note in his journal. "I need to remember to talk with him. His pain is as bad as mine."

"The service will end about 2, and then we'll have the procession to the train station for the trip to Scotland," Josh said.

"We've sent the notifications to all our embassies, with instructions for what government leaders would be attending," Trevor said. "The Foreign Minister is coordinating that. We'll know by tonight who's coming. We've also worked up the list of family and friends that we thought would want to come, and they've been notified by email or phone as well."

"Arrangements are underway for the burial service at Holyrood," Jay said. "The Queen will lie in state there beginning Friday at 6 a.m. through Sunday at midnight. The burial service, which will be for family and close friends, will be on Monday at one. The archbishop and Reverend Ward will again officiate, assisted by Archbishop Brimley of Edinburgh."

Josh cleared his throat. "Michael, there's one thing we do need to clear with you. Even with the extended visitation hours at the Abbey, we won't be able to accommodate everyone who will want to tell Sarah goodbye. So, we thought that, once the service ends, you and the family could travel in cars or carriages behind the Queen's coffin from the Abbey to the train station. It's about three miles. It would give the people who weren't able to see her the opportunity to bid farewell."

Michael looked from Josh to Jay and then back to Josh, not speaking.

"If you'd prefer not, of course, that will be fine," Josh said.

Michael shook his head. "It's not that, Josh. It's a fine idea. I'd like to make one change. The family can ride; I'd like to walk behind the casket."

"Michael, it's three miles," said Josh.

Michael nodded. "I'd like to walk."

"Sir," said Jay, "other family members may want to walk if you do."

"You're thinking of Ma. And you're right. I'll tell her she'll have to ride in the car." He saw them exchange glances. "That's assuming, of course, that I have a ghost of a chance of her listening. The family is gathering here this afternoon at 3. I'll talk with them then. Can you coordinate this with Mr. Mitchell in Security?"

By the time the family began arriving at the palace, Michael had received word that friends were coming from all over the world: Michael's Olympic friends Lucio Pena and his wife Marcia from Chile and Moses and Florence Akimbe from Kenya; and the whole San Francisco contingent – Brian and May Renner and their three children, Hannah, three months younger than Hank, Joseph, who was 9, and

Jeffrey, 7; Frank and Abby Weston; Father John Stevens, now retired, and his wife Eileen; Milly Hensley, still secretary at St. Anselm's in San Francisco; and Paul and Emma Finley. Michael also heard from the Italian branch of the family – Damiano and his wife Sylvia, Stefano and Carolina, and Maria, along with 85-year-old Mama Sophia, Michael's grandmother, would all be coming.

If anything, the initial news reports understated Britain's grief, rising up like a great wave and showing no sign of abating. On Sunday, Britain came to a virtual standstill as people clustered together around television sets in their homes and pubs. Sports and entertainment events were cancelled. Regular television programming disappeared, replaced by ongoing reports about the royal family and retrospectives on the life of Sarah Kent-Hughes. Church services were packed all over the country.

The anguish spread quickly to the continent, North America, and beyond. The prime minister of Canada, along with the Dominion countries, ordered flags to be flown at half-mast, and the President of the United States followed suit. Mourners from around the world began leaving flowers and notes at the British embassies and consulates.

Davey Malone has set up an extensive food-and-drinks buffet in the palace ballroom. People kept arriving all day, well before the official 3 p.m. start time, and everyone was guided to the ballroom, where Michael and the children greeted them.

Standing apart from the crowd, Tommy watched the people in the ballroom. Last night, when he'd found his father crying, he'd tried to speak and discovered his voice was gone. Terrified at first, he didn't know what was happening to him and thought he might have gotten cancer, too. He searched online for what might be happening. The closest thing he could find was something called hysterical shock, which he didn't fully understand. So far, no one had realized he couldn't talk.

He watched the crowd. The sadness felt like swimming in a deep pool of tears. Tommy considered going back to his room when he spotted Ellen McFarland, sitting by herself on the steps of the raised platform where bands and orchestras usually played. He walked over and sat next to her. He could see both kindness and sadness in her eyes.

Ellen put her arm around him. "My heart aches for you and for me, Tommy. I know how much Sarah loved you, and she'd been my good friend these 14 years."

He leaned against her, just as her mobile buzzed.

"That had better be Tommy McFarland," she said, "telling me he's on his way here. He's got to come for Michael."

As she looked at the text, Tommy saw her frown and then open it. "What in heaven's name is this? Call a detective in Glasgow?" She punched in numbers for a call, and then identified herself. He watched her face go from puzzled to horrified to shocked.

Tears began pouring from her eyes as she almost gasped for breath. She turned to him.

"Tommy's killed himself," she said in heaving breaths. "He's dead. Tommy's dead."

The boy fell back from her. Staring at her with his mouth open, he felt like he couldn't breathe. He crawled and then stumbled away, finally running toward the door of the ballroom. He pushed through a group just arriving and kept running.

He heard Ellen scream behind him. "Michael!"

Ellen's scream sounded across the ballroom. Michael, at the other end of the room, hurried to her. She was almost incoherent and was shaking uncontrollably.

"He's dead!"

"Who's dead, Ellen?" Michael said.

"Tommy," she said, gasping. "He killed himself."

"No," Michael said, shaking his head. "It can't be. There must be some mistake."

"The landlord sent a text," she said. "He said to call a police detective. That's all he said." She handed Michael her phone. "I called, and the detective said he was sorry to tell me that Tommy's body had been found in the flat. He hadn't been at work in several days and the office called the landlord and asked him to check." She dissolved into tears; Betsy, who'd accompanied Michael, put her arms around Ellen to support her. "He left a note and letters. They're dated two days ago."

Ellen's daughter Emily had joined the group with Hank and Gavin.

"They're wrong," Emily said, her voice getting progressively higher. "They've made a mistake. He would never do that. Never."

Michael pulled out his mobile. "I'll have Mr. Mitchell here check with Glasgow Police." Mitchell said he'd check and call back.

By this time, the guests had coalesced around the group with Michael and Ellen. They all stood in silence, Emily's face red with emotion and Ellen feeling as if she would faint.

"The detective said the building manager told him that Tommy's girlfriend, the one from the office, had moved out on Monday," Ellen said. "Tommy hadn't been at work since."

Michael's mobile buzzed. "Yes, Mr. Mitchell?"

As he listened, he began to shake. "Thank you for checking," he said, his voice breaking. He looked at Ellen and Emily. "The Glasgow police confirmed that the body of a man was found hanging from an exposed pipe in your flat. The manager identified him as Tommy, but there will need to be a family member to confirm identity."

Ellen sagged against Betsy, and David grabbed her before she fell to the floor. Emily began to wail and sob, and Gavin took hold of her. She first beat her fists against his chest, and then she, too, collapsed against him, sobbing.

"Tommy's parents may not know," Michael said. "I'll need to call them." He pulled out his mobile again, but his hand was shaking so badly he couldn't look up the number.

"Michael," David said, still holding Ellen, "sit in a chair." He looked at Jim. "Jim, get a bottle of something strong like whisky from the bar and bring three glasses." Jim dashed off.

Fifteen minutes later, and after a few sips of whisky, Ellen and Emily had calmed but looked shell-shocked. Michael was sitting, saying nothing, his eyes almost glazed. At one point, he looked up at Jason. "Jas, I don't think I can handle this. Not Sarah and Tommy."

David looked around the group. He spotted his own children, Hank, Sophie, and Helen. "Has anyone seen Prince Thomas?" he said, using the boy's title to avoid saying "Tommy."

Ellen looked up. "Oh, no," she said. "He was sitting here with me when I called the detective. I just blurted it out. He was the first person to hear it and he ran off. Oh, help me, Lord, please, oh, no. I'm sorry, Michael, it was a terrible thing for him to hear."

At that, Michael stood. "We have to find him. Jason, alert Security and see if they've seen him or can spot him on any of the Security cameras. Get them to start a check of the palace." Michael, David, Hank, and Jim hurried from the room.

"I'll check the loft," Michael said. "Most likely he would've gone there." As they hurried down the hallway, they met Josh and Zena walking toward the ballroom. Michael explained what had happened.

After the shock registered on Josh's face, he moved right into his chief of staff role. "Hank, check with the guards' quarters. Tommy spends time talking with the palace guardsmen. If he's not there, check the bowling alley and the gym in the basement.

"David, you and I will check the staterooms and the rooms on the first floor. We'll start at opposite ends and meet in the middle, and then we'll head upstairs. Michael, you and Jim tackle the loft and the guest rooms outside the loft entrance." He pulled out his mobile and called. "Mr. Mitchell, we'll need a security team to begin looking in the gardens for Prince Thomas. And check the outbuildings." He turned to his wife. "Zena, go to the ballroom and see if you can help

Betsy with Ellen and Emily. Call me if you hear anything, and I'll do likewise. Okay, let's go."

Michael and Jim took the elevator to the top floor. They first checked the guest rooms immediately outside the family loft but found no trace. Inside the loft, they looked at each room, closets, storage areas, and even cabinets and wardrobes. Tommy wasn't there.

"I'm going downstairs to help search the grounds," Michael said. "The light is starting to fade, and it's a lot of territory to cover. Can you wait here on the chance he finds his way to the loft?"

Jim nodded. "I'll stay here. We'll find him." He paused and pointed down the loft hall. "We didn't check Mom's studio. Could he be there?"

Michael shook his head. "We locked it when she left for the hospital. I've got the key. She didn't want anything disturbed." He pulled a key ring from his pocket. "It's still on my key ring." Michael left to return downstairs.

Jim decided to recheck each of the rooms. He was a little wary of Michael and Sarah's room. He had been in it many times before, but it seemed too private and personal now. The need for certainty overrode his qualms, and he meticulously checked any place in the room Tommy might be.

Jim was 22 and serving as a pilot in the RAF, soon to be promoted to captain. He'd been stationed at Basra for the past four years, during two terms of overseas duty. From the time he was 10, he knew he wanted a military career.

Of all the members of the family, Jim had lived with Michael the longest. He and his mother Jenny had met Michael when Jim was enrolled at St. Anselm's School in San Francisco. His mother had been an exotic dancer and a prostitute. She'd given birth to Jim when she was 12 and living in Los Angeles. She was 20 when she'd been killed on orders of her pimp; she'd found faith at St. Anselm's and had quit her former life. Unknown to Michael until he learned it in court, she'd named him Jim's guardian. Jim and Jason had both been adopted by Michael and Sarah not long after they'd married.

Jim was five foot eleven, with sandy hair and a lanky frame. He'd never known his father; Michael assumed he must resemble whoever his father was because he looked completely unlike his mother. He was friendly, personable, and popular with his unit in Basra. He was also a devout Christian; he was often kidded by his military mates for how much of his off-duty time he devoted to Bible study. His friendliness and encouraging attitude had won him friends throughout his unit.

In Michael's bedroom, Jim saw a small alcove next to the bathroom. He seemed to remember a storage closet being there before, with a curtain drawn across it. He walked to the alcove and saw a light switch on the wall, so he flipped it on. A small spotlight came on in the alcove, and it shone directly on a curtain hanging not on a window but an interior wall. He opened the curtain and saw a narrow door, one that just might accommodate a hiding boy.

He opened the door. The narrow space contained a painting, leaning against the wall. He pulled it out, and what he saw made him gasp.

It was a painting of Michael, and it was obviously painted by Sarah. It was a full-length portrait, with Michael posing to the side and slightly away from the viewer.

Jim had never been interested in art; when he was a child, he privately thought Jason and Sarah were crazy to spend so much time painting and going to museums. But even Jim could tell this painting was stunning, among Sarah's best work. And he knew why it was hidden away. It was a nude portrait of Michael. It wasn't full-frontal, but it was a nude portrait. It was one of the most beautiful things he'd ever seen.

He pushed the canvas back in the closet, pulled the curtain closed, and turned out the light. He felt almost shaken. He also felt he had accidentally and deeply intruded into Michael and Sarah's personal life.

He finished checking the room, looked in the bathroom and the linen closet, and then turned to the other rooms. After 15 minutes, there was still no sign of Tommy. He looked at the door to the studio and decided to make sure it was locked.

It wasn't. He pushed it open and turned on the light. Fading natural light was still coming through the windows at the end.

The studio was large but not huge. It was mostly as he remembered it the few times he'd seen it. Sarah's easel was set up, holding a blank canvas. There were a few half-finished canvases, works Sarah had started and apparently decided not to complete, leaning against a wall. There was a small storage cabinet for paints and brushes, and the door was open. There was no place anyone could hide, no matter how small.

A sofa and chair stood off to the side, and there was a small chair, possibly a child's chair, positioned behind the stool where Sarah would sit to paint.

"Tommy?" Jim said. "Are you here?"

He heard a noise behind the sofa. It sounded like a strangled whimper.

Jim pulled the sofa away from the wall. Tommy was in a small recess behind it, looking at him with frightened, teary eyes.

Jim knelt on the floor. "Hey, little buddy. I'm really glad to find you. We've been looking all over. Are you OK?"

Tommy stood, still looking at him with fear in his eyes. He shook his head.

"Are you hurt?"

Tommy again shook his head. He pointed to his mouth.

"Is something wrong with your mouth?"

Tommy nodded again. Tears were welling up in his eyes.

"Tommy, can you speak?"

Tommy shook his head, and then began to cry openly. Without a sound.

Jim felt unnerved, but he knew enough to pull Tommy to him and hug the boy. "It's OK, little buddy. We'll figure out what the problem is. You had quite a shock a little while ago."

Tommy clung to his brother.

"I'm going to call Dad and let him know I've found you. A lot of people are looking for you right now."

Tommy straightened up and began to pull Jim toward the door.

"You don't want Dad to know this is where you were," Jim said, guessing.

Tommy nodded, and Jim let himself be pulled out of the studio.

"Can you lock it, or was it already unlocked?"

Tommy pulled a key from his pocket.

"Was this Mom's key?"

Tommy nodded.

"Do you need to put it back some place?"

Tommy shook his head. They had entered the central family living area of the loft.

"She gave you the key?"

The boy once again nodded.

"Okay. You lock the door to the studio, and I'll call Dad. He's going to ask me where you were, and I can't lie to him. I'll tell him I found you hiding behind the sofa." To make his point, Jim sat on and patted the family room sofa, which was placed against a wall. The back was curved just enough that a small boy might hide there.

Tommy smiled through his tears.

"But Tommy, I'll need to tell him about your voice. It may need to be checked by a doctor. You can't speak at all?"

Tommy shook his head.

"When did this start?"

Tommy held up his index finger.

"A day ago. Yesterday, at the hospital?"

The boy nodded. And then he found a piece of paper and wrote a note, handing it to Jim. "Please don't tell Dad."

"Tommy, it needs to be checked."

Tommy wrote on the paper again. "After the funeral."

Jim saw the pleading look in the boy's eyes. "You're afraid of Dad finding out."

Tommy nodded and wrote again on the paper. "He's angry with me. About Mummy and the studio. She let me watch her paint and it made him angry."

"All right. I don't understand what happened here, but I won't say anything until after the funeral. He might find out, you know.'

Tommy wrote "Thank you."

Early Monday evening, Hank knocked gently on Michael's bedroom door. His father opened it to see both Hank and Tommy in their suits. Hank was fully dressed, but Tommy was holding his tie in his hand.

"I tried but can't get his tie to work right," Hank said.

"You need some help with the tie?" Michael said, and Tommy nodded. "Both of you, come on in."

The family was getting dressed for the visitation at Westminster Abbey. The coffin had been placed in the Abbey, and that morning David and Michael visited the church to view the body and make sure an open coffin was appropriate. David had wept tears he didn't think he had left in him; Michael had remained dry-eyed but had been barely able to speak. In the coffin, Sarah's face had looked thin but had an almost translucent beauty. Michael gave the OK to continue with the open coffin plan.

While Hank stood to the side and watched, Michael had Tommy stand in front him as they faced the mirror. "They call this the

Windsor knot. It'll be some trouble to get it right the first few times, but eventually you'll learn it." He began to tie the knot.

Michael was thankful that Ellen had plucked up the fortitude to call Tommy McFarland's parents, to tell them what happened. Michael had called a few hours later; Mr. McFarland had just returned from the police mortuary and formally identifying the body. Michael asked if the funeral might be delayed until after Sarah's burial on the following Tuesday. Mr. McFarland agreed, and Michael in turn agreed when Mr. McFarland asked him to speak during the service.

"We both have a heap of sorrow, Michael," he said. "I don't know why Tommy did what he did, no matter how low he was feeling. I'm sorry to ask you to speak so soon after your own sorrow, but you're the one he would want, I think." Michael didn't say he might know what happened; Tommy had normally been irrepressible and buoyant, but that was balanced by occasional times of deep depression. Even in college, Michael had suggested Tommy get some professional help, but his friend always avoided it.

"There," Michael said, finishing Tommy's tie. "That looks just fine. We'll find some time to practice a bit later. We'll have this again for the service on Thursday and next week in Edinburgh."

He put his arms around both boys. "I know this is hard. I know it was hard to hear what you heard last night. I wanted to run and hide, too, Tommy. But both of you need to remember this. No matter what happens, your mother loved you and your sisters more than life itself. And I love you more than life itself. And God loves you more than anyone." He paused. "Tommy, if I could have given my own life to save your mother's, I would've done it. But that's not how it works. I wish it could, but it doesn't."

Tommy leaned his head against Michael, while Hank put his arm around his father's waist.

The viewing by the family and close friends was scheduled for 7 p.m. The cars left the palace, slowly making their way on The Mall, through Admiralty Arch, and then turning on Whitehall. The crowds lining the streets were enormous and silent as they watched the caravan proceed by.

They arrived at the Abbey and were greeted by Paul Nkane, Archbishop of Canterbury, and the Abbey dean, Roy Wilton. They made their way down the nave and approached the coffin, positioned right before the altar platform. Michael glanced at his children, to make sure they were ready. And then he nodded.

The entire visitation was being broadcast by BBC, Sky News, and a camera pool for the U.S. and other networks.

The family – Michael, Iris, Hank, Sophie, Helen, Tommy, Jason and Jane and their two boys, Jim, David and Betsy and their two children, Scott and Barb Hughes and their adult sons Scottie and Hondo, Iris McLaren, and Michael's cousins from Italy, all walked forward. They bowed their heads for a few brief moments, and then stood to the left of the coffin. Chairs were available for seating. They were followed by Trevor Barry, Josh Gittings, Jay Lanham, and their spouses, several cabinet heads, and members of the advisory House of Lords. Right after them came the palace staff, led by Brent Epworth and including a tearful Davey Malone. The diplomatic corps followed the staff.

An hour passed; the official mourners had all viewed the casket. The family walked back to the coffin. After a few moments, they turned to walk back up the nave to the cars waiting outside. As they started, Tommy turned around and walked back. The entire family stopped and turned, watching the boy as he reached the coffin and stood there.

If the nation's heart had not been broken before, the sight of six-year-old Prince Thomas Michael McLaren Kent-Hughes holding his hand against the side of his mother's coffin, and then leaning forward to kiss it, broke it now.

Tommy

Seven years later

"So, Sophie's planning on Oxford and Helen's talked you into drama school." Hank speared a forkful of salad. "This food, by the way, is not our normal fare. The usual grub's not bad but I suspect we have a bit of a Potemkin Village here for the families, so thank you." He grinned.

"You're remarkably well informed about what's happening at the palace," Michael said.

Michael had spent the morning at the Sandhurst parent day program, including a brief tour of the military college. He was sitting with Hank, now 19, who would be invested as the Prince of Wales in two years' time. They were at an informal lunch in the mess hall with the other parents and students.

Hank, who rarely used the more formal "Henry," had spent the last year at Sandhurst, following his graduation from International Christian School. He'd considered going straight to university but decided to do military service first. Michael hadn't pressured his son to join the military, although it was something that, historically, members of the royal family did as a matter of course. Michael himself had been an ordained priest before becoming king and had no military experience.

Hank had made the decision on his own. Following graduation from Sandhurst in two weeks, he'd be enrolling for the summer term at the University of Edinburgh. The young man had a gift for business and finance, much like his namesake and uncle, Henry Kent, murdered during The Violence of 19 years before.

Lunch was the first time that day Michael had to talk with Hank alone; they both were enjoying every minute.

Hank nodded. "I've some great sources. They tell me that Sophie wants to read history, specifically Spanish history. And they tell me that, despite grave concerns by her father, approval has been given to Helen to study acting."

Michael laughed. "Yes, her father has grave concerns, but I've been overwhelmed by the daughter's histrionics and a strategic reminder that I've told all my children, with the exception of the heir to the throne, they're free to pursue their adult lives apart from the palace. And, as you've reminded me more than once, even the Prince of Wales-to-be has been given the freedom to pursue business and finance. Is Sophie telling you this?"

Grinning, Hank shook his head. "Sophie sends me a detailed email every Sunday, updating me on what's happening generally but not personally. Helen, as you might imagine, is rather scattershot in her communications, a short email here, a postcard there, long stretches of nothing, and then a whole pile of emails and notes. And they're usually about her latest heartthrob or the part in the next play she's trying out for."

"That sounds exactly like your sister."

"Jason and Jim send notes, at least weekly, usually by email. No, my chief informant is my brother, HRH Prince Thomas."

"Really?" A slight frown crossed Michael's face.

"I was surprised, but Tommy is my most faithful correspondent. I get almost daily emails, and he sends texts as well. Once or twice a week we talk on Skype or Facetime. He's remained a consistently faithful communicator, and I can't tell you how much I appreciate it. Even with my mates here, and I've made some good ones, and with emails, texts, and letters from Hannah, it can still get lonely at times." Hannah Renner, a native of San Francisco and now attending Harvard, had been Hank's love interest for the last 18 months.

Michael looked down, saying nothing.

"Is something wrong?"

"Tommy is grounded at the moment, and confined to the palace, except for school."

"What happened? He's said nothing about it."

"It happened yesterday," Michael said. "The mother of one of his friends at school got hold of me. It seems the boys have been exchanging pornography by email."

Hank looked shocked. "Dad, I find that difficult to believe. I know it's far from unheard of for 13-year-olds to do that, but Tommy's the Puritan in the family. I tell him that his name should have been Cromwell or Cranmer."

"Well, Puritan or not, that's what happened. When I confronted him, he denied it, which made a bad situation worse. And I grounded him until he tells me the truth."

"Dad, today was the speech tournament, the one at Westminster School. He'd been practicing his dramatic recitation for weeks. He did get to go to that, didn't he?"

"No, Hank, he did not. He's confined to the palace. He was emailing pornography and he lied about it, and I won't stand for it."

"Did you see what the material was?"

Michael shook his head. "I saw the emails with the subject lines. The other boy's mother found the emails on her son's computer and was shocked."

"Who was the boy he was emailing with? Was it Sebastian Coombes?"

Michael looked surprised. "Do you know Sebastian?"

"He's sometimes part of our email and online talks. They'd been working on a final joint project for a history class about the soldiers who fought during the Norman Conquest, both the Anglo-Saxons and the Normans. Tommy drew a lot of pictures of what the soldiers might have looked like, how they might have been dressed out based on a considerable amount of research. They're quite good, in fact."

"Tommy draws, Hank?"

Hank nodded. "You didn't know? He's sent several to me, and I printed them off and put them on the wall in my room. He put my face on one of the Normans, as a joke. Several of my mates here were so impressed they commissioned him to do the same for them, except wearing their contemporary dress uniforms. They sent him photos and he based the drawings on them. He's made himself quite a few pounds, in fact."

"I'd no idea."

"I even nicknamed them, with a slightly off-color name. I call them his ASS pictures. It's become quite a joke with Tommy and Sebastian."

Michael paled. "ASS pictures?"

"Yes. It's an acronym for Anglo-Saxon Soldiers."

"Do you have one on your phone? Could I see the email and the drawing?"

Hank powered on his mobile and handed it to Michael. "Here's one email. Just click on the attachment."

Michael saw the email's subject line, "ASS picture No. 11." He clicked on the attachment, and what appeared on the screen was what he could see was an astonishingly detailed drawing of a Viking.

"It's a Viking Berserker, from the Battle of Stamford Bridge. The Vikings had invaded near York a few weeks before William landed near Hastings with the Normans."

Michael looked almost white. "How many of these drawings has Tommy sent?"

"Quite a few. At least 30 or so. He's given some of the drawings to the guardsmen at the palace as well. Some of them served as models."

"I feel sick. I've done your brother a terrible wrong. Mrs. Coombes apparently never looked at the pictures themselves. They all had this ASS acronym in the subject line, and she must have assumed they were pornography." Michael glanced at his watch. "The speech tournament at Westminster School, do you know what time it started?"

"At 9 this morning, Dad. You didn't know? It was scheduled to be over at 1."

Michael pulled out his mobile and punched in a number. "Ms. Abbott," he said. Paula Abbott was the security director in charge for the weekend at the palace. "Did Prince Thomas go to the speech tournament this morning?" He listened for a moment, said "Thank you, no, nothing else, thank you," and then ended the call.

"He didn't go. He stayed at the palace." He closed his eyes. "What have I done?"

"He was supposed to be reciting from *Beowulf*, using the Tolkien translation, I believe." Hank paused. "Dad, you need to return to London. The program here is over with lunch anyway. You need to talk to Tommy."

In the car back to London and the palace, Michael showered recriminations upon himself. His security officer for the day, Albert Hankins, riding in the back seat with him, wisely decided to say nothing and only listen.

"He kept telling me it wasn't porn, and I wouldn't listen. He offered to give me his laptop and let me see for myself, and I refused. I told him I wouldn't look at such filth. I chose to believe Mrs. Coombes; she was so upset I thought she must have seen what the boys were sending.

"And the speech tournament, it was an elimination round. I remember Tommy's teacher saying something about it. The final round is in a month, at Methodist Hall near Parliament. You miss any round, and you're out of it. And there's no make-up round." He paused. "How can I atone for this? I can't." He looked out the window. "What this really points out is that I haven't taken the time to get to know my own son. I'd no idea he was even doing drawings. I only knew about the Anglo-Saxon project because his history teacher said something about it a few months ago." He paused. "I feel sick. I hope I haven't crushed his spirit."

It had been almost seven years since Sarah's death, and Michael remembered her words about Tommy. *Hold him within your love, Mike.* Michael, now 44, hadn't remarried; he either avoided events or functions where he needed a partner or simply arrived by himself, figuring no one would show the king to the door. Despite Sarah's urging, he hadn't put himself in a position where a possible romantic interest might arise. For a time after Sarah's death, the media had speculated about the king and possible marital plans or partners. But after two years, with Michael steadfastly doing nothing to feed speculation, media interest had died.

As they neared London, the Saturday afternoon traffic slowed considerably.

"I'm sorry, sir," the security chauffeur said, "but it's a rather typical Saturday for traffic into the city. And an accident on the Battersea Bridge has the bridge closed and traffic snarling Chelsea Bridge and Vauxhall; I'm seeing if we can outflank the jams and get to Lambeth Bridge."

Michael's mobile rang. "Yes, Ms. Abbott. We're in traffic headed home." He listened. "All right. Does anyone in the family have any information or idea, Helen or Sophie or Mrs. Richards?" He listened again. "Right. Thank you. We should be there within the hour. Keep me informed, even if there's no news. And, yes, open the envelope." He powered off.

Michael addressed Hankins. "Tommy's not in the loft. They're searching the palace and the grounds. Mrs. Richards discovered Tommy was gone." She was the family's housekeeper.

"He's likely still within the palace, sir," Hankins said.

Michael shook his head. "The public palace tours continue until Oct. 5. The first tours started at 8 a.m., and Ms. Abbott says it's been extremely crowded, especially with the good weather. He might've found his way out through the crowds." He paused. "I'm hoping he disobeyed me and went to the speech tournament."

"We can track his phone. It's equipped with a GPS device."

"He left his phone, tablet, and laptop in his room. With an envelope addressed to me. I told her to open it to see if it might say where he's gone."

Twenty minutes later, they'd neared the Imperial War Museum. As traffic thickened, the chauffeur took back streets to get over to Lambeth Road.

Michael's mobile buzzed. "Yes, Ms. Abbott?"

"Sir, I need to read you the letter he left. We've not found him anywhere in the palace or on the grounds, and the letter indicates he may've left the site altogether."

"Go ahead." Michael enabled the mobile speaker so Hankins could hear as well.

"Dear Dad," Abbott read, "I know you won't believe me, but we didn't send any porn pictures. It's my drawings for our history project. I've left my mobile, iPad, and laptop for you to check. The passwords are below. Or Mr. Mitchell can check the palace server if you think I've deleted anything.

"I was bringing the pictures for you to see, and I heard what you said last night about autism and a special school. I looked the school up to be sure. I'm not autistic. I know what it is. My best friend is autistic. I'm not going to a special school. But it sounds like it's what you're thinking.

"I'm sorry for the mess with Mrs. Coombes, but Sebastian texted me through his sister. He's grounded, too. His mum never looked at the pictures. I know you won't believe me, but please ask Hank. He knows.

"I'm sorry. I have to go. You said if I couldn't admit about the porn, then I wasn't part of the family. I don't want a new school. I'm going somewhere safe until you talk with Hank.

"Your son, Tommy."

"He overheard a conversation I had last night with the counselor from when he couldn't speak. He only heard the first part. Ms. Abbott, I'm not sure what safe place he might be referring to. Perhaps it's with a school chum?"

"We've his list of his classmates, sir. And it's not Sebastian; we called and checked. Do you know who else he might be close to?"

"No, Ms. Abbott, I don't. Tommy is much the introvert, and Sebastian is the only friend I've been aware of. Helen or Sophie might have some idea."

"We've asked the princesses. Princess Helen didn't know. Princess Sophie said a young man in her class who serves as Tommy's upper-class mentor had heard nothing. He said he'd call if Prince Thomas contacted him, and he said Prince Thomas doesn't really have any close friends at school. Princess Sophie also said there was a boy in his class that he'd helped out of a scrape at school, but she didn't know his name."

Michael looked at his watch. 4:30 p.m. "Do we know how long he's been gone?"

"Mrs. Richards reported him missing from the loft about 12:15. She'd knocked on his door for lunch. When he didn't answer, she checked and saw he was gone. She searched the loft premises and called the security duty officer immediately. We're now reviewing all of the CCTV from the public tour areas of the palace. We've several hours of tapes from 12 different cameras inside the palace, and another eight outside the building on the grounds." She paused. "Sir, we've also advised Scotland Yard, and an officer has arrived at the palace. Through the police, they're checking the CCTV for Grosvenor Street at the rear of the palace and the Palace Road cameras by the Mews. The public tour exit on Grosvenor is the most likely way for him to take; the gates from the palace grounds to the Mews are locked during the public tours, as are the front gates. The only other exit is through the security check for the tours."

"All right. We're right by Lambeth Palace now and should be there shortly." He powered off his mobile. "I don't know what he means about his best friend being autistic. This is the first I've heard of it."

Tommy hadn't initially considered running away. But after hearing his father on the phone talk about autism and a new school somewhere in Worcestershire, he knew he had to leave.

Prince Thomas Michael McLaren Kent-Hughes had just turned 13. He'd always been a quiet, private child. Born one month after his father had become the British government, Tommy hadn't seen much of his father during that period, known as The Long Recess. But he did see a lot of his mother, his older brother Hank, and his twin sisters, Sophia and Helen.

The adult male stabilizing influence in his life had been and remained his Uncle David Hughes, twin brother of Sarah. David lived in Scotland, but he assumed a large role in Tommy's life when he, his wife Betsy, and their two children had moved to London from Edinburgh and occupied quarters in the palace for two years. David and his son Gavin spent considerable time with Tommy; for his part, Tommy idolized his uncle.

Unnoticed for two weeks after Queen Sarah's death and the funeral services in London and Edinburgh was that Tommy had stopped speaking. David had been the first to realize it, although Jim, when he learned the family knew, told Michael that it had started the day of Sarah's death. Doctors and psychologists eventually diagnosed hysterical shock. The boy often tried to speak, but he was always left in tears and frustration. Two years after Sarah's death, his voice returned.

For some time, no one except his Uncle David realized what had happened during those two years. The boy had taught himself Old Norse and Old English, using both texts and audio CDs. David had suspected he might have a gift for languages and had given him old textbooks and language CDs. Tommy copied the CDs on to his tablet and computer. When he began speaking again at age 8, he was able to tell his uncle verbally what he'd learned. It was three years later that David, realizing the rest of the family was unaware, mentioned to Michael that his son had not only learned Old English and Old Norse but had since learned Old Icelandic as well, to the point that some of the top professors in Edinburgh often consulted with the then-nine-year-old when the boy visited his uncle.

"He's something of a language prodigy," David had said.

Michael had been dumbfounded. The boy who couldn't speak for two years had taught himself multiple languages. Experts had been consulted, and they all agreed that Prince Thomas was something of a savant when it came to Germanic languages. At 12, he shocked everyone again when he learned Finn-Ugric, decidedly not a Germanic language.

The scene with his father over the alleged pornographic pictures had been ugly. Tommy had adamantly denied doing any such thing; Michael was just as adamant that the boy had collected and sent them. Refusing to look at the supposedly offending emails and files, Michael had grounded the boy until he admitted the truth.

That Friday night, banished to his bedroom, Tommy had cried himself to sleep. Mrs. Richards had brought him a dinner tray, and he begged her to believe him that he hadn't done what he was accused of. She comforted the boy as best she could, and later risked a rebuke from the king, asking him to at least look at the boy's laptop and mobile devices. Michael refused; he believed the report by the friend's mother was sufficient. "Why would she make this up?"

Tommy had spent weeks practicing and rehearsing his memorized recitation from *Beowulf*. He had drawn pictures of himself as Beowulf, battling the monster Grendl, to help visualize the specific passages. On Saturday morning, after Michael had left for Sandhurst and Tommy knew his case to be hopeless, he'd torn the drawings into pieces. His only thought was leaving.

He set his mobile devices aside and wrote the note for his father. He packed two changes of clothes in his backpack, along with some portable food quietly purloined from the loft's kitchen. From his chest of drawers, he retrieved a large gift bag from the palace gift shop. Months before, someone had left it on the palace terrace, and he'd brought it to his room. He didn't know if he'd ever need it, but the bag was new and unused.

Into the bag went various language primers and the book he was currently reading, on the history of the kingdom of Mercia in Anglo-Saxon times, along with his iPod which contained several language tracks. From a clothes drawer he withdrew an envelope containing 230 pounds, the proceeds of his earnings for selling the pictures to Hank's friends, teachers at school, and even a few of the palace guardsmen and security officers.

He opened his door and listened carefully. Mrs. Richards was the nominal governess for Tommy and the twins, but that now mostly consisted of keeping track of their meals.

About 9:15 a.m., he heard Mrs. Richards say something to herself out loud about needing to do a room clean. He made his move, quietly closing his door, tiptoeing to the loft's main door, and slipping quickly down the hall. His plan was to get to the concealed stairway that allowed the monarch to travel from the residence floor to the stateroom floor. The door opened behind a screen in the Yellow

Room, and he could watch until no one was looking and blend into the crowd of tourists. He and his siblings had taken this stairway dozens of times during hide-and-seek games.

It turned out to be easier than expected. The staterooms were unusually crowded. He joined the tourists, positioning himself close to a family with children near his age and following them, his sweatshirt hood pulled over the back of his head. He knew where the CCTV cameras were and made sure he didn't turn to face them.

Reaching the ground level, he headed for the terrace exit, where tourists turned in their audio guides and retrieved checked bags. He knew there was some danger in being spotted with a backpack before that point, but no one challenged him. The crowd's density helped.

He followed another family as they left the refreshment tent for the large bathroom facility. He waited for that family or one like it to leave and head for the final stop, the big palace souvenir tent. Once he reached that, he knew he could walk with the crowds the rest of the way to the rear exit on Grosvenor Place. He tagged along with yet another family.

As it turned out, no one paid any attention to the boy in the hooded sweatshirt carrying a gold Buckingham Palace shopping bag. He reached the rear exit, saw the attendant was mostly greeting adults, and slipped outside the gate. Hoping to leave a trail of confusion on the CCTV if he were spotted, he first turned to the left, as if headed toward Buckingham Palace Road or Victoria Station. Seeing a crowd of tourist families walking north, he turned around and fell in with them, heading toward the Wellington Arch and the Hyde Park tube station. It was 10:14 a.m.; he'd made good time. If the tube were operating normally, he'd ample time to reach his train at 11:40 at King's Cross station. He wouldn't even have to change tube lines.

At the Hyde Park Station, he used a 10-pound note to buy an all-day transit pass for the underground. He rode the escalator to the platform. Two minutes later, a train arrived, and Tommy joined tourists, students, and residents on the move to fulfill their Saturday plans.

He could only remember taking the tube three or four times at most. Within London, the royal family always had to travel by car, usually with an additional security car in front or back. He quietly observed the people he was sharing the crowded tube car with – teenagers and tourists mostly, but adult Londoners as well. People were chatting among themselves, reading, or pointedly avoiding eye contact. He blended in better than he could've hoped.

Sixteen minutes later, he exited at King's Cross and followed the signs to the trains. He checked the big schedule board and then found the automated ticket machines. Standing in line for an attended ticket window might be easier, but it also increased the chances of his being spotted, a young teen traveling by himself. It took him a few minutes to figure out how to use the machine, but soon he'd inserted 75 pounds and received a one-way, standard fare ticket. He had 20 minutes to spare before boarding and another 15 before the train left, so he looked around the food shops and bought water, a sandwich, and biscuits. With the food stowed in his backpack, he believed he had sufficient stores for the trip.

Edinburgh was only five hours away. Another hour or two after that, and he knew he'd be safe with Uncle David and Aunt Betsy in St. Andrews.

Arriving at the palace, Michael's car stopped at the private entrance just inside the interior courtyard arch; the main arrival portico was part of the public tour and was crowded with visitors. Michael hurried to the security offices.

He spotted Ms. Abbott as soon as he entered the office. "What do we know?"

"Sir, there's no update. But at Assistant Superintendent Crossling's suggestion, we're checking all CCTV tapes from the time the tours started. We've drawn a blank from 11:30 onward. He may've left earlier than we realized."

Michael shook hands with Crossling.

"Sir," Crossling said, "has Prince Thomas ever done anything like this before?"

Michael shook his head. "Never. His sister Helen did it twice and was caught within 30 minutes, both times by Security tracking the GPS on her phone. He's likely heard those stories."

"Sir," Abbott said, "at Mr. Crossling's suggestion, I called Mr. Lanham for communications support. He's in route to the palace now. With the Yard and the London police involved, media are bound to hear the prince is missing."

An hour later, Michael returned to the family loft, with the promise of regular security updates.

He went to Tommy's room. He picked up his son's note and read it. He felt desolate at being the cause of the boy's flight.

As he stood to leave, he noticed the rubbish bin by the desk. He could see torn pieces of paper. Sitting again at Tommy's desk, he fitted the pieces together, discovering three different drawings. As soon as he looked closely at one, he knew it was a representation of Beowulf battling the monster Grendl, except it was a Beowulf who looked recognizably like Tommy.

A few minutes later, Mrs. Richards found him, taping the picture back together while tears streamed down his face.

She handed him his mobile. "Your majesty, It's Ms. Abbott."

Michael wiped his eyes. "Ms. Abbott?"

"Sir, we've spotted him on the CCTV."

Michael raced to the security office. Abbott led him to one of the young security officers, Simon Fredericks.

"Officer Fredericks?" Michael said.

"Here, sir, we're fairly certain it's him. We've gone over this tape several times, and finally noticed something unusual." Fredericks pointed to the screen. "This is the area where tour visitors exit the palace building, turn in their audio guide headsets, and retrieve bags."

Michael watched closely.

The officer stopped the video. "Right here, a family is crowding at the desk with their headsets. This individual in the hooded sweatshirt seems with them." He stopped the video and enlarged the picture. "You can't see his face like you can the other members of the family, but do you see what's different?"

"He already has a backpack. And it looks like he's holding a bag. Is that a souvenir bag from the gift shop?"

Fredericks nodded. "Yes, sir. It's too soon for anyone to be wearing a backpack at that point or holding a giftshop bag." He switched to another screen and pointed. "Here he is again, waiting outside the WC area. We still can't see his face, as if he knows he needs to face away from the cameras. A family comes down the walkway from the WCs, and he follows. It's a different family. And here he is again." He switched to another video. "It's outside the gift shop. He's waiting and follows yet another family on the path to the exit on Grosvenor Place. The last we see of him on the palace CCTV is turning left at the exit."

"What time was this?"

"It was 9:40, sir," Abbott said.

"But that was more than two hours before we thought he might have left. Are we sure it's him?"

Crossling nodded. "Once we had the time, we had the Met check the CCTV along the street. You can watch it here." And he nodded to Fredericks, who opened a fourth screen.

Michael could see the boy in the hooded sweatshirt walking toward Palace Road. As he passed a large group of people, he suddenly did an abrupt about-face and followed them, close enough to suggest he was part of the group but not too close for anyone to wonder what he was doing. He kept his head down, as if avoiding the CCTV camera, but enough of a glimpse showed it was Tommy.

"Where does he go next?" Michael said.

Crossling answered. "The CCTV is spotty here, unfortunately. The last we see of him is taking the under-street stairs to the Wellington Monument at 9:44. We're checking the CCTV for the monument area at that time, but it was really crowded with tourists heading for Apsley House or Hyde Park, and a large bicycling group was crossing over to the park."

"Any guesses as to where he might've gone from there?"

For a moment, no one spoke. Crossling shook his head.

Then Officer Fredericks spoke. "If it were me, sir, trying to get away from the palace, I'd head to a bus or the Hyde Park tube station. Everything's right there. Is he familiar with the tube?"

"I don't think so. It's not Security-approved for any of us."

"Well, sir, the station is on the Piccadilly line. Westbound, it ends at Heathrow. Eastbound, it goes for quite a way, but it does stop at King's Cross. And in both directions, it connects to other lines, so that he could get to Waterloo, Victoria, Euston, and Paddington stations with only a single change of trains."

Michael looked at Crossling. "Do you think he's left London?"

"I don't know, sir," Crossling said. "Earlier I would've said it was highly unlikely. But watching him on the palace CCTV and then outside, I'd say the prince knew exactly what he was doing and had a definite plan."

"So, what do we do next?"

"We're checking the CCTV for the Piccadilly line and the Hyde Park station," Crossling said. "We've an approximate time so that helps us narrow things quite a bit."

Michael looked at his watch. "It's been more than nine hours since he left. He could be anywhere, even out of the country."

Abbott shook her head. "We have his passport in Security, sir. Wherever he is, he hasn't left Britain."

"Sir," Crossling said, "if I could make a suggestion. We're continuing to check CCTV on the tube and the possible train stations. Why don't you see if you could get something to eat and we'll call you if we find anything?"

David

Betsy Hughes looked up from her needlework and watched her husband David. He was diligently reading and grading papers and tests from the courses on Scottish history he taught at St. Andrews University, and entering the grades on his laptop. The school term had just ended, and David was marking up student papers for final grades. She knew he hoped to finish the grading this weekend, submit the grades through the school's online portal, and leave Monday for a several-day hike in the Highlands. Their son Gavin would usually accompany him, but this year, David would be by himself. Gavin had left for a mission trip sponsored by his university theology program.

She also knew David would read each paper painstakingly, to make sure he was giving a proper and fair assessment.

At one point, he looked up at her and smiled. "We should be a painting, entitled 'Picture of Domesticity, with Man Reading and Woman at Her Needlepoint.'"

She grinned. "How about, 'Woman at Needlepoint and Man Reading, with Woman Wondering if Man Would Make Her a Cup of Tea." He laughed but dutifully got up and soon brought back two cups. He returned to his grading.

It was at moments like this one, children away, royal relatives in London temporarily forgotten, all the prizes and honors for both his books and his teaching out of sight in his study, that she believed she loved him most. They'd met on a blind date as third-year students at the University of Edinburgh, she an education major and he a year-abroad student from the States studying history. It was an instant attraction, and from that moment on they'd been almost inseparable. She'd been surprised that she'd fallen so quickly and so deeply in love, and with an American. But that's what'd happened. It had been a glorious year, with their friends Tommy and Ellen and Michael and Sarah, David's twin sister. The sister who'd eventually married Michael and become queen when Michael became king. The sister who'd died.

Michael and their children had been devastated. Almost unnoticed in the midst of all the national grief was David's desolation. He and Sarah had been close. And then she was gone, dead at 35. And Tommy was gone now, too, and Ellen remarried.

At the end of that glorious university year, she and David decided to get married, despite her parents' concerns that they were too young and still had more school ahead, particularly David, facing several more years for advanced degrees. He'd eventually achieve a doctorate in history and become a professor at St. Andrews, an American who loved, taught, and breathed Scottish history better than most Scots.

Those early years had been hard, but Betsy cherished them. Now, they had a good income with his university position and the royalties from his books. But they could've only afforded their current home with the inheritance David received when his grandmother and father died six months apart. Sarah declined her part of the inheritance, given Michael's extraordinary financial position. It was a generous move, allowing the estates to be divided between David and his older brother Scott. Their house sat on four acres, some four miles north of central St. Andrews, and even had beachfront.

David and Betsy had two children, Gavin, 20, and Eleanor, 18. Both had good heads. Eleanor would be starting her first year at the University of Edinburgh, intent on studying biology. Gavin, however, worried his parents. He'd been a classic overachiever since grammar school, taking on far more than he should've but had always managed to pull it off. So far. But they worried. David wondered if he was trying to compete with his famous royal cousins or even his father's recognitions. Gavin had been going on summer mission trips for years; this summer he was doing two, one to Haiti and the other to Albania. It was because of the Haiti trip that he was missing the hike with David.

Her husband hadn't said anything, but she knew he was disappointed. He always enjoyed the time alone with their son. Despite his hectic teaching and writing schedule, he'd always been there for her and the children. She looked at his chiseled American good looks and his wavy sandy hair that was starting to show a light dusting of gray. Physically, he was a handsome man. Eleanor favored her father in looks, while Gavin seemed a spitting image of Betsy's father, dark-haired, square-jawed, and solidly built. He was now in his second year of theology studies and starting to work on a book about faith and missions. Yes, they worried he was taking on too much.

Betsy also knew David was troubled about Michael, his brother-in-law. A few weeks earlier, David had tried to talk with Michael about Prince Thomas and his need to be with his dad more. Michael had been offended and cut the conversation short, and likely, she thought, because David had been spot on. He and Michael hadn't talked since. David called and sent emails but received no response.

She knew he was deeply hurt but rather typically blamed himself for the estrangement. "I could've handled it better."

She knew how close Tommy was to her husband. It was to David he'd turned when his mother died. And Tommy, who favored his mother physically in looks, also physically favored his uncle, with the same wavy blond hair and a rounded boy's face now giving way to that chiseled look. Because of Tommy, Betsy knew what David looked like as a boy.

And it was to his uncle whom Tommy turned whenever he faced a serious problem.

She set aside her needlepoint just as David closed his laptop. "Finished?"

"All done," he said, smiling but tired. "I think I'll be able to do my hike on Monday."

"So, this year, it's just you and Rolfe?"

"Just me and Rolfe." Rolfe Solveig was a native Norwegian but had lived in Scotland for years, operating a tour guide business that included both bus tours and hiking expeditions. "I wish Gavin could've come, but this Haiti trip was important for him. This year, just me and Rolfe, which he's doing as a personal favor. He's really too busy running the business but he wanted to do it." They hiked different routes each year; this year it was the Great Glen Way from Fort William to Inverness, a hike David had never done before.

David glanced at his watch. "It's going on 8. Do you want any more tea?"

As Betsy shook her head, the doorbell rang.

David frowned. "Are we expecting anyone?"

"Not that I'm aware of."

David walked to the door and checked the camera screen just inside to see who it was.

"Tommy?" He opened the door. And the boy stepped into his uncle's arms.

On his way back to the loft, Michael's mobile buzzed. He glanced at the caller ID and saw it was his brother-in-law.

"David, I owe you a call. Actually, I owe you an apology. I'm sorry for my rudeness when we last talked. But if I could, might I call you back in an hour or so? We're having something of a family emergency."

"Michael, is it about Tommy?"

"Do you know something? Have you heard from him?"

"Tommy's with us here in St. Andrews. He arrived a few minutes ago."

Michael stopped and leaned against a wall, relief overwhelming him. "Is he all right?"

"Physically, he's fine, Michael. More than a little tired and rather hungry. Betsy's fixing him a rather robust tea. But he's physically fine." He paused. "He explained why he came."

"Can I speak to him?"

"Just a moment, I'll get him. Michael, please be careful. I know you're likely at your wits end but be careful with him. He's not in good emotional shape."

A moment later, Michael heard his son's voice.

"Dad?"

"Are you all right, son?"

"I'm not going to that school. If you say I have to go, I'm staying here with Uncle David."

"Tommy, I know what you overheard. I understand why you reacted the way you did, but you only heard part of the conversation. I'm not sending you to that school or any other. You're staying at ICS."

On the St. Andrews end of the conversation, David and Betsy could both see that the boy was on the verge of tears.

"And I know about the pictures. When I had lunch with Hank, he told me. I owe you a huge apology, and there's nothing I can do to make up for your missing the speech competition. I'm so sorry. I've completely screwed this up."

Tommy handed the phone to David and left the kitchen. David nodded at his wife and Betsy followed the boy out of the room.

"Michael, it's David again. He's shook. Betsy's with him."

"David, I need to let Security and Scotland Yard know Tommy's okay. Can I call you back in an hour?"

"That's fine, Michael. We'll be here."

"Did he say how he got to St. Andrews?"

"He caught the 11:40 from King's Cross. It's mostly an express, I believe, with only a couple of stops. He figured out the fare machines on his own. Once he got to Waverly Station in Edinburgh, he took the train to Leuchars and then the bus to St. Andrew's. He bought a map and walked to the house, mostly along the beach."

"That must be, what, three miles?"

"Right at four. He decided not to take a taxi or a bus because he was afraid the word might already be out and the police looking for him."

"I'll call back in an hour, David. Thank you. All he said in the note he left was that he was going to a safe place. If I'd have been thinking clearly, I would've realized that his safe place was with you and Betsy."

For a moment, David said nothing. "I'll be waiting for your call, Michael."

"One last thing, David. Tommy left a note, and he mentioned that his best friend was autistic. Do you have any idea whom he's talking about?"

"Yes, Michael, I do. But that's his story to tell, unless he gives me leave to share it. I'll ask him."

Ringing off, Michael walked back to the Security offices.

"He's in St. Andrews with David and Betsy," he told the group, now some 20 strong. "I've talked with him. I'll be talking with David in an hour to decide what we do next."

"We're glad he's safe, sir," said Abbott. "Officer Fredericks here was just asking if he might have gone to family outside of London, like Prince Henry or the Hughes in Scotland."

"Well, that's exactly what he did." He paused. "Thank you all for your help and hard work. We've had a good result."

"Sir," said Ms. Abbott, "we'll need to dispatch security officers immediately to Dr. Hughes' home at St. Andrews. It's the protocol.

We can send two officers from the team at McLarens." Palace security included an office in the barn at McLarens.

Michael nodded. "When I call David back, I'll let him know. I'll likely be flying up there tomorrow."

Michael called David at 9 p.m. precisely.

"He's asleep," David said. "He's had himself quite an adventure. It was relatively uneventful, but I think the new experience quite wore him out."

"I assume he took the tube to King's Cross?" said Michael.

"Right," David said. "He didn't want to leave a trail on his own phone or computer, so he used Helen's to get directions. She doesn't use a password, because she keeps forgetting it. He checked underground lines and the schedule for the trains at King's Cross. He learned what he needed to do to access the ticket machines, and the BritRail web site has some easy-to-follow videos. He apparently had money from selling some of his pictures, and that's what he used to buy his tickets. I can't imagine the anxiety and trouble you've gone through today, but what he did is rather impressive for a 13-year-old."

"And he fled because he thought I was sending him to a school for autistic children?"

"It was what pushed him over. He was already upset over what'd happened with the pictures, and when he heard your conversation on the phone, he became terrified, I think. You need to understand why. It wasn't an irrational reaction. And it has to do with his friend, Angus. I checked with him, and he said he was okay for me to tell you about Angus. I think you'll see why Tommy panicked."

"This is the autistic boy he calls his best friend, what he said in the note?"

"Yes. Two years ago, when Tommy spent a few weeks with us, he met Angus at church. It's quite a story."

David and Betsy had taken their then-16-year-old daughter Eleanor and Tommy to their Wednesday evening church program. Their 18-year-old son Gavin had left the week before for a new student orientation at university. The program began with an informal buffet dinner, followed by classes for adults, the teen youth group, and choir and music practice for singers and musicians. The year before, Tommy had joined the musicians. Brent Epworth, master of the house at Buckingham Palace, had given Tommy guitar lessons, and the boy had taken to it immediately. Epworth also gave him an old guitar, which he'd brought with him to St. Andrews for his visit.

When they arrived at the church, David noticed a woman standing uncertainly at the entrance with a boy of about Tommy's age. He could see immediately the boy had some kind of developmental disability; his mother was holding his hand and the boy was leaning and staring down at the ground.

Eleanor peeled off to find her friends, and David introduced himself, Betsy and Tommy to the woman.

"I'm Evelyn. This is my son Angus. He heard one of your music programs on the radio and he's been desperate to visit." David and Betsy could both see she was extremely nervous.

"Why don't you sit with us for dinner? There's no cost," David said, and Betsy nodded. Betsy later told David that she had immediately recognized Evelyn from their days at the University of Edinburgh.

With food from the buffet line they were soon seated and eating. David and Betsy talked mostly with Evelyn, but the adults could see that Tommy was managing to keep a rather one-sided conversation going with Angus.

When they finished eating and the time for the program started, Tommy addressed the adults.

"Angus has decided he'll come with me to music practice. I told him I have a guitar, and he thinks he can play it."

For a moment, Evelyn looked terrified. "Wait, I'm not sure, he's –"

Tommy politely interrupted. "I know. But Angus knows he'll be fine with me. We're already becoming great friends."

Evelyn stood motionless, clearly torn. Should she listen to the handsome boy and run the risk of an epic Angus meltdown or should she grab Angus by the hand and run from the room? Then she slowly nodded. The three adults watched Tommy take Angus by the hand and leave the dining area.

"Angus is autistic," Evelyn said. "I've had him for a time in a residence school in Edinburgh, but it turned out rather awful; he was constantly bullied, and it made him turn inward even more than he already was. And he got seriously ill. He's been at home, attending a special needs program at school. He never indicated any interest in music until he heard the radio program. He found the church on the internet and brought me a map he'd printed. I've never seen him so trusting with anyone before, not like this with your nephew."

She'd been in the kitchen at home; Angus was listening to the radio in the front parlour. He'd darted into the kitchen, grabbed her by the hand, and dragged her to the radio. It took time, but she finally realized he was captivated by the music, which sounded to her vaguely American country western and would turn out to be bluegrass. She wrote down the name of the program; Angus navigated the internet to find the church musicians who'd recorded it and the church's location.

"You need to know," Betsy said, "that Tommy, as David said, is our nephew from London, staying with us for a few weeks. His father is King Michael."

Evelyn nearly bolted. "Oh, no, you don't know about me."

"I think we do, Evelyn, and it's all right. We were in education together at university."

"It's Evelyn McLin, Michael," David said. "She and Angus had moved to St. Andrews from Edinburgh, and she's now a full-fledged member of our church. There's no father around; Angus was the result of an affair with an older married man and he turned his back on her once she became pregnant."

"I don't recall anyone mentioning Angus or Evelyn." Michael had known Evelyn from childhood; she'd relentlessly chased Michael through school and at the University of Edinburgh. She'd been instrumental in sabotaging Michael and Sarah's relationship, and she'd later been recruited to claim she and Michael had an affair in college.

"I know it has to be disconcerting, but Tommy's had a huge impact on Angus, a boy his doctors and teachers wrote off as virtually unreachable. The night they met, Tommy took him to the music practice room, introduced him as his new friend, and handed him his guitar. What happened next shocked everyone. Angus took a few moments to sound the strings, and then launched into exactly the music he'd heard on the radio. Everyone was stunned. They were even more stunned to learn he'd never played the guitar before. Someone found him a fiddle, and he and Tommy played together. You've no idea how it's changed Angus. It's been utterly amazing." David paused. "They perform here at the church, whenever Tommy's in town. And they practice together via Skype and Facetime. Tommy eventually persuaded him to play together at the church but with Tommy by long distance from the palace via an iPad. Angus won't play without Tommy."

"David, I'm flummoxed. I didn't even know Tommy played guitar. And to help this boy like he did." He paused. "Why haven't you mentioned this before?"

"Tommy asked me not to, Michael," David said. "He knew the story about Evelyn, because she'd told him. He was afraid you might make him break off his friendship with Angus. But you should know that Evelyn was so overwhelmed by Tommy reaching out to Angus that it led her to faith. And Angus has progressed remarkably. Yes, he's autistic, but he's done so well that he's been mainstreamed into a local school here. Evelyn said it's like an entirely different child walked out of church that night, and now she believes the sun rises and sets with Tommy."

"I'm feeling a bit overwhelmed with all this. And it's my own son."

"Michael, Tommy has an almost uncanny ability to sense where a lot of people are, like he can read their minds, or perhaps their hearts."

"It's what his counselor said, in the part of the conversation Tommy missed last night. He said that, while it might appear he has a degree of autism, it's actually a case of Tommy being a highly developed empath. He reminded me of something he told me when Tommy couldn't speak after Sarah's death. He said it was as if Tommy had absorbed the totality of the family's grief, and coupled with his own, his mind couldn't handle it. So, his speech just shut down as a defense mechanism, that his mind was actually trying to protect him."

"Do you know where he learned to draw?"

Michael was silent for a time. "Yes, David, I do. I know he never had art classes at school, but I came home early one day and found him in the studio with Sarah. It was two years before she died, so he must have been four."

"I asked him, and he told me he learned from Sarah. I was amazed. I know she never let anyone in her studio when she was painting. He remembers sitting quietly while she painted and just watching her. One day she noticed him drawing, much like the story I heard about Jason. And she'd talk with him, guide him, even give him some assignments." He paused. "Michael, I think Tommy could almost crawl inside Sarah's skin. At least when it came to her painting."

"I know. David, it led to one of the biggest fights Sarah and I ever had. She'd never let any of us see her painting. Only once before had I seen her do a sketch, and that was at university, and her subject was my calf. When she started painting at UCLA, scores of people watched her. But after that, no one was allowed. I came home one day and the door to her studio at the palace was open, and I heard her talking. I looked in and saw she was with Tommy. His hands were all different colors, because she'd been teaching him about pastel drawings."

"How did that cause an argument?"

"I asked her why she let Tommy watch her when she never let any of the rest of us. She said it was because, other than Jason, Tommy was the only one in the family who understood what she was trying to do with her painting. It escalated from there. I said I'd always been interested, more than interested. I'd supported her and encouraged her, but she'd still never let me watch her paint. The truth is that I was jealous of my own son. He'd been able to be a part of her life that she'd never let me enter."

He almost said what Sarah had told him about Hank, Tommy, and the throne. But he held back.

For a moment, David said nothing. Then he spoke. "I think I can understand it, Michael. I mean, why you reacted the way you did. It might help explain some other things, too. The day before she died, she asked Tommy to do a drawing of her. It's of Sarah in her hospital bed."

Michael heard the catch in David's voice.

"I'm sorry, Michael. It's still hard for me to talk about, and it was almost seven years ago. He gave me the drawing. It's a very simple pen-and-ink drawing. I have it framed in my study here. You won't believe how good it is, and to have been drawn by a six-year-old is rather mind-blowing. He captured Sarah exactly, and not just her illness. He caught the love in her eyes."

"How did I miss all of this, David? It's almost as if we're talking about a stranger. How did I not know what was going on in my son's life?" He paused. "Perhaps I can answer my own question. Of all my children, he's the one I feel the least close to. And while a lot of things contributed to it, it was mostly about Sarah. I was jealous of my own son."

"Michael, I don't know. You can probably figure it out better than I can. In my last conversation with Sarah, just the two of us, she asked me to look after Tommy, because she said he'd take her death as badly as you would, because he was so much like you. It confused me; I always thought of Hank as the one most like you. When I asked her to explain, she said Tommy had the same capacity for faith and love for others that you did, that both of you were far beyond herself and the rest of the family in that regard. 'But they won't see it in each other, David, and that could become a tragedy.' Maybe all of what's happened this weekend is a bit of divine intervention."

Michael felt the tears on his cheeks. "How is he doing really, David?"

"He adores you, Michael. You're the most important person in his life, and I'm not sure you've known that. When you confronted him about the pictures, his world split apart. He was devastated, far beyond how any child would be if wrongly accused. He believed you could do nothing wrong, that you'd never falsely accuse him, and yet he knew he hadn't been exchanging pornography. He couldn't hold those two contradictory thoughts together." He paused. "Michael, his relationship with you is very close to broken. I don't think it's irretrievably broken, but that could happen."

"What do I do, David? I'm afraid that anything I do might make it worse."

"Michael, I'm no expert here. I have my own struggles with children, especially Gavin. My son is a gifted young man who's trying to do everything at once and become everything at once and I'm scared that he's taking too much on and he'll crash and burn one day. I'm not the expert on children, and I doubt anyone is."

They were both quiet for a time.

"You might," David said slowly, "consider something. I know you likely have a hectic schedule, but what if you come here, tomorrow say, and come to church with us tomorrow night. Tommy and Angus will be playing, unless you think Tommy must return to London. In fact, most likely the word's already traveled like lightning around the church that Tommy's here; he called one of the musicians at church and asked if he could play with them tomorrow at worship and tomorrow night. I expect the evening service to be packed once people find out. And they usually do a music program after the service, as a public outreach.

"But you could come and hear him and Angus play; it would mean seeing Evelyn as well, so fair warning. And perhaps spend a few days with him. If you like, I can take the two of you hiking in the Highlands. I've already scheduled the hike for myself. Tommy's hiked with me and Gavin before, and we might even see if Angus will come. You'll have plenty of time to talk with him. Michael, Tommy's a marvelous young man. You need to see and know the child you and Sarah created."

"My schedule's packed, but I'll cancel or postpone everything. I'll come tomorrow. Ms. Abbott told me that two security officers have been dispatched to your house and should be there soon. They'll stay outside, but it's protocol to have protection in place for any family members when they travel."

"We'll make room. I want you to stay here with us as well. And Michael, don't hinge everything on what happens in the next few days. Consider it a start, a beginning. And don't build a lot of expectations. Just come here and we'll do our hike, and you can enjoy your son for the person he is. You may not realize it, but you've had more to do with who he is than you know. Many's been the time I've gotten a glimpse of his father when we were at school together."

When they finished the call, Michael walked to the loft to find Mrs. Richards.

"I'm going to St. Andrews tomorrow. My schedule is crazy busy this coming week, but it'll have to be put off or rescheduled. I have to go to Scotland." He paused. "All of this comes from things I've done and not done, and I'm learning that God has been blessing me with a child I've never felt close to."

David emailed a list of hiking clothes for Tommy, and Michael turned it over to Mrs. Richards to pull together. Sophie and Helen decided to tag along on the plane ride, but they would go on to McLarens and stay with Iris. Michael also called Hank and Jason, updating them on Tommy and letting them know of the hiking plans.

Rearranging his schedule he left in the hands of his secretary, Carrie Waldman, and Josh Gittings and Jay Lanham. Since the restoration of Parliament, Josh, Trevor Barry, and Jay had returned to normal palace service. Trevor was spending more time at his legal chambers; his legal and consulting practice had mushroomed since the end of The Long Recess. He now supervised six attorneys directly and shared the legal work with several others, turning his chambers into one of the largest and most sought-after practices in the country. He remained the monarchy's legal consultant; his son Andrew had joined his chambers as a barrister.

Both Trevor and Josh were approaching 60, and Michael knew that Josh, at least, was beginning to think about retirement, or a partial retirement. Jay was now 48, supervising the palace communications staff even though he, too, could likely be successful as an independent communication consultant. For now, however, he seemed to prefer and rather enjoy the reduced duties of the palace compared to the massive job of managing Government's communications.

Paula Abbott assigned Simon Fredericks as the king's personal security officer for the trip to Scotland. She'd been impressed by his work on the tracking of Prince Thomas, and after a phone conversation with Security Chief Ryan Mitchell, wanted to see how Fredericks did with fieldwork.

On Sunday, the royal plane landed first at Edinburgh airport, with the two princesses departing for McLarens. A short flight followed to Leuchars Air Force Base near St. Andrews. A car was waiting, and Michael soon arrived at the Hughes home.

David and Betsy met him at the door, with Tommy standing behind them. Michael and his son looked at each other for a moment, before Michael walked over to the boy and enfolded him in his arms.

"I'm so sorry, Tommy."

Michael held him and kissed the top of his head. Tommy's arms stayed at his side.

David had thrown Rolfe Solveig a bit of a curve for the hike by adding Michael, Tommy, and Angus, plus three security officers who would accompany them and a team tracking them with vehicles. But Rolfe quickly recovered, and he was able to make changes in their accommodations for the 73-mile hike from Fort William to Inverness along the Great Glen Way. Fortunately, it was early in the hiking season; accommodations were plentiful. Because the group included members of the royal family, Rolfe expected and received a number of phone calls from palace security. Sunday became a day of making new reservations, without naming who was in the party, and ongoing phone calls with Ryan Mitchell and Paula Abbott at Buckingham Palace.

Evelyn McLin, once she recovered from meeting with Michael at church and profusely apologizing for her past behavior, had been concerned about Angus tackling the 73 miles of the hike. Michael watched as Tommy reassured her.

"We'll be together the whole time, Mrs. McLin. Security will be with us and tracking us in the vehicles, and if something happens, they can move very quickly."

"Angus," she said, "you would like to do this?"

Angus nodded, speaking haltingly. "I can do it. I'll be with Tommy and Mr. Hughes."

Separately, both David and Evelyn marveled at how well Angus could communicate, and how much had changed during the past two years.

"I'll be responsible for him, Mrs. McLin," Tommy said. "We'll be fine. I'll have him call each morning before we set out. And I'll call if we run into a problem."

That, and learning several security officers would be in the group, convinced her.

After the boys had gone to sleep at the Hughes' home Sunday night, Michael noted the discussion with David as they sat in the family room. "Evelyn seems to have great confidence in Tommy."

David nodded. "Angus could barely speak when Tommy met him. He looked like a boy with serious problems, and he'd only nod or shake his head. He was also given to tantrums. Everything changed when he met Tommy. Music opened up the world for him, and Tommy was there to encourage and support him. When we first met them, Angus's problems were immediately obvious. Now, you have to be around him for some time to know he's autistic. How Tommy's helped him is astounding."

They left for Fort William before dawn on Monday, and found Rolfe waiting for them at the small office at the trailhead. David made the introductions, Rolfe inspected their equipment and boots, and then, in his soft Norwegian-and Scottish-accented English, explained the route, displaying a large map.

"The total hiking distance from here at Fort William to Inverness is 73 miles. We'll do about 12 miles each day, sometimes a little less and sometimes a little more. The first leg, from here to Gairlochy, is fairly short and easy, and we'll spend the night there. It's a beautiful view of Loch Lochy, and tomorrow we'll walk around it to South Laggan on Loch Oich. On Wednesday, we'll walk to Fort Augustus, on the southern end of Loch Ness, and we'll be traveling along Loch Ness for most of the rest of the hike. Thursday we'll reach Invermoriston, Friday we'll stop in Drumnadrochit, and then on Saturday we end in Inverness."

Simon Fredericks stood and addressed the group. "Security vehicles will be tracking us on both sides of the lochs and available within 10 minutes at all times. We've also arranged for a helicopter service that can reach us even faster. Three of us will be part of the hiking group. The places we'll be staying overnight know the size and makeup of our group – six adults and two teens – but they haven't been told identities. That relative anonymity will likely become harder to maintain as the hike progresses, but we hope to keep it all the way to Inverness."

"A word about overnight accommodations," Solveig said. "Because of the size of the group, we have reserved the largest rooms available for each overnight stay. Most are generally shared rooms and shared bath facilities. We'll work out with security what's appropriate at each stop."

Angus, sitting next to Tommy, leaned to his friend and said, "We shower together?"

Tommy reassured him. "It'll be okay. We'll work out a scheme for privacy."

Solveig continued. "We'll maintain a moderate pace each day. The hike is relatively easy for first timers, and extremely easy if you've hiked before. The winds will be at our back; it's why we start at Fort William and head to Inverness. Each town where we stay overnight has food and supplies available, with the best selection available at Fort Augustus, about the halfway point. Where we're staying there is a new facility with quite a few features, including hot tubs and a very good restaurant. If you have special dietary needs or need some kind of special assistance, please let me know. If you have questions or concerns at any time, just ask.

"It's time we got on our way."

Mary

Mary Penniman frowned at the printed reservation sheets for Wednesday and Thursday. It was the slow time for the hiking season; overnight guests would usually be few if any at mid-week. Yet a party of eight was booked for tonight and would be joined at dinner by four more.

She called to her brother in the next room. "William, did you see tonight's reservations?"

"Yes. Party of eight overnight and 12 for dinner?"

"Have you ordered supplies?"

He walked into the room. "Yes. Rolfe Solveig called Sunday. Originally it was him and one other, but the group expanded at the last minute. They're from St. Andrews. I almost asked Mum to stay and help but figured with Ciara and me in the kitchen and me and you serving, we could manage. Just. Did I tell you how glad I am you're here?"

The year before, 36-year-old William Gill had quit his London advertising job and invested a good chunk of savings in a guesthouse at Fort Augustus on Loch Ness. It needed some serious rehabilitation; he'd spent months on the work, using local tradesmen for plumbing updates, new electrical wiring and fixtures, new flooring, and new cabinetry. Most of the rest of his savings had gone to new kitchen equipment and furniture for the bedrooms and living areas. The restaurant could seat 25 at a time, and an outdoor deck could accommodate 15 more. Dinner was a set meal, with breakfast and lunch set up buffet style.

A stay at Gill's cost a bit more than the other guesthouses in the area; it was also a cut or two above. A builder helped William figure out how to afford three hot tubs and several other amenities. And while he hadn't been overwhelmed with guests, he'd made enough to tide them over through winter and spring. And the main hiking season was barely getting underway, heavy on weekends. Soon, reservations would also begin to fill weekdays.

Rolfe's unexpectedly large party was a pleasant mid-week surprise.

William's sister, Mary Penniman, had driven up from London with her 13-year-old son Mark, stopping in York to get her mother. Mrs. Gill had taken Mark and William's two children, Quinn and Alana, to Inverness and then the Orkneys for an end-of-school-term holiday. The preponderance of Irish names in William's family was attributable to his wife, Ciara; she was a native Dubliner. They'd met in London, working at the same firm.

Mary had stayed in Fort Augustus, helping her brother and sister-in-law with whatever needed doing. Serving food. Washing dishes. Laundry. Making tea. Checking in guests. It was unpaid work, but, for Mary, it was a break from London and her job at the British Library, where she worked in translations. She loved Scotland, she loved the area around Loch Ness, and she loved the idea of her brother throwing over his London career and doing something he truly wanted to do.

William was more than grateful for his sister's help. He also worried about her. Several years before, her husband John had been killed in Iraq a week before he was to come home. She'd been devastated, and William knew she still mourned him deeply, to the point of wearing her wedding ring as if she were still married. She also refused to talk about John to anyone, including her son. It was as if she had made a pretense of his still being alive and stationed overseas.

John's father had set up a trust to pay for Mark's education at International Christian School in Notting Hill and beyond. Mary never would've been able to pay the tuition, but the trust would cover Mark thorough graduation and university. John had been an ICS graduate, and his father had been so impressed that he wanted the same opportunity for Mark.

Mark's first year had gone extraordinarily well. Disaster struck at the beginning of this last year. A new student had enrolled in Mark's class, and the boy had decided Mark would make a perfect target for pranks and abuse. He had wheedled Mark's friends away one by one and then started the bullying in earnest. Mark grew withdrawn and clearly depressed.

Then, suddenly, everything had changed. Another student in Mark's class had happened upon a bullying incident in the hallway, collared the bully, shamed the other boys, and marched the bully to the headmaster. The bullying had stopped. Mark began to look forward to school again. The headmaster had called the offending student's parents to the school and told them the bullying stopped or the boy would have to leave. He had a separate meeting with Mary.

When she asked Mark who'd intervened in the hallway, he answered her with two words.

"Prince Thomas."

The first day's walk hike had been relatively short, just under 12 miles. Rolfe had been concerned about the level of physical activity the group would be undertaking, but he was surprised to see his royal guests and the security team keep up extremely well, including the two boys. David had told him that Angus McLin was autistic, but the boy was a real trooper.

When Rolfe had asked Tommy if he thought his friend could keep up, Tommy nodded. "He's a walker. At home, he walks for blocks and blocks, often along the beach. I think he'll do fine."

And so far, Angus had done exactly that, to the point where Rolfe stopped worrying.

When they reached the guest house at Gairlochy, Rolfe went inside with a security man while the rest of the group remained outside, resting and admiring the view. The two boys slipped to the side by themselves.

"David," Michael said, nodding toward the boys, "do you have any idea what they're doing?"

David looked. Angus had slipped an arm from his sweatshirt and was holding it up for an inspection by Tommy. Then they saw Tommy do the same thing.

David grinned. "I think, Michael, that Angus is experiencing physical changes in his body, and is asking Tommy's help in figuring out what's happened. And Tommy is showing him the same thing has happened to him, and there's nothing to be concerned about."

Michael was silent. He continued watching for a moment and then turned away. He had a sudden vision of him and Tommy

McFarland, up in the hills behind McLarens, and Michael doing the same thing as Angus. He'd been terrified he had some serious disease.

"You didn't know that Tommy had started puberty."

Michael shook his head. "No, I didn't."

"He called me a few months ago. He'd started seeing physical changes, and while he was fairly certain what was happening, he wanted to make sure."

"A father should've noticed."

"Michael, don't start beating yourself up over this. He'd talked with Hank quite some time ago, and Hank had explained what to expect. But he'd forgotten. He called me to verify that his body hadn't suddenly started going crazy. And he hasn't started the big growth spurt yet, but I suspect it's not far off. Angus is about four months behind him in the process. It's a blessing that Tommy can explain it and reassure him."

A little later, Tommy pulled Michael to the side and told him he needed to get some supplies. "Angus needs some deodorant."

Michael nodded. "And you're okay with yours?"

"Yes, sir. I'm fine."

Michael nodded. He knew David was being more than kind, but he also knew that he simply shouldn't have missed this in his son's life.

The hike to South Laggan had afforded a beautiful view of Loch Lochy, a short overland walk, and then a view of Loch Oich. It was a bit longer than the first day's hike, but everyone in the group seemed to be holding up well. Michael found himself tired at the end of the day and ready for dinner and a good night's rest. But he felt more relaxed than he had in years. Tommy seemed to sense a lessening of the tension with his father, and Michael watched his normally introverted son become talkative and more outgoing than he'd ever seen him. He wondered if Tommy was an introvert only around him.

A hearty dinner was served by the elderly couple who operated the guesthouse and who were pleasantly surprised by their guests. Afterward, they all turned in, with Security maintaining watch.

Sleeping in the large common room, Michael awoke in the darkness to the sound of thunder and rain. A storm seemed to be rolling up the mountains, following the wind across the lochs to Inverness. He decided to settle himself back under his warm covers when he heard what sounded like the whimper of a wounded animal.

Simon Fredericks, in the single bed next to Michael's, also heard the sound, and sat up, looking around. Everyone else seemed asleep, including Tommy, who was in a single bed on the other side of Michael.

When Michael's eyes grew accustomed to the dark, he saw the source of the whimper. Angus was sitting up, back against the wall and hands over his ears. Another peal of thunder led to the boy beginning to shake and whimper a bit louder.

Michael got up, walked around Tommy's bed, and sat on the side of Angus's.

"It's just a loud storm, Angus. And I have to say it scares me a bit, too. But it's only a storm. I'll sit here with you until it passes."

At that moment, thunder boomed so loud that the walls seemed to shake. Angus, with a strangled cry, dove straight for Michael and wrapped his arms around his waist. The boy was shaking.

Michael put his arms around Angus. "It's okay, Angus. I'm here with you until the storm passes. And it will pass." Each succeeding peal of thunder caused Angus to tighten his hold on Michael. And Michael kept reassuring the boy. At one point, he looked across at Tommy and saw his son was awake as well, watching them.

As the storm faded, Angus gradually relinquished his grip. After several minutes, with only the sound of a gentle rain on the roof, Michael was able to settle Angus back in his bed.

The next morning, shortly before they were to leave, Michael was standing by himself, soaking up the view of Loch Oich. Tommy walked up and stood next to him.

"Thank you for helping Angus last night."

"He seemed quite frightened by the storm."

Tommy nodded. "He's always been afraid of thunderstorms. When he was at that school in Edinburgh, there was a storm one night. The boys who bullied him dragged him out of bed, pulled off his pajamas, and locked him outside in a courtyard. He was left there for hours, until one of the staff saw him lying naked on the ground. He got really sick with pneumonia and almost died. It took him weeks to recover, and Mrs. McLin brought him home for good. She filed some kind of action against the school. He's still frightened by storms."

"Where's Angus now?"

"Uncle David's helping him get dressed after his shower. Thank you for helping him."

"This is why you became so upset when you heard me on the phone and thought I was going to send you off."

Tommy nodded again. "Angus told me what happened to him."

"You're a good friend to Angus."

"He's a good friend to me, too, Dad. He helps me as much as I help him. He's my friend for life."

Michael put his arm around Tommy's shoulder. "You're a good lad, Tommy Kent-Hughes."

They heard a noise behind them, and both Michael and Tommy turned. Angus was standing there, grinning.

"Tommy's my best friend."

The route grew slightly more rugged. The previous night's storm had left little trace of itself, other than a few wet spots. They were between Loch Lochy and Loch Ness, heading for Fort Augustus, the approximate halfway point. As he had the previous two days, Rolfe told them stories of the history of the area, along with some of the folklore.

"What about the Loch Ness monster?" David said.

"The stories about Nessie have to wait. We have two-and-half-days of walking along Loch Ness, and plenty of time to hear about Nessie. I can't tell them all now or we'll have nothing to talk about tomorrow."

They found a spot for lunch that had portable bathrooms.

While they ate, Rolfe described where they'd be staying in Fort Augustus.

"Gill's is a new old place. It used to be called Campbell's, but the owners retired, and it sat vacant for a time. Last year, a man from London decided to give up the city life, bought the property, and put a fair amount of cash into renovating the place. I've stayed there a few times, and it's one of the most comfortable places you'll find. William and Ciara Gill are the owners, and you'll find yourselves in for a treat. Ciara is a fine cook, and what she doesn't know about food, her husband does. The bathrooms have been renovated, as well, and –" casting a glance at Angus – "you'll find the rooms have private showers."

Angus beamed.

"Before we set off," Rolfe said, "let's do a check. Is everyone still feeling fit? We'll be gradually climbing a bit before we descend into Fort Augustus, and I want to make sure you're not feeling sick, or nauseated, or lightheaded. Everyone OK?"

They all agreed; everyone, including the boys, felt fine.

As they set off, Michael and David walked together for a time.

"It's a fairly easy walk Rolfe has us on," David said. "And he's maintaining a slower pace than he might, likely out of deference to you flatlanders."

Michael laughed. "And we flatlanders appreciate it. I grew up in hills not much different than these, but it's been a while since I hiked them."

"Those self-massages for the calves that Rolfe showed us are wonderful."

"I fully agree."

"You seem more relaxed than I'm used to seeing."

124

Michael nodded. "I feel more relaxed. The exercise, the fresh air, the scenery, and the companionship are all like a tonic, as Ma would say. I've been spending some time with my son, too, and that's been good. I needed this more than I knew, and I have my brother-in-law to thank for it."

David smiled.

Fort Augustus, according to Rolfe, had a population of 646, until the Gill family arrived and rounded it up to 650. The town was heavily dependent upon tourism; it had several small hotels and guesthouses. Gill's was located on Station Road, close to the Caledonian Canal. "If you're interested," Rolfe said, "the Fort Augustus Abbey is well worth a visit, and there are several shops in town that are all things Loch Ness and Nessie."

Gill's was once a fairly substantial private residence. It had two floors, and the renovation had added handicap access, new bathrooms and an expanded kitchen, and substantially refurbished sleeping quarters. There was no dormitory; instead, they would be sleeping two to a room, and each room had its own private shower. Security had already determined the sleeping arrangements: Tommy and Angus; David and Rolfe; Michael and Simon Fredricks; and the two remaining security officers. No other guests were scheduled for the night they were staying, except for William Gill's sister.

William welcomed them, and then looked dumbfounded to see the king among the party.

"I, uh, I didn't expect you, your majesty," he said, stammering. He immediately thought of the food Mary was still collecting at the shop and Ciara was already preparing and wondered if it would be adequate. "Welcome to Gill's, sir."

Michael looked at Rolfe and then William Gill. "Mr. Gill, this week, we've been on a wee bit of vacation, hiking the Great Glen Way with my brother-in-law and my son and his friend. Yes, we've our Security officers with us; that comes with the job, even on vacations. But we're here to hike, eat some good Highlands food, and enjoy being with each other. So, whatever you've planned for your regular guests will be more than fine for us."

"If you'd like to step into the lounge, sir," William said, "we have some refreshments." He glanced at his watch. "It's about 3 p.m., now, and dinner is at 5, so there's time for drinks and then seeing you to your rooms."

Mary Penniman had volunteered to pick up extra food and cooking supplies at the market. She'd brought a portable rolling cart, but she should've asked Will how much he'd actually ordered. Two full bags occupied the cart, and she was carrying a third bag that was packed. She kept hoping she'd make the three blocks home before the bag split. Her arms were sweating, her hair was trying to come undone, and she worried about being back at the inn before the hiking guests arrived.

Reaching the inn, she used the handicapped entrance in the front to avoid hauling the cart up the steps. Coming through the front door, she caught her foot on the sill and tripped, the bag flying out of her arms right into the middle of the newly arrived guests. She closed her eyes, expecting to hear a crash, but heard nothing but a grunt. She looked up; a man who looked remarkably like King Michael had caught the bag, creating a flurry of sudden activity behind him. And standing next to him was the boy Mary knew to be Prince Thomas, because she'd met him at ICS in London.

Tommy stared. "Mrs. Penniman? Is Mark here as well?"

After depositing their backpacks in their rooms and cleaning up, they assembled in the dining room for dinner. William and his still-embarrassed sister served the meal, which consisted of grilled salmon, salad, vegetables, and homemade bread that Ciara had made that morning. Dessert included shortbread, oat cakes, and sticky toffee pudding. Ciara hovered at the serving of each course to make sure everything was all right.

"You've outdone yourself, Ciara," Rolfe said. "This was excellent."

Michael agreed. "I don't think I've ever had better salmon, and it was kind of Angus and Tommy to leave the rest of us some dessert." They all laughed. After that meal, all of the hikers were in a mellow mood, and Will and Ciara were both more than relieved that the meal had been a success.

"I know you're likely tired," Will said, "but tonight is the start of the annual Fort Augustus Abbey fete. It continues through Saturday, and they've a band, all the booths are open, and there are some carnival rides as well."

David looked at Rolfe. "How early do we leave tomorrow?"

"We actually have a late start. Tomorrow is the shortest leg of the hike, ending in Invermoriston. So, if you're up for it, the fete tonight is very doable."

"Can we, Dad?" Tommy said.

Michael nodded. "It sounds like a plan."

"The abbey is only about four blocks," William said, "so it's an easy walk. Mary here can escort you down there while we clean up here." He smiled hopefully at his sister.

Mary thought she'd like nothing better than a hot shower, but she had planned on attending the opening night of the fete. "I'll be glad to, your majesty."

"How about we reassemble in the hall in 15 minutes?" Michael said. "Does that work for everyone?"

As Mary quickly changed for the fete, she considered the man the world knew as King Michael of Great Britain. He looked just under six feet, with what had once been fully black hair now competing but losing with gray. His sky-blue eyes were just as she remembered them, when she'd actually met him years before. *Mesmerizing.*

He was a handsome man. No, she thought, that's not quite right. He's a beautiful man, with the kind of presence that makes you feel safe and that everything will come right in the end. He'd deftly caught the bag of groceries and been nothing but gracious.

She'd never met David Hughes in person, although she'd read two of his books. What immediately struck was how much Prince Thomas looked like his uncle, with the exception of the sky-blue eyes.

Those were his father's. She was a bit mystified by the prince's friend, Angus. He seemed extremely shy, almost as if he had some disability.

Michael's catching of the bag and then joking about it, to put her at her ease and cover her red face and deep embarrassment, wasn't something she'd normally associate with a king. He seemed a very kind, gentle man. And a beautiful one. Definitely a beautiful one.

She felt slightly confused. She hadn't been physically or emotionally attracted to any man since John's death seven years ago. Until now. And it was ridiculous. He was the king, for heaven's sake. A king who'd insisted on helping her carry groceries to the kitchen.

"We drove up from London last weekend." They were walking to the abbey and Michael had asked when she'd arrived. They could already hear the music from the band. "I hired a car; we usually don't need one in London and it's too expensive anyway. Mark and I drove to York to get my mother and then here. Mother took Mark, and Will and Ciara's two children, to Inverness and then to the Orkneys for a little holiday. I stayed to help Will and Ciara and to get a little holiday myself."

She looked back at Tommy, walking behind Michael. "Mark will be sorry to have missed you."

"Are you and Mark school chums?" Michael asked his son.

"We've gotten to know each other a bit this year."

Michael saw that Mary had started to say something and then stopped. He also glanced at her hand and saw her wedding ring. He wasn't quite sure why he'd looked, but he knew he'd been quite taken with Mary Penniman as soon as she stumbled through the door.

She's married, Michael, so back off, he thought. Why are you even thinking about her?

He knew why. She was a beautiful woman with an engaging personality. He guessed her age about eight years younger than he was. She'd light brown hair with blond highlights, a narrow face with high cheekbones, and emerald-green eyes that were almost astonishing in their beauty. She was about 5'8". What he noticed immediately, even as she sprawled on the floor, was her presence.

You're not looking for a relationship, Michael, he told himself, and you're especially not looking for a relationship with a married woman. But he was attracted. He had not felt this way with any woman he'd met in the last seven years, and he barely knew Mary. He tried to show only politeness as she talked, but he was hanging on to her every word.

Perhaps it was the Highlands air.

He also knew they'd met before. He wracked his brain to remember any possible meetings at ICS, but he knew it was somewhere else. He just couldn't put his finger on it.

The fete was in full swing at the abbey. Mary explained that the abbey was no longer a functioning Benedictine monastery but converted to apartments. The owner still maintained a museum and visitor center, the beneficiaries of the annual fete.

The hiking party's arrival nearly brought the festivities to a standstill. Michael was recognized immediately, greeted by the owner and fete emcee, and introduced to the crowd. David and the others heard people in the crowd talking about what a coup it was to get the king for the abbey fete. Simon Fredricks heard the comments as well and told David and Rolfe that it might be best to let people think he was here for that instead of the hike. "Some might be apt to follow us tomorrow."

The normal activities gradually resumed. The band struck up a slow tune, and Michael surprised himself when he asked Mary to dance.

"I haven't danced in years, your majesty."

"Mrs. Penniman, neither have I, so we're starting as equals." He offered her his arm, and, after briefly hesitating, she took it. They entered the area that had been cordoned off and joined other dancers.

"You may have not danced in years, but you dance beautifully. Please call me Mary."

"You're rather good yourself, Mary."

"I know Prince Thomas from school. And I was going to blurt it out earlier, but I was afraid I'd embarrass him." She told him about what had happened with Mark's bullying. "Other students had seen it and knew about it, but it was Prince Thomas who intervened and put a stop to it. He likely didn't make any friends in the process."

"Except perhaps for your son, and I suspect that was worth it." He smiled. "I keep learning new things about my youngest child."

The song ended. They stood talking for a moment, until the band erupted into a highland fling. Michael put one hand on his hip, raised his other hand in the air, and began the intricate steps that was Scotland's national dance. Mary stood back and began to clap.

Suddenly, Tommy was standing next to his father and joined in the dance. David followed. And then Angus, carefully watching Tommy, joined in as well.

The dance ended with a roar from the cheering crowd.

"And where did the king of Great Britain learn to dance the fling?" Mary said, laughing and applauding.

"I was brought up in Scotland, by a Scot. He made sure I knew the traditions. What I'm not as certain about is where my son learned it."

Tommy grinned. "Uncle David taught me."

Michael laughed. "And my American brother-in-law dances a rather wicked Highland fling himself!"

David reddened but smiled. "It's hard to stop your feet when you hear the music."

Michael was up early the next morning. Followed by Simon, he made his way downstairs, found coffee in an urn in the dining room, and poured himself a cup. He could hear noises in the kitchen, presumably someone getting their breakfast together. He walked to the back porch, a large screened-in affair facing the canal and the tall hills behind it.

Mary Penniman had been seated but, startled, jumped up.

"I'm sorry, I didn't know anyone was already up." He looked at the table next to her chair. It held a Bible and a notebook. "I interrupted your Bible study?"

"No, I'd finished. I was sitting here, enjoying my tea. Did you sleep well?"

"I slept like the proverbial rock. The hike and then the dancing did the trick, I believe."

"You certainly put on a show. And we all enjoyed it."

"Might I ask you a question? I've the distinct impression that we've met before, but it wasn't at ICS. Am I mistaken?"

For a time, she didn't answer. "No, you're not mistaken. We have met. It was five years ago, at the Tate exhibition."

And then Michael remembered.

The Exhibition

It started four months after Sarah's death.

Jason and Jane had invited the family for dinner at their house in Mayfair. Jim, now stationed at the air base at Norfolk, was on weekend leave. Palace commitments and appearances had been reduced to almost nothing because of the official mourning period, but Michael and the four children still arrived slightly late. Michael had been caught up with what at first seemed a major roadblock but had turned into a minor snag in the preparations for the parliamentary elections scheduled for May. At long last, the Government emergency would be ending, with Michael resuming the normal duties of the monarchy.

He wished Sarah was there to see it.

He apologized and explained to Jane. "Fortunately, Trevor, or I should say your dad, stepped in and resolved the crisis before it became a crisis."

After dinner, with the children and Jason's two boys watching a movie on television, Jason, Jane, Jim, and Michael sat in the dining room, drinking wine and reminiscing.

"Something interesting happened at work yesterday," Jason said.

"Yes?" Michael said.

"They brought in new wallpaper and everyone thought it was the next exhibition?" said Jim, grinning. The family knew of Jim's antipathy to art museums, like the Tate Modern where Jason worked;

his comment was a facetious reference to his general opinion of most contemporary art.

"Cretin." Jason gave his brother a malevolent look. "Every Friday, a staff member gives an informal talk on something in the museum's collection. It's usually something they know about or are involved with. It can be connected to an exhibition, an individual painting, or really anything the Tate is doing. And while it's mostly a staff thing, the talks are open to the public. We typically have 35 or 40 people tops, unless there's a big exhibition underway, and then we'll get more. That one of Edvard Munch bumped the lecture number up to about 300.

"Anyway, it was my turn in the barrel yesterday. I talked about the two paintings by Mom that the museum owns."

They were all silent for a moment, and then Michael spoke. "I would've liked to have heard it."

"I talked about how she painted," Jason said, "how she managed her time, the subjects of the painting, how she came to paint them, and how the Tate acquired them."

"This is leading to something, isn't it?" Jim said.

Jason nodded. "More than 2,500 people showed up for the lecture. We had to move it from our large meeting room to Power Hall and quickly rig up a microphone and speaker system. They also filmed it, noted its availability on the web site, and in the 24 hours since the lecture, the Tate's received more than 30,000 orders. This level of interest is unheard of." He paused. "I ordered a copy for you, Dad."

"Thank you. It's encouraging that so many people responded. Sarah's work deserves to be better known. And I'll watch the lecture as soon as you have it."

"The executive director of the Tate was here this afternoon," Jason said, "on a Saturday, no less. They want to do an exhibition of Mom's work. As much of it as we can assemble for a show. Preferably all of it. They've asked me to curate it."

"Jason, that's wonderful. When will it be held?"

"I haven't said 'yes,' yet. I'm not sure what I think about it. If it goes forward, it won't be for possibly two years, perhaps 18 months if they let me work it full-time."

Michael nodded. "I see two good things here. First, it will give Sarah the recognition her work deserves. And second, it will boost your career, will it not? Aren't you rather young to curate an entire exhibition? If you decide to do this, and I think you should, I'll help in any way I can."

Jason ultimately agreed to curate the show, and the Tate assigned him to the project full-time. Several corporate sponsors stepped forward immediately. The exhibition involved four primary lines of work. First was finding the paintings and gaining the agreement of the owners to lend them. Second was considerable research in Colorado and California, where Sarah was born and attended school. Third was the writing of the exhibition catalog. Fourth was the planning of the publicity and exhibition opening. An ambitious target date was set for the second anniversary of Sarah's death, barely 18 months away.

He started with Sarah's personal notebook, where she recorded every painting started and the completion date, plus to whom it was sold or given. She'd listed 101 paintings as completed, and Jason set about tracking each one down. It was, at times, tough sledding – making contacts with owners, tracking down subsequent sales or transfers, often paying personal visits. He made several trips to Denver and California, meeting with the gallery owners in Santa Barbara and San Francisco who'd first exhibited her work. He also began to structure and continually revise text and illustrations for the catalog, including commissioning several art critics and museum curators to write essays.

"He's pursuing this like a personal passion," Jane said to Michael, "and that's what it is, really."

At the end of 12 months, Jason had secured contract agreements for 99 identified paintings, an almost staggering success rate. The paintings included some 14 that were part of the family's personal collection.

But two works simply refused to be found. From Sarah's journal, Jason knew they were the last paintings she'd done. Disposition had been left blank. Jason couldn't determine what'd happened, whereas Sarah had meticulously accounted for each of the previous 99 paintings. One painting notation simply read MN, suggesting it was one of Michael except for the "N." The other was simply labeled "T."

One evening at the palace, Jason, Jane, and Jim were sitting with Michael after dinner. Jason was talking through where the exhibition stood and fretting over the two unaccounted-for paintings.

"Dad, do you remember what painting she was working on at the end? I recall you saying she told you about her illness while she was painting in the garden."

"I didn't see it. I know it was a bit larger than her normal-size canvas, and I assumed it must be of me, because she had me sit to get some detail exactly right. But the news about her illness took my attention completely away from the painting."

"Was anyone else there? A security officer?"

"Officer Matson. He was her personal security person. In fact, he knew before the rest of us did about her leukemia. He'd accompanied her to the various doctors' offices." Michael picked up his mobile and called Security. "Can you tell me if Officer Matson is on duty this weekend? He is? Wonderful. Can you ask him to come to the loft? We've a question about what Sarah was painting at the end. Great. Thank you." He looked at the group. "He'll be up shortly."

When Matson arrived and heard Jason's question, he thought a moment before answering. "I carried it back to the house, sir," he said. "I know she asked His Majesty to sit so she could get some details right, but I seem to remember the subject was a child. I'm afraid I didn't examine it closely; the queen was rather particular about looking at works in progress."

"A child?" said Jason. "I wonder where it would be. I've been through everything in her studio, and there's nothing like it there." Michael thanked Matson, who left to return to Security.

"So, we have a hint of one of the two," Michael said.

Jim cleared his throat. "I may've seen the other one."

Michael, Jason, and Jane all looked at him.

"I stumbled over it accidentally. Do you recall the day after Mom's death when we heard the news about Uncle Tommy, and discovered Tommy had run off after Aunt Ellen had blurted it out?"

Michael and Jason both nodded.

"After we searched the loft, Dad, you asked me to stay here while you joined the search of the grounds."

Michael nodded. "And you found Tommy behind the sofa."

Jim was clearly uncomfortable. "Well, yes and no, but that's another story. Before I found him, I did another search of the loft, including your bedroom. There's a narrow closet in an alcove, and it looked just right for Tommy to hide. I opened it, but he wasn't there. What was there was a painting, a rather large one I'd never seen before."

Michael frowned. "A narrow closet? Ah. The utility closet. It has an electric box."

"That's it. That's where I saw the painting. And I seem to recall a mounted metal box at the end of the closet."

"I doubt if I've opened that closet in years," Michael said.

"What's the painting's subject?" Jason said.

Jim hesitated before answering. "It's Dad."

Jane poked Jim, who was sitting next to her. "What are you not saying?"

"You'll have to see it. I think it would be best for Dad to see it first, by himself."

Michael stood. "Well, no time like the present." He walked to his bedroom.

"What's the mystery here, Jim?" said Jason.

"Jas, I don't think that's my question to answer. Let's wait for Dad."

Ten minutes later, Michael returned. He looked shaken.

"I found the painting. I'd no idea she'd done this. She must've done it from memory because I never posed for it." He poured himself another glass of wine. "It's incredible. I'd like you to see it, and then give me some counsel on what I should do."

"Jane as well?" Jim said.

Michael looked at his daughter-in-law. "Yes, I think so. I think we'll need a woman's perspective here."

Mystified, Jason and Jane followed Michael and Jim to the bedroom closet. The door was concealed by a curtain, making it easy to miss in the overall room décor and its location next to an exterior wall. Michael pulled back the curtain, opened the door, and pulled the 4' by 6' painting out.

Jason's eyes widened. Jane gasped. For several moments, no one spoke.

"It's extraordinary," Jason said finally. "It's clearly Mom's work, in her style. You can see in her later paintings that she was moving toward something new but hadn't quite reached it. She reached it here. It's stunning."

Michael looked at Jane. "Jane, what do you think?"

"I think Jason is right. It's stunning. But can you include it in the exhibition? There's potential fallout here, I mean for the monarchy. Wouldn't there be?" She looked at it again. "But it's gorgeous."

"I understand her lettering designation," Jason said. "The M stands for Michael, and the N stands for nude. Dad, the son in me says this needs to stay within the family. The art critic and artist in me says it must be in the show. It follows the works she'd been developing; I can see how she was evolving her style." He paused, tears suddenly appearing in his eyes. "And it tells me what we might've had if we hadn't lost her." He put his arm around his wife.

"Even being the official art cretin that I am," Jim said, "I could see that this was a wonder. My first thought was how much Mom loved Dad."

Jason looked at his brother. "Which is more perceptive than you might realize. You're speaking like an art critic."

"God forbid."

Michael laughed. "Now we know what painting #100 was, which leads to the next question. Does it go in the exhibition? I'd like to think about it. I'd like us all to think about, before we make a decision." Michael returned the painting to the closet.

They returned to the living area, and each was quiet for a time.

"Jim," Michael said, "you implied something about that night. Didn't you find Tommy behind the sofa?"

Jim nodded. "But it wasn't the sofa here. It was the sofa in Mom's studio."

Michael frowned. "But that door was locked."

Jim shook his head. "I tried the door to make sure. It was closed but unlocked."

"But I had the key. How—"

"Tommy had a key. Mom had given it to him. When I found him, I realized he'd lost his voice. By writing notes, he asked me not to say anything until after the funeral. And he was terrified that you'd find him in the studio. He said it would make you angry."

Michael stood and began to pace. "He was right. It would've made me angry. It still makes me angry, and it's irrational and wrong of me to react that way."

Jason, Jane, and Jim looked at one another. They'd never seen Michael like this.

Finally, Jane spoke. "Is it possible that painting #101 is of Tommy? If the designation is 'T,' Officer Matson remembers a child, and she asked you to sit to get details right, could she have been painting his eyes or eye color?"

A few minutes later, they were standing on the palace terrace. Michael's four children and Jason's two were playing chase, with considerable squealing and laughter. Michael called them to come to the terrace.

"Tommy?" Jason said, and the boy looked up from where he was helping himself to a cold drink in a cooler. Eighteen months had passed since Sarah's death, and Tommy still wasn't speaking. He and his teachers had figured out how to manage at school, and Michael's children and grandchildren had adapted.

Before they came outside, Michael and Jason had agreed to let Jason take the lead.

"Tommy, did Mom ever paint a picture of you?" Jason said.

Instead of answering, Tommy looked at Michael.

"It's okay, Tommy," Michael said, "we're just trying to figure out if we've accounted for all the paintings she did, for the big show that Jason's doing. Do you remember her doing a painting of you, right before she got sick?"

At this point, all of the children began to pay attention to the conversation.

"What's going on?" said Hank, and Michael shook his head.

Tommy looked at Michael again, and then nodded his head at Jason.

"Do you know what happened to it?" Jason said.

Tommy nodded, pointing at himself.

"She gave it to you?" Jason was working very hard at being patient. He didn't want to unduly upset his little brother.

Tommy nodded again.

"Is it in your room?"

Tommy shook his head.

"But you know where it is. Can you show me?"

With another glance at Michael, Tommy stood staring at his brother, nodded, and then took Jason's hand to walk back inside the palace.

The family all followed, including the children. Tommy walked to the northern administrative wing and down the utility stairs to the areas that included a small bowling alley and several storage rooms. One room was designated for the children's old toys, clothes, and baby furniture that they wanted to keep even though they'd outgrown them. It was this door that Tommy opened.

The room was filled with rocking horses, a toy carousel, trunks with each of the children's names on them, boxes, and several items covered with sheets. The family crowded in behind Tommy and Jason.

"The room is temperature-controlled for preservation," Michael said.

Tommy looked at his father, and then walked over to a large number of boxes stacked against a wall. He moved several out of the way and extracted what clearly looked to be a painting wrapped in brown paper.

"May I open it?" Jason said, and the boy nodded.

What came to view first was the back of the framed canvas.

"There's an envelope here, marked 'certificate of ownership,'" Jason said. Before turning the painting around, he opened the envelope. "It's in Mom's handwriting. She notes the date it was completed and says she's given ownership to Thomas Michael McLaren Kent-Hughes." He looked at Tommy, who nodded at him. "It's dated the day before she went into the hospital."

Jason turned the canvas around.

Sarah had painted individual pictures of the entire family. Each of the children had a portrait by their mother, including Tommy. The portraits hung in the hallway outside the family loft. Even Jason's two young sons had portraits there.

What Jason saw was almost haunting. He knew immediately that this was the last painting Sarah had done, and it spoke to what level she had achieved in her art. Tommy, and it was clearly a painting of Tommy, sitting very straight and wearing a jacket and tie. The background looked like the Green Room, looking through the door to the throne reception room. Tommy was holding on his lap what looked like a ball.

Jason heard a noise, and he turned to see his wife with tears running down her face. Hank was staring openmouthed. Sophie had her hand to her mouth. It was Helen who broke the silence.

"It's beautiful. It's the most beautiful painting I've ever seen. It may be the most beautiful thing I've ever seen."

"It looks alive," Hank said. "It's like Tommy's going to step outside the picture."

Jason glanced at Michael. His father's face was almost unreadable, a full range of emotions running across it.

Tommy touched Jason's shoulder, and indicated he wanted paper and pen. Jim quickly tore out a sheet from his calendar book and handed it and his pen to Tommy.

Jason read the note. "'She got the eye color wrong.'" He looked at the painting. "But it looks exactly right, Tommy."

Tommy wrote another note.

"'She couldn't get it right, so she used Dad,'" Jason read. He looked back at Michael. "That's why she asked you to sit, so she could get the details right."

A sob broke from Michael's throat. He turned quickly and left the room. He almost ran down the hallway toward the stairs to go up to the ground floor. And then he stopped, sitting on the stairs. He knew what Sarah had done in that painting. It was the portrait of a young boy, his son, their son. But it was more than that, and it wasn't a ball he was holding.

In the storage room, Jason turned back to Tommy and saw sheer panic on the boy's face.

"It's okay, Tommy. All of us, and most of all Dad, loved Mom very much." He felt tears on his own cheeks. "We're learning something new about her. She wasn't just a good artist; she was a great artist. And had she lived, she might've become known as one of the greatest. This painting of you may be the best thing she ever did, and she loved you so much she wanted you to have it."

Tommy nodded again. He wrote another note. "'That's what she told me. She said it was about the future. And she said to put it away, out of sight.'"

Jason saw the tears in the boy's eyes, and he pulled Tommy into a great hug. And then he realized what the painting was, and why Michael had fled the room.

The six months leading up to the exhibition found Jason in a permanent state of feverish activity. The people he'd carefully selected to write the catalog essays produced what turned out to be unsatisfactory, with little about Sarah and more about contemporary and modern art. Jason decided, with virtually no time to spare, to write the entire catalog himself, combining biography, art criticism, and personal observations about his adopted mother's work.

The finished product was idiosyncratic for an exhibition catalog, and his supervisors at the Tate Modern were concerned that it would likely blow up in all their faces. But Jason remained obstinate, and the fast-approaching exhibition opening date finally silenced the museum critics, some of whom, Jason knew, were hoping for a disaster. This was the art world, after all.

Michael had made the decision to allow the nude painting to be included. He reasoned that, first, it wasn't full frontal, although it was highly suggestive, and second, to leave it out would be misleading as to where Sarah's art had been moving. He expected some public shock; Jay Lanham worked with Jason and the museum's PR staff to develop a crisis plan.

The painting of Tommy had been more problematic. Michael, as Tommy's parent and legal guardian, could've decided to include the painting or not. Instead, he allowed Tommy to make the decision. Jason initially kept his thoughts to himself, but it was this painting he wanted to feature on the catalog's cover, the exhibition web page, and all the promotional materials. He'd realized, as had Jim, that Sarah's art was a serious tension point between Michael and Tommy, and Tommy was almost frightened to allow the painting to be included. What finally convinced the boy was a long talk with his Uncle David, in town for a conference at the British Library, who told him the painting was a beautiful portrait of his mother's love and he wanted to see it included, if Tommy was agreeable.

The chatter about the exhibition had been phenomenal. When it was announced, tickets were sold out for the first two months, leading the Tate to a decision to expand opening hours and extend the exhibition by another six weeks. While the intention had been primarily an exhibition for London, the Metropolitan in New York and the San Francisco Museum of Art put up serious investment money to host the exhibition as well. And then, through lobbying by Michael, the Tate accepted a final showing at the Scottish National Museum of Modern Art in Edinburgh, but most of the agreements with the various owners of the paintings had to be amended to accommodate the expanded exhibition dates.

The funds paid by the three museums already covered the entire cost experienced by the Tate and the corporate sponsors to assemble the exhibition.

When the publicity materials featuring the portrait of Tommy went public, a media and public sensation resulted. The painting had never been seen before, and its quality and beauty, even in printed brochures and on the web site, created a huge critical buzz. Both American museums asked for extensions of time, given the advance ticket sales.

In the catalog, Jason omitted any reference to what he believed the painting of Tommy might be about. He told Michael what he thought; Michael said he didn't know. Jason doubted the answer but didn't press it.

The morning before the opening, Michael and the family had a private showing. The children already knew about the nude painting, but Michael wanted to make sure they saw it in the context of the exhibition. They'd already been shown the painting in the loft, and at the time Michael had noticed the older three were surprised, while Tommy clearly wasn't.

"You've seen this before?" Michael had said to Tommy, and the boy nodded.

"When?"

At first, he hesitated. And then Tommy had written on the notepad he carried with him and handed the sheet of paper to Michael. "'She let me watch her paint it.'"

Michael had a sharp intake of breath and clenched his fists, crumpling the paper, before forcing himself to calm down. He only nodded back at Tommy. But Tommy had seen the reaction.

Now, months later in the exhibition hall, Jason walked the children through the various rooms. The children had been silent as they looked at the paintings and read the description cards. The paintings were in chronological order, starting with Sarah's first painting of Michael given to Ian and Iris McLaren and the one of Michael's hand during her final year of college, and ending with the portrait of Tommy, right after and next to the final painting of Michael.

The exhibition was especially overwhelming for Michael. It was reliving his entire relationship with Sarah. Jason had captured something in the display than no one else might've seen – the overarching story of the love and marriage, including the tension between them in the final years before her death. Or, as Michael realized, Jason had allowed the paintings to tell the story.

"What you've done here is extraordinary," Michael told his son. "As much as we talked about the exhibition, I wasn't prepared to see it in its fullness. I'm in awe of what you've accomplished."

As flattered as Jason was, he was more relieved than anything. Michael was one of the two people whose reactions he'd been most concerned about. The other was Tommy.

"I know I'm here tomorrow for the official opening," Michael said. "But might I come back by myself, say about 5 this afternoon? I won't stay long: I'd just like to walk through once more before the crowds come."

"Of course, Dad," Jason said. "I'll let museum security know and be waiting to escort you."

"Jason, this is simply fantastic. I don't think I have enough superlatives. I'm personally overwhelmed, and I'm so proud of what you've done."

They both suddenly heard a panicked cry form Hank. "Dad!"

Michael ran to the children. Tommy was standing in front of the final two paintings, clutching his throat and seeming almost to be gagging.

Michael grabbed his son's shoulders. "Tommy! Are you choking?"

Tommy frantically shook his head. Michael and the others could see he was trying to mouth something with his lips. He finally choked it out.

Mary Penniman was aggravated. The book from the Tate Modern Library that was supposed to have arrived days ago had yet to be sent for her translation project at the British Library. The Tate librarian had apologized, citing all the hubbub and upheaval over the exhibition of the Sarah Kent-Hughes paintings. Mary understood, but she was still a bit annoyed about what should've been a simple operation.

She decided to get the book herself.

It wasn't the easiest destination to reach by tube, especially when a breakdown in one of the tube lines snarled traffic in several others. She finally was able to exit at St. Paul's station and walk across the Millennial Bridge to the Tate, with its imposing industrial powerhouse structure facing the river and its trapezoidal tower behind. She reached the library a few minutes before the museum closed. The book was waiting for her at the library counter.

Tucking the book safely in her briefcase, with the cover note from the librarian for the checkout, she stopped briefly in the restroom. Coming out, she took a wrong turn. When she finally realized she was going the wrong way, she doubled back, found a staircase, and headed down.

She knew she shouldn't go all the way down but couldn't remember which floor was officially ground level. She thought it might be three or four. She guessed three, went through the door, and suddenly found herself in the main exhibition hall.

The doors were open for the exhibition, which she and all of London knew opened the next day, including a ceremony with the king. She had a ticket for about six weeks from now. She could see paintings inside, and, giving in to impulse, she walked into the exhibition.

Mary had met Queen Sarah at John's funeral. The queen had arrived with one security man. No official entourage, no media in her wake, just the queen.

She knew that Sarah did this as a kind of ministry; John's funeral was far from the first the queen had attended. And she knew King Michael was in Paris, negotiating a ceasefire, when John had died. The ceasefire had finally been signed, but it had come too late for John. Sarah's presence had somehow gotten both Mary and her son through the funeral.

Mary wandered through the exhibition rooms, forgetting about time, the museum closing, or anything else. She'd seen a few pictures of the queen's paintings, but she'd never seen the real thing.

In the final room, she saw the two last paintings positioned side by side. They both left her almost breathless. She sat on a bench in front of the two, and was sitting there, crying, when a man sat next to her.

It was the king.

Jason had been waiting for Michael at the underground security entrance and escorted his father to the elevators and to the exhibition rooms. When they entered the last room, Jason was shocked to see a woman sitting near the last two paintings. He started to move toward her when Michael stopped him. "Let me talk with her. She's crying."

He sat next to her. For a time, neither said anything. She began to stand but he motioned her to sit.

"I apologize, your majesty. I took a wrong turn and ended up here, and I couldn't stop looking."

"I understand. I was here this morning with the children, and I knew I had to come back before tomorrow."

"She loved you. She loved you desperately. It plays all through these paintings, right down to these two. That's your youngest, Prince Thomas, isn't it?"

Michael nodded. "Yes."

"It was genius to place these two paintings together. It reminds me of that old T.H. White book about King Arthur, what was it, yes, *The Once and Future King*."

Michael gripped the edge of the bench so hard he thought he'd break it.

"I know I shouldn't be prattling on like this, but I know what it is to love someone with every ounce of your being. She painted exactly that love right here, with these two paintings. I didn't mean to cry, but I know what it is to lose someone you love. These paintings, especially these two, speak somehow of loss but also about hope. Did you pose for this one?"

He stared at the two paintings. "No. Sarah must have painted it from memory."

"You'll likely be criticized for allowing a nude portrait to be exhibited, but it's a magnificent painting; it needs to be here. What she painted was the tenderness, the gentleness, and also the underlying strength." She paused. "And that one of Prince Thomas. It's a portrait, but it's also a glimpse into the future, and I can't explain exactly why."

Mary stood. "I'm sorry, I should go, I'm babbling on and you need to be by yourself."

"Wait. What's your name?"

"It's Mary." She hesitated. "I met Queen Sarah at a funeral three years ago. She was beautiful."

And then she hurried off. As she passed him, Jason signaled to the security man to escort her to the entrance.

Michael and Tommy

The present

"I remember now." Michael looked across the Caledonian Canal and up at the hilltops behind Fort Augustus. "You'd taken a wrong turn and ended up in the exhibition rooms. You were sitting on the bench by the final two paintings. You said you met Sarah at a funeral, likely a military funeral she attended."

"You remember it exactly. And, yes, it was a military funeral. She sat with the widow and her child. She even went to the cemetery."

"It was something she always insisted on doing. She'd say these men and women had given everything for the rest of us, and it was the least she could do to acknowledge that in the only way she knew how."

"I attended the exhibition about six weeks after I saw you. I'd gotten tickets and went with a friend from work. It was better when I didn't feel like I was sneaking in."

Michael smiled. "Jason and the Tate had a huge success on their hands. The catalog stayed on the bestsellers list for more than a year, and in four countries – the U.K., the U.S., Canada, and Australia. Translated into 14 languages, too. And the exhibition broke attendance records here and in America. Jason did his adopted mother proud."

"I've read my copy of the catalog three times. What I didn't know was how much her art was wrapped up in her faith and in her love for you. The book makes both very clear."

"Jason didn't create the typical exhibition catalog. And he stuck to his guns when his bosses at the Tate wanted something more standard. His steadfastness made the museum tens of millions of pounds, and I hope they're grateful." He paused. "Something else happened because of that exhibition."

Mary waited for the king to explain. Whatever it was, she thought, judging by the king's face, it was something deeply emotional.

"Tommy started speaking again. He'd been unable to speak since Sarah's death; the doctors had diagnosed hysterical shock. But when I took the children to see it before the opening, he croaked out a word in a hoarse little voice. He was standing in front of those final two paintings, and at first we all thought he was choking or having a seizure."

"What did he say?"

Michael could feel the emotion rising in his chest even now, five years later.

Michael looked down. "He said 'Mummy.'"

Mary's eyes welled with tears. She could see he was speaking with great difficulty; those two extraordinary paintings had additional meaning that went beyond being paintings, even outstanding paintings. She put her hand on his arm.

William stuck his head in the door to the porch. "Mary, could I borrow you for a few moments to help get breakfast set out?"

She stood quickly, wiping her eyes with her sleeve. "Of course." She looked at Michael. "It was good talking with you, your majesty. And thank you for the dance last night."

Michael also stood. "Thank you for listening; I hope I didn't burden you. Perhaps we'll meet at ICS. And you'll have to introduce me to your husband."

"Yes, of course," she said, looking down, and then excused herself.

She began moving a chafing dish with eggs toward the dining room when William stopped her.

"You didn't tell him about John."

"I know. I just can't talk about it, Will."

"Mary, it's been seven years. Wouldn't John want you to find someone?"

She shook her head and hurried to the dining room.

At 10 a.m., the group readied to leave for the next leg of the hike, this one along Loch Ness to Invermoriston. They said their thanks and goodbyes, and as they started to the footbridge over the canal, Michael turned around and waved. Mary waved back, and he was still close enough that she could see him smile.

William noticed the wave. "I think our king might be interested, Mrs. Penniman."

"That makes one of us, William." She knew full well she wasn't telling the truth. Michael had unexpectedly opened a small part of his soul to her, and she thought that at the precise moment, she might have fallen in love with him. But it was simply impossible.

As she started to return inside, she turned and watched the group crossing over the canal and moving toward the hiking trail. She wasn't certain, but she thought she saw him look back again.

It was cloudy and cool, but no rain was in the forecast. As they walked, Rolfe told stories of the Loch Ness monster. "The first report of a monster associated with the loch was in 565 A.D., a man's death reported by Saint Columba. Columba was historical, but we're not so sure about the monster." He went on to explain how the legend grew.

As they ate their lunch, Tommy pointed out the obvious to Michael.

"You danced with Mrs. Penniman last night. You haven't danced since Mummy died."

"Well, that's right. But it was only a dance or two. The fete was rather fun, don't you think?"

"I won a Nessie," Angus said, opening his backpack and pulling out a small carved-wood replica of what someone thought the Loch Ness monster looked like. "At the ring toss."

"Congratulations are certainly in order, Angus," Michael said, smiling at the boy. "That'll be a nice keepsake for the hike."

As they were preparing to resume walking, Michael pulled Tommy aside. "Do you know what Mr. Penniman does? Has Mark ever said anything?"

Tommy looked at his father in surprise. "Mark's father is dead. He was killed by a roadside bomb in Iraq during the war."

"That can't be right. I talked with Mrs. Penniman about him this morning, and she agreed when I said I'd like to meet her husband."

"He really died, Dad. Mark told me that he's not allowed to talk about his father at home, and that his mother never speaks of him. I'm certain I've got that right."

"That's really odd. I wonder how I confused it?"

Their lodgings in Invermoriston were spartan but serviceable; they once again worked out a schedule for Angus to have a private shower in the communal bathroom while Tommy stood guard. The weather held for the trek to Drumnadrochit, the final overnight before they reached Inverness Saturday.

Michael could see that they were all tired, even Rolfe, but it was a good, companionable kind of tiredness. They arrived early enough in the village to take the last Loch Ness cruise of the day; they all enjoyed sitting in the cruise ship, refreshed with coffee, tea, and an array of edibles. The cruise narrator kept everyone on board laughing with a quite informative discussion of the loch and Nessie.

For their last night, the inn where they stayed provided room accommodations much like the Gill's in Fort Augustus. The furnishings weren't quite as sumptuous, but the dinner was excellent. Rolfe had also arranged an evening treat – a small bonfire with dessert provided by David. "Where I come from," David said, "you can't have a respectable bonfire without s'mores." He demonstrated the fine art of roasting marshmallows, and then instructed the group on how to combine them with chocolate between graham crackers.

Angus, melted marshmallow dripping down his chin, spoke for them all. "This is the best dessert ever."

They were sitting on benches in silence, watching the fire, when Tommy spoke.

"Dad, can you tell me about Uncle Tommy? I know I'm named for him and I know he died, but I really don't know much about him. I remember he had red hair, and he was always laughing. But I don't know much about what happened to him."

David looked over at Michael. It was a subject Michael generally avoided, and he could be quite abrupt in avoiding it. He saw Michael blink a couple of times, and then he drew himself up to speak.

"Tommy was my best friend, son. When I was brought to Scotland after the death of my parents, Ma and Da enrolled me in the local school. I was on the small side, I was new, and I was English. I was something of a natural target for the school bullies. And bully me they did."

Angus sat up, listening intently.

Michael noticed. "I think you know what I'm talking about, Angus?"

The boy nodded. "Did they throw you in the storm?"

"No, but if there'd been a storm, they likely would've done."

Tommy walked over and sat next to Michael.

"The bullying got particularly rough one day, and I thought I was really in for the worst of it. Suddenly a boy with the reddest hair I'd ever seen jumped into the middle of everything and began punching the ringleader. I must've become inspired, because I began fighting back as well."

"Did you whip them?" Tommy said.

"No, I'm sorry to say that seven against two was poor odds, and Tommy and I both ended up with a lot of bruises and black eyes. All the parents were called to the school, and Ma and Da came. I can tell you that Da looked quite cross, and I thought I was going to be punished when we got home." Michael laughed. "Instead, Da took me to the barn. He told me that he didn't countenance fighting, and the school certainly didn't countenance it. And then he showed me the best ways to defend myself, including how to use my fists and my feet."

The group engaged in a collective laugh.

"From then on, Tommy and I were best friends. We were inseparable. Ma worried about Tommy being a bad influence, but he never was. We went trekking in the hills, we skinny-dipped in the mountain creeks, we teased girls together, and we generally got into all the mischief you'd expect boys to get into. We slept at each other's houses more times than I can count.

"When it was time for college, it was a no-brainer. We were both going to Edinburgh, and we were going to be roommates. That was five years, with me studying for theology and my seminary degree and Tommy in his five-year architecture program. It was right at the beginning of that fifth year when one of the dormitories had a fire, and we found ourselves saddled with a roommate, a third-year American named David Hughes."

Tommy and Angus, as well as Rolfe and the security officers, all looked at David, who smiled in remembrance. "Your father and Tommy were very kind to take a homeless student into their room. The fire had destroyed all my clothes, and all I had left was my backpack, my books, and my laptop. They loaned me clothes and made me feel welcome, even though I knew I had to be a bother."

Michael grinned. "We didn't kick you out, so you must've had a few good qualities. Anyway, I met Sarah entirely apart from David; I didn't immediately know they were brother and sister. Your mother and I started dating, Tommy and Ellen were already engaged, and Ellen arranged a blind date for David, a lovely young woman named Betsy."

"Aunt Betsy?" Tommy said.

"The very same," David said.

"I was best man at Tommy's wedding, and he was best man at mine and at David's. He and Ellen lived in Glasgow, where he was an architect and she was a teacher, while David and Betsy were in Edinburgh, finishing up studies and David preparing for graduate school.

"You've heard the stories of what happened during The Violence. Tommy was in Chicago for an architects' conference, and the president of the United States arranged to have him flown in a fighter jet to San Francisco. While I was in surgery on the operating table, he was with your mother, coaching her through the birth of Hank.

"When we got to London, I asked Tommy and his firm to assess and undertake the renovations of all of the royal properties, including Buckingham Palace. Everything needed work, and it was Tommy who designed the family loft we live in now. The work brought considerable attention to their firm. They grew rapidly,

Tommy was traveling a lot, and I think this was where things began to go wrong.

"Son, he was my best friend, and because of that, I knew he'd have dark times. Most people would look at Tommy and see the life of the party, the one always telling jokes, always finding a good insult aimed at England, a kind of Mr. Scot Personality. But he could be very sad, with almost black moods. I talked to him more than once about getting some professional help, but he always dismissed it as 'quacks with a degree.' But he needed help.

"Not long before your mother told us about her illness, Tommy got involved with a woman who wasn't his wife. He left his family and began living with her. He was a professing Christian, but somehow, he was able to justify to himself what he'd done. We didn't know any of this was happening until your mother was in the hospital. I don't know what I could've done, given what was happening with your mother, but I could've at least talked with him."

"We knew," David said. "Betsy and I knew. Ellen had come to Betsy almost hysterical when she found out. I tried several times to reach him, but he wouldn't talk. Ellen and Emily stayed with us for a few weeks. She'd left Tommy in their flat. She said she couldn't bear to go back. She'd just found a new place to live a few days before Sarah died."

"I remember," Tommy said. "I remember being with her when she got the call that he'd died. She told me what had happened, and I ran and hid."

Michael nodded. "She wasn't thinking when she blurted it out. It's not something you should tell a six-year-old, that his namesake and the man he calls Uncle Tommy had just killed himself."

He looked at the fire. "Tommy, it was a hard year. Looking back, I can say that it was the worst year of my life. Da had died two years before, leaving a big gaping hole for all of us. Your mother got sick, and then we learned the day after she died that Tommy was dead as well. Two of the people I was closest to were both gone at the same time, and a third wasn't there to lean on."

The group around the fire had gone completely silent. None of them had ever heard Michael speak about this, not even David. The only sound at this point was the logs crackling with flame.

Tommy leaned against his father's chest, and Michael put his arm around Tommy's shoulders. "What did you do, Dad?"

"I prayed a lot, son. I leaned on my staff and friends at the palace. I leaned hard on your Uncle David here, who lost the man he considered his second father, his sister, and his good friend the same time I did. Ours was a mutual loss, and we cried a lot together and prayed together and supported each other."

"You don't know, Michael," David said, his voice partially choked with tears, "how much you carried me through all that. It was a dark, dark time."

"We carried each other, David."

On Saturday, the eight hikers arrived at the trailhead at Inverness to find transportation waiting. Rolfe Solveig introduced his wife, and Michael and David both hugged their tour guide. Michael had already emailed Jay Lanham at the palace, asking him to arrange for a royal warrant to be sent to Solveig Scottish Tours and Hikes.

David and Angus were dropped off at their homes in St. Andrews, and Michael and Tommy were driven on to McLaren's outside Edinburgh. They spent the night there with Iris and the twins.

"How was the hike?" Sophie said at dinner.

"To quote my friend Angus, it was the best ever," Tommy said.

"Dad?" Sophie said.

Michael first looked at his son and smiled. He turned to his daughter. "It was the best ever, Sophie. The best ever."

Michael and Mary

The present

The new ICS fall term began three months later. Parents Night was Oct. 2, and Michael found himself once again planning the evening with all the intensity of a military battle. This would be his seventh Parents Night without Sarah. His secretary, Carrie Waldman, Sarah's secretary until her death and then the successor to Michael's secretary when she retired, helped him map out what he called his battle plan.

On his way to the school that evening, he looked at Carrie's neatly typed page. Helen and Sophie were in the sixth form, their final year at ICS; he tried imagining them in graduation gowns, but it was still beyond him. His two little girls would soon be going off to university, Sophie to Oxford and Helen to the Royal Academy of Dramatic Art.

Tommy was in the second form, the last year of lower school. The trick was that all three children had different teachers for their subjects, although Sophie and Helen shared some classes. His schedule, which he and Carrie had worked on for almost two hours, was hectic, frenzied – but doable. Michael would be in three buildings for the upper and lower schools, and he was going to get some exercise racing up and down stairs. He was thankful that Jane and Jason were taking care of the grandsons' schedules. He also remembered that the headmaster had talked with him about advancing Tommy at least two grades, noting that the boy was already at the fifth and sixth form level in most of his studies.

Because of the size of the expected crowd, Simon Fredericks and a new officer, Charlie MacArthur, were assigned for security for the king, with an additional two outside with the car. For a number of years early in his reign, Michael's usual security officer had been Paula Abbott. But Paula had married and then had to be reassigned when she became pregnant. Now the mother of two children, she managed the administrative side of the security office, reporting to her chief, Ryan Mitchell, although she occasionally worked the king's security detail. She'd arranged for Simon to attend the king; Michael had been impressed with the young man's work during the hike in Scotland.

The driver dropped Michael, Simon, and Charlie in front of the school. They joined the crowds moving through the front door, were acknowledged by the parents around them, and eventually found their way to the auditorium. Simon sat next to the king while Charlie stood in the aisle next to a side wall. All three knew the drill; with three alumni children, and three children and two grandsons currently at ICS, Michael spent a considerable amount of time at the school.

Jason and Jane arrived and sat directly behind them. Jane leaned forward and touched Michael on his shoulder, letting him know they'd arrived.

Generally, both parents of students were expected to attend Parents Night. The date was publicized well ahead of time; the school was borderline insistent that both attend if possible. Michael, already feeling the odd duck because of his position as king and the deference he was paid by the other parents, teachers, and administrators, felt even more odd being by himself. There were extraordinarily few single parents at ICS. This wasn't by design but more by the fact that this was a Christian school, comprised entirely of Christian families, which tended to be the traditional nuclear families.

After seven years without Sarah, I should be used to this by now, Michael thought.

The assembly ended and the marathon sprint, as Michael called it, began.

Carrie's notes for each session were of enormous help. She'd typed a short paragraph explaining each teacher and class, which of his children they taught, and which subject. The notes not only helped Michael navigate the crowded schedule; they helped keep all of it straight in his head. He made a mental note to give her some flowers.

At 8:30, Michael arrived at the last session of the evening before tea, punch and biscuits at 8:50. It was Tommy's British history class. As Michael and the two agents entered the room, the teacher, Neville Sampson, smiled and bowed slightly to the king. As was the experience in the other classes, Michael's arrival created something of a buzz among the parents.

He smiled when he saw the folder on his son's desk, with Tommy's name written in his clear and attractive handwriting and decorated with hand-drawn Norse runes. To accommodate both of a student's parents, most of the desks had an additional chair placed next to the student's desk. Tommy's did not.

As Mr. Sampson began his welcome to the class, Michael glanced at the empty desk next to him, and saw the folder with the name Mark Penniman. At that moment, the door opened, and a flustered Mary Penniman came in, apologized to Mr. Sampson, and finally reached Mark's desk. Her eyes widened when she saw the king; she did a small curtsy, smiled, and sat down.

She's a beauty, Michael thought. Her green dress highlighted her green eyes. There seemed to be an air of sadness and reserve around her, one he'd missed before, as if she was bearing up under a great loss, but only just. Michael's heart skipped a beat; he was startled by the instant attraction to the woman sitting across the aisle, remembering what he'd experienced at Fort Augustus.

As if reading his thoughts, she glanced his way, saw him watching her, and smiled.

There was no chair next to Mark Penniman' desk. Michael did a quick glance back and saw the wedding ring on her hand, wondering whether Tommy had been right or not about Mark's father.

When the session ended, Michael spoke.

"How have you been? Any more problems with groceries?"

She smiled. "No. I've been careful to try to avoid being my usual clumsy self."

They walked together to the reception in the school cafeteria, chatting about Scotland, her brother, and her work at the British Library.

When they reached the cafeteria, she asked him to excuse her. "I'm sorry, but I need to find a restroom."

"Of course. It was good seeing you again. Please give my regards to your brother and sister-in-law." He watched as she quickly moved through the crowd.

Later, while he was chatting with Jason and Jane, he saw her again, talking with other parents. From where he stood, he could see both her slenderness and her full attractiveness. She may or may not be married, but it seems clear that she's not interested, he thought. He turned his full attention to the conversation with the group around Jason and Jane.

Mary could barely contain her panic, and she'd no idea why she even was panicking. She wasn't interested in King Michael. She wasn't interested in any man. There'd been only John, and she was content with that. She'd forgotten she'd likely see the king at the school; to find herself sitting next to him had completely flustered her.

He was seven years older than she was; she had looked up his birth date shortly after the hiking group had left and then gotten mad at herself for doing that. She'd misled him about having a husband; she simply wasn't ready to consider a relationship, and she knew she never would be. John had been sufficient for her, even the few short years they had together. She had her work, her son, and the quiet life she wanted. She didn't want to complicate it with a man, and especially a man with all the trappings of Michael Kent-Hughes.

But seeing him, talking with him, and even taking that short walk with him to the cafeteria had unnerved her. She could almost sense his presence. His easy smile and the way he cocked his head when he grinned made her want to reach and touch his face, his handsome, beautiful face that held the barest hint of crow's feet by his eyes. And she knew she wanted to touch more than his face.

She glanced to her left and saw him standing with his son and daughter-in-law and a group of people. He suddenly turned towards her and saw her looking at him, and he gave a small smile. She turned away. It was time to leave. She had a short tube ride to Paddington Station and then a train ride home. It was simply time to leave.

A week later, Tommy found Michael in the loft's small study and asked if he could invite a friend for the weekend.

"And who might that be?"

"Mark Penniman. He sits next to me in Brit history. We've gotten to be good friends. He's on the lower school football team with me, but he doesn't ride a bike."

"He doesn't? Well, maybe we'll have to have him over and get him up on one."

"This weekend, Dad?"

"That should work, Tommy. We've no plans. But make sure it's all right with his parents, or I should say his mother, and if she'd like, I'll call." He paused. "By the way, the headmaster and your teachers think you should be advanced two forms. The headmaster called again today. What might you think about it?"

"I think I'd like to do it, Dad. I think I can, but I won't know unless I try it, right?"

He stopped, but Michael could see he almost had more to say. The boy excused himself to make his call to Mark.

Michael considered what the headmaster had said. Tommy was not only performing two forms at least ahead of his class; in most subjects he was already at sixth-form level, equivalent to his sisters. Michael had called David; he wasn't surprised to learn that Tommy had already talked with his uncle about it.

"To be sure, it's a dilemma, Michael," David had said. "On the one hand, you don't want to needlessly hold him back. On the other, you want to make sure he has the emotional maturity to handle older classmates. If it were my child, I think I would work out a plan with the headmaster and the teachers. Accelerate his classes and what he's learning. Perhaps enroll him in a university class; University of London has several for gifted teens. See how he does this coming year. Have him take university advanced placement exams. And then the two of you make the decision, together.

"But Michael, my own experience with him is that, intellectually and emotionally, he could start university now."

Michael decided the best short-term course was to pray.

"You're invited to spend the weekend with Prince Thomas?" Mary said.

Mark, visibly excited, nodded. "Tommy invited me. We're project partners for the fall term, and we're doing a study of the old kingdom of Mercia. It's frightfully complex, Mother, because there are no primary sources; you have to rely on what other kingdoms said about them. Tommy speaks and reads Old English, just like the Anglo-Saxons did, and we're going to work through some of the old chronicles."

"It is just the project?"

"I get to see the palace, Mother. I get to spend time with the royal family. It'll be brilliant."

"We'll need to work out the arrangements." Mary realized this would give her the opportunity to get her mother in York and bring her back to London for a few weeks. Her mother had brought a visit up often enough. "I should expect someone from the palace to call?"

Mark nodded. "Tommy said his dad would call. King Michael will be there the entire weekend."

Mary felt her heart start pounding. She smiled and nodded at Mark.

Michael called Mary the next evening.

"Mrs. Penniman? This is Michael Kent-Hughes. I understand our two rascals have been conspiring to get together this weekend."

"Yes, your majesty, that's what I understand as well. Is this all right? Are you sure it's no trouble?"

"Not a bit. The children often have their friends over for a weekend. If I understand Tommy correctly, Mark will come home from school with Tommy on Friday, and then we'll bring him home on Sunday, say about 5? Does that work for you?"

"Yes, that works fine."

"Good, then. If you happen to take off for the weekend, is there a number where we can reach you?"

"My mobile. I just might get away for a night, to pick up my mother in York for a visit here, but you can reach me via my mobile." She gave him the number.

Michael decided to ride with the Security car to pick the children up at school. He was slightly surprised to see that Mark Penniman looked nothing like his mother. The boy had black hair and dark brown eyes. *Must take after his dad.* He was shorter and a bit stockier than Tommy, but then Tommy had clearly started a growth spurt. And Mark was a quiet, almost shy boy, seeming younger than his 13 years.

As they rode through Friday afternoon London traffic, Michael glanced over at Tommy. The boy was already entering young manhood. He was shaving once a week now, and he was growing taller. After talking with David, Michael had brought up the subject of puberty with Tommy. They'd had long talks about the physical and emotional changes the boy was experiencing. At first embarrassed to talk with his father about it, Tommy had overcome his embarrassment and had routinely come to ask his father an array of questions, some of which embarrassed Michael but which he answered truthfully and factually. At times, their mutual embarrassment in their conversations had given way to laughter. *Thank you, Father, that this son of mine feels comfortable enough with his Dad to talk with me about this.*

He glanced at the girls, talking animatedly with each other about their day. Jane had become a kind of surrogate mother for Helen and Sophie, for which Michael was exceedingly thankful. He wouldn't even have known where or how to have begun to explain puberty to them. Jane had taken them in hand when they were about 11 and started talking with the girls about the physical and emotional changes they should expect. He looked at them now; they were well on their way to becoming attractive, poised, confident young women. They were vastly different in their temperaments and emotions; some days they seemed almost polar opposites of each other. He loved them both dearly.

Hank had been the school football star, serving as captain for both of his last two years. While Tommy loved the sport, Hank was the better player. But Michael had been pleased that his younger son chose to join the lower school team and, from what the coach had told him, played with all his heart.

Arriving home, Michael saw that Mark was wide-eyed in wonder at the palace's scale and grandeur.

"Tommy," Michael said, "after you throw your stuff in your room, why don't you take Mark on a tour? And make sure you stop off in the kitchen for one of Mr. Malone's snacks." Since Sarah's death, Davey Malone had been bringing the family's dinner to the loft each day at 6 p.m. sharp. When she'd been alive, Sarah had usually cooked for the family. Michael's skills in the kitchen were vastly and famously more limited, and the children had unanimously voted for meals supplied by Mr. Malone.

At dinner, the family planned out their weekend. Tonight was games night. On Saturday morning they'd first give Mark a few bicycling lessons, and then take a spin around the gravel walks of the palace gardens and possibly nearby Green Park. When asked what he might like to do, Mark had responded with such a quick "Could we see the Imperial War Museum, sir?" that Michael readily agreed. The girls had their own plans for Saturday, so Michael told Security to plan for a jaunt to the museum on Saturday afternoon, including only Michael, Tommy, and their guest.

Michael also called the grounds crew and asked them to be prepared to help the family erect sleeping tents in the garden for Saturday night.

In the games room on the ground floor of the palace, Michael was surprised to find Mark generally staying anywhere Michael was.

The boy didn't say much, but he played Michael a credible game of ping pong, watched closely as Michael rode his stationary road bike, and sat next to him when the kitchen cook brought popcorn and other snacks. But when Tommy challenged him to a game of one-on-one basketball, Mark readily took off with his friend.

"I think he likes you, Dad," Sophie said to Michael.

On Saturday morning, Michael, Tommy, and Mark were up early for the bike lesson. They pulled out the bike Hank had used when he was younger, and Michael adjusted the seat for Mark's height. Michael could see the boy's apprehension, embarrassment, and desire fighting for control.

"When I was a boy learning to ride," Michael said, "it took me days before I could find my balance."

"I fell down the first eight times I tried to ride," Tommy said. Michael gave his son a small smile of thanks.

"So, don't think of the bike as some alien monster who's trying to defeat you," Michael said. "Think of it as a friend you're getting to know for the first time. And you don't know each other very well, and you're both trying to decide whether to be friends or not. And you're wondering if you have to spar a little bit to see what's up between you."

Mark's first two times up, Michael ran alongside the boy holding on to the seat. As soon as he let go, Mark went over, the first time into the grass but the second time scuffing his knee on the gravel walk. Michael doctored it with his first aid kit, and then got Mark back up on the bike.

"Okay, so you've had a scuffle with your new friend here. And he got the best of you this time. But you're going to show him that you're coming back, and he better be ready, because now it's going to be different."

Holding the seat, Michael ran alongside the boy, and kept running alongside, even when he had let go. Mark, unaware that he had found his balance, thought Michael was still holding him steady.

"Now speed it up a bit, son." When Mark accelerated, Michael stopped running alongside.

When Mark realized Michael wasn't there, he wobbled a bit, but then righted himself and kept going. Michael and Tommy cheered and danced a victory jig.

They watched Mark brake, and then stop. Getting off the bike, he turned it around, remounted rather awkwardly, and then rode back to them. When he stopped, Michael and Tommy high-fived him.

"Outstanding!" Michael said.

Mark's face was flushed with accomplishment. "It seems hard, but it's not. You have to find that spot where you balance."

"Exactly. Now we're going to work on turns. Tommy, get your bike. Take it slow and let Mark follow you when you do some turns."

For the next hour, the two boys rode around the palace gardens together. Simon Fredericks joined Michael with coffee, and the two men watched the boys ride.

"It's something, isn't it, sir," Simon said. "He's taken right to it."

Michael nodded. "I think we've found the world another cyclist."

Finally, he called the session to a halt. "We need to get some breakfast and plan our trip to the war museum."

While they ate, joined by the twins, Michael and Tommy told the girls about Mark's prowess on the bicycle. The boy beamed.

"We'll have to get you a helmet," Michael said. "We'll stop at Tony's bike shop on the way to the museum and pick one up."

Tony's Cycles was a bike shop south of the Thames, not far from the Imperial War Museum. Tony Simpson had been the chauffeur for Michael's birth parents and the man who had taught Michael to ride a bike. When his parents had been killed in a car crash, 6-year-old Michael had been ordered out of the house by his half-brother Henry. Tony had driven him from the family home in Kent to Michael's designated guardians, Ian and Iris McLaren in Edinburgh. Shortly after his coronation as king, Michael had been traveling to a speech when the car was stopped in traffic. He saw the bike shop and startled his security agents by saying he needed to check on some things and leaping from the car. Michael and Tony had been reunited after more than 20 years, and Tony's shop now bore the royal warrant on its front window. Michael bought his own as well as all of the children's bikes here.

Tony, now 72, was semi-retired, and his son and grandson tended to most of the shop's day-to-day operations. Michael hoped they would find him at the shop on a Saturday, when he liked to come in and work on bikes needing repair and chat with the customers.

This Saturday, Tony wasn't there. "His arthritis is kicking up," Tony's son Leo said. "It's that old bike injury from more than 40 years ago." Tony had been a professional racer until his bike fork disintegrated on a downhill slope. The resulting crash had left him partially crippled and ended his cycling career; his father had found him the chauffeur's job with Michael's father.

"Give him my best, and tell him I'm coming to visit, so not to be surprised," Michael said. They bought the helmet for Mark, and added a water bottle, a pair of gloves, and an air pump.

Michael spotted a bike, a bright-red hybrid. "Mark, why don't you sit on that one there to see what kind of fit we might have?"

The boy sat on the bike, and Tommy helped steady it while Tony's grandson Derek quietly took seat height measurements. When Michael glanced at Leo, he gave a quiet nod, indicating to add it to the ticket. Paying for the helmet and other items, Michael asked if they might pick the bike up on their way back from the museum. A quiet nod from Leo told Michael they would have it ready.

They ate an early pizza lunch at a shop down the street, and then drove to the Imperial War Museum. The museum had been damaged during The Violence 19 years earlier, but the building had been fully restored and expanded with a sizeable addition.

"Have you been here before?" Michael said

Mark shook his head. "Only on the internet."

The visit repeated a common practice Michael had started at the beginning of his reign. He preferred to show up at museums and art galleries like any other visitor, to avoid any big to-do from the staff. Sarah, in fact, had started the practice the day after they'd arrived in London, when she took Jason and Jim along with the then-baby Hank to the Tower of London.

Inside, Michael and Tommy attracted almost as much attention as the exhibits. The crowds were friendly and enthusiastic; Michael's group was stopped twice due to prolonged applause and people shaking Michael's hand.

All of the Kent-Hughes had been to the museum several times before. But Mark had not, and he was awed. The World War I Gallery captivated him, but it was a special photography exhibit on the war in the Mideast that captured his complete attention.

Some seven years before, Michael had led and concluded the negotiations that, while not officially ending the war, provided for an extended ceasefire. So far, the ceasefire had held. Michael, as not only the acting head of government but essentially Government itself, had been able to bring most of the British troops home. Jim's RAF squadron had returned a year later; Michael's adopted son had spent four years involved in the conflict. Jim was now officially assigned to a base in Norfolk but he and other veterans had been given an extended leave of absence in recognition of their service.

Michael's accomplishment was no small thing; the war had lasted a good 18 years. Reports of his nomination for the Nobel Peace Prize surfaced but hadn't happened. For Michael, the important thing was that most of the British soldiers and airmen had come home.

Mark wandered through the photography exhibit, which provided a chronology of the entire war. Included in the earlier photographs was a photo of a younger Michael, Sarah, Jason and Jim, with the baby Hank, visiting the British base at Basra the day after the coronation. Mark recognized them in the photo, read the inscription card, and turned and looked very seriously at Michael.

"You went there, didn't you?"

Michael nodded, "Several times. That was the first, the day after we were crowned."

The boy precisely followed the exhibit's timeline, examining each photo closely. Michael could see that Tommy was getting impatient and pulled him aside.

He whispered to Tommy. "It'll be a great blessing to let Mark get through this. I know there's a lot to see, but this is particularly important to Mark, and it's likely because of his father. So, let him be and we'll see if he says anything."

Later, in the museum shop, Michael allowed each boy to pick out one item as a keepsake. Tommy selected a book on Anglo-Saxon warfare, to add to his growing collection on the subject. Mark had trouble deciding, but finally chose the photography exhibit catalog, which included all of the photographs with a much fuller description for each than in the exhibit itself.

Michael told the chauffeur to stop at Tony's on the way home, and while the boys waited, went inside to get the bike. The security man riding with them readied the bike rack on the car's roof, and helped Michael secure it for the ride home. At first saying nothing, but watching Mark from the corner of his eye, he could see the boy's eyes had gotten huge.

"Every boy needs a bike," Michael said. "And this one had your name written all over it, Mark."

Mark expressed his shocked thanks, while Tommy simply grinned.

On the final leg of the drive, Mark suddenly spoke. "My dad was in the Royal Engineers. My granddad told me he had an engineering degree, and he'd joined the army after graduation. My mother doesn't talk about it, and she won't allow me to talk about it or ask questions. I barely remember what he looked like. I remember his funeral, with all the flowers. Queen Sarah held my hand."

Tommy whispered to his father, and Michael called to the chauffeur. "One more stop, Alan, if you please. The Guards Museum Shop on Birdcage Walk."

"Yes, sir."

The shop was a small building nestled close to the fence, about 50 feet away from the museum entrance.

Michael nodded toward the steps to the underground museum entrance. "We don't have the time to visit the museum today. It'll be closing in 30 minutes. But let's stick our heads in the shop."

The shop was all things Guards and military, but it featured a wide array of toy soldiers from several periods of Britain's history, including contemporary military units. Tommy went to the salesclerk and asked what they might have in the way of Royal Engineers, and the clerk showed him one of the cases. He signaled to Mark and showed him the figures. Mark's eyes widened.

Tommy told him to pick one. "It'll be my present to you."

Mark finally selected a Royal Engineer in full military uniform, and the clerk retrieved one in its box from the storeroom.

"Tommy, thank you. It's like seeing what my dad looked like." Then he embarrassed himself when the tears welled up.

Returning to the palace, they watched Mark ride his new bike and then joined the grounds crew in setting up the tents in the forested area of the garden. The weather forecast now called for clear skies through Sunday morning.

Michael called Jason and Jane to invite the grandsons, Paul and Timothy. He also invited Jim, but Jim had a date with a young woman he'd recently met. It was Michael, Tommy, the two grandsons and Mark, along with two security agents, who prepared to camp out.

Once the tents were erected, the children collected their sleeping bags and pillows. Davy Malone sent out food for cooking over the campfire, and Michael wisely let Simon Fredericks do the cooking honors. After they ate, they toasted marshmallows and mashed them with chocolate and graham crackers, repeating David's dessert from the hike in Scotland.

At lights out, they went to their assigned tents. The two grandsons went with Michael, while Mark and Tommy were in a nearby tent. The two security agents had one tent, but they rotated shifts so that one would always be awake and on duty.

The next morning after church, they returned to the garden to disassemble the tents. When they finished, Michael suggested a bike ride up Constitution Hill to Hyde Park. The entire family, including the twins and Paul and Timothy, got on bikes and followed Michael through the palace gates and into the park. Four agents accompanied them. Mark was thrilled to go on his first official bike ride on his new bike.

After lunch, Jason picked up his sons while Tommy and Mark worked on their Anglo-Saxon project. At 4, Michael went looking for the boys to announce it was time to get Mark home. They weren't in Tommy's room. Thinking he might have to have Security check the palace and grounds, he heard voices at the other end of the loft.

He followed the sound to Sarah's studio. The door was open, Tommy was showing Mark the studio, explaining how his mother painted, where she kept her paints and brushes, and how she stretched her own canvases.

For a moment, Michael said nothing. He was surprised by the old, familiar churning at seeing Tommy in Sarah's studio. He thought he'd resolved this, that this feeling about Sarah, Tommy, and himself was long gone, but it was suddenly clear to him that nothing was resolved. And Tommy still had Sarah's key. Michael finally cleared his throat.

"It's time we get ready to leave to bring Mark home."

Tommy looked around and caught the edge in his father's voice. "I was only showing Mark where Mummy painted. We were just looking. We didn't touch anything."

Mark felt the tension between Michael and Tommy but looked confused.

"Let's get ready, shall we?" Michael said.

The Pennimans lived in northwest London, a bit farther out than Trevor and Liz Barry and not far from the Northwest London Cycling Trail.

The neighborhood was one of neat suburban houses. Mark's house was on a cul-de-sac, which Michael pointed out was ideal for practicing his cycling.

As they stopped in front of the Penniman's house, Mark looked at Michael. "Do you think I could surprise Mother with my bike? I could ride by on the walk."

Michael grinned. "Do you think she'll be okay with it?"

"I think so."

Michael and Simon removed the bike from the rack while Mark strapped on his helmet and gloves.

"You go up a house or two while I ring the bell," Michael said. Tommy positioned himself at the bottom of the front walk to signal to Mark when his mother answered the door.

Michael rang the bell. Mary Penniman opened it and smiled at Michael. An older woman resembling Mary was standing behind her. Tommy signaled to Mark.

Michael smiled. "Mrs. Penniman, I think we have a wee bit of a surprise." He nodded at the older lady.

Mark came down the sidewalk, yelling a "Hallo, Mother!" as he sped by.

Mary's eyes widened. She stepped further outside the door as Mark came back, waving at her. Soon he was off the bike and rushing it up the front walk.

"Mother! It's been grand! I can ride a bike, and King Michael got me this new one. We camped out last night behind the palace and we did a cook-out and slept in tents. And I got to go to the war museum yesterday." And then he stopped, knowing he'd said too much.

Mary Penniman had been looking a bit overwhelmed with seeing Mark on a bike and then the non-stop information flowing from her normally quiet son. But her expression suddenly changed.

She looked at Michael. "The war museum?"

Michael nodded. "We gave the boys their choice of what they might like to do, and Mark was keen on seeing the war museum. In fact, there was one exhibit he became absorbed in –"

"I don't allow him to visit the war museum, or anything else that glorifies death and destruction. He knows this."

"Mrs. Penniman, I don't think that's what the museum is about. In fact, if anything, it's just the opposite –"

"I don't care if you are the king, and even if you were the one who finally stopped that abomination in the Mideast. You'd no right to take Mark to that place."

"Mrs. Penniman, I'd no idea –"

"Exactly. You'd no idea. You'd no idea what that war has done to us."

Mark tugged on his mother's sleeve. "Mother –"

"Mark, please go inside. Now." She turned to Michael. "And take this bike away. If I think he needs to ride one, I'll buy one. You'd no right to do this."

"Mother, no!" Mark said with a cry. "The king gave it to me!"

"Inside, Mark. Now!"

In tears, the boy looked at Michael and then fled inside.

Michael was stunned almost speechless. He finally turned to Tommy, who was staring openmouthed. "Son, take the bike to Simon."

"But, Dad –"

"Tommy, take the bike to Simon and wait in the car."

Michael waited until the boy walked the bike down the sidewalk. He turned to Mrs. Penniman.

"I'd no idea that any of this might offend you. I apologize. I won't trouble you or your family again." He turned and started walking down the sidewalk. And then he stopped, turning back to her.

"I don't think this is about the bicycle or the war museum. I don't know what I originally did to offend you, but it must've been something colossal. So, I'll go all the way.

"If Mark's to become the man you want him to be, you need to let him be the boy that he is. He's a great boy, and he needs to do the things that boys do. And you're not the only woman who lost a beloved husband in the war."

Michael turned and walked quickly to the car, getting in and shutting the door. Mary Penniman, her mother beside her, stood on the porch, two bright red splotches on her cheeks.

"Let's go," Michael said, and the car moved from the curb and down the street.

Mary rushed inside, and her mother, Amanda Gill, followed, shutting the door behind her. Amanda leaned against it, closed her eyes, and began breathing deeply, trying to calm her own emotions before tackling her daughter.

Mary was furious and shouting. "How dare he! I don't care who he is. How dare he lecture me like that!" She stomped to Mark's room. The boy was sitting on his bed, an angry, obstinate look on his face.

"Mark, we have to talk."

He looked at her but didn't say a word.

"I know you had a good time with your friend," Mary said, "but there are certain things we don't do in this family."

"Like talk about my father."

Mary's voice rose. "You'll stop that right now!"

Mark stood. "I learned how to ride a bike! I did it. The king taught me, and I did it!"

"You will not speak to me that way!"

"Why won't you talk to me about my dad?" he said, in the angriest voice she'd ever heard.

Amanda walked in from the hall just as Mary slapped her son's face.

This time it was Amanda who shouted. "Mary Penniman! Stop this!"

"Don't you start, too, Mother. Our wonderful king takes Mark to the war museum, of all places. The war museum! The one place I've told Mark he's not to go."

Amanda looked at her grandson, still wearing his helmet and biking gloves, his face sporting a large red mark from the slap.

"He even gave him a bike to bring home! He'd no right to do this!"

Her mother saw the look of shock and devastation on Mark's face. "I think, Mary, that I'd like you to come to the kitchen and have some tea."

"Mother, I have to talk with Mark."

"It can wait. Come to the kitchen with me."

"Mother, I have to deal with this."

"Mary, before you inflict even more damage, you need to come to the kitchen. Now!"

Mary was so shocked by the edge in her mother's voice that she turned from Mark and stared after Amanda. She followed her to the kitchen.

"Sit at the table while I fix tea," Amanda said. Mary sat. She hadn't been addressed this way by her mother in 20 years.

Amanda put the kettle on to boil.

"I've held my tongue for seven years, but I'm not holding it any longer. You're going to destroy that child because you can't deal with John's death. He died, Mary, he died in a crazy, stupid, useless way on that road outside Basra. A mine blew up their vehicle, and he died. And part of you died with him. And you've been trying to let all of you die with him. Wouldn't he be thrilled to see that you're stifling that son he loved so much? Wouldn't he just love how you've shut yourself up? That your life is now confined to a small office at the British Library, taking Mark to school, and your bedroom here?"

"Mother!"

"Don't pretend to be shocked. You know it's true. What's shocking is that I haven't said anything before this. Go in there and look at that boy. He was thrilled to be riding a bike. What can possibly be wrong with a 13-year-old boy riding a bicycle? Instead of castigating the king you should be thanking him. What other man is around here to do that? And so what if they went to the war museum?

Did it occur to you that you refusing even to acknowledge there was a war has forced Mark to find out what happened to his father in other ways? Of course, he's going to be interested. I'm sure he's already looked all over the internet."

Mary didn't respond, but only stared at her mother.

"Mary, it's time for you to rejoin life. Let that boy ride his bike. Talk to him about his father. Apologize to the king. And take off that wedding ring. Your husband died, Mary. You're not a nun. And John would be furious with you."

Mary burst into tears and fled to her room.

The teacup in her slightly trembling hand, Amanda walked to Mark's room, to find him asleep on his bed. She set her cup down, and as quietly as possible removed the bike helmet. She decided to leave his gloves on. She covered him with his blanket and sat looking at him. He looked so much like his father it took her breath away. *And for the first time since he saw his father almost seven years ago,* she thought, *a man paid attention to him. He taught him to ride a bike, took him to the museum, and did a campout. Mark must've thought he'd died and gone to heaven. Oh, dear Lord, please help my daughter come to her senses and start living again, and please help this boy.* And then she noticed something clenched in Mark's hand. She gently opened his fingers and saw the toy soldier. Because she'd seen John in his uniform many times, she knew exactly what this figure represented. She closed the boy's fingers over the figure and began to cry, silently.

As Mary lay on her bed crying after her mother's words, she suddenly had a startling clear picture of Michael Kent-Hughes touching her face, and her trembling at his touch.

So, Mary, be honest with yourself. Was it the war museum, or was it the attraction you feel for the man that you don't want to acknowledge? Shocked by the way her mind was working, she focused to force the thought away. Despite the friendship of their sons and the school, her world and that of King Michael's existed in entirely different universes. She wasn't going to get involved again. That part of her life was locked away.

She gradually fell asleep.

In the car, Michael inwardly seethed. *Of all the pig-headed, stupid people. She thinks that because it's got "war" in the name that it's a temple to Mars.*

Tommy, seeing the anger on his father's face and having heard the mutual shouting, said nothing.

Still angry, Michael finally spoke. "Perhaps some people don't like to be surprised, but this takes the cake. You take a boy to a museum and she goes nuclear."

"It's because Mark's dad was killed in the war," Tommy said.

"Don't defend her. Her behavior was abominable. And while we're on the subject of behavior, the studio is off limits to your friends. And when we get home, I want your key."

"I was just showing him where she painted."

"It is for family only. I don't want anyone else in there. In fact, I don't want anyone in there, and that includes you. You'll give me your key when we arrive home."

In the front seat, Simon Fredericks sat on his hands. He had great regard for the king, but he wanted to take him to the woodshed. Simon had heard the shouting exchange as well, and he was amazed at how two people could both be wrong. And now this with Prince Thomas; all the good from the hike seemed to have washed away in seconds.

It struck Simon that the king was still angry over the death of his wife, that he'd yet to come to grips with it after so many years, with Prince Thomas bearing the brunt. And if Simon valued his job, he couldn't say anything.

The next day, Mark at first claimed he was sick and couldn't go to school. Mary refused to listen, and told him that, sick or not, he was going. She knew he was afraid of what Tommy might say, or if Tommy had told anyone about what happened.

When they arrived at school, they found Tommy waiting for Mark. He greeted Mary politely, and then he and Mark walked together to their building.

Tommy glanced over his shoulder to make sure they were away from Mary. "We're still saving the bike for you. Maybe your mum will come around."

"Is your dad still mad about the studio?"

Tommy nodded. "It goes back a long time, to when I was four. He got mad one day when he found out Mummy allowed me in the studio while she painted, and no one else."

"You were only four?"

"I know it makes him sound bad. I think there was a lot more to it, but I'll likely never know the whole story."

"What do you do when he's mad at you?"

"I stay out of his way, if I can." Tommy paused. "He made me give him my key to the studio. But I've a copy."

Mary's relations with her mother remained tense; they were barely on speaking terms.

Ten days later, the lower school football team had an after-school game with Central London Grammar School. Mary arrived from work after the game had started. She saw the king standing with his security contingent, watching Tommy on the field. Mary decided to ignore his presence.

Michael had noticed Mary's arrival and decided to stay focused on the game.

In the game's final seconds, the ICS team was ahead 1-0 when something went wrong. From the parents' vantage point, it appeared that one of the players had tripped, right where the ball was, and three more had rushed in to try to gain possession. Two more went down. The referees called time and the game ended. When the boys began to stand up, everyone breathed a sigh of relief. Except one boy didn't get up.

Mary looked to see where Mark was. When she couldn't see his number or his hair, she began to hurry toward the downed boy, right on the heels of the coach. Michael knew immediately it was Mark who was down and ran on to the field. He'd been close to where play had stopped and reached the downed boy first.

Mark was clutching his leg, which was a mass of blood. In the free-for-all tumble, someone's cleated shoe had clawed Mark's leg, ripping deeply. Though the cleats were plastic, one player's shoes had sharp, jagged edges. Tommy was kneeling next to his friend.

Seeing the blood, Mary went white. Michael, wearing his standard business suit for public appearances, went to his knees in the mud next to the boy. He immediately saw the fear and pain in the boy's eyes.

"It's all right, Mark. We'll get this taken care of." Michael covered the wound with his hand and pointed to the penalty flag in the referee's back pocket. "Can you hand me that flag, ref?"

Michael tied the flag around the wound, to staunch the flow of blood. "We need a first-aid kit." The coach sent one of the boys running to the bench.

"Tommy, tell Simon and Charlie we need the car, and to drive it as close to the field as possible." Tommy sprinted off, just as the player with the first-aid kit returned.

Michael pulled out the antiseptic. "Mark, it's going to burn, so if it hurts too much just hit me on my arm." Mark and the other boys laughed.

Mark grimaced when Michael applied the antiseptic, bandaged the wound with gauze and tape, and wrapped tape around the whole of the bandage.

The coach looked with admiration at the bandage. "You're pretty good at this, your majesty."

"I've a brave patient here, and I learned emergency first-aid a long time ago, when I spent a summer in Africa. And I kept it up; it's almost mandatory when you've six children and two grandchildren." The coach and the parents gathered around all laughed in agreement.

Tommy came running up, with Simon Fredericks and Charlie MacArthur right behind him. "The car's here, Dad."

"Okay. Simon, I'll need you to come with us to the hospital. Charlie, can you call Mr. Mitchell and arrange for a car home for Tommy?"

"Yes, sir. I'll do it now."

"I'm staying, Dad. Mark's my friend."

"All right." Michael turned back to Mark. "Mr. Penniman, we've got a short walk to the car, and I'm going to carry you. Charlie, can you get Mark's and Tommy's things from the locker room and arrange a ride back to the palace with Mr. Mitchell?" Without waiting for a response from Mark, Michael picked him up in his arms, and he and Tommy starting walking toward the waiting car. Then Michael stopped and called over his shoulder, to where Mary was still standing, almost in shock. "Mrs. Penniman, we need you to come with us as well."

Mary quickly caught up with them. "I can get a taxi or call for an ambulance."

Michael shook his head. "You wait an hour for a taxi during Thursday afternoon rush hour or several hours for a National Health wagon to show up? I think not."

He gently placed Mark on the car's back seat, and then folded down the two riding seats that faced it. "It's not comfortable but it will have to do. The patient gets priority, I'm afraid." He helped Mary into the car, motioned Tommy to the front seat with Simon, and then sat in the other facing seat. Michael touched the driver on his shoulder. "Kensington Hospital, Alan."

"Yes, sir."

"That's a private hospital," Mary said. "My National Health doesn't apply."

"It'll be taken care of, Mrs. Penniman. Mark needs a good specialist to take a look."

Michael turned his attention to the boy, who could sense the tension between his mother and the king.

"Sir," said Mark, "do you think this will leave a scar?"

Michael looked at the bandaged leg and thought a moment. "Well, most likely, I think. If you're lucky."

Mark beamed. "Cool!"

Michael pointed to the scar on his own cheek, faded but still visible. "I got this one at the Olympics in Athens, when a German cyclist hit a flat piece of rock on the road, went airborne, and planed down on top of me."

Mark stared at Michael, wide-eyed in admiration.

"Tommy's got a few from some bike spills, and I've got some on my legs from old road rash injuries, but it wouldn't be polite to show them in mixed company."

Mark laughed.

Mary didn't understand what had just been said but figured it was some kind of male bonding thing. She was also unsure why they were going to Kensington Hospital. "I can't afford a private hospital."

"It's all right, Mrs. Penniman." Michael continued to focus his attention and conversation on Mark.

Reaching the hospital, the car pulled up right at the emergency entrance. Michael quickly carried Mark inside.

The sight of the King of Great Britain carrying an injured boy in his arms, followed by a bewildered woman and Prince Thomas, galvanized the emergency room staff. Mark was placed on a wheeled stretcher and whisked into an examination room. Michael and Mary followed the attendants and stretcher into the room.

"I'll wait outside," Michael said. "If you need me, let me know."

He joined Tommy and Simon in the waiting room.

"Mark will be all right?"

"I think so, Tommy. But the injury's more serious than it appeared. The gash in his leg exposed the bone."

Simon looked at the king. "And you had to move quickly to keep him and his mother from seeing it and panicking."

Michael nodded. "That reminds me, I need to check them in." Simon and Tommy watched as Michael sat with the admitting officer, and Simon realized that Michael was going to cover Mark's expenses.

An hour passed. Then two. Finally, Mary Penniman walked into the waiting area. She looked exhausted.

"He's gotten stitches. They're admitting him, at least for tonight. The wound was worse than it looked." She paused. "The doctor said that someone's quick thinking and action kept it from being worse."

Michael nodded. "I expect you'll want to stay with him tonight. So, here's what I suggest, and this is only a suggestion, I'm not trying to interfere. I can have our driver take you home to get what you need for tonight, and we'll will stay with Mark until you get back. You might want to get something to eat while you're home, even if you don't feel hungry."

She looked at Michael. "You're not trying to interfere? You're already interfering. You brought us here in the first place, and they tell me the expenses are covered."

Michael nodded again. "As soon as I saw the wound, Mrs. Penniman, I realized he needed expert care." He paused. "And you're right. I'm interfering."

"I can't let you do this."

"Mrs. Penniman, consider it a gift to Mark. That's all." He paused. "Tommy told me about your husband. I'm sorry. And I apologize for my harsh words at your house."

At first, she didn't answer, but looked from Tommy back to Michael. "My husband died seven years ago, your majesty, outside Basra." She paused. "Queen Sarah came to his funeral while you were in Paris negotiating the ceasefire."

Michael looked at her hand with the wedding ring, and then at her. "It's what Sarah would do. I'm sorry, Mrs. Penniman. I know what it is to lose someone you love because of the glorification of a cause. For me it was my brother."

She'd seen him looking at her wedding ring, and she moved her hand out of sight. "I'm sorry. I'm sorry for what I said before." She looked toward Tommy, and then back at Michael. "On the field. And in the car. You knew his leg was worse than it appeared."

Michael nodded.

"That's why you were joking with him. That business about the scars. It was to keep him calm and distracted. And me as well."

Michael smiled. "I've never forgotten the bicycle crash at the Olympics. There were a lot of similar injuries among the cyclists."

She looked at his clothes and touched his tie. "Your clothes are ruined."

There was blood across Michael's shirt, tie and coat, and the knees of his pants were stained with dried mud where he'd knelt on the field.

"It's all right, Mrs. Penniman. Let Alan drive you home. We'll stay with Mark."

In his room, Mark was awake but slightly groggy from the pain medicine they'd given him. Michael sat next to his bed, Tommy stood next to his father, and Simon stood near the door.

Michael explained where Mary was, and asked him how he was feeling.

"Woozy, sir. Might I have some water?"

Michael poured some from the bedside pitcher into a cup and held Mark's head up while the boy sipped his water. Mark held his hand to Michael's around the cup.

"Thank you, sir," the boy said. Michael noticed that Mark's hand lingered on his own. He returned the cup to the tray, and then put his hand on Mark's.

"They'll be bringing you some food soon. Eight o'clock is late for hospitals to feed patients, but the nurse said they're making up a special tray." Michael had told Simon to get something for himself and Tommy before the cafeteria closed, but Simon reminded the king that he couldn't leave Michael by himself.

Simon watched the king talk with the boy. *He's unbelievable with children,* he thought. *Of course, he's had lots of practice with that family of his. But he touches something in children. Like they know he accepts them for who they are and treats them with respect. Mark here is falling in love with the king; you can see it all over the boy's face. I just wish the king could accept his own son for who he is.*

"Sir, those times you went to see the troops in the Mideast, would you have met my father? His name was John. John Penniman."

Michael looked thoughtfully at the boy. "Mark, I don't believe I did. A lot of troops were there."

"Yes, sir. I just wondered. I can't remember what he looks like, and I don't have a picture of him. My mother won't talk about it."

"I can't tell you about your dad, but I can tell you what it was like, the places where our troops were." Michael began to talk about the military bases, the climates at different times of the year, and some of the people he'd met.

A little after 10, Mary returned with an overnight bag, necessities for Mark, the book from the war museum, and a large shopping bag. Seeing the book, Michael smiled.

"Mark," she said, "why don't you look at your book with Tommy while I talk with King Michael for a few minutes."

As they left the room, Michael gave Mark a thumbs-up and a wink.

"I didn't know if you'd had a chance to eat," she said, "so I brought some sandwiches for you, Tommy, and the security officer." Simon, who'd been dealing with a rumbling, hungry stomach for the last two hours, felt his morale instantly soar.

"You didn't have to do that, but it's most appreciated."

Michael called to Tommy, and the three of them walked with Mary to the nearby waiting area, where Mary opened the shopping bag, filled with sandwiches, crisps, biscuits, and bottled water.

"My mother fixed them while I got things together. The sandwiches are one of our family's favorites, ham and apple slices." She sat with them while they ate.

"Words can't say enough for what you've done. The doctors had nothing but praise for your first-aid technique and told me how fortunate Mark was to have someone around who knew what to do."

Michael smiled and shrugged his shoulders. "Perhaps I'm a frustrated medical technician."

"How did you know to come here? There are a lot of hospitals in London."

"It was the closest. My two girls and Tommy here were also born here. And this was the hospital where," he hesitated before going on, "where Sarah died. I'd spent so much time here that I got to know a lot of staff and see the quality of medical care. I knew this was the place to get Mark's wound attended to."

Mary watched him while he finished his sandwich. *I love watching him eat,* she thought. *I'd love to see him come in sweaty after a bike ride and help him out of his jersey. And feel his sweaty back and chest. Mary! Stop this!*

Tommy had found a second sandwich in the bag and was working his way through the crisps and biscuits.

"I think we need to head home." Michael stood as he collected the wrappings. "Mark's going to be fine, although he may miss the rest of the season. But a suggestion, if I may. Let him come to the games and dress out with the team, even with his bandage still on. The coach will find things for him to do. But even though you'd like to see him as far as possible from a football field, let him be with the team. It'll mean the world to him, and he'll know he'll be back for spring training."

She nodded. "I don't know how to repay you for your care and kindness."

"There's one thing you can do, Mrs. Penniman. And I'm going to be interfering again. If you could talk with Mark about his dad, it would do more for him than you'd imagine. And it would mean a lot to me as well."

She stared at him without speaking.

"And now we must go."

"Thank you for the sandwiches, Mrs. Penniman," said Tommy. "The food was great."

"And thank your mother, too. That ham and apple combo is terrific," Michael said.

Mary smiled. "She'll be glad to know you enjoyed it." She watched them walk down the hall to the elevator.

Alan Sykes, Michael's regular driver in London, was waiting near the main entrance.

"Did you get something to eat, Alan?" Michael said.

"Yes, sir, I had one of those sandwiches Mrs. Penniman brought along."

As they moved into the night traffic, Michael stared at the lights of the buildings and the passing cars. It was almost 11. He looked over at Tommy, who'd already fallen asleep.

Michael should've felt exhausted. What he felt was exhilarated.

Mark's doctor decided to keep the boy in the hospital for a second night and discharge him on Saturday. On Friday at lunch, Mark had a visit from Dr. Owens, the ICS headmaster, and Coach Rowling, who had three members of the team with him, including Tommy and a palace security officer. Mary could see the boys were in awe of the bandage on Mark's leg and his hospital room, and even more in awe of the crutches Mark would have to use for at least two weeks and possibly longer. She realized that in the strange world of 13-year-old boys, her son had acquired celebrity status. On Friday evening, Amanda came by with fresh clothes for her daughter and things for Mark to wear the next day.

Mark was discharged on Saturday at 10, with a follow-up appointment for Tuesday. A nurse wheeled the boy in a wheelchair to the front door, where they found a car waiting to take them home. The king's driver, Alan, smiled at them. "His majesty would like to offer you a ride home," he said. Alan helped Mark into the car, and placed his crutches on the floor, next to Mark's backpack and clothes and books retrieved by Charlie from the locker room. Mary called her mother and told her they were on their way.

When they reached home, Amanda came down the walk, and was surprised to see the king's car.

"He offered us a ride home," Mary said to her mother, as Alan helped them bring their things inside.

Amanda Gill looked at the car, and at her daughter, and smiled.

"Mother," Mark said, "may I have my book?"

Mary nodded. "It's right here."

After getting the boy settled and having lunch, Mary walked into her bedroom and found the photograph album she'd hidden at the bottom of her closet. She brushed the dust away. Then she walked to Mark's room and sat on the side of his bed.

"I need to tell you about your father." She and Mark spent the rest of the afternoon talking. Part of it she spent in tears, as she explained each photo to Mark and told him about his dad.

That evening, after Mark was asleep, Mary got ready for bed. She looked at the wedding ring she was still wearing. She stared at it for a few moments, and then took it off, placing it in her jewelry box. *I still love you, John, more than life itself. I always will. But Mother's right. I think you'd want me to get on with my life.*

Weeks passed. Mark was indeed out for the rest of the football season, but Coach Rowling had him dress out with the team and serve as an assistant while his leg recovered.

Michael and Mary often saw each other at the games, and talked together, trading stories about their sons and the school. Mary agreed to accept the bike for Mark, and, once the stitches in his leg dissolved, Mark got the doctor's okay to start doing short rides.

Michael's conversations with Mary, while frequent, remained on a pleasant, fellow-school-parent level. Mary gave no indication of being interested in anything else, and Michael was wary of pushing too much or too hard, so he ended up not pushing at all. Several times he came close to asking her out, *for a coffee or something, anything would do*, but he held back.

For her part, Mary found herself still strongly attracted to Michael, but the gulf in their positions seemed too wide. Still, seeing him at school events gave her a warm internal glow, and she felt herself blushing every time he walked up.

On a Friday afternoon in mid-November, as Mary arrived at the school ball field, she mentally ticked off the games left in the schedule. *There's today, and there's next Friday, and then we're done.* Mark's leg was healing nicely, and she could see him standing next to the coach. The late autumn afternoon was unusually chilly. All of the parents were either huddled in the seats with blankets or standing along the sideline and regularly stomping their feet to keep warm.

Mary was hugging herself to keep warm and trying to move about. She was thankful for the heavy wool coat she was wearing, but she'd forgotten to bring gloves. Her hands were freezing.

Suddenly she felt the glow of knowing the king was standing nearby. He was next to her, offering her a cup.

"We have tea and coffee. No sweetener or milk, I'm afraid.

"Anything warm will do. Thank you. Tea would be wonderful."

Extracting a thermos from a basket next to him, Michael poured the steaming liquid into her cup. She sipped the tea, feeling its warmth meet the internal glow.

Michael sipped his cup. "I'm the coffee drinker in the family. Everyone else takes tea, even Jason and Jim."

"My husband was a great one for coffee. My family drank tea, but John loved his coffee. Especially Starbuck's. I can hear him now, ordering his 'Venti non-fat latte.' No sugar, just coffee and steamed milk."

She saw confusion on Michael's face.

"Is something wrong?"

He shook his head. "No. The coffee I'm drinking is non-fat latte. From Starbuck's. No sugar." He sipped his coffee and smiled. "I've drunk Starbuck's since I was at university. It got to be a kind of joke. 'Mike loves Starbuck's.'"

"Mike? Somehow I can't see you being called Mike."

He looked out at the players on the field and saw Tommy's attempted goal get deflected.

"Sarah called me Mike. Everyone else calls me Michael."

"I'm sorry, I didn't mean –"

"It's okay. For a time after she died, I couldn't talk about her. I couldn't bear it. It was too raw, too painful. It's like I died with her, or at least the part of me that was most alive. I'd wake up at night, reaching for her and only finding an empty bed. Or I'd wake in a panic, and I'd rush into the children's bedrooms to make sure they were there and safe." He looked at Mary. "I'm sorry. I don't mean to burden you."

"You didn't. What happens is that you wake up, and want to feel her next to you, and not just anyone, because just anyone wouldn't do. It has to be her. You want the one you loved, the one you held in your arms and who held you, the one who made love with you." She stopped abruptly, unsure whether it was the embarrassment or the tears in her eyes.

"That's it exactly." He turned to the game, tears in his eyes.

On the way home, he discovered Tommy had been paying attention to more than the game.

"I saw you talking with Mrs. Penniman. She's turned out to be quite nice."

"She has indeed."

"Have you thought about asking her out, Dad? You seem to get along. You might think about it."

Michael and Simon were both surprised by Tommy's comment.

Michael looked at his son, and realized he'd never apologized to Tommy for the studio incident and what he'd said in the car, and that Tommy's words about Mary Penniman were the most the boy had said to him for the past few weeks.

"Tommy?"

Tommy turned from staring out the window. "Yes, Dad?"

"I owe you an apology. Actually, I owe you two apologies."

In the front passenger seat, Simon Fredericks smiled, until the boy responded.

"Dad, I think there's always going to be this rock between us. I don't remember all of what happened that day you came home, when I was in Mummy's studio. I remember a lot of shouting. But I think the rock's going to be there, and I don't think we can fix it. So maybe we should just tell ourselves it's there, it'll always be there, and we just have to go around it or ignore it." He paused. "We may not ever be close, not like you and Hank or you and the twins. But it doesn't mean I don't love you and you don't love me. It's just something that's there, and we'll work around it." The boy paused again. "Right before Mummy died in the hospital, she told me that I had to remember you'd always love me, and that I was to always love you. She said sometimes we'd each be unlovable, and those were the times we needed to love each other most."

Facing straight ahead, Simon kept waiting for a response from the king, but the lengthening silence told him there wouldn't be one.

What Simon didn't see was Tommy's staring again from the car window, tears in his eyes.

It was the following Friday, after the final game of the season, that Michael offered Mary and Mark a ride home, and asked if they'd like to stop for supper with him and Tommy. Four months later,

Buckingham Palace announced the engagement of King Michael and Mary Penniman of London.

Iris

Two years later

From the family room, Iris heard the car door slam, and she stood up, ready to greet Tommy, arriving for a week-long visit. Usually, the grandchildren each took a turn with a visit of four or five days. This year, Hank was in training for the Olympics, Sophie was in Spain for a university course, and Helen had a small role in a play at the Hampstead Theatre in London. This year, only 15-year-old Tommy was visiting, and he would be starting university at St. Andrew's in early September.

She was a wee bit disappointed that the other three were growing up now, but she knew it was the natural order of things. Still, she was more than glad to see Tommy. Of all of her grandchildren, he was the one who brought back the memories. He looked the least like his father and acted the most like him, with the same quiet, serious demeanor. Like Michael, Tommy had always been a reserved child, taking in far more than most people realized.

Iris was 78 but felt and acted years younger. Life had certainly slowed down, but it was still life, and she was determined to enjoy every minute of what time she had left. She loved visits by the grandchildren; two weeks after Tommy, Jason's two boys would be arriving. And if she managed to last, the newest grandchild, Michael and Mary's David, would be coming along in a few years.

She was often amazed at how the four children of Michael and Sarah were so different. The outgoing Hank could put everyone in a room at ease and find time to flirt as well. Caretaker Sophie was serious-minded but had a streak of fun and mischief in her. Helen often forgot that the entire world wasn't really a stage. And Tommy, the quiet one, with his brilliant mind and healthy American good looks, preparing to enter college two years ahead of his peers.

Michael had told her that Tommy would be entering as an almost third-year student, because of his performance on advanced placement tests. "There a list of colleges as long as my arm that have been after him, Ma," Michael had said. "But he decided on St. Andrews."

She knew why, and she suspected Michael knew why as well. St. Andrews was where David Hughes taught, and Tommy was closer to his uncle than he was to his father. He even looked like his uncle, reminding Iris of when David and Sarah first visited McLarens, all those years ago.

Aye, Tommy brought the memories.

She heard the door open, and Tommy set his artist portfolio down and hugged her.

"Let me look at you," she said. "Thomas Michael, you've gotten as tall as your brother and father."

"A little taller than Dad and almost at Hank's height," Tommy said, grinning.

"Well, get your bags up to your room and let's have some tea," she said. "I think I have a pie or cake waiting."

After getting settled and sharing a slice of Iris's raisin cake, the two sat in the family room and talked. Tommy sat with his sketch pad, drawing a picture of her as they talked. She had several of these drawings. She knew that, with Michael in London, Tommy felt free to draw and sometimes paint. There was a tension between the boy and his father about painting, and Iris suspected it went back to when Sarah was still alive. When she had asked Michael about it, he'd shrugged it off, which told her she was right.

She thought back to the scene in the hospital waiting room, when the little boy flung himself at his father, blaming him for his mother's death. And then his silence. Like everyone else in the family, she'd missed it; the family had been too caught up in grief over Sarah and Tommy McFarland to notice for some time that the boy had stopped speaking.

She'd even missed it during the funeral ride from Westminster Abbey to King's Cross Station. The four children had crowded into the car with her, with Michael and David deciding to walk behind the car carrying Sarah's casket. Tommy had watched them, and then he surprised them all, opening the car door and hurrying to where his father and uncle were standing. As the cars started, he walked between them, with the crowds standing silently along the route. Whenever there was a stop, to clear traffic ahead or do some security check, Tommy would walk to the crowd and silently shake people's hands, giving a little nod.

It had been several stops before Michael, wrapped up in untold pain and grief, noticed what the boy was doing. David had seen him first and touched Michael's arm, nodding toward Tommy. Michael had stared, and then moved to the opposite side the street, replicating Tommy's shaking of hands. David had joined Tommy.

There had been no stops for the final mile to the station, and the crowds and the group in the car noticed when Tommy took his uncle's hand. Michael appeared not to notice.

And then there had been that train ride to Edinburgh. The family, seated, seemed encased in individual cocoons of grief. As the train left and began to pass stations along the way, it was again David who noticed what Tommy was doing, as the boy stood at a window. He was waving.

"Tommy," David had said, "who are you waving to?"

The boy pointed. When David joined him, he turned to Michael. "Michael, you need to see this."

Michael, Jason, Jim, and the three children joined them at the window.

People were lining the way, behind fences along the tracks. At stations, people were 10 and 15 deep, and the train slowed as it reached each one. At two stations, Cambridge and York, the funeral train stopped to await the easing of traffic ahead. And while there were gaps, people could be seen lining a considerable part of the way.

Michael just kept staring. "They're seeing her home," he said finally, his voice breaking. He sat and sobbed.

The sun was setting as the train reached the Scottish border, but people continued to line the way. Many had torches; bonfires had been lit in several places.

As the train pulled into Waverly Station in Edinburgh, there had been an overwhelming sense of light. People waiting for trains held lit candles, and Iris could see a huge glow toward the station's main terminal.

Tommy, moving away from the family and security guards, began to walk quickly toward the terminal, and then broke into a run. Two security officers dashed after him, but the boy was quick and had a good head start. As he entered the main terminal, there was an open space in the middle of thousands of people, each holding a lit candle. For several minutes, Tommy, with tears running down his cheeks, walked to people and shook their hands, nodding his head. When the rest of the family caught up, they were at first stunned by the crowd, and even more stunned to see the six-year-old boy walking along its edge, shaking hand after hand.

Iris had turned to Michael, and she saw the look of almost shocked recognition on his face. Michael spoke to the rest of the family.

"Tommy is showing us that the people have their grief, too, and we must honor that."

Michael strode to the crowd and began to shake hands, following his son's lead. The other children and other family members soon followed.

Iris stared at the 15-year-old boy sketching in front of her and marveled at what he'd understood at so young an age.

"Are you ready to start university?" she said.

He looked up from the sketch pad and nodded. "Dad's a wee bit concerned, but I feel ready, Ma."

"And you plan to read history?"

"History and languages of the Anglo-Saxon era," he said. "Perhaps with a focus on the Vikings." He bent over his sketch again, and it was then she noticed something about him she'd never seen before. He was tapping his foot, almost nervously.

The two spent the next day in Iris's gardens; she had Tommy plant several rose bushes supposedly suited for the Scottish climate. For dinner, Security drove them into Edinburgh, to a French restaurant that Tommy had suggested after searching online. They eventually began talking about Ian, as she knew they would. Tommy simply couldn't hear enough about Ian McLaren, who'd died when Tommy was four. The boy had been in the room with David Hughes and her when Ian had passed away. And she still wondered about the words Ian had whispered to her right before he died, words about Tommy.

In the car on the way home, she noticed the boy fidgeting, touching his fingers to his thumb over and over again and still tapping his foot.

The next morning at breakfast, she decided to say something.

"You've something on your mind."

"I'm sorry, Ma. Things just seem strange right now."

"Strange?"

He nodded. "Not here, not with you. It always feels right to be here. It's more with me, like there's something I forgot to do, or I'm supposed to remember something. It's very odd."

"Is this something new?"

"It's been happening off and on for a few weeks. The only way I know to describe it is that I'm in a room with someone, and they're saying something important. But I can't hear the words. They're telling me I'm to do something, something I'm meant to do. Do you think I might have the wrong major at St. Andrews? Should I be studying theology at Edinburgh instead?"

"Whoa," Iris said, "you just connected two things and left out the bit in the middle. Where did theology come from?"

"I don't know. I'm not even sure it's that. But it's like being called to something." He paused. "It's stronger when I pray."

Iris tried to keep a bland face, but Tommy caught the almost shocked expression.

"What?" he said. "Do you know something?"

She didn't answer immediately. "No, I don't, Tommy. I'm just reminded of something that happened to your father at about your age." She paused. "Have you talked with David?"

Tommy shook his head. "When I go to stay with them after I leave here, I'm doing a hike with him, Gavin, and Angus. I'll talk with him then."

"Your Uncle David always has good counsel," she said. "And one thing you could do to help get the thoughts out is hike up in the hills here, up to the overlook. I haven't done it in years, but it was always a good place to clear my head."

An hour later, she watched him as he walked through the gardens toward the hill trail, followed by a security officer. He looked like he still had some growing to do. He was blond, already tall, with none of the awkwardness of a teenager. Tommy had a natural grace about him that again reminded her of his father.

And that look on his face when he nodded at her suggestion of the overlook. She remembered the fidgeting of Michael at the same age. And she'd seen the same look on the face of his father, when he'd hiked up that trail and came back to tell her and Ian that he was being called to the Anglican ministry.

She watched Tommy until he disappeared from sight.

Noah

Six years later

Under the canopy, he knelt with his trowel, brush, and small pick, carefully sectioning a square-foot layer of dirt. The indication so far was nothing would be found here, with the most likely area about four to five feet over, but the area had to be cut away and examined. This kind of sectioning wasn't the most glamorous part of the dig, but as project manager, he felt he needed to do the work considered more like drudgery. And it would help the main focus of the work to have this section cut away and examined first. He'd been at this for most of the day, and he was tired.

He also owned the property, but very few people knew that.

The island of Broughby, the northernmost of the Orkneys, was small, invariably bypassed by tourists and the tour ships because of its remoteness and lack of attractions. There wasn't much to see or do; no old, ruined abbeys or castles or exotic bird migration zones. The island was home to 300 people, almost all involved in fishing, like their parents, grandparents, and ancestors going back to the times of the Celts.

The one village on the island, also called Broughby, was served by a ferry three days a week. The ferry connected to the main Orkney islands and the ports of Aberdeen and Inverness. A one-room school, with a teacher whose husband was a fisherman, served younger children; those aged 13 and up boarded at a school in Kirkwall on the main island. The stone houses and shops of the island were old, built in the late 18th century or early 19th as replacements for what had been in place before. A few dated to the early 17th century, including the pub and the house occupied by the doctor.

The village had been blessed with the presence of a fairly young doctor, Dr. Elijah McCrae, who'd moved to Broughby from Glasgow for reasons unknown and unasked, although villagers knew from seeing him in the pub that he was fond, but not too fond, of his drink. He managed to stay fit by a daily run on the island's one road. But the villagers were thrilled to have him there and didn't question their good fortune.

The island's only other significant architectural feature was the manor house, simply referred to as "the manor." Built of stone in the 1920s by a London millionaire as a hunting getaway on an island without much to hunt, it had been vacant for years, managed by a property firm in Glasgow, until early the previous year, when it was sold along with the rest of the small island. The villagers had been ready to take up arms when they discovered the sale included the village and the land occupied by their houses, although, legally, everyone in the village was a tenant.

To their surprise, an attorney had arrived from Glasgow, rented a room with the doctor, and called a meeting at the Broughby Pub (including a round of free drinks), where he proceeded to explain that the new owner was interested primarily in the manor and surrounding land as an archaeological site, and wanted to lease the residential and commercial property in renewable 99-year leases to the residents for the sum of one pound, assuming they were interested. A surveying team arrived, mapped out property dimensions, and in due time the townspeople had become full leasers of the buildings and land they occupied. The one area not included was the ferry landing facility, which was soon refurbished and updated at the new owner's expense.

No one knew the identity of the owner. The lawyer and the surveying team said they'd received instructions from a firm in Edinburgh, managing the island on behalf of a foundation, in whose name the manor and the rest of the island was listed. Some guessed it was an American billionaire from Silicon Valley, or Middle Eastern sheiks, or even the Chinese. But whoever it was, he, she, or they had the thanks of the villagers.

A few weeks after the attorney had departed, two young men arrived, introduced themselves as Thomas McLaren and Noah Bennington of the University of Edinburgh. They explained they were the advance team for a university-level archaeology group arriving the following spring. Personable and friendly, McLaren was blond, tall, and slender, with a neatly trimmed mustache and beard. Bennington was broad-shouldered and muscular, with close-cropped dark hair, and slightly shorter than his friend. Villagers thought Bennington looked more like a soldier than a graduate student. He was also considerably more reserved than McLaren. Both spent time with the villagers during the evenings at the pub, and both were known to occasionally stand for a round of drinks. They even stayed through the Christmas holidays, sharing a Christmas dinner with the doctor and a few others at the pub.

The manor house had been extensively renovated. Whoever owned it had poured serious refurbishing money into it. People wondered if it might be turned into a hotel or resort, but locals employed in the renovation said the manor now looked more like a school dormitory, and the bathrooms had been expanded to include two individual shower rooms. It wasn't a likely site for a hostel, so the villagers remained somewhat mystified until McLaren organized a slide show of what was happening at the manor to accommodate the dig.

In early April, the first wave of the archaeological crew joined the graduate students. Leading the group was a professor, whom the villagers searched online to find Farley McNeill, Ph.D., a history professor at St. Andrews, specializing in the late Anglo-Saxon and Viking periods. With him was a young man, Angus McLin, introduced as the logistics coordinator. McLin seemed slightly odd, with difficulties looking people he'd just met in the eye until the second or third meeting and occasionally having a bit of halting speech. When the doctor was asked for his opinion, he said it might be a slight case of autism or possibly a stroke, but that McLin seemed an amicable sort and should be welcomed like the rest of the crew.

A few days later, the group was joined by Dr. Evan Elliott, a professor of archaeology at the University of Cumbria and considered Britain's top Celtic specialist in the archaeology field. Dr. McNeill had recruited him for the project, to direct the work of the dig itself and help interpret any findings or discoveries.

There would be a larger student group arriving on May 1 to work until mid-August. McNeill had come early to make arrangements for supplies from the mainland and to supervise the installation of beds and other furnishings. He hired local villagers to transport and set up all the materials and furnishings from the ferry to the manor, a distance of about five miles. And he paid well.

The island of Broughby was some nine miles long and three miles at its widest. The manor was roughly in the middle but closer to the northern end, and the village was at the southern end. Both were on the more protected eastern side; the western side was subject to heavy snows in the winter and sometimes in the other seasons, as well as the full brunt of North Atlantic storms. In between manor and village were a few small crofts scattered among the hills, rented from the manor.

If Broughby was known for anything, it was for fishing and its hilly, almost mountainous landscape. A gravel road wound its way along the shoreline from the manor to the village, and the villagers were pleasantly surprised one morning to discover ongoing loads of gravel and roadbed materials arriving by small transport ships at the ferry port, along with small trucks to transport it, to resurface the road and the village streets. Whoever the owner was, it was someone demonstrating a high level of care.

The locals were more than delighted. The pub owner looked forward to increased business, as did the owners of the food and other small shops. There weren't many shops in Broughby to begin with, but they'd all experienced an increase in business with the renovation of the manor and anticipated more to come with the spring and summer.

What the townspeople didn't know was that Noah Bennington was no student. As some suspected, he was military, a former captain with the SAS, the Royal Army's elite fighting force. His assignment was to provide security for Thomas McLaren, now 21, known to his family and Britain as Prince Thomas Michael McLaren Kent-Hughes.

The prince had agreed with his father King Michael and Buckingham Palace Security to use part of his name as an alias for the duration of the dig. If he was going to be beyond the immediate reach of the palace security services for an extended period, they wanted precautions taken to help ensure his safety. Prince Thomas merely shrugged. If that's what it took to do the work, so be it.

He'd also grown a beard, which made him almost unrecognizable from the very few public photos of him that existed. For Prince Thomas stayed as far from the public limelight as he could. He was the most private of all of King Michael's children, with no interest in assuming royal duties of any kind. He was rarely if ever seen in palace publicity photos or on the palace balcony for celebrations. Occasional gossip columnists had suggested that he and his father were estranged, but neither Prince Thomas nor the palace ever commented. He'd graduated ICS at 15, and through advanced placement tests earned enough credits to receive his B.A. from St. Andrews University at 18.

Prince Thomas was also the tallest of Michael's children, standing 6 foot 2 in his bare feet; his slender, muscular frame made him appear taller. Complicating his desire for privacy were his almost movie star looks. The fact was that, wherever he went, he turned heads. He had a chiseled face, dark blond hair, and the trademark royal blue eyes. But what people found even more attractive than his looks was his demeanor – kind, quiet, a bit shy but engaging when you spent more than a few minutes with him. He liked people and was an ardent listener.

Over the winter months, he, Noah, and Dr. MacCrae had become good friends, sharing a pint or two most evenings at the pub. MacCrae suspected that McLaren was something more than he said he was but never asked; the doctor himself had a past he preferred remained buried back in Glasgow.

Tommy McLaren didn't really believe his identity could be kept secret for long, but he went along with the palace's plan. His move to Broughby had been without the approval of palace security or his father, and he'd listened to King Michael's irate words on the subject. He told his father that Noah Bennington, given his background and training, was more than capable of providing any security needed.

Tommy had used resources from his own extensive wealth to buy the island for a well-researched reason. Records in Edinburgh, London, Oslo, Reykjavik, and Copenhagen suggested Broughby was the site of a significant Viking settlement with several tantalizing characteristics, including odd references to very early Christian influences, unlike any other Viking settlements. Prince Thomas had been awarded an M.A. in history at 19 and was working on his Ph.D. thesis, which would be submitted in September and defended in the late fall at the University of Edinburgh. He'd used his historical knowledge and his fluency in five languages – Old Norse, Old English, Old Icelandic, Finn-Ugric, and Latin – to ferret out clues about Broughby and specifically the manor property.

If his research was right, his Ph.D. would upend all conventional wisdom about Viking and even early British history. He had enough to argue his thesis now; what he hoped to find at Broughby was confirming evidence. The descriptions in the records all pointed to the more northern end of the island as the site for the Viking settlement, and a scouting expedition had shown the most likely location for a Viking village was down a path from the manor and close to the shoreline.

Using a land management firm owned by his brother Henry, the Prince of Wales, Tommy had first tried to buy only the manor property. The owner, who had the firm in Glasgow manage the island for him, decided he wouldn't sell unless he could unload the whole island. Tommy had paid 25 million pounds, about two percent of his total net worth. The legal, surveying, and renovation management team had moved quickly because Tommy had studied and planned the operation months before the final sale papers were signed.

"Tommy," Noah Bennington said, walking down to him from the manor house, "it's late. We've a lot to do tomorrow to prepare for the students' arrival on Saturday. You need to eat and get some sleep."

Tommy stood up and stretched. Dr. Elliott and Dr. MacNeill had retired to the manor an hour before, pleased with Tommy's careful work. Neither had expected to find anything in this spot, but Tommy promised to stop if anything was uncovered. Nothing had.

Noah was right; he'd already put in a long day. And it might be nice to take a shower and replace his t-shirt and dirt-smudged cargo shorts with a clean shirt and jeans.

Tommy saw Noah as his security officer, but he had also come to know Noah as surrogate big brother. Noah was 32 but looked younger, just about young enough to pass as a graduate student. He'd been assigned to the prince for the past two years, after deciding he needed out of the SAS and talking with Ryan Mitchell, the palace's security chief. And his first meeting with the young prince, then 19 to

Noah's 30, happened in circumstances seemingly ideal but turned into anything but.

Two years earlier

It was the annual Christmas holiday get-together at McLarens outside Edinburgh. Noah Bennington had literally just joined the palace security service and was told to report to the family residence in Scotland. His parents and older sister and her family had been disappointed; Noah had been expected to be with the family for Christmas. The Benningtons were English, but his father had retired from the army and moved with Noah's mother to a small farm outside Glasgow. His sister, her husband, and their two girls were coming up from London.

Noah hated to miss the family at Christmas, but he was also a bit thankful. His father hadn't been pleased with Noah's decision to leave the SAS and the army and join the team at the palace. Noah was sure to hear an earful throughout the holiday; the reporting duty was something of a deliverance.

He'd arrived at McLarens a day before the royal family and was put through his paces by Ryan Mitchell, the head of the security team. Mitchell was on duty for the Christmas holiday, and he always made a point of training all new hires.

Noah didn't know his assignment until Mitchell told him.

"You're being assigned as the personal security officer for Prince Thomas," Mitchell said. "And it's a relatively easy job. He's at St. Andrews University, working on his M.A. That he's only 19 and is due to receive his degree this spring should tell you something about his mind. He listens and more importantly heeds instructions and suggestions from Security. He always tells you his plans and where he'll be. He doesn't try to avoid or get around security protocols, as some of the other royal children tend to do."

Noah knew that was an indirect reference to the prince's older sister, Princess Helen, who saw security protocols as something to be challenged, avoided, ignored, and overcome at every turn. He'd already heard the stories; he'd hoped to avoid that assignment.

"You were hired and selected for specific reasons," Mitchell said. "Your record in the SAS is exemplary, including a commendation for bravery under fire. While we don't expect you to be called to that kind of action, the prince will be on a course of study and research that will often put him beyond the reach of our regular security services, and his father is a bit anxious about it." And then he explained the prince's planned research trips to various Nordic capitals and the longer-term plan for an archaeological dig in the Orkneys.

Left unspoken but understood by both men was that Noah had been selected also because he was not married, had no children, and would likely be called upon for extended periods of work with the prince.

"We're looking at two to two-and-a-half years for this assignment," Mitchell said, "and then you should expect to be moved to another. What makes this particularly pleasant is that the prince is nothing like you'd expect a prince to be. He's quiet but engaging; some call him an introvert but he's far more than that. In fact, he's the most liked of all the royal children by the security officers." Mitchell had paused, looking very directly at Noah. "He's also religiously devout; he takes his faith very seriously, as we know you do, and that was a major plus from the king's perspective."

McLarens had originally been about 80 acres but had grown with strategic purchases of land and neighboring properties by the king to more than 800. The king's mother still lived there; she was now 80, with the normal infirmities of age but still sprightly, gardening every day when weather permitted and having an active sense of humor.

Noah saw the family arrive in waves. First were King Michael, Queen Mary, the Princess Helen, Prince David, and Mark Penniman, Queen Mary's son. Princess Sophie was with the Spanish royal family in Madrid for the Christmas holiday and wouldn't be coming to Scotland. That afternoon, Jason and Jane Kent-Hughes, now the Duke and Duchess of Norfolk, and their two teenaged sons followed, along with Jim and Laura Kent-Hughes, the Duke and Duchess of Sussex, and their two young daughters.

Early Christmas Eve, David Hughes, the king's brother-in-law, and his family, including his wife, a son, a daughter-in-law, a grandson, and a daughter, arrived, along with an Angus McLin for whom the Hughes had guardianship. Prince Thomas had traveled with them from St. Andrews. Henry, Prince of Wales, and his wife Hannah arrived from London about the same time.

The main house had long ago been outgrown by the burgeoning family, another reason for the expansion of the property to include extensively remodeled farms and houses nearby. The families were each assigned to a house; the young men, including Prince Thomas, Mark, Angus, and the two teenaged sons of Jason Kent-

Hughes, would sleep in a small dormitory of private rooms adjacent to the barn. The barn served as the center for security and property management. Noah and three other officers were assigned to drive family members to and from their sleeping quarters, but the primary activities would happen at the main house.

The small dorm was within easy walking distance of the main house, so Noah didn't meet Prince Thomas immediately.

Shortly before lunchtime on Christmas Eve, the men and boys of the royal family piled into the black SUVs for a shopping expedition into Edinburgh. Mr. Mitchell explained that this was an annual tradition, going back more than 40 years to when Ian McLaren took the young Michael Kent into town to get them both out of the way while Iris McLaren prepared Christmas dinner. Mitchell also explained that Noah would be one of the four security officers remaining at McLarens, both for security duty and any chauffeuring that might be needed. The women and girls of the family generally remained at the main house.

It was when the caravan returned from the shopping trip that the trouble started.

Standing by one of the SUVs, waiting for the Duchess of Norfolk to leave the main house to return for something forgotten at their assigned house, Noah witnessed the blowup. He heard the rest of the story later from Mr. Mitchell and a few bits from Prince Thomas later that evening.

At 4 p.m., the family followed another tradition, the opening of a single present of each person's choice. Iris McLaren was always the first to open a gift. She selected one to her from Prince Thomas, saying that she'd been intrigued when it and quite a few similar packages arrived by courier several days previously. The gift was a small painting, a beautifully done portrait of King Michael and Queen Mary. Mitchell later said the prince certainly had a talent.

While Iris and Queen Mary loved it, for some reason the painting offended the king. He didn't say anything but stood and walked out into the back garden. That's when Noah saw him and stood at attention. The king looked furious.

Prince Thomas followed.

"Dad, what's wrong?"

"You know what's wrong!" the king shouted. "It has to be a painting, doesn't it?"

"Dad, it's of you and Mum. It's for Ma," the prince said. Noah saw the genuinely perplexed look on the prince's face.

"Perfect," the king said. "You have to keep jabbing your finger in my eye, don't you? You have to keep reminding me and everyone else of what happened."

"That's not what I was doing," Prince Thomas said, his own voice rising. "You make this into something it's not. You do this every single time. You have to keep digging the old hole, and then a few days or a few weeks later, you apologize. And everything's warm and cozy until you do exactly the same thing all over again, and I never know what's going to set you off."

"You think you know what happened, but you don't!" the king shouted back. "You have no idea what you step into and yank me into every time you do this!"

"So why don't you tell me, or will it be just like all the other times?" the prince shot back.

Noah looked at the windows of the family room, filled with faces of the family, watching. He stared straight ahead, as if at attention, not knowing what else to do.

The king suddenly walked off, heading for the path and the trail that led into the hills behind the main house. Mr. Mitchell, who'd been inside the house, came rushing out and followed the king. Prince Thomas stood in place for a moment, and then he turned toward the barn. He saw Noah, gave a slight nod, and entered the barn building.

Two minutes later, the scheduling officer came out of the barn and walked to Noah.

"You need to get your kit. Prince Thomas is returning to St. Andrews and you're to accompany him. I just talked with Mr. Mitchell, who's still climbing up the trail behind the king. I have the duty officer getting your protection equipment together, so see him. But be quick; the prince is adamant about leaving immediately."

Noah returned to sleeping quarters, grabbed his satchel, hurriedly packed his clothes, and reported to the duty officer, who handed him a second satchel.

"Kevlar vest, unloaded pistol, and ammunition box. You won't need it, but it's required under security protocols. If you go outside the prince's home with him, you're required to wear the vest and the pistol to be loaded."

"Yes, sir."

"Officer Robbie Norton's driving the two of you to St. Andrews, so best be out there."

Noah had barely a minute to wait with the driver when the prince appeared, carrying a suit bag and small suitcase and with a computer bag strapped on his shoulder. Noah took the bags and placed them in the trunk of the SUV, next to his own, and then held the door open for the prince.

The Prince of Wales came hurrying from the house. "Tommy," he said, "please don't go. You know he'll apologize."

"I'm sorry, Hank. This time he went too far. Please give my apologies to Ma and the family. And tell Angus I'll come to visit in a couple of days when they're home." Tommy got in the back seat, closing the door. "Let's go now, please, Robbie."

They'd been on the road to Edinburgh for 10 minutes when the Prince spoke. "You must be Noah Bennington."

Noah, in the front passenger seat, turned his head to the prince. "Yes, sir."

"Mr. Mitchell had told me I was getting a new security officer. I'm sorry you had to witness that display of family warmth back there. For that matter, I'm sorry I had to witness it. And I suppose I've messed up your Christmas even more than it'd already been messed up."

"It's my job, sir."

"Can you tell me about your background?"

Noah told him about his family, growing up on army bases, joining the army, and applying for and being accepted in the SAS. When the prince asked, Noah noted his tours of duty in Northern Ireland, Iraq, and Afghanistan. He explained his decision to leave the SAS, some connections made to Buckingham Palace Security ("my dad served with Brent Epworth in Iraq"), and then his joining the palace security group.

"It's rather rude of me to ask, but was your father all right with your leaving the army?"

Noah didn't immediately answer. "No, sir, he wasn't. And he isn't. He made the call to Mr. Epworth, but he wasn't pleased."

They were driving around outer Edinburgh now, heading for the bridge over the Firth of Forth. After crossing the bridge, Robbie took the A907 to Kirkcaldy and then the A915 to St. Andrews. As they approached the town centre and their destination of the prince's flat in a stone building off Market Street, Noah's mobile buzzed. It was Ryan Mitchell.

Noah listened and turned to the prince. "His Majesty's been trying to call you, sir."

"I turned my phone off, and I won't be turning it back on until after Boxing Day."

"I heard," Mitchell said. "All right. I'll explain to the king that Prince Thomas doesn't want to be reached for a time. You need to know about the weather, too. A winter storm is coming in tonight, and most of Scotland may get socked in. Tell Robbie to get back here quickly; he should have more than sufficient time before the storm arrives, but he needs to keep an eye out."

They arrived at the house and retrieved the luggage from the trunk. Robbie wished them a Happy Christmas and left to return to McLarens.

Tommy pulled his key from his pocket to open the door. "I've really guaranteed you a miserable Christmas, haven't I?"

"It's all right, sir. I've been in far worse places for Christmas." He paused. "Do you have sufficient supplies for the storm?"

"We better check. Likely not. And look, as long as it's just the two us, please call me Tommy."

What Tommy called a three-bedroom flat was actually a townhouse. Kitchen, dining room and parlour, with a half bathroom, were on the ground floor. The first floor included two large bedrooms, each with their own bathroom ("The security officer on duty sleeps in that one," Tommy said, pointing, "and mine's just opposite"). The second floor included a bedroom and bath and the room Tommy used for a study and for painting.

"It's about 250 years old," Tommy said, "and updated many times, including by palace security." The duty officer had provided Noah a map of the premises, including the locations of doors, all with deadbolts, and the alarm system. "I've lived here for three-and-a-half years now, and I hate the idea of giving it up when I move to Edinburgh next summer."

"Do you mind having a security officer always underfoot?"

"You get used to it. And it's good to have someone else around."

The kitchen was checked and needed supplies noted. Tommy told Noah to wear something besides a suit and tie, since no formal appearances were going to be necessary. After changing and putting on his vest, with the pistol under his coat, the two of them walked over to a food shop that was still open on Market Street. The temperature had noticeably dropped, and the air felt heavy with moisture.

Tommy sniffed the air. "I imagine we're in for it with the snow."

Returning to the flat, Noah volunteered to get supper together and fried up sausages and sliced potatoes.

"This is quite good. You might consider a second career as a chef."

Noah laughed. "My mother insisted that both my sister and I had to learn how to cook, saying it was nonsense to call it a woman's job. So, I learned."

"Tomorrow, depending upon the weather, I'd like to attend worship at Holy Trinity. It's literally right around the corner, and it's been my parish church since I've been here. Will that be a problem for you?"

"Not at all, sir. I'm a believing Christian. Which is another bone of contention with my father, because he and the rest of my family are not. It'll definitely not be a problem; in fact, I look forward to it."

"That's perfect, Noah. I'm sorry about your family. That's one thing I don't have to worry about with mine."

Noah hadn't been quite sure what to expect from King Michael's youngest; so far, he was pleasantly surprised to find a quiet, unassuming scholar who was incredibly intelligent, kind, and decidedly non-royal, or at least different from the stereotype that existed in the public mind. He was more than pleased to find Tommy personable, down-to-earth, always willing to listen and, if needed, obey security instructions.

What struck Noah most about the prince was his faith. Noah was a devout, practicing Christian, and he was pleased to discover his charge was as well. Beginning on Christmas morning, Noah offered, and Tommy accepted, the sharing of devotions and prayer. It would continue, whenever possible, through the move to Edinburgh and for the next decade, including daily morning times during the archaeological dig on Broughby.

Noah would come to be fully accepted and trusted by Tommy, the Hughes family, Angus, and Professor McNeill. Tommy, the talented, multilingual young scholar and artist, who also happened to be a royal prince, would become the closest of friends with Noah, the muscled, broad-shouldered former SAS captain, who'd been to war and seen and done things people could only guess at. It was an unlikely friendship, bound by a shared faith.

The present

On Saturday on Broughby, 12 students and two additional workers would be arriving on the ferry. The students were from various universities around Britain. They'd applied for work on the dig, attracted by the credit hours offered, all expenses paid, and even a small stipend. Professor McNeill had interviewed each, checking their academic references with personal phone calls or actual visits. Each applicant had been vetted by palace security via Noah and all final resumes and applications had been reviewed by Tommy and Dr. Elliot.

The two non-students in the group were a cook and an additional security officer, the increased security presence a concession to Tommy's father.

"By the way," Noah said, "Professor McNeill said that there was a phone message received at the pub for you. Your Uncle David asked you to call him." Within the next three days, satellite phone service would be operational for the project and all workers; in the meantime, outside phone calls came through the pub.

"I'll drive down to the village to make the call," Tommy said, referring to the manor's van purchased for the project. "If you want to come, we can get a pint and likely some dinner as well."

"Brilliant proposal."

McNeill, Elliott, and Angus joined them, and within an hour the five, joined by Dr. MacCrae, were ordering their sandwich and crisps dinners, with a cola for Angus, who didn't drink alcohol, and pints for the other five. Tommy, carrying his pint with him, went to the pub's phone booth and called his uncle.

At this time of day few villagers were present; that would change within an hour, when the locals would crowd the pub after dinner. The few who were there greeted the manor team warmly; what they called "McNeill and his crew" were already well liked. No town and gown issues had emerged during the entire month of April. Two weeks before, McNeill and Tommy had organized a meeting in the village, explaining the scope of the archaeological project, answering any and all questions, and promising regular updates through the summer. Tommy privately thanked Jay Lanham at the palace for creating a communication plan that included building relationships with the village.

Reaching his uncle at St. Andrews, Tommy soon learned that he was being asked to expand his work force.

"It's Gavin, Tommy," David Hughes said. "He's been going non-stop for years, and all of us, including Emily, were worried he was taking on too much." Gavin Hughes was, at 28, one of the youngest head pastors of a major church in all of Scotland. His charismatic speaking style had attracted numerous people to the church in Edinburgh, he'd been working on his second book, and he was married to Emily McFarland, with a three-year-old son and another baby on the way. Tommy was godfather to the three-year-old, Lucas.

"What's happened, Uncle David?"

"Three weeks ago, he was preaching on Sunday like he usually does. In the middle of the sermon, he suddenly stopped and stared around the auditorium. Then he sat on the steps of the platform and began to sob." David paused, and Tommy could tell his uncle was still upset. "It unnerved the congregation and terrified Emily, who called us. We had doctors and a psychiatrist examine him; they concluded he'd suffered a nervous breakdown, most likely from overwork. It was what Betsy and I'd always feared."

"What do the doctors say?"

"He needs to be completely away from his church and his other commitments for a period of four to six months. The church elders agreed to allow Emily and little Lucas to stay at the manse until she finds other accommodations, but the pressure is on for her to move. They've already hired an interim pastor until Gavin sorts himself, and they need the manse space. Officially, Gavin's on an unpaid leave of absence, but they're covering some living expenses. We offered, and Emily will be staying with us; the baby's due in five months and her mother and Jeff, as you know, live in Singapore." Ellen McFarland had eventually remarried after Tommy McFarland's suicide; her husband, an American working in the oil business, had been transferred by his company a year before.

"What I'm asking is a huge imposition. It's actually Emily's idea. Could you take Gavin on as a worker on your dig? He's not trained in archaeology, of course, but you said you'd assembled a team with quite varied backgrounds. I wouldn't ask this of you, Tommy, but we're at our wit's end. If that won't work, Gavin may have to be institutionalized. I don't think he needs something that extreme, and neither do the doctors, but he needs to be involved in something entirely different, something more routine, where he'd need coaching and be less inclined to overachieve."

"Of course, he comes here, Uncle David. We've all kinds of things he could do. And Broughby is about as far as he could get from the bustle of Edinburgh and his work. When will he come?"

"Today's Thursday. I could get him on the ferry next Tuesday, which would put us in Broughby on Wednesday after the stopover in Kirkwall. I'll come with him, if that's all right, just to make sure he gets settled, and then I'll return."

"It's a plan. I'll be waiting for you when you arrive. I believe the ferry gets in about 3 in the afternoon. The Wednesday ferry overnights here so you could return on Thursday." He paused. "We'll be at capacity this weekend with the students arriving Saturday, so if it's all right with you, I'll rent you a room with the village doctor."

Even before he'd rung off, Tommy mentally had started counting bedrooms and beds, and he realized that he'd have to share his private room with Gavin. But they'd manage. The only other single-occupant rooms were for Angus, the two professors, and Noah. Angus needed a room by himself. He was a fully functional adult now, but he was still almost rabid on the subject of privacy. Tommy knew he could probably persuade Angus to share a room with him, Tommy, but it'd be easier for Angus to be alone and easier for Tommy to keep an eye on Gavin. The professors by right of rank needed private rooms, and Noah had to have one, because that was where all equipment related to security was stowed, locked in a closet, and the second security man arriving with the students would room with him. Gavin would have to become Tommy's roommate.

"He'll room with me, if that's okay. Angus has a room to himself, but it's the smallest bedroom, and you know how Angus is about privacy, even if he thinks of Gavin as his brother."

"I know exactly. Tommy, I know this is an imposition. I don't know how to thank you."

"Uncle David, I'm as much a part of your family as I am of mine, if not more. Angus isn't the only one who thinks of Gavin as his brother."

Returning to the group and the just-delivered dinners, Tommy waved his pint glass at the pub owner for a refill and explained that Gavin Hughes would be joining them, providing a barebones explanation of why. He saw Angus wrinkle his forehead with the housing implications.

"Angus, Gavin will be bunking with me, so we'll need to get that spare single bed set up in my room. Can you manage that, say sometime during the weekend?" Tommy knew that Angus would do whatever he was asked, and do it brilliantly, but, as he'd explained to Professor McNeill and Noah, Angus always needed very specific, literal instructions.

"Yes, Tommy, I will do it." The look of relief was so obvious on Angus's face that Tommy almost laughed. "I'll be glad to see Gavin, and I'm glad he's your roommate." This time, Tommy did laugh.

Farley McNeill was in his early 50s. He'd taught at St. Andrews for almost 25 years and was one of the best-loved professors at the school. He was close friends with David Hughes, and almost exactly the same age, but with his shock of snow-white hair, ruddy complexion, and expanding waistline, he looked older. He'd never married and lived alone in his rooms at the university. He had a penchant for beer and ale, and he loved nothing better than holding court on Anglo-Saxon and Pictish history for faculty and students alike at a pub on Market Street.

McNeill had first met Prince Thomas at a dinner at David and Betsy Hughes' home. The boy had been almost 16, and David introduced him by explaining that Tommy would be attending St. Andrews for the fall term, intent on reading history and specializing in the Anglo-Saxon and Viking period, which was McNeill's own specialty. Michael had been somewhat opposed to Tommy graduating ICS early, questioning whether he had the emotional maturity to begin college at 16. David had convinced him.

"I've read your books, sir," Tommy said.

McNeill eyed him as he lit his pipe. "Indeed. Which ones?"

"All of them, sir."

The ensuing conversation almost shocked the professor; the 15-year-old son of King Michael was fluent in five languages besides English and knew his British history as well as McNeill did. The two had talked for hours, until David reminded them that Tommy needed sleep. Joining David and Betsy for a glass of whisky, McNeill told David that Tommy was already light years ahead of almost every specialist in Anglo-Saxon history McNeill had heard of.

David smiled. "He's amazing, isn't he? Farley, his IQ is off the charts, he soaks up research and reading like a sponge, and he's already got ideas that the academic history establishment will find unsettling. You should know that Oxford, Cambridge, Harvard, and several other schools actively recruited him, but he chose St. Andrews because you taught here."

McNeill flushed, feeling simultaneously flattered and embarrassed. "I suspect it was also because of a certain uncle teaching here."

"That, too, but you were the deal clincher. He made his decision after reading your last book."

"The one *The Times* called 'intriguing but flawed'?"

"Do you want to know Tommy's assessment?"

"Please."

"Tommy said you were likely 100 percent right but didn't have all the evidence you needed."

McNeill had stared at his friend. "It was my own assessment as well." He paused. "His father must be very proud of the boy."

He was surprised when David glanced at Betsy before answering.

"He is, Farley. I'm talking family here, so it's somewhat out of school. Tommy and Michael aren't estranged or at daggers' points. They're just not close. It goes back a long time, to when Sarah was still alive. This has more do with Sarah than it does with Tommy. It also has to do with Michael being Government at the time Tommy was born."

"Ah, I'd forgotten that."

"Michael was Government for almost the first seven years of Tommy's life. It took Sarah's death to kick Parliament back to existence."

"It was likely the most stable seven years in Britain's history."

"And that was part of the problem. Nobody wanted to go back to the chaos of parliamentary democracy. And, physically, it nearly killed Michael. Few know what it cost him in terms of his family. One of those costs was Tommy."

McNeill sipped his whisky. "I didn't realize how much he resembles you, in looks, I mean."

"Anyone who sees us together says that. I suppose it's true. We also share an interest, which will likely become Tommy's vocation, in academic scholarship. Farley, I believe you can nurture that in the right way. I'm his uncle, his mother's twin brother, and it's difficult, if not impossible, for him to separate who I am from what I am. I've taken him about as far as I can, and I'm hoping you can take him even further. He deeply admires your works, and I know he's only 15, but he's an exceptionally brilliant 15. What he sees in your scholarship is a willingness to push against prevailing wisdom, challenge authority, and create an entirely new and different understanding, even if it's unsettling."

"Your words?"

"His."

At St. Andrews, McNeill had immediately assumed a mentorship role with Tommy, who took to McNeill like a beloved grandfather. They'd worked together, studied together, argued together, and critiqued each other's work. David could see his nephew flourishing under McNeill's tutelage.

Initially, Tommy had been something of a celebrity on campus, the youngest student by two years as well as a royal prince, but that eventually faded.

McNeill knew where Tommy's thinking and studies were heading, and he knew it would turn the academic establishment at St. Andrews and beyond on its head. When Tommy came to him about the Broughby references he'd found in his research, McNeill encouraged his work. When Tommy laid before him the plan for a dig at Broughby, McNeill had signed up, to the point of requesting his first sabbatical ever and joining the project as a full-time member. He was gratified when Tommy had offered a stipend, but he would've done it without pay.

And when Tommy had showed him the extended outline for his thesis, McNeill had been struck silent. And he knew that, in a short five years, the roles of teacher and student had reversed themselves.

For Farley McNeill understood better than anyone that Prince Thomas Michael McLaren Kent-Hughes was on the brink of transforming the academic and public understanding of British history.

Erica

She wasn't sure she was grateful or not that the train from London to Cambridge was on time. Had it been late, canceled, or interrupted in any way, she'd have taken it as a sign that the trip to Edinburgh was a mistake, and she needed to return home and her regular studies.

Erica Larsson, 22, was reading English literature at Cambridge. She'd read across the breadth of both British and American literature, but her special focus was the Middle Ages, early, middle, and late. She loved *Beowulf*; she could recite chunks of Chaucer in the original Old English. She'd also spent considerable time studying the history of Britain in the so-called Dark and Middle Ages, the era of the Anglo-Saxons and Vikings, including the Norman Conquest period. She'd learned that you couldn't study literature without studying history. And while she'd impressed her history tutor with her grasp of the material, it was literature that she loved.

Erica wasn't sure what she'd be doing after taking her bachelor's degree. Possibly teaching, or more likely, staying on for her master's. But she knew she wanted to write fiction.

She'd inherited her father's blue eyes and her mother's slightly rounded face and blondish hair color. She herself called it blondish; the bright blond of her childhood had darkened somewhat in her teens. She usually wore it tied back in a ponytail, to keep it out of her face.

Her parents had divorced 12 years before. They were separated seven years before that. She'd been reared primarily by her maternal grandmother. It was complicated; Erica's father was closer to her grandmother than her own daughter was.

Thinking of her mother always brought a sigh. Erica might see her for Christmas or Boxing Day, or she might not. Her mother might, or might not, remember Erica's birthday. This time, she hadn't seen her mother in six months, which meant her mother had missed Christmas, Boxing Day, and her birthday.

Her mother, Billie Larsson, moved with what in an earlier era would've been called a fast set. Her mother's involvement with them had a single purpose: to meet King Michael. Her mother was in love with royalty: the idea of it, the lifestyle of it, virtually everything about it. Erica wasn't sure where this near obsession had come from; her grandmother said it had started about the time her parents divorced. Whatever its origins, Erica always considered what her mother called her "hobby" with distaste. It seemed pathetic to spend all your waking hours in a pursuit of meeting the king, or another member of the royal family if the king wasn't available, and you'd no good reason to meet him anyway.

Erica prided herself on her more democratic sensibilities. She wasn't quite sure that Britain needed a king, even one like King Michael. She occasionally attended meetings of anti-monarchist groups, which sprouted, died, and resurrected themselves with great regularity at Cambridge.

Erica's father Jenner Larsson seemed her mother's polar opposite. He hated society events. He appreciated the tradition represented by the monarchy and he highly respected Michael Kent-Hughes, but he wasn't going to spend every waking moment plotting how to meet him. Jen was also a naturalized Briton. A native Swede, he'd attended the London School of Economics and fell in love with London and Britain. He'd met Erica's mother at a student conference in Cambridge; instant physical attraction led to marriage two months later. By the end of the first year, they both believed they'd made a mistake, but having a baby kept them together for another two years.

He was now a businessman, CEO of an Anglo-Swedish steel company, and he spent his days navigating tariff threats, labor contracts, economic downturns and upturns, construction markets, and anything else concerning the steel industry. Erica saw her father and his second wife Ann regularly, at least once a month if not more often. And he always remembered her birthday, although she wasn't sure if he or Ann did the remembering.

Erica had attended a public school in Cambridge before attending the university. Cambridge was her mother's hometown and where her grandmother still lived. It was the same house where her mother and now Erica herself had grown up. Erica was most deeply attached to Nan, her 70-year-old grandmother. They lived close to the university, in a small freestanding house a block from the Fitzwilliam Museum. Her grandmother owned the house outright, but the taxes were astronomical, and Erica knew it must be her father who paid them. Otherwise, it would've been sold long ago.

It was her university tutor who in early December had handed her the brochure about the dig at Broughby in the Orkneys. The advisor knew Farley McNeill, and said that if he was involved, it had to be a top-tier project. And, he said, it seemed to fit Erica's own academic interests and studies.

She fully researched McNeill, Broughby, and what little could be found about the project. If she applied and was accepted, she'd be spending May, June, July, and the first two weeks of August on one of the remotest parts of the British Isles. Broughby's population was 300, which suggested there was very little to do other than work at the site, or fish.

She set it aside for a week, and then her boyfriend Derek, who was reading Classics and resembled a young Brad Pitt, had announced they needed to see other people. That shock was bad enough, but the next day, her closest friend and roommate Alison moved out of their shared room and in with Derek.

Erica had been stunned. She and Derek had been seeing each other for more than a year and had lately been planning their future. Together. She was confident in his regard, no, his love, for her, and she knew that she loved him. Other friends eventually told her that Derek and Alison had been sleeping together secretly for months.

She felt betrayed by both her boyfriend and her best friend. She'd gotten physically ill, and her grandmother had been almost frantic. Nothing Nan said could comfort her. Erica had known Derek for two years and she and Alison had been school chums since they were seven.

That's it, she thought, *I'm done with men. Especially the lookers like Derek. I'm done with relationships.* She picked up the application for the archaeological program from her desk. What better place to be done with men than Broughby? She could get away with a bunch of fellow study nerds and leave Derek, Alison, and Cambridge behind. Erica knew she was still angry. But she'd channel her anger into the dig in the Orkneys.

She sent in her application and a reference letter from her tutor. Not long after, a letter arrived from Professor McNeill, asking her to come to Edinburgh for an interview in January. It explained that she'd be provided with an overnight stay at the Edinburgh Hyatt Regency, her meals, and her transportation costs.

At the interview, she found McNeill both charming and rather endearing. He described the living quarters, what she'd be doing, the daily lectures by himself, another professor, or his graduate teaching assistant, and that she'd have a roommate who would also be a woman. Twelve people were being selected. He said she'd incur no expenses, earn 15 credit hours, and be paid a small stipend toward any expenses not covered by the program. When she asked about the sponsor, he directed her to the manor property's owner, a philanthropic foundation that used a management company to operate the house and associated activities. He said the entire course of work had been certified by St. Andrews University, which would be offering the credit hours.

Just to be sure, she had her father check into the foundation.

"They're known in philanthropic circles," Jen Larsson said, when he called her about what he'd learned. "While they're new to archaeological projects, they have a solid track record in a number of philanthropic projects in Scotland and Wales. And don't tell your mother, but they're so highly regarded that even members of the royal family are among their contributors."

Erica laughed. "Mother would want to accompany me to the ends of the earth if she thought she might meet a royal."

"Just one thing, Erica," her father said. "For security reasons, I need you to keep your connection to me and the company confidential. There's been an uptick in terrorist activity near some of our facilities in Sweden and Brazil. We have nothing near Broughby, but it's never bad to be cautious. If you're asked about your family, could you simply say I work in the manufacturing industry and not say anything about me being a CEO?"

"Not a problem. I doubt the subject will even come up. If it does, I'll just muff it up a bit."

Ten days after the interview with Professor McNeill, the letter advising her of her acceptance arrived. If she accepted entry into the program, she had to sign a letter of agreement and complete registration papers for the course, including a medical certificate. She did both and mailed them back. In early March, she received her welcome kit, including a list of recommended clothes, a questionnaire about any special dietary needs, a 25-page Project Design document, and contact information for family. She also was given a diagram of the manor, with her bedroom marked with an X, and highlighting the women's shower rooms, dining room, exercise room, and kitchen. The package included photos as well, and she could see exactly what her assigned room looked like.

She was told that her roommate would be Julia Heaton, a junior-year student at Newcastle University and a history major specializing in late Roman and early Anglo-Saxon history. She and Julia had been given each other's email address and were encouraged to talk before the trip. They connected by email and then by phone and Facetime, and Erica was encouraged by both Julia's seriousness and by her sense of humor. She and Julia agreed that the project sounded almost too good to be true, but Professor McNeill's reputation assuaged any doubts.

Reading the Project Design document, she decided that Professor McNeill or someone he employed was a fine writer, indeed. The paper was jargon-free, in very readable and very clear English.

The train from London was on time, and Erica found herself heading for Edinburgh and away from all the personal heartbreak in Cambridge.

At Waverley Station, she retrieved her two checked bags, found the taxi stand, and soon arrived at the Hyatt Regency. A specially appointed desk clerk for the group welcomed her, smoothly checked her in, and handed her a key.

He also handed her an envelope with her name on it.

"From Professor McNeill," he said. "It's instructions for tomorrow. There will be a bus at 5:30 to transport the team to Aberdeen, and there will be light breakfast, tea, and coffee aboard. It's an early start to meet the ferry for Kirkwall at 9:30."

"Do you know how long a ferry ride?" she said.

"From Aberdeen to Kirkwall is about six hours. You'll have overnight accommodations in Kirkwall, and then the ferry the next morning at 8 for Broughby. It's not as far as the route from Aberdeen to Kirkwall, but it makes stops at Eday and Westray before going on to Broughby. It's another six-hour trip, give or take.

"After you settle into your room here, there's a hospitality suite for the group in the Burns Room on the third floor. It includes drinks and light food. If you have supper here at the hotel, simply charge it to your room. If you go out, keep your receipt for expenses, and you can give it to the group leader tomorrow morning. Have you visited Edinburgh before?"

Erica nodded. "A few times, most recently in January. But I don't know the city very well."

"If you need directions or recommendations, our concierge will be glad to assist."

She and her luggage were soon in the room, and she was impressed with its appointments, wondering if they were being treated first class as a kind of farewell to civilization. She freshened up and took the elevator to the third floor to the Burns Room. The door was open; she could hear voices in conversation. She took a deep breath, knowing she'd be meeting the people she'd be spending the next three-and-a-half months with.

Six or seven of the group were there, about evenly divided between men and women. A tall man she guessed was in his 30s was wearing a suit. He spotted her and walked over.

"Ms. Larsson, I'm Simon Fredericks. Welcome to Edinburgh and welcome to the Broughby Dig. Let me get you a nametag."

A young woman with dark brown hair and deep brown eyes walked up.

"Erica! I'm Julia Heaton. I'm so glad to meet you in person!"

The two chatted. Simon returned with a plastic name tag with her name and university embossed on it, and then he introduced her to the six others in the room. She heard a blur of names and universities, and she silently thanked whomever had the idea for nametags.

"We're asking everyone to wear the nametags for the first week," Simon said, "until you know each other. If you lose it, we've a spare for each."

"What's your university, Simon?" she said.

He smiled. "I don't have one. My job is security."

"For the hotel?" Julia said.

"No, actually it's for the project. I'll be living at the Manor on Broughby with you. We don't expect any security issues, but you might say I'm there as a reserve. I'll also be helping with the dig."

Erica and Julia milled about through the crowd. Erica found people to be friendly and excited. More than one person noted the expense the foundation was going to; all would've been happy with a hostel bed but instead found themselves in a first-class private room in a luxury hotel.

By 6:30, all 12 students had arrived. Simon explained they'd be joined in the morning by Mrs. Norah Bixby, serving as their cook on Broughby and traveling with them to the island. She was spending the night with a sister who lived in Edinburgh.

"Rule 1," said a young man, whom Erica could see had a nametag with 'Alan Bishop, University of Rochester,' on it, "is always be nice to the cook." They laughed.

"For dinner tonight," Simon said, "if you don't have other plans or prefer to be on your own, we have reservations at 21212 in New Town."

Alan Bishop's eyes popped. "Sign me up. I'd never be able to afford that, and if you're offering, I'm available." Everyone else, including Erica and Julia, agreed. Looking around at the group, Erica was inwardly pleased and more than a bit relieved that she'd guessed right; all of them, including herself, were study nerds. No one even remotely looked or acted like Derek.

After dinner, which Erica believed might have been the best restaurant meal she'd ever eaten, they returned to the hotel. Most of the group decided on a drink in the bar, but Erica and Julia both decided to turn in.

"Did you notice something about Simon?" Julia said, as they walked from the elevator to their rooms on the tenth floor.

Erica shook her head. "No, what?"

"He has a bulge under his left arm. He's carrying some kind of gun."

"Do you think he'll need it?"

"Let's hope not."

On the ferry to Kirkwall, Erica found herself sitting with Julia and Mrs. Bixby, who had been waiting in the Hyatt lobby as they assembled for their 5:30 bus. A few bleary-eyed students must've stayed up late in the bar; they looked a bit green.

She'd hoped the ferry ride would be smooth, for their sakes. When the sea turned choppy and then a bit on the heaving side, she and Julia both decided to sit with Mrs. Bixby and avoid the spate of sickness coming from their colleagues.

Erica found Norah Bixby delightful. The woman was in her late 50s, about 5 foot 3, with a mass of auburn-colored curls that must've been assisted by something from a bottle. She was lively and chatty and full of helpful advice for seasickness.

"Get them some lemons," she said to Simon Fredericks, who had found a pail just in time for one of the students. "There are probably some in the bar, and it'll be open."

"Perhaps we should help," Erica said, tentatively, and Julia nodded.

"I call it virtue rewarded," Mrs. Bixby said. "My guess would be that both of you went to bed early last night and skipped the bar."

Julia laughed. "Guilty as charged."

"I don't mind my warm milk with a little rum before bedtime," Mrs. Bixby said, "and I have occasional need for a medicinal, but I never imbibe before a sea trip."

File that one away for the future, Erica thought.

Norah Bixby's entire working career had been spent at St. Andrews University, she told the girls. And all of it in what the university accountants called food preparation and what she called feeding the students and staff. Two years before, her husband Morris had retired as the university's head of custodial service, and he'd convinced her to retire as well. They'd planned a number of trips around the U.K. and Ireland. After a trip to Cornwall, they had gone to Skye, where they went to bed one night after a lovely day of sightseeing. Morris didn't wake up.

"Heart attack, right there on the Isle of Skye while he's sound asleep. I could've brained him, leaving me in a strange place to figure out how to get him home to St. Andrews." She'd quietly checked to see if she might have her old job back, but it was filled, and the replacement's job backfilled. So, she focused on her church, her garden, and staying in touch with family. The Bixbys had no children of their own, but she did have several siblings and a number of nieces and nephews.

"And then one morning, who do I bump into at the post office – I was mailing a birthday card; I know it's old-fashioned with all these internet cards, but I still like to feel a birthday card – but Professor McNeill. We got to chatting – sweet man, he remembered my cakes – and he asked me what I was doing, which was nothing, of course, and then he asked me if I'd ever heard of Broughby. Which I hadn't, so he told me about the project and wondered if I might consider coming along as a cook. He said that at full complement the group would be 14 or 15 people plus occasional guests, which was absolutely no problem because I was used to cooking for 400 to 500 at a time. And I thought, well, why not? It might be something of a lark, going to the ends of the earth and all."

She paused, as if seeming to catch her breath before going on.

"So here I am." She patted the briefcase beside her. "And I've planned menus and food orders, and I've had the most delightful conversations with the grocer and the pub owner in Broughby. The one thing we won't lack will be fish; it seems the boats in Broughby catch quite a fair amount and we can get it at almost wholesale prices. And not just cod, either."

"Professor McNeill said we'd be scheduled to help occasionally in the kitchen," Julia said.

"It won't be anything too strenuous, I can assure you," Mrs. Bixby said. "But everyone, including the professors and our security man, will take a turn. It'll mostly be chopping vegetables, cutting up fruit, perhaps helping with some of the baking. But I promise it won't be much, and it's only occasional, once every two weeks or so."

Erica thought that was more than reasonable.

"And if we have special events, like visitors from the mainland or the community, Professor McNeill says we can hire some local help, too."

"Do you know any of the students, Mrs. Bixby?" Julia said.

"I know two, the two graduate students, Tommy and Noah. And Angus, of course."

"Angus?" Erica said.

The woman nodded, smiling. "Angus is an absolute dear. I think Professor McNeill has him doing logistics, which probably means the work of a general factotum. You'll see for yourself, but Angus was born autistic. But to meet him is to know one of the gentlest souls God put on this earth. I understand he had considerable problems when he was young, but music helped change his life. He's a fully functional adult who can do all the things you or I can do. And he's the sweetest boy, although I should say he's the sweetest young man because he's 21."

What Mrs. Bixby didn't say, because Professor McNeill had cautioned her, was that Angus had told her his story. He was enrolled in a few classes in what was called university college, mostly classes for working adults. He was greatly partial to Mrs. Bixby's scones with strawberry jam. He told her about how he met Tommy, how they had played music together at church, how they still played music together, and the hike on the Great Glen Way with King Michael, Tommy, and Dr. Hughes. Angus also explained that Dr. Hughes and his wife Betsy had assumed guardianship when he was 14, after his mother died from ovarian cancer. He said Tommy had remained his best and steadfast friend.

Mrs. Bixby didn't need Angus to tell her that. She'd seen Tommy and Angus together at St. Andrews. Angus wasn't a full-time student like Tommy, but Dr. Hughes had arranged for Angus to attend the St. Andrews classes for adults and take several music courses. She'd watched how tenderly and yet equally Tommy treated Angus, and how he wouldn't let Angus use his autism as an excuse for not doing something. Angus would struggle until he did it. Norah Bixby had watched, listened, and closely observed. She found herself falling a little bit in love with both Prince Thomas and Angus McLin.

She reminded herself to call Prince Thomas by his Broughby name, Thomas McLaren, just as Professor McNeill had said.

After spending the night in Kirkwall, where no student stayed up late in the hotel bar, the group sailed Saturday morning to Broughby. It was a smaller ferry than the one from Aberdeen. The seas were just as rough as yesterday, and they all felt the rolling more than the previous day, but the group seemed to have found its sea legs.

The boat slowed as they approached the island, and they could all see that the village was indeed a village, with stone houses and a few commercial shops backed up the hillside from the harbor. To their right they could see some 30 or so fishing boats in the docks.

As they entered the ferry facility from the boat gangway, Erica could see and smell the newness of the building. It had obviously been recently remodeled, and while it was small, it was as contemporary as anything she had seen in Aberdeen, Kirkwall, or the stops earlier that day.

A small group waited with a "To the manor we're borne" sign, which Erica thought was rather clever. She immediately recognized Professor McNeill from her meeting with him, and Professor Elliot from the photo in the welcome kit. From Mrs. Bixby's description, she guessed that the shorter, dark-haired young man looking very nervous was Angus.

And then there were the two graduate students. "Things suddenly have become very interesting," Julia said quietly, "above and beyond the dig itself. I claim the dark-haired one with the big muscles."

Erica hadn't noticed the dark-haired one or his muscles. The one she noticed was the blond one with the beard and mustache, and one of the warmest smiles she'd ever seen on a man. Derek had been good-looking, but he didn't hold a candle to the young man introduced to the group as Tommy McLaren.

He was tall, slender, with a chiseled face and a neatly trimmed beard and mustache. He shook everyone's hand, with a word of welcome for each of them. He was wearing jeans, a light-blue t-shirt, and a jacket; the weather was a bit on the cool side, which the welcome kit had emphasized. He struck Erica as confident and gentle, and a man who'd no idea of the effect he had on women.

And his eyes, like an ice-blue or a sky-blue.

She watched him hug Mrs. Bixby, telling her he was so glad to see her again. She could tell by his voice that he was perfectly sincere.

And she knew that she'd just done what she'd been determined not to do after Derek. She'd fallen in love at first sight.

She had to stifle these feelings. They were simply likely a physical reaction to Tommy McLaren's good looks, she told herself. She would not, could not, be hurt again. Plus, why would he be interested in her?

"Our van, while sizeable," Professor McNeill said, "will not hold all of us and the luggage. It's only a 10-minute ride, about five miles, but we're going to take half the group at a time, alphabetically. I think we have this right, so if your name begins with H through Z, you're in the first group. Tommy and Noah will drive you and then return for the rest of us."

Their luggage was loaded on the top and in the back, and then they moved toward the seating. Angus, looking slightly to her left, smiled and opened the front row door for her.

"Welcome," he said shyly.

"Thank you." She looked behind her and saw that Julia was already seated next to Muscle Man, also known as Noah.

"You'll need to slide over to the middle," Tommy said, sitting in the driver's seat. "Angus will be riding shotgun."

There was nothing to it but to slide next to Tommy McLaren. Angus climbed in after her.

Sitting this close, she could feel his presence like a series of small electric shocks. And she could smell his scent of light sweat from hauling luggage, the wool of his jacket, and what distinctly reminded her of apples.

Get yourself under control, girl, she thought, closing her eyes. *You need to push these thoughts away. You're not ready for anything like Tommy McLaren, not now and likely not ever.*

Introducing himself to the members of the group, Tommy thought the pictures that had accompanied their applications did justice to the real people, with one exception.

The photograph of Erica Larsson showed a studious young woman, blondish hair pulled back in a ponytail. Her eyes had been framed by glasses.

The young woman named Erica Larsson who stepped off the ferry had nearly knocked him over.

She was beautiful, but not in the conventional sense of what most people considered beautiful. She had expressive, dark blue eyes and an almost oval face. It wasn't the kind of face you'd find on a fashion model or a movie star; it was something deeper than that, an intelligent, interesting face. Her blondish hair was loose and slightly windblown from the ferry trip.

Tommy had shown little to no interest in girls, either at ICS or St. Andrews. Graduating early, he'd missed the junior and senior year dances. At St. Andrews, it was all about studies, research, and work. He'd been on very few dates. He didn't feel uncomfortable around girls or women; he did grow up with two older sisters, after all. But dating seemed to interfere with his studies; the research trips to

Reykjavik, Oslo, Stockholm, and Copenhagen; his master's thesis; and now his Ph.D. thesis.

In one momentary glance, he'd been bowled over.

And it couldn't have come at a more inconvenient time. Not to mention he knew little about her beyond what was on her application and what the security checks had turned up. He knew her parents were divorced; she was living with her grandmother while reading English at Cambridge. She'd been dating some months ago, but it had ended suddenly. She was something of a writer; nothing published beyond a few stories and poems, but her professors and tutors had great regard for her work and her mind. And he knew her father was CEO of an Anglo-Swedish steel company that was one of the largest in the world.

She was also something of a republican; she'd been known to attend anti-monarchial meetings organized by political activists at Cambridge. Simon Fredericks, increasingly seen as the most likely successor to Ryan Mitchell as head of palace security whenever Mitchell retired, had flagged the republican tendencies, but Tommy had pointed out that's what you did at college, and she'd done nothing more than attend meetings.

Tommy had seen Noah's quickly masked reaction when Simon came down the ferry gangway. No one had said which security man was coming, but neither Noah nor Tommy had expected Simon. Simon, Tommy knew, had been the one who most closely tracked Tommy's fleeing to Scotland when he was 13 and had accompanied them on the hike through the Great Glen Way. He was also the security officer most frequently assigned to accompany Tommy's father for everything from laying ceremonial wreaths at Westminster

Abbey to official visits to foreign capitals. His arrival in Broughby added a wrinkle; Noah would take it as a vote of no confidence. Tommy suspected it had less to do with Noah and more to do with keeping an eye on Tommy for the king.

In fact, that was exactly what King Michael had asked Simon to do. Ryan Mitchell had said Noah was perfectly capable of doing his job, but Michael said he wanted some direct feedback, and he thought Noah might feel conflicted.

Palace politics, family politics, and now the beautiful young Erica Larsson. Tommy could not be distracted from the work. He simply couldn't.

But when she sat next to him in the van, he smelled jasmine.

Breakfast on Sunday was served promptly at 7:30. Mrs. Bixby had assembled a full English breakfast, buffet-style. Professor MacNeill had assigned kitchen duty for the day.

"There's a church service in the village chapel at 9," Tommy told the group. "Attendance is entirely voluntary. We can all fit in the van if necessary, but I know Professor McNeill has kitchen duty and Professor Elliot will remain here."

Seven hands went up; four students, and Noah, Simon, and Angus. An eighth hand went up when Julia changed her mind.

Erica had already raised her hand.

This time, she didn't sit next to Tommy but found a seat in the back of the van. She noticed that Angus was once again riding in the front seat with Tommy driving. She could see a connection between the two, but Mrs. Bixby hadn't said anything about it on the ferry. Perhaps it was recent.

She was slightly surprised when she saw Tommy and Angus carrying instrument cases inside the chapel. Tommy's was a guitar case, while Angus's was smaller, like a violin case. Both sat on chairs on the small platform close to the pulpit. About 100 people were in attendance, including the group from the manor. The chapel couldn't hold many more.

One of the villagers was serving as the pastor; Erica was fairly certain he was a fisherman from the looks of him. He opened the service in prayer, and she was taken aback by the man's beautifully deep speaking voice.

A time of worship in song followed. The congregation began with "Be Thou My Vision" accompanied by Tommy on the guitar and Angus on the violin. The two had obviously played together for a long time, deepening the mystery of their relationship for Erica. She watched them as they signaled each other with cues, and both knew exactly when to let the other do a solo section. She glanced at Julia next to Noah, and she could see her roommate was as taken as she was. Then she saw Noah, singing with his eyes closed as he held a well-worn Bible, and she realized that Muscle Man was a devout Christian. She wondered if Julia knew.

When they returned to the manor after the service, they discovered Mrs. Bixby, with assistance from Professor McNeill, had prepared a Sunday feast.

"On Sundays," Mrs. Bixby said, when the entire group was seated, "this will be the main meal of the day. Sunday evening meals will be light and informal, set up on the sideboards here, from 5 to 7. Enjoy!"

As they ate, Erica leaned over to Julia.

"This is so good I may have to think about some exercise this afternoon."

"If all the meals taste this good. I'll have to join you." Julia ate a small bite of roast. "What did you think of the service? Surprised at our musicians?"

Erica nodded. "A bit. The music and the pastor's words were powerful." She leaned closer to whisper. "And Muscle Man's voice is quite good."

"I may have to rethink my original impression. Muscle Man turns out to be quite the believing Christian."

After lunch, Erica decided a short nap might be in order. She went upstairs to their shared room and looked out the window at the hills. Their room was on the back side of the house, facing fairly tall hills.

A movement on the terrace caught her eye. It was Tommy McLaren, carrying a large portfolio of some kind under his left arm and a smaller case with his right. He was walking toward what she saw was a path leading up through the hills. She watched him until he rounded an outcropping of rock and disappeared.

She tried to nap, but sleep eluded her.

The program Monday morning started at 9 a.m. and set the pattern for their work for the rest of the spring and summer. They assembled in a room adjacent to the dining room, with tables and chairs arranged classroom style. Professor McNeil, alternating with Professor Elliot, began with a lecture on Celtic settlements in the Orkneys. The lecture assumed they had all read the 25-page Project Design they'd received in the welcome kits. Then Tommy followed with reports of research in national, regional, and private libraries in the U.K. and Europe. The libraries included those in a number of churches and monasteries. It took a week before Erica realized that it was Tommy who'd done the research he was describing.

They'd break at noon for lunch and then head to the dig site, down a short walk from the manor. Again, it was Tommy who described the site, laid out the parameters of the day's excavation work, and explained they'd first be getting lessons in excavation.

"This will be for the first three days of this week. I know it might seem excessive to learn how to use a trowel, shovel, and knife, but we have to move slowly and deliberately. We want to make progress each day, but we must be careful. And we need both photographic and written evidence for each section, so please remember to check the methodology and take photographs before and after with the cameras provided. And note the numbered section in your journals."

"What are we specifically looking for?" one of the students said.

"We think this area was the outskirts of a Viking or Norse village," Tommy said, "with most of the village lower down close to the shoreline and likely washed away by the sea. Tomorrow at lecture we'll see slides of some of the crude maps drawn by monks and others of what we think is the general area. If we're right, we might find evidence of a structure made from the trees which covered the island at one time. Evidence of postholes, actually. It's possible that we may find a rubbish heap, which would be a great find."

He paused for a moment, debating on whether or not to tell them they might find a Viking tomb. "There's a possibility of finding a tomb. A few of the accounts of what we think is Broughby describe a tomb. It might be stone, or it might've been wood. If it was wood, it'll likely not be found, having been worn away by decomposition."

They didn't do much digging work that first day, but, after supper, Erica was ready to turn in. Julia was lying on her bed, reading the welcome kit report.

"He knows his stuff, doesn't he?" Julia said. "I'm quite confident that Tommy's the author of the Project Design."

Erica had finished toweling her hair dry after a shower. "You may be right. The way he described that 9th century manuscript in Oslo sounded like he'd been the one reading it."

"In Old Norse, no less. You know, there may be more to Mr. McLaren than we realize, aside from his Oscar-winning looks."

On Wednesday, Erica noticed Tommy leaving the dig site early. Thirty minutes later, she heard the van start up and saw it backing out of its garage in the area between the dig site and the manor. She could see Tommy was driving.

"He's getting Gavin," Angus said, working nearby. He'd heard the van as well and saw her look up. "Gavin's our new worker, but he won't be rooming with me. He rooms with Tommy."

267

And then Angus had turned his attention back to his soil section.

Tommy was waiting at the dock when the ferry arrived. He waved when he saw David and Gavin standing at the rail.

Watching them come down the gangway, Tommy saw that his cousin looked frail, as if he were recovering from a serious illness. Gavin had lost weight. Dark circles under his eyes suggested he hadn't slept, or slept well, in a long time. His face was drawn, in keeping with the lost weight. The buoyant, outgoing, every-person-I-meet-is-my-friend Gavin looked almost a shell of himself.

Tommy hugged his uncle first, and then turned to Gavin. "I'm glad to see you, cousin."

"Not quite what you expected," Gavin said, with a wan smile, "judging by the look on your face."

"I didn't know what to expect, Gavin, and what I see is someone who needs the bracing air of Broughby and the opportunity to get some dirt under his fingernails at an archaeological dig."

Gavin gave a small laugh.

"How was the crossing?" Tommy said to David.

"Smooth from Aberdeen to Kirkwall yesterday, but a bit choppy most of the way today from Kirkwall."

Tommy picked up Gavin's bags, and the three walked to the van.

Tommy pointed down the street. "We'll pass Dr. McCrae's house, where you'll be staying tonight, Uncle David. You'll be eating dinner with us at the Manor, and I'll show you what progress, or lack of it, we're making at the dig. Gavin, you're rooming with me for the duration, and I'll explain the class, work, and meal schedule later."

"I'll be going to class?"

Tommy nodded. "It's part of the deal. You work here, you have to know what we're doing. You're not registered for the program, so you don't have to do papers, reports, or presentations. The classes run from 0900 to 1100 five mornings a week. We get an hour for lunch, and then we spend 1300 to 1600 at the dig. I've asked Angus to show you the dig scheme, and how we photograph and document each section."

"How is Angus, Tommy?" David said. "I've had a couple of emails, but we both know he's not much for details."

Tommy laughed. "Angus is doing brilliantly. I asked him if he wanted to come meet you, but he said he had to work to the end of the shift. You know how he is, give him a task, set a time, and he's on it. But he'll be glad to see you."

Tommy got them seated in the van, and they headed down the street toward the manor road, stopping in front of Dr. McCrae's house. "Uncle David, I'm going to drop you here to get settled, rest a bit if you want, and then I'll come back to get you and Dr. McCrae for dinner." As if on cue, McCrae came out the front door and Tommy made the introductions.

"Beautiful views of the sea," Gavin said, as they traveled the manor road.

"They're even better from the upper floors of the manor. You can see the sweep of the coastline all the way to the village."

"It's bigger than I expected," Gavin said, as they pulled into the manor's circular drive.

"Even better, it's completely renovated and modernized. Showers and bath facilities, kitchen, heating, electrical, and water systems, everything is up-to-date and meeting code. And an exercise room."

Gavin followed Tommy up the stairs and down the hall of the first floor, stopping at a door near the center.

Tommy opened the door. "This is us." He set Gavin's bags down, and Gavin followed him in.

The room was about 20 by 20, with three windows facing toward the sea. Angus had rearranged the furniture, adding a single bed and a desk that matched Tommy's own.

"Angus remembered you liked two pillows."

Gavin smiled and nodded, and then sat on the side of his bed. He began to rock back and forth slightly, his left hand shaking until he used his right to stop it. Tears came down his cheeks.

"I've made such a mess of things, Tommy. I've messed up the church. I've messed up Emily. Lucas is totally confused that his daddy is gone. Mom and Dad have gone to no end of trouble. And now I've complicated your work here. How much convincing did Dad have to do to have me stay with you?"

"None." Tommy sat and put his arm around Gavin's shoulder. "He told me what had happened, asked if I could do this, and I said absolutely. We can always use an extra pair of hands, and if you need to get away, it'd be hard to find a more remote place than Broughby."

Gavin calmed. "I don't know if I can return to preaching. The mere thought is terrifying."

"That may not be the goal. It may be something else entirely. The important thing is to heal. Then you can decide what you need to do."

"Emily's scared."

"Of course, she is. She lost her dad. She's afraid of losing you, too. She loves you, Gavin, she and Lucas and this new baby need you, and she wants the two of you to get old together."

Tommy stood. "I'm going to show you where the bathroom facilities are. Why don't you splash your face and get some of the sea salt off, and I'll take you down to the dig and introduce you. Not to mention the fact that Angus will be quite anxious to see you. And remember –"

Gavin smiled. "Yes, I know. Always ask his permission before I hug him or shake his hand."

"Right. Oh, and here's your name tag. We've asked everyone to wear theirs for the first week or so until we all connect names to faces."

Gavin looked at his. It read, "Gavin Hughes, Edinburgh Theological Seminary."

"We all have an education designation on our tags. But yours is the only seminary."

Gavin nodded and clipped the tag to his shirt pocket.

Dr. McCrae showed David to his room. The two then sat in the small sitting room for tea.

"I was wondering," Dr. McCrae said, "if you might not mind signing three of your books?"

David's first thought was that he was likely giving Tommy's real identity away. "Of course. I'll be glad to."

Dr. McCrae stepped out and returned with the books. "I'd figured out who Tommy was not long after he arrived. I've never asked him, and he's never spoken of it. But I once met his father when he toured my hospital in Glasgow, and I remembered the eyes. Very few people have that eye color."

"I don't think Tommy cares about his identity being known one way or the other. It's Michael, who was concerned that Tommy wouldn't be within easy reach of security. He insisted that Tommy adopt an alias. Except for you, it seems to have worked so far."

"I don't believe anyone else here knows. There's been considerable speculation about who owns the island, along with considerable surprise when that lawyer arrived and offered the renewable leases to homes and shops. And all the renovation work on the road and the manor, too. Not to mention the repaving of the streets here in the village." He sipped his tea. "I might venture a guess that either the king or Tommy is the ultimate owner."

David smiled. "And you would not be far off. All I can say is that it's not the king."

McCrae refilled David's cup from the teapot.

"Has Tommy said anything to you about Gavin?"

"Only that a new person was joining the team. He was very circumspect. Has your son had a breakdown?"

David nodded. "Too much work. That is, taking on too much work. A chief pastor for a large megachurch, book published and another underway, a growing family with a toddler and a baby due in October, trying to be a good husband, constant demands on his time, and trying to meet those demands. It was all too much."

"Officially, unless he asks, he's not a patient. But I'll keep an eye on him. I'm usually up at the manor a couple of times a week; I've gotten to be good friends with Tommy and Noah. Speaking of which, I suspect Noah's not a graduate student?"

David shook his head.

Dr. McCrae smiled. "And this new man, Simon Fredericks. I've the impression he unexpectedly cannonballed into the pool."

"He's the man who usually accompanies the king. I met him about eight years ago when we hiked the Great Glen Way. I didn't know he'd come to Broughby."

"He arrived Saturday with the student group. I met him at the pub."

"That's a bit perplexing. I've known Noah for the last two years, and I'd trust him with my own life and the lives of my family without a second thought." He paused. "So, Dr. McCrae, what's your story? How did a young doctor leave Glasgow and end up on one of the remotest spots in the United Kingdom?"

For a time, Dr. McCrae said nothing. He looked away, toward the room's window, which was reflecting the waning afternoon sunlight.

"You've been open with me, and you deserve no less." He cleared his throat. "The people here have all wondered but never asked. The fact is, my wife killed herself. She'd a high-powered job, up and coming young professional, the usual story, and I was too busy at work to see the crash coming. She'd started drinking more than she ever had, to deal with the pressure, she said, but she insisted she could handle it. I believed her and I shouldn't have. She couldn't. One night, she got into a bath of warm water and slashed her wrists, and she did it vertically on her arms because she was playing for keeps. I came home and found her. And I couldn't deal with it, David. May I call you David?"

David nodded.

"Fairly or unfairly, perhaps both, I blamed myself. I still do. I couldn't stay in Glasgow; I really wanted to stop practicing medicine altogether. I was the doctor who couldn't care for his own wife. She was only 30." He looked down at his teacup. "She'd been fired from her job. The drinking had caught up with her. She'd been missing meetings, oversleeping, forgetting client appointments. They found several empty and partially empty bottles of scotch in her office. She hadn't told me about being fired, but it was only a matter of time before I'd find out. She'd never failed at anything before, and she couldn't handle it.

"So, I decided to leave Glasgow. I sold our house, quit my job at the hospital, and lived with my parents in Aberdeen for a week. I saw an ad in the newspaper for sub-leasing this house we're sitting in, and I signed for it by telephone, sight unseen. The lease is owned by the pub owner. That was three years ago. The people here know I'm a doctor, and that's all that matters. I keep up my certifications by mail and the occasional seminar. Most of what I'm called on to do here is handle injuries associated with fishing and the occasional childbirth."

The two men sat in silence for a while.

"I haven't told anyone that story. You're a good listener. When Tommy asked about your staying here, he spoke of you with great regard."

"He's always seemed like a son. Thank you for telling me your story. I think that, at some point, you might consider telling Tommy."

There was a knock at the door.

"And that, I suspect, is Tommy himself, to take us to our dinner. You'll find Mrs. Bixby quite the accomplished cook."

Erica was glad it was almost four and time to stop. She could see that even Angus looked tired, and they were all probably anxious to get a shower or find a nice tub. They'd made good progress on the sections today, but it was still nothing but dirt.

She saw Tommy coming down the walk, accompanied by a slightly shorter man who looked a bit older than Tommy. He had dark hair and looked like he should be built more solid than he was, or like someone just starting recovery from a long illness.

"If I could have your attention," Tommy said, and everyone looked up. "This is Gavin Hughes, who's joining our team. He's a graduate of Edinburgh Theological Seminary, including a master's in church history, and he's taking a bit of time off to join us with the dig.

Erica smiled at Gavin and heard several welcomes. Next to her, Angus suddenly stood and walked over to Gavin, staring at him intently, and then surprised the entire group.

"Gavin," Angus said, "may I give you a hug?"

The next morning, Tommy drove the van to Dr. McCrae's house and met David. He was surprised to see the two men embrace.

"Got along, did you?" Tommy said, when David climbed in the van.

"We did. We talked long into the night. He's a good man."

"He's become a good friend."

"He told me that," David said, as they arrived at the ferry terminal. About 10 people were waiting to board.

They stood at the ferry gangway.

"I'll watch over Gavin, Uncle David. He'll heal. He's made of good stuff."

"I'm glad we said our goodbyes last night. I don't think I've ever been so frightened, Tommy. When we first saw him after the church breakdown, he couldn't stop the tremors in his hands. And this was the little boy I carried and tossed in the air."

"It'll be good for him to be here. No one expects anything of him except to work the trowel in the dirt and listen politely while his cousin drones on. And Angus will be good for him as well."

"I know," David said, and threw his arms around his nephew. "They're sounding the departure bell, so I better board."

"Give Aunt Betsy, Eleanor, and Emily my love. And give my little godson a huge hug."

"I will." David walked up the gangway. He stopped and turned around. "And thank you, Tommy."

Tommy gave him a thumbs up.

Under Professor Elliot's and Tommy's guidance, the group began making progress. Section by section, the soil was being carefully removed, sifted, and rechecked. Tommy had shown them digital slides of a 9th century drawing from an old manuscript. They could all see the rough outline of a smallish rectangular structure, with an "x" marked next to it.

The students soon realized that, even with the full participation and discussion by the two professors, the content of the course and the direction of the dig were all based on Tommy's work. He answered questions and posed them. He pointed but didn't direct. He could answer their questions, or if he couldn't, he offered possible answers. Professor McNeill was the overall coordinator, Dr. Elliot was the archaeological expert, but Tommy was the intellectual force.

The surprise, for Erica, at least, if not the entire group, was Angus. He worked like a beaver. He was fast and accurate, and he was painstaking about the photos and journal entries. He rarely spoke while he worked, but his intense focus kept the rest of them on their toes.

Gavin always seemed to work near Angus or Tommy, although not as feverishly as Angus worked. He was quiet, always polite, but saying very little about himself or his background. His physical appearance was already improving, with the circles gone from around his eyes and Mrs. Bixby's food helping to fill him out a bit. A few times Erica spotted Gavin in the village, talking with Dr. McCrae.

For the next three weeks, Erica avoided Tommy as much as possible. She had to see him in the classroom, but she made sure to work a part of the site that was well away from where he was working.

It was during the excavation session three weeks later that a confrontation erupted, right before a startling find at the dig.

Erica was working near Angus, using the knife, brush, and trowel in a section of soil that seemed looser than what she had previously worked. Julia was also close by. Tommy came over from the section he was working and knelt next to Erica. He'd seen her massaging her lower arm.

"If you turn your wrist and hand like this," he said, "you'll find it a bit easier." He placed his hand on hers and turned it slightly.

Erica felt his touch and a warmth flooded through her. His touch was gentle; his hand was strong and, she thought, beautiful.

She jerked it away. "Don't touch me," she said through clenched teeth.

"What? I'm sorry." Tommy pulled his hand away. "I was trying to –"

"Just don't touch me," she said vehemently.

Tommy stood and turned to Julia, who with the rest of group, including Angus, was watching.

"Julia, would you show Ms. Larsson how to hold her trowel and brush properly so she doesn't strain her wrist and risk carpal tunnel syndrome?" And with that, he walked off and left the area.

Everyone was staring at Erica. She felt the redness on her face. Julia was sitting, looking at her uncertainly.

"Hold your arm like this,' Julia said finally. "It'll actually feel better."

"That's what he said to do," she said, feeling an anger she couldn't explain.

Julia nodded. She hesitated before speaking. "He was right, Erica."

Erica turned back to her soil section. She felt foolish, embarrassed, and angry. She knew she was being irrational. She might blame it on tiredness, but she knew that wasn't it. He'd simply been trying to help, while she was trying to keep him at arm's length. He was refusing to stay where she wanted, and, needed, him to stay. And then his touch unnerved her.

"Something." Angus stood up and then knelt down again. "Something."

They all looked. He was brushing dirt away from his section. They crowded around, but not too closely; Angus, they knew, didn't like people too close.

It was the edge of a stone. It extended back into the dirt. Angus had exposed about six inches of its length, but it was clearly longer.

"Tommy!" Angus said at the top of his voice. "Tommy!"

The entire team kept working into the night. Noah and Simon rigged up lights so they could see. The six-inch edge uncovered by Angus grew to more than six feet and extended down two feet by the time Tommy said they had to stop to rest. Gavin worked as hard as any of them.

They could see what looked like part of a monument or a tomb. It was located right where the "x" had been marked on the old manuscript in Oslo. What was even more striking were the runes from the Norse alphabet carved on the stone.

Mrs. Bixby had kept dinner warmed until they came inside, exhausted and yet bubbling. The talk at the dinner table was excited and ranging over all the possibilities.

"So, here's a question for our professor friends," one of the students said. "If what we've found is a tomb, how could it have Norse runes on it? Wouldn't that imply that at least one Norseman is buried there? I thought they sent their dead off to sea in fired longboats."

"They did," Professor McNeill said, "for some leaders. But they also had boat burials on land, especially for kings. This clearly isn't a boat. It might be something other than a Norse tomb, like a memorial. It might be a tomb for a conquered leader, and the Norsemen added the runes." He glanced at Tommy. "Although I've never heard of Norsemen building tombs or memorials for others."

"The runes look to me to be ninth century," Professor Elliot said, "which would mean early in the Norse invasion period. We need to uncover more of the carvings to be sure, and I'll need to send photos to several specialists and see what they say."

Julia looked at Tommy. "And what does our lecturer say?"

"If it's a tomb, it might mean that the Norseman or Norsemen buried there were Christians," Tommy said.

"But that could put an entirely different slant on a lot of things," Alan said.

"Tomorrow morning," Tommy said, "I'll give you a complete briefing on the research from the libraries that applies here."

As they headed upstairs for bed, Tommy founded himself walking by Erica.

"I'm sorry. I should've asked permission to show you."

She said nothing but nodded, and then hurried to her room.

Nightgown on, she was brushing her teeth when Julia arrived.

"Big day today," Julia said. When Erica didn't respond, Julia said, "Are you OK?"

"A lot of things happened today."

"Erica, I think Tommy was just trying to help. I don't think he was hitting on you."

"I can't get involved. I just can't."

"Who said anything about getting involved? I think he was just trying to help. And he was right about the repetitive motion." Realization suddenly dawned. "Ah, you're attracted to him. Well, why not? He's smart, a bit on the beautiful side, well, more than a bit, and he seems unattached."

Erica told her about Derek and Alison. "And, yes, I'm attracted to Tommy. Who wouldn't be? But it would be nothing more than me finding someone on the rebound."

"Has he said or done anything to suggest he's interested?"

Erica shook her head. "No, not really. There's no reason to think he would be interested in someone like me, anyway."

"Which may be putting your finger on the problem. You're attracted to him, he hasn't shown any reciprocal interest, so you build a wall to justify his lack of interest. You tell yourself you can't get involved because it's too soon after a previous relationship. He does something to help and you react negatively. It makes a kind of sense, really."

"Did you just psychoanalyze me?"

"No. Well, yes, I suppose I did. But it makes sense, doesn't it? Why don't you try to relax around him, and see what if anything develops?"

But Erica couldn't relax. Getting too physically close to him in the classroom, at meals, or on the dig created a tension inside her that she could barely stand. She did her best to avoid him, and he seemed to accept that. She'd occasionally notice him watching her with a bewildered look in his eyes. She'd quickly turn away.

The tension between Tommy and Erica soon translated itself to the broader team. Erica would enter the classroom each morning, and the temperature in the room would seem to drop. No one was quite sure what had happened, most of all Tommy. Erica listened to his lectures and took notes, but she stopped participating. When asked, including by Professor McNeill, she'd say nothing was wrong. Julia knew, and she'd occasionally suggest that Erica needed to figure out what to do, but Erica would shake her head and say everything was fine.

The next Saturday was an off day from the dig, and the group was encouraged to do anything that might interest them. Tommy spent the morning with the two professors, reviewing progress, considering next steps, developing a plan for involving additional consultants via long distance, and preparing the project grids for the next round of the dig. The edge of the rectangular stone had now grown to 16 feet long, with an additional two feet dug down the width. It was more and more resembling the side of an out-of-the-ground tomb-like structure, and the team had started uncovering soil across what was likely the top.

The runes had come into a more complete view, and the three agreed that they were definitely earlier than 900 A.D. Norse inscriptions. Tommy had started a translation effort, and he'd contacted Old Norse experts in Copenhagen and Oslo for assistance. Complicating the translation was that the runes appeared to be a variant of Old Norse, one neither the professors nor Tommy had seen before.

Most of the students decided to go into the village; Noah volunteered to drive them in the van and pick them up when they sent a text or called him. Gavin and Angus remained at the manor, taking a walk along the shoreline below the dig.

Four of the women decided to hike into the hills behind the manor; Erica had suggested the idea, privately wanting to see where Tommy might be taking off to. Mrs. Bixby packed them a lunch, and Professor McNeill cautioned them to avoid any small farms they might see or pass. "People live there, and we need to respect their privacy. If they see you and call you over for a visit, that's fine. But be careful to avoid trespassing."

They hiked for a good two hours, and then stopped to reconnoiter. They were approaching the crest of the hills, and Erica wanted to see what might be on the other side. One path led to a small forested area up the hill, but Julia thought she saw the outline of a cottage in the trees. Remembering Professor McNeill's caution, they paralleled the ridgeline for another quarter mile before stopping for lunch. But they still hadn't seen over the top of the hills to the western face of the island. They'd heard the views were spectacular, but they were all tiring. Erica was the only one who wanted to go on.

Tommy, Noah, Gavin, the professors and Angus were eating lunch when Simon came in, holding a printed piece of paper.

"We've a report from the weather bureau in Kirkwall that a storm is brewing and headed toward the Orkneys. The west side of Broughby will catch the full impact, but we may get some serious rain and wind on this side. And it may last for a couple of days."

"Where is everyone?" Tommy said.

"Eight of the students are in the village, likely having lunch at the pub right now," Noah said, glancing at his watch. "They're supposed to call when they're ready to come back."

"The other four?"

"Hiking," Simon said. "I saw them leave. It's four of the women. They wanted to see if they could reach the top of the ridge. In hindsight, I wished we'd known the weather forecast before they left."

"OK," Tommy said. "Simon, could you drive the van to the village and get our eight, and alert the village if they haven't already heard? The fishermen will need to secure their boats. Noah and I will head into the hills and bring the other four back. How much time do we have, do you know?" He looked out the dining room window. "It looks all sunshine at the moment."

"No more than an hour," Simon said. "Let's get to it."

Tommy grabbed his hiking backpack, stopped in the kitchen for power bars and water, and started for the terrace to meet Noah. Gavin stopped him on the stairs. "What can I do?"

"When Simon returns with the students, can you work with them to secure the site? And then can you stay here with Angus? You know how he is about storms. If it's a bad one, he'll get hysterical. If you could be here and sit with him if and when it starts, I'll be grateful."

Gavin nodded, and Tommy raced to the terrace. He and Noah followed the path, fairly certain the four young women would have followed it as well.

They'd been walking for 40 minutes when Tommy noticed the clouds beginning to build up overhead. "Looks like the weather report was correct."

"I see the girls. They're headed our way." Both of them felt enormous relief.

Two minutes later, they were face to face with three of the women, and they explained the approaching storm.

"Weren't there four of you?" Noah said.

Julia nodded. "We got tired, but Erica wanted to keep going. She said it shouldn't be much farther to the top. She was keen to see the view."

Tommy felt the first signs of panic. The overhead clouds were turning darker, and the winds were picking up.

"Noah, take them back to the manor. If you're quick, you'll miss most of the storm. I'll keep going ahead to find Erica."

"Tommy, I can't let you go by yourself. You know the protocol."

Julia looked at the two young men. *The protocol?*

"Yes, I know the protocol, but there are times you have to ignore it. You head back. And you need to get going. The storm's getting ready to break on top of us. I've got more hiking experience, and I know the terrain. I'll go on ahead. If Simon kicks up a fuss, I'll talk to him."

Noah stared at Tommy for a moment, and then turned to the three girls. "We need to leave. And Tommy, keep in touch with your mobile."

"Will do." Tommy left the group and continued climbing up the hill.

He guessed the spot where Erica would've gone, just over the ridge line and about a quarter of a mile from where he was, and fairly close to the stone cottage he used for his getaway place. The cottage sat in an isolated area, near the crest of one hill and the base of another. The winds were really beginning to kick up as he climbed. The sky had turned an ominous shade of dark gray tinged with yellow, just as he saw the cottage to his left. He knew they were in for a bad one, and, hearing a roll of thunder, he hoped that Gavin was sitting with Angus.

He began calling Erica's name, but heard nothing in response. He kept climbing and shouting her name, unsure anyone could hear him with the rising winds.

At first, he thought it was the wind, but then he heard the noise again, and realized it was a cry.

"Erica!" he shouted. This time he heard an answering cry.

"Help!"

"Keep calling so I can find you!" he shouted, and he heard the cry again.

He slowed as he reached the ridgeline, and then he saw her, clinging to the other side of the ridge and lying perilously close to its edge.

He realized what had happened. She'd come over the ridge and immediately saw the spectacular view. She likely had been so focused on the view that she didn't realize the steepness and took a tumble down the side.

"Erica!" he shouted again.

Holding on to a small shrub, she looked up and saw him. "Tommy!"

"Hang on!" he shouted.

He pulled off the backpack and quickly opened a side pocket. He almost cried in relief to see the nylon rope still tied neatly inside. He found a gnarled stub of a tree on the ridge, shook it to test for strength, and, satisfied, tied one end of the rope securely around it. He then tied the other end around his waist, gave a few pulls to make sure the tree would hold, and began to rappel down the steep face of the hill.

He finally reached Erica and grabbed her hand, just as the shrub she'd been holding on to uprooted and slipped down the drop. He could see she was nearly hysterical.

"I need you to calm yourself." He pulled her close to him. "I know it's frightening, but you need to calm yourself. We have to focus everything on getting to the top of the ridge, and we have about 20 feet to get up."

"But the storm—"

"Forget the storm. Focus on anything. Focus on me. Put your arms around my waist and hold tight. Keep telling yourself you won't let go. And do everything I tell you to do as I pull us up the slope."

As he slowly pulled them up, he could hear her whispering, "Don't let go. Don't let go." At one point, he thought he felt the tree give slightly, but he hoped it was his imagination.

Finally, they reached the top, and both fell to their knees. The first thing he did was put his arms around her. "It's okay. We made it. We're safe."

She held on to him desperately, sobbing almost wildly.

"It's okay. You're safe."

He felt something sting the side of his face, just as a huge peal of thunder sounded overhead.

Hail. And then the cold rain mixed with it.

"We have to get to the cottage. It's about a hundred yards. We need to run now."

"I can't. I think I sprained my ankle," she said, still sobbing.

He slipped the backpack on, stood and pulled her to her feet. He could see she was in pain. The hail was coming harder.

He picked her up in his arms. "Put your face on my shoulder. Don't expose it to the hail." She quickly obeyed, and he started walking, hurrying as fast as he could. He kept his head down as much as possible, partially covering hers, but he could feel the hail hitting his head and his hands.

Reaching the cottage, he set Erica down, pulled the key from his pants pocket, and opened the door, pushing her inside but still supporting her so she wouldn't fall. Inside, he looked back through the door, and saw the hail suddenly become golf-ball size.

He supported her to a chair, and then let her slowly sit in it. She was shivering, her hair was wet and bedraggled, and tears were streaking down her dirty face.

He removed his jacket and pulled off his sweatshirt. "Put the sweatshirt on. It's mostly dry. I'll build a fire, but first I have to call Noah and let him know we're safe."

"You have blood on your face. Your right cheek."

He put his hand to his cheek. "Likely the hail. And it's still coming down," he said, pointing to the window. He pressed No. 2 on his speed dial.

"Noah, I found her. We're in the cottage. We're both safe, but the storm shows no signs of letting up. And it's hailing golf balls at the moment. And I mean golf-ball-size hail."

"Everyone else is here. Simon read me the riot act for letting you go off by yourself."

"I'll talk to him. It was an emergency and we did what we had to do. Stuff the protocol. We're safe, so I'll check back in a bit. How's Angus?"

"Gavin's sitting with him in his room. The last time I checked, Angus was holding on to him for dear life."

"Good. Thanks. I'll call back. When the storm passes, ask Angus what he might suggest for transporting someone with a sprained ankle and who can't walk."

"Erica?" Noah said.

"Yes. He'll come up with some ideas." Tommy powered off.

Erica looked almost swallowed in his sweatshirt, but he could see she had wrapped it tightly around her.

"Now we need a fire. I've plenty of wood in a protected area by the back door. Kindling, too."

"This is your cottage?"

"I come here when I need to think and work alone."

After a few minutes, he had the fire going, small at first but gradually building to where they could both feel the warmth.

"Now, I have to check your ankle. I need permission to touch your leg."

She nodded. "I'm sorry. For what I said before. I'm sorry."

He placed his hand on her right ankle, and then removed her hiking boot. He felt the bones in her foot.

"I'm trained as a Red Cross Master. My father is rabid on the subject of first-aid training, and our entire family has been through the courses." He smiled. "This is the first time I've used it. Nothing feels broken, but you likely do have a nasty sprain. Which means you need to stay off that foot. When we get back to the manor, we'll get Dr. McCrae to take the official look and do an x-ray. In the meantime," he said, walking over to a chest of drawers, "I'll get out my trusty first-aid kit and find an ace bandage."

"You need to doctor your face."

"There's a mirror in the bathroom. I'll check it in a minute."

"There's a bathroom?"

He nodded. "We had a septic system installed."

"Well, that's a good thing, because I need to use it. Can you help me get there?"

He supported her as she hopped on one foot, and then he had her wait while he retrieved the chair. "You can use the chair to support you when you use the basin." He quietly closed the door. Walking to the kitchen area, he did a quick inventory of food supplies. Two tins of sausages, three tins of peach halves, and four bananas that he had left a few days ago and were still apparently in good enough shape to eat. He also spotted not- quite-stale bread in a bread safe, next to a box of cereal. And power bars and water in the backpack.

We'll survive, he thought.

She came out, using the chair like a walker.

"You didn't tell me my face looked like a mud pie. Now take care of that cut on your face."

"After I bandage your ankle."

While he tended to his face, she sat and looked round the cottage. It was one room, maybe 25 feet by 35 feet. The fireplace dominated one wall, with the door to the bathroom in one corner and the kitchen area in the other. A small table and a chair were in the kitchen area; she was sitting in the other chair. Near the large front window was an artist's easel, currently covered with a cloth.

His sweatshirt smelled like him, like sweat and that odd smell of apples.

She was sitting in the chair when he came back, a small adhesive bandage on his cheek.

"The fire feels good."

"We've enough wood for a week, so we should be fine."

"When did you know about the storm?" she said, and he told her about Simon receiving the report.

He walked over to the window. "The good news is that the hail stopped. The bad news is that the snow has started, and right now it's so thick I can't see 10 feet from the window." He pulled out his mobile. "I've got plenty of battery time left, but we need to conserve it. Do you have your mobile?"

"I didn't bring it. Julia had hers."

"I'm going to call Noah and tell him we'll call only if there's an emergency." He made the call.

"Noah says Mrs. Bixby is fixing a special storm dinner."

"I hate to ask this, but is there anything to eat here?"

He grinned. "Well, it's not up to Bixby standards, but I have tinned sausages and peaches, a few bananas, some power bars, a loaf of almost-stale bread, and I think I even have a box of corn flakes. No milk, though."

She looked around the room. "There's a canvas and easel over there. Do you come here to paint?"

"When I need to. I use painting to relieve tension, refocus, and help me get my mind off my work when I'm feeling overwhelmed."

"I can't imagine you feeling overwhelmed. You're always so in control, with a solution to every problem and an answer to every question."

"Appearances are deceiving. When it come to the work we're doing here, yes, I know it solid. But other things, well, not so much."

She knew she was borderline prying, but she went on. "Like what?"

He didn't answer right away. He walked back over to the window and looked out at the blinding white outside.

"Like my relationship with my father. It's been strained since I was a child, and it had a lot to do with my mother. Painting is a good way to relieve the tension and stress." He could've said that painting was also a way to stay connected with his mother, and that he never mentioned his painting to his father. But he didn't.

"What does he do?" Erica said.

Tommy hesitated only briefly. "He's in government service in London. I live in Edinburgh, so I don't see him that much."

"Does your mother work?"

He shook his head. "My birth mother died when I was younger. My father eventually remarried, but not right away. And it's none of that ugly stepmother business you read in the fairy tales. I really like my stepmother, and she's been nothing but kind to me. What about your parents?"

"They're divorced. My father lives in Birmingham with his second wife, and my mother, well, she travels a lot. I might see her two or three times a year."

"What does your father do?" He asked but already knew the answer.

This time, it was Erica who briefly hesitated. "He works for a manufacturing company. He's involved in sales and stuff related to that. I don't really know much about his business."

Tommy knew from the security report exactly who her father was. For whatever reason, Erica was misleading him, perhaps for the same reason he'd misled her. He felt a great urge at the moment to yell at his father for the whole stupid security charade.

"I'll get us some dinner together. We'll call it Bixby's North."

She laughed. "I'd offer to help but I'll only be in the way, and not much use at that."

She could still feel his touch on her ankle and foot. He'd been gentle; each touch had sent that warmth through her again, just like when he'd touched her hand at the dig. All her defenses were down now. She couldn't keep pushing him away, and she didn't want to.

She pointed to the covered canvas and easel. "What are you painting?"

She was close enough to see him blush. And then he turned quickly to the food cabinet.

"It's a portrait." He paused. "Sometimes an image or a face gets such a powerful hold on my mind that I have to paint it."

"May I see it?"

He stood for a moment, and she could see he was considering his answer. He nodded, walked to the easel, and carefully removed the cloth serving as a cover, and turned it around so she could see it.

It was unfinished, but she could see it was nearly done. Her eyes widened.

The painting was good, so good, in fact, that it was stunning.

And it was a painting of her.

At the manor, it was a quiet group at dinner. The team had secured the dig site in light snow that had turned somewhat heavier, and they could hear the winds. The stone with the runes had been covered and secured with a tarpaulin.

"Of all of us," Alan said, "it would be the two who get along the least who'd be stuck together."

There were a few smiles.

"They like each other," Angus said.

Every head around the table turned to Angus.

Disconcerted with the focused attention, Angus looked at his plate. "They like each other. A lot."

The others, including the two professors, looked at each other in surprise.

"One thing about Angus," Professor MacNeill said, "is that he's one of the most perceptive people I've ever known."

After dinner, Simon pulled Noah to the side.

"Leaving Tommy to look for Erica was a violation of security rules, and I'll have to report it. I'll also explain that I've been with Prince Thomas, David Hughes, and the king on two extensive hikes, and the prince is by far the most experienced hiker in this entire group here at the manor. And while it was a violation of the rules, I would've done the same, it was the right decision, and it probably saved the girl's life."

"I might've found her," Noah said.

"I know, but the prince knew exactly where to look, didn't he? The storm was almost here, and the other three had to be taken to safety. The four of you arrived soaked to the skin as it was."

They sat at the small kitchen table, eating their sausages warmed over the fire. The tinned peaches turned out to be surprisingly good as well.

Neither had said anything about the painting.

"I've started writing a story. After Julia falls asleep, and she's a sound sleeper, I've been writing a story by hand. It's far from finished, but I'm trying to visualize what the tomb might mean, assuming it is a tomb." She looked up at him, and she could see he was listening closely.

"It's about a young woman, a teen, really, who lives with her father on a small island north of Scotland, an island like Broughby. Her mother died in childbirth, and she and her father live quietly in a small cottage with a thatched roof. He fishes with the rest of the men in the village, and she tends a small garden, keeps house, and manages a few livestock like goats and chickens. And a few pigs as well. She's well-liked by the other women in the village, but they think of her as something of a dreamer. And she dreams, especially when she looks out to sea. She has light hair and deep blue eyes.

"One day, she's dreaming of the stories she's heard about lands beyond the sea, when she sees sails. She looks closely, and she's never seen fishing boats built so long and fashioned with strange figureheads on the front. She doesn't know what they are, but they look ominous. What she's seeing is the arrival of the Norsemen, and her life will change forever.

"There's more, but that's the start."

"I'd like to read it. Or rather, I'd like to hear you read it to me." He understood what she'd just done. She'd responded to his painting of her with her own kind of painting. He'd shown her his vulnerability, and she'd responded the same way.

"I will. It's in my room at the manor."

He stood and gathered up their dishes. "I've an extra toothbrush, and you'll find it and toothpaste in that small cabinet in the bathroom." He paused. "And obviously, there's nowhere to sleep, except I do have a large sleeping bag. It's padded and not entirely uncomfortable, but it will be better than trying to sleep in the chair here. And it will provide some warmth."

He helped her to the bathroom and then settled her in the sleeping bag for the night, close enough to the fire to keep her warm. He put on his jacket over his t-shirt and pulled a chair near the fire.

"The sleeping bag is huge. I think it's big enough to share."

He looked at her.

"I trust you, Tommy. And you'll get sick without some extra warmth."

She was right; the sleeping bag was considerably oversized, and the cottage wasn't airtight from the cold and the storm's winds still howling outside. He knelt and then got in the sleeping bag as well. As they faced each other, a foot of space separated them.

"When I came to Broughby, I'd left a ruined relationship only a few months before. I'd been deeply hurt by a boy I thought I was in love with and the girl who'd been my best friend since we were children. I was determined that would never happen again. Coming down the gangway at the ferry, I saw you standing there, smiling, and I've been at war with myself ever since. That spilled out on you, and

I'm sorry. You never did anything wrong. It was me. I was afraid for all kinds of wrong reasons."

"I've dated very little," he said.

"You must be joking."

"I'm serious. It's been all work. I graduated from school in London at 15 and started at St. Andrews, specifically to study under Professor McNeill. Everything's been focused on work and study, and recently on my Ph.D. thesis at Edinburgh."

"How old are you?"

"I'm 21."

Erica partially sat up. "You're younger than I am. I turned 22 in February. And you're preparing for your Ph.D. defense?"

"I turn my thesis in in late September at the University of Edinburgh and defend it in November. But what I was saying is that I didn't date much. I can count real dates on less than two hands, actually less than one hand, if I'm honest. When I saw you on the gangway, well, I've never experienced a reaction like that. I felt almost drunk, or at least like my life had suddenly lurched out of control." He paused. "You're beautiful, Erica."

She shook her head. "You're the beautiful one here, Tommy." She reached for his hand and brought it to her lips.

Tommy leaned over and kissed her forehead.

"That's all I trust myself with at this moment," he said. "We should try to get some sleep."

"Why do you always smell like apples?"

"Apples?"

"Yes, apples. Even that first day when I sat next to you in the van."

He smiled. "Ah. It's the soap I use."

She held on to his hand, the hand that had touched her ankle. The hand that had saved her life.

She kissed it again.

Erica woke to the sounds of kitchen noises.

Tommy saw her stirring and lifted her up, helping her to the bathroom.

"I talked with Noah," he said. "They hope to get up here by noon. The snow has considerably melted lower down the hills, and it's melting here as well. He tells me that Angus has rigged up a trolley of sorts to help get you down to the manor."

When she "chaired" her way back to the kitchen table, she saw he'd poured cereal in bowls and also had opened the last of the peaches.

"I'm afraid there's no milk," he said, "And I could really use a cup of tea right at the moment. Memo to file: get tea bags and a kettle for the cottage. I'm willing to try what corn flakes with bottled water might taste like."

She laughed. "I'm so hungry I could eat it dry."

"How's the ankle?"

"Really sore but I can't see any swelling. And the bandage is still in place."

"I'll say grace." When he finished, he opened his eyes to see her staring at him. She suddenly leaned forward and kissed him.

He returned it.

Shortly before noon, they both heard voices calling out. Tommy opened the door to see Noah and Simon, along with Gavin and two of the students from the team. They were carrying a stretcher made of wooden slats, two blankets, and a pillow.

"Angus did this?" Tommy said.

Gavin laughed. "He worked on it most of the night, and you know how he is when he sets his mind to something. Watch out world! And Mrs. Bixby sent along a thermos of tea and some scones."

Fortified by Mrs. Bixby's supplies, they made their way down the hills. It wasn't lost on any of them that Tommy walked alongside Erica's stretcher the entire way down, except when the path was too narrow. The snow had melted considerably, but there was still evidence of the storm all around them.

During a rest stop, Noah looked at the two of them. "Are you going to tell us what happened up there? We were worried that only one might be left alive before we arrived."

Tommy smiled. "Nothing happened, Noah." He looked at Erica. "But everything changed."

She reached for his hand and squeezed it.

"Angus was right," Gavin said.

When they reached the manor, and were welcomed by the rest of the team, Tommy supported her as Erica thanked Angus for the stretcher.

"Angus," she said, "may I give you a hug?"

He looked at Tommy, who nodded.

"Yes," Angus said, "you may."

They had a quick lunch, and then Noah drove Tommy and Erica to Dr. McCrae's house. Erica said she wanted Tommy along.

"No broken bones." Dr. McCrae looked at the x-ray. "And I'm wondering who my competition is."

"Competition?" said Erica.

McCrae pointed to the ace bandage. "Yes, whoever it was who wrapped your ankle."

They all laughed.

The next two months were almost a golden period for the dig team, the sudden change in Tommy and Erica's relationship breathed an air of relaxation and camaraderie into the group. The lecture/dig work schedule continued as before, but with a nightly reading added, for any who wanted to listen. The entire team gathered after supper to listen as Erica read her story, however much she'd been able to finish since the last reading. They listened as they drank tea or hot chocolate.

Twice a week, the team drove down to the village after supper, and Erica would read at the pub, repeating what had been read at the manor to catch the villagers up on the story.

"You've become our team bard," Tommy told her one night, as they drove back to the manor. "Perhaps even the village bard. Everyone's trying to figure out which character they are."

Erica had to force herself to focus on the work. What she wanted to do was watch Tommy. He had a natural grace and an easy manner. She'd occasionally catch herself staring at his legs, as he knelt

301

or squatted with the work. They all wore shorts when it was warm, and Tommy wore shorts even when it was cool. She could see how muscled his legs were.

She also noticed his gentleness, and especially with Angus. It wasn't just the music they played together at church; she knew they had to have known each other for a long time, which Tommy acknowledged when she asked.

"We met at church when we were 10. We connected over music. He has a genius for it, and no one knew it until he came to church that night. We've been close friends ever since."

"Is the autism a barrier?"

"Only when Angus lets it. Which isn't often. I don't let him get away with much."

Erica suspected that Tommy had had a lot to do with Angus's success.

They made an effort to avoid public displays of affection, but the entire team knew they had fallen for each other. On movie nights, she'd sit close to him, his arm around her. She felt like they were basking in each other's presence.

Two weeks after the storm, the team was scraping off centuries of accumulated dirt from the top of what was clearly a large, rectangular flat stone structure whose edge Angus had first uncovered. It was larger than they'd first estimated, six feet by eighteen feet, and at least a solid six feet deep. Professor Elliot had arranged for a small crane from Kirkwall large enough to lift the covering stone. It would be arriving on the next ferry.

Gavin was brushing the final areas of dirt away from the stone, and they could see a design emerging.

"It's a cross," Gavin said. "A quite beautiful Celtic cross."

The entire team crowded around and stared.

"A cross on a stone with Norse runes on the side," Professor Elliot said. "Assuming they were carved at the same time, the implications are huge."

The team all looked at Tommy, who'd told them the research and old manuscripts had pointed directly to this.

"Vikings who were Christians," said Professor McNeill. "If this bears out, it'll have been a century earlier than the earliest reports, and those are conversions that happened after the Norsemen settled in England."

He lifted his gaze from the cross on the stone to Tommy. "I don't know what else to say, Thomas McLaren, except that we're right on the verge of proving your theory right. This is stunning. I knew your head was right, but to see this is simply stunning."

"There are Norse myths," Tommy told the group, "largely dismissed by most scholars, of men from the west bringing a warrior against Odin. The myths may actually be stories of Celtic or Irish monks bringing Christianity to the Norsemen."

Off duty, Tommy and Erica were spending considerable time together, taking walks, reading together, sitting next to each other at meals. Early one Saturday morning, after her ankle had mended, they hiked back to the cottage, accompanied by Noah.

"I know you'd much prefer to be alone, but I have to come," Noah had told Tommy.

Tommy had finished the painting, and this was the trip to retrieve it and bring it to the manor. He brought along a portfolio to transport it, and he was glad Noah was with them. He and Noah between them carried the painting back down the hills. Noah asked if Tommy wanted it displayed, and he shook his head. "No, for now it stays in my room."

A week later, the team had finished excavating the stone structure. They waited a day for weather to clear, and then removed the tent over the excavation site. The small crane was positioned in place, and cables attached. They all stood back and watched the crane lift the stone top, which Professor Elliot had estimated to weigh about a ton. Carefully, the crane operator set the stone on level ground. And then they looked to see what the stone had been covering.

It was indeed a tomb. They could see the remains, much deteriorated, of two bodies, lying side by side. One was smaller than the other, suggesting a married couple.

"We're going to need an archaeological forensic specialist," Professor Elliot said. "It looks like the remains are preserved enough to be able to do an array of tests."

"Not to mention a specialist in 9th century gold and silver artifacts," Professor McNeill said, "given what's in here."

"And jewelry," Julia said. "The amount of jewelry by itself suggests someone high born. I think there's an expert on Viking jewelry at the British Museum. That jeweled sword alone is amazing. And they're both wearing crowns."

"And the crosses," Tommy said. "Both have jeweled crosses. That's not likely to be Viking jewelry, at least as we've understood it. We're looking at two people, two people of high rank, possibly Vikings, who were both buried as Christians."

"We need photographs," Professor Elliot said. "A lot of photographs. Then we need to secure the tomb and develop a plan for examination of what it contains. We also need an informal agreement among ourselves, to keep this news here and not broadcast what we've found. This may be the most remarkable find since Sutton Hoo, and we have to ensure we don't get overrun with government monitors, news media, and even tourists wanting to take a look.

"And Tommy," he said, "we also need a plan for Broughby. The news will eventually get out, and the island needs to be prepared to be overrun. This is going to change lives here, and it could change them drastically. We'll need to get the village involved."

For a moment, no one spoke.

Erica put her hand in Tommy's and leaned against his shoulder. "We thought it was a project, Tommy. This looks like a career."

The next morning, Tommy had an announcement for the team.

"Some extraordinary things have happened. Some I was confident of, some I hoped for, but none like what's been found. We're going to celebrate. Bright Wings has a concert in Kirkwall in two weeks, and we're going to go, the professors and Mrs. Bixby included. We're going to rent a high-speed boat, and spend a weekend in Kirkwall, celebrating."

The room erupted in cheers.

That afternoon, after work at the dig had concluded for the day, Tommy and Professor McNeill were drinking tea on the terrace.

"I believe you have what you need for your thesis, Tommy," the professor said. "But I expect you won't include the whole of what we've found here."

Tommy nodded. "The stone tomb by itself is more than sufficient," he said. "But we have to do some serious planning about the contents. We need security for it, especially while we're doing our weekend in Kirkwall. I have to talk to a lot of people, including about how we announce it, and when. We have to talk to the village, which will mean we're essentially going public; no one will be able to keep this news secret for long. Including our team. And we have to do this right, professor.

"Erica was right, but perhaps not in the way she realized. It is a career, because I think there's a lot more here than the tomb. We know that part of the village was washed away, but the corollary to that may be that part of it wasn't. And I don't think that tomb was placed far away from the village. In fact, I suspect it was almost in the middle of the village."

"A find like this comes along every two or three generations," Professor McNeill said. "It'll make the name and reputation of every single student on the team and be like a gold-plated career ticket." He paused. "Have you thought about life after Ph.D.? And have you considered the need for a long-term manager for the property?"

"Assuming my Ph.D. is awarded," Tommy said. "I'll be looking for an academic post, preferably in Scotland because it's close to Broughby. But the academic world isn't exactly overflowing with job possibilities at the moment, especially in 9th century history. And your advice on a manager is good, I think. It'll mean finding just the right person who's comfortable living on a remote island. But apart from this, my future is with Rikki."

Professor McNeil smiled as he relit his pipe. "Rikki, is it now?"

"She's about the last thing I expected to happen here. I feel so incredibly blessed. A few short weeks ago, I saw myself being forever content with my research. Now, well, she's changed everything." He smiled. "I'm going to spend the rest of my life with her, and I can't imagine anything better."

Tommy arranged for the weekend rental of a good-sized home in Kirkwall. The high-speed boat made the journey on a Friday afternoon in late July from Broughby to Kirkwall in under three hours.

When they reached the rental home, Tommy handed out room assignments. Angus was a bit apprehensive about the trip but was comfortable enough now with the team to give the trip and the concert a go.

Tommy handed Gavin his key. "I hope you find the room to your liking."

"I'm sure I will." Gavin walked up the wide stairs, found his door, and opened it. The first thing he saw was another suitcase, and he thought there must have been a mistake. And then he saw Emily, and a little boy running to him yelling "Daddy!" Gavin embraced his family.

At dinner at the Foveran restaurant, Gavin introduced Emily and Lucas. Emily came up to Tommy and hugged him.

"It's a miracle," she whispered to him. "He's healing. You did this."

"Gavin did this, Emily. I gave him the opportunity, but he did this. And God. How are you feeling?"

"Like you feel when you're almost seven months pregnant – fat and increasingly miserable. Gavin says he's coming home in August, when the project ends. And he wants to make a lot of changes. He's been thinking about the ministry, and he says he's not going back to the church. He wants to do some different things." She hugged him. "I was so scared, Tommy. All I could think about was Dad. But Gavin's phenomenal." She hugged him again.

After dinner, the group strolled around the town, checking shops and stores. It was something of a novel experience for both Tommy and Erica, being together on a non-dig weekend. Tommy discovered he liked being with her anywhere. She was funny, poking fun at him and herself. He loved watching her look over local woolens in one store and thought he would laugh out loud when they happened upon a cheese shop with free tastings, and, like a child in a toy store, she confessed to having a cheese addiction.

On Saturday morning, the group visited St. Magnus Cathedral and the Orkney Museum. They had lunch at a small café near the waterfront. Then they returned to the rental to get ready for the concert. An early buffet dinner was set up in the home's dining room, and then they boarded a bus for the Pickaquoy Centre for the concert. Professors Elliot and McNeil and Mrs. Bixby had decided to forgo the concert and instead went back to the town center; Angus decided he would go but stay near Gavin and Emily, who brought Lucas with them.

Pickaquoy was crowded. They found a space on the field near the front, and soon the concert was underway.

Bright Wings was a popular band, well-known across Europe for what was called electro-swing music, and it immediately had the place rocking. Tommy and Erica danced and sang, until they were spotted by the lead singer and called to the stage. And there, before 2,000 concertgoers, they danced a 1940s swing dance that had the concert fans standing and applauding.

"Where did you learn to dance like that?" Erica said, when the song finished.

"I have an aunt who loves swing music." He almost added "Gavin's mum," but stopped short, remembering that no one except Angus, Mrs. Bixby, and Dr. McNeill knew Gavin was his cousin.

"You should tell her she's a marvelous teacher," Erica said, laughing.

The Broughby team had cheered them on. Julia recorded the entire dance on her mobile, thinking it would make a great Facebook post. When she uploaded it, she noted the connection to the team at Broughby.

They left Kirkwall at 10 on Sunday morning, with a lunch already packed on board, and soon arrived back at the Broughby ferry landing.

On Monday at the classroom session, Tommy said that they'd catalogue and photograph what they'd found in the tomb but halt the work after that. "We'll have less than two weeks before the program officially ends, and you have papers and reports to write, as well as the final lectures by our professors. We're going to recover the tomb with the stone, and then we'll plot out what we do for next spring and summer. If we do another program like this one, you'll be the first to know, and we'd welcome back any and all of you. We'll also be working with the foundation for a small, permanent staff here, with a site manager, a security program, and perhaps a groundskeeper or two.

"When we decide to announce the news about the tomb, we'll let each of you know ahead of time. And you might need to consider the possibility of being asked for media interviews, because this will likely be major news for a time and your schools might want publicity.

"This has been a great project. You've all been simply brilliant."

That afternoon, Tommy and Erica sat on a large rock on the pebble beach below the manor.

"You and I have some talking to do. I want to talk about life after project."

"I want life after project, Tommy."

"After I turn my thesis in, I'll likely be partially here and partially in Edinburgh, getting everything in motion for next year. I'll also have to make a trip to Norway; that Norse variant we found on the tomb might also be at a couple of sites near Bergen. Professor McNeill will remain involved in some way, and Professor Elliot is talking about a student group from his university to help with the work next year. And we have to find a site manager."

"What about Gavin? He knows the work, and he's got administrative skills, I think we've all seen that. And he's told a few of us about his ministry and that he's leaving it, but he's not sure what he'll be doing next. Even if it were for a temporary period, he might be ideal."

"That's a smashing idea. I'll talk with him. But then there's us. You've your last year at Cambridge, I've the work here and then my thesis defense at the end of November. And you're going to finish that book you're reading to us and get it published. Erica, you're too important to me now. I'm not letting go. I want our relationship to grow. I want to be part of your life, a big part, if you'll let me."

She leaned against his shoulder. "You're already a big part of my life, Tommy," she said, "and getting bigger all the time. I want that to continue."

"We'll call it life after Broughby. I don't want to plan everything out, but I do want to see you on a regular basis, like all the time."

She laughed and kissed his cheek. "We'll work it out, but that will be the target. And now I'm going back to my room and get ready for supper."

He remained for a few minutes, watching the waves come into shore, and then returned to the manor.

Early Wednesday morning, Tommy, Noah, and Simon were in the dining room, sitting at a small table away from the main dining table. Tommy had called them together.

"I want to tell Rikki my identity. The project is nearly at an end, and this will all be public as soon as I turn in my thesis. There's no good reason for her not to know, and she won't go shouting it from the rooftops."

"I'll need to check with the palace," Simon said. "I'll send a text now. I don't expect there to be a problem."

The two professors and the other students started arriving for breakfast. Gavin and Angus were both helping in the kitchen.

"And I want leave to tell the rest of the team before they head back," Tommy said. "It's only a few days."

"I'll check that as well," Simon said, "but I really don't think there will be any objections. Mr. Mitchell may want to do a quick courtesy check with your father."

In her room with her stomach rumbling for breakfast, Erica had just completed a last look at a report and submitted it by email to the two professors. She looked up as Julia hurried into the room, holding her open laptop.

"Erica, I need to show you something. I filmed your dance with Tommy at Kirkwall and posted it on my Facebook page."

Erica could see Julia looked troubled. "What's wrong?"

"It's been shared. It's been shared a lot. Like tens of thousands of times. Several news media have picked it up."

"It must've been a slow news day. A dance?"

"You need to see it. Did you know about this?"

Looking at Julia's iPad, Erica saw the headline from the Glasgow newspaper, "HRH Prince Thomas Cuts a Mean Rug at Kirkwall."

"There must be some mistake," she said, "or a misidentification." She saw the other stories, from BBC, ITV, Edinburgh, and several from London.

Then it all clicked in her mind. Her face turned red, and she rushed from the room.

"There," Simon said in the dining room, looking at his mobile, "I've sent it. Mr. Mitchell will get back to us shortly, I'm sure."

Erica burst through the door and nearly ran to their table.

Tommy could see she was trembling with anger. "Rikki, what's wrong?"

She pointed to Noah and Simon. "Who are they?"

Everyone in the room turned towards them, and Mrs. Bixby, Gavin, and Angus came from the kitchen, bearing food trays but stopping when they heard Erica. Julia arrived, following Erica.

"Who are they? What are their real names?"

"Their real names are Noah Bennington and Simon Fredericks."

"And who do they work for?"

Tommy stood. "They work for Buckingham Palace Security."

"Buckingham Palace Security! Why do we need Buckingham Palace Security on Broughby?"

Tommy looked at her calmly. "Because of me. Because I'm Prince Thomas Michael McLaren Kent-Hughes, and my father is King Michael."

There were audible gasps from around the room.

"You lied to me!" she said, shouting. "You lied to all of us! We thought you were a student like the rest of us when you're HRH Prince Thomas! You knew how I felt about liars; you knew it! I'd been down that road with liars before! And you did it anyway to protect yourself and your precious royal connections. What else have you lied about?"

"Rikki, I had to –"

"Don't even start! And don't call me Rikki! We're done! We're finished! I never want to see you again!" She turned and rushed from the room in tears.

Tommy started after her when Simon stopped him, catching his arm. He handed him his mobile. "It's Mr. Mitchell. And he needs to speak to you. It's urgent."

Still staring after Erica, he took the mobile. "It's Tommy."

"Your royal highness," Mitchell said, "I need to alert you to two things. First, the video of you and the young lady dancing has gone viral on social media, and a few enterprising reporters saw it and recognized you. Several online news stories have been posted, and all make the connection to you and the island of Broughby."

"I didn't know there was a video."

"Mr. Lanham has sent the link from palace communications. Second, several reporters and television camera crews are on the ferry that's due to dock at Broughby in exactly one hour. They got up rather early in the morning to catch the boat."

"Mr. Mitchell, I can't have the news media invading Broughby, not yet, anyway. We're not set up to handle it and the excavation hasn't been secured." Tommy felt his heart beating rapidly; everything was going wrong that could go wrong.

"I have Mr. Lanham in the office with me, and I'm putting you on speaker phone. He has a suggestion for how you might deal with this."

"Mr. Mitchell, I'm turning on the speaker on my mobile as well so Simon and Noah can listen."

"Your royal highness, it's Jay Lanham. You've got a gaggle of media on their way via the ferry. If your concern is the project, I'd suggest you meet them at the ferry. You're waiting to board the return to Kirkwall. You're surprised by all the attention, but the project is winding down and you're headed back to Edinburgh. That immediately poses a quandary for the media. Do they stay on the ferry and return with you, or do they stay on Broughby to see what stories they might ferret out? Since the next ferry won't be for two days, my guess is they'll return with you, and it wouldn't hurt to mention the ferry schedule.

"The downside, of course, is that they have you for several hours on the ferry, until you arrive in Kirkwall. And they'll be tired and cranky. They'll want individual interviews, and they'll want a group press conference. It'll keep them away from the project, but you're the sacrifice."

Tommy glanced at his watch. "The ferry docks in 45 minutes." He looked at Simon and Noah. "Okay, the ferry it will be. Noah, I need you to stay on Broughby, just in case any of the media remain and try to get hold of Rikki. Simon, you'll need to come with me to Kirkwall. Mr. Lanham, I need 15 minutes to get some things together, and then Noah will drive us to the ferry. I'll call you while we're driving, and I'd appreciate a crash course on how I might best handle this."

"I'll be here." Lanham powered off.

"Julia," Tommy said, "can you find Erica and ask her to meet me at the van?" Julia nodded and rushed from the room.

Tommy hurried upstairs, accompanied by Noah and Simon. He grabbed his laptop and began stuffing some clothes in a carryall. "Noah, I have some files here that I'll need but not today. Can you make sure they're boxed and come with you when you leave?"

The group rushed back downstairs. Noah climbed into the driver's seat and Simon, with his own bag, got in behind the passenger seat.

Tommy stood waiting, hoping to see Julia and Erica at any moment. Julia finally came running through the front door.

"Tommy, I can't find her. She's not in our room, she's not down at the dig or the shore. She may have gone into the hills."

Noah leaned from the driver's seat. "Tommy, we have to go. The ferry arrives in less than 20 minutes."

Tommy glanced at the front door and then turned to Noah. He climbed in the passenger seat.

"Let's go."

As the van got underway, Tommy called Lanham in London.

"It's Tommy, Mr. Lanham. Anything you can do to guide me in Operation Sacrifice will be greatly appreciated." He listened intently, taking notes, occasionally asking a question and then answering questions posed to him. They arrived at the landing, but the ferry wasn't yet in sight.

Tommy thanked Jay Lanham and rang off.

"Noah, I need you to do something. Give the painting to Erica. She'll likely refuse it, so tell her I said if she wouldn't take it, I told you to destroy it." He looked toward the area where the ferry would appear. "And you probably need to leave with the van before the ferry arrives, so it looks like we've been waiting impatiently for it. The reporters don't need to know there's a van on Broughby."

Noah handed Tommy his sunglasses, "Here, wear these. They'll think you're trying to sneak past them. And Tommy, remember you're a Kent-Hughes, and you have more leadership abilities in your little finger than most people have in their entire bodies."

Tommy hugged him. "I'll see you in about 10 days, if not sooner."

Two minutes after Noah left, the ferry came into view.

Simon patted his carryon bag. "Mrs. Bixby packed a quick lunch and a thermos of tea. I have it with me."

"Bless Mrs. Bixby." Tommy stared at the incoming ferry.

Phenomenally angry, Erica had gone up into the hills behind the manor. She followed the path that she knew would eventually lead to Tommy's cottage. She had no reason, or rational reason, for going to the cottage, but she was drawn there. She didn't stop to think that it might be locked until she arrived. She moved the lever, expecting locked resistance, but the door opened.

She sat by the now-cold fireplace. She rocked herself back and forth, crying, until she remembered the conversation they'd had here. She'd asked him what his father did, and he asked about hers. And they'd misled each other, probably for the same reasons. She'd done the same thing she'd accused him of.

Then she asked herself if that changed how she felt about him. She knew the answer.

It was time to go back to the manor and find Tommy. And apologize and talk. But first apologize.

An hour later, she reached the manor's terrace, to find Julia crying and Mrs. Bixby trying to console her.

Erica sat next to Julia. "What's wrong?"

Julia shook her head. "This is my fault. I filmed that stupid video, and I posted it and linked it to Broughby. Any idiot who knew what the prince looked like would've been able to pick him out. All of this blew up because of me."

Mrs. Bixby patted her hand.

Erica stood. "Julia, I have to apologize to Tommy. I hid the same thing from him that he hid from me, and I'm nothing but a hypocrite for getting angry at him. What's done is done about the video. Do you know where he is?"

"He's on the ferry to Kirkwall," Mrs. Bixby said, and explained what had happened.

"Six hours with the news media?"

Mrs. Bixby nodded. "A man at Buckingham Palace suggested it. They had to do something dramatic to draw the media away from here. We weren't even remotely prepared for reporters and camera crews swarming the manor and the excavation site. The tomb is still uncovered except for the tarpaulin."

Erica walked inside, followed by Mrs. Bixby and a still tearful Julia. She found the rest of the team in the rec room, focused on the large-screen television. She watched for a few seconds before she realized what it was. One of the television networks was broadcasting a live interview with Tommy on the ferry.

"He's never been interviewed before," Noah said. "He's really good. He looks so at ease and polished." He turned and saw Erica. "Hello, Erica. Tommy tried to find you before he left, but he had to make the ferry."

She watched him. Noah was right. Tommy was good, almost as if he did interviews for a living. He answered questions and raised interesting points the reporters didn't know to ask. He made jokes, mostly at his own expense. He talked about the Celts and the Vikings, noting they sounded like American sports teams, and explained what they were trying to learn at the dig. He laughed with the reporters, and she could see the smiles all around.

Only once did she see the barest hesitation. He was asked about his dancing partner at the concert, and if there was any sort of relationship. She watched him smile as he adroitly deflected the question.

"She's a member of our team, one of 12 students from around Britain. It's a good group. Actually, what I should say is it's a brilliant group, the best team I could've been part of. Working with all of them has been a real blessing."

The live broadcast was ended by the reporter at that point, with a basic summary and extremely kind words about how charming and personable the prince was, "the most private and least-known of King Michael's children." The report then changed to a flashback of Queen Sarah's funeral, when the six-year-old Prince Thomas had kissed his mother's coffin.

Erica felt the tears in her eyes.

Noah walked up to her. "Tommy asked me to give you something."

Expecting a note or short letter, she followed him upstairs to Tommy's room and waited at the doorway. Noah brought her the wrapped painting.

She stared. "I can't accept this."

"He wanted you to have it."

"I just can't accept it, Noah."

"Tommy said that if you refused it, I was to destroy it."

She gasped. The tears spilled over, and she finally reached to accept the painting.

"Did he say anything else?"

"No, I left before the ferry arrived. I'm sorry. We had just sent a message to palace security when you confronted him. He wanted to tell you who he really was, and we had to get clearance from security and the king."

Carrying the painting, Erica slowly walked to her room. She knew the painting conveyed a message, and it sounded a lot like goodbye.

When the ferry arrived at Kirkwall, several palace security agents and local police officers were waiting. Tommy and Simon were escorted through the crowd, with people waving, applauding, and shouting questions about where he learned to dance. Tommy was quickly learning that he was now likely to be recognized everywhere.

In the car to the small Kirkwall airfield, he realized how utterly exhausted he was. The reporters had all been friendly, with few if any barbed questions or comments. But after an almost solid six hours of a group interview and then 12 individual interviews, he felt mugged.

But he said a prayer, silently asking God to bless Jay Lanham, who had anticipated every single question he'd been asked and explained it all in that short 15-minute phone call. The project had been protected.

Reaching the airfield, the car drove directly on to the tarmac and up to the waiting plane. Tommy saw it was Michael's royal plane. "I take it we're going to see my father?"

Simon nodded. "Next stop is City Airport, London. Your father needs to see you."

"Lovely."

He had no idea of what to expect from Michael, but at least he'd have a chance to thank Jay Lanham and Ryan Mitchell in person.

When they were on board and seated, the steward walked up, holding out a warm, moist face cloth in tongs. "Would you like something to drink, sir? We also have light snacks."

"Some tea would be nice. No, change that. I'd like a small whisky."

Ninety minutes later, Tommy arrived at Buckingham Palace. The last time he'd been here was a year before, when he came down for a short visit from Edinburgh.

Ryan Mitchell and Jay Lanham met the car at the arrival portico in the courtyard. They both greeted Tommy with a nod of their heads.

"My profound thanks to you both," Tommy said. "The initial warning and that instant media training prevented the disruption of a very important chunk of work. You'll know eventually what it is, but I owe you both more than I could ever repay." He turned to Simon, standing behind him. "Simon, thanks for all your help. You kept the dogs at bay on the ferry."

Smiling, Mitchell nodded. "Your father is waiting in his office, sir."

"An official discussion, is it? Well, I can't keep his majesty waiting."

"You did very well, indeed, with the media, sir," Lanham said.

"Thanks to you, Mr. Lanham. Only thanks to you."

Tommy made his way to Michael's office in the administrative wing. He remembered the night he walked these same hallways, holding the pictures of the soldiers to show it wasn't porn in his email and then overhearing the discussion about autism.

He knocked, heard his father's "Come in," and walked in. He was immediately relieved to see his stepmother Mary sitting by his father's desk.

"Your majesties." Tommy bowed his head, following protocol, and then walked forward to embrace Mary. His father came from behind the desk to shake his hand.

Michael grinned. "Our newest media celebrity."

Mary smiled. "You look wonderful, Tommy, so tanned and healthy. Obviously, you've been working outside."

"It's the dig. We have a tent over the excavation area, but we're still outside a lot."

Mary went into mom mode. "Sunscreen?"

"Every day. The team, too."

"We watched you on TV on the ferry," Michael said. "You're a natural at this. Jay told me you've never done an interview before."

"We had 15 minutes before the ferry arrived. Mr. Lanham focused everything, and it was a huge help. I've thanked him profusely."

"Have you considered doing more of this, possibly for family appearances?"

"No, Dad, I haven't. I think this was something unusual. I don't expect most of my work to result in this kind of media interest, or at least I hope not often."

Michael shook his head. "I wasn't talking about your work. I was talking more about royal appearances and public events."

Tommy looked from Michael to Mary and back again; his stepmother was looking down at her lap.

"We've discussed this before, Dad. You said we each had the freedom to pursue our skills and gifts. Sophie has her Spanish studies, Helen is on the stage, and even Hank is seriously involved in his business ventures. And Jason has his art and the Royal Academy and Jim his military career."

"I know, Tommy, and that hasn't changed. I'd just like you to think about the possibility of doing some royal family things. That's all. We can talk about it another time. So, your uncle tells me you may be up to major things on that island of yours. He hasn't said much, but he said it may be exciting for the history world."

Tommy nodded. "We've a lot of work to do yet. I'm returning to Edinburgh to start arrangements for a full-time crew at the site, then a week in Norway to meet with experts there and check some runes. After that, I go back to Broughby for some weeks. I have to manage it all around my thesis, but it's doable." He paused. "And, yes, there are some pretty exciting things coming. We'll likely have some intense media interest for a time, so all those interviews today might have some benefit after all."

"David also says Gavin is doing incredibly well."

"He is. He seems a whole different person than when he arrived."

"That's wonderful. One other thing, Tommy. I've asked Mr. Mitchell to replace your personal security man. Simon sent in his report, and he made very clear that, given the circumstances, he would've done the same thing. But the fact is that security protocol was violated. We need to make a change."

"No. You can un-ask Mr. Mitchell, Dad, because Noah remains in place. We made a split-second decision, and I overruled Noah's own objections. I was the one who violated security protocol. Because I did, a young woman is alive today."

"Do you think you're overstating what happened?"

"You weren't there. I knew exactly where to find her. We'd no time to get three women back to safety and then go look for the fourth. The storm was upon us, and it was fierce. I found her hanging on the side of the ridge, holding on to a shrub, at the edge of a drop-off of more than 50 feet. No, Noah stays my security agent. If it's not Noah, then I'll refuse to accept any security protection."

The room felt heavy with tension.

Mary intervened. "Michael, you have Trevor, Josh, and Jay coming any time now. I'm going to borrow Tommy to walk with me in the garden. We can talk again at supper." She stood, and Tommy stood with her. He nodded to his father and left the room with Mary.

Neither said anything until they crossed the palace terrace and were walking on the gravel path toward the trees in the garden.

"How's Mark? We stay in touch by email and the occasional phone call, but I haven't seen him since I've been at Broughby."

"He's fine." Mary slipped her arm through Tommy's. "He's finishing engineering school this coming year, and then he's on active duty with the Royal Army Engineers."

"I miss him. I miss that laugh of his."

Mary laughed. "It is rather distinctive."

"And loud."

"And loud." She paused for a moment. "Tommy, I'll talk with Michael about Noah. I thought we were past that. Michael relies greatly on Simon and even Simon said the right call was made. Your father has a lot on his mind."

"We're like oil and water. It's been this way ever since I can remember. We make progress and then something like that happens and blows it all apart again."

"There's something of a royal problem, Tommy. It was behind his question about royal appearances and likely the comment about Noah. Sophie had to renounce her claim to the throne to marry Charlie, as you know; the Spanish royal court insisted, and they were right to do so. Helen told Michael that she's done the same; she and Willem are getting very close to being engaged, even with things being a mess in the Netherlands right now. His sister the queen hasn't been heard from in weeks, and the Muslim government may have her under house arrest. If a revolt happens, and it's successful, Willem may be the next king, and Helen has already gone with her heart and signed away her succession rights."

"I don't understand. What does this have to do with me? Hank's the Prince of Wales."

"Two weeks ago, Hannah miscarried for the third time."

"Oh, Mum, I'm so sorry to hear that. I know how much they both wanted this baby."

"This time, there were complications. The doctors had to perform a hysterectomy."

They were in the palace woods now, and they continued walking in silence. Mary said nothing, allowing the implications to sink in.

Tommy stopped. "Wait. That means –"

"Yes, it means a lot of things. The news has been contained so far, but that's what Michael's meeting is about right now. Hank and Hannah won't be able to have children."

They resumed walking, reaching the small palace lake. The water was catching a few dying rays from the sun.

"Michael wanted to tell you himself, but he was worried. Tommy, he's as aware as you are of the distance between the two of you. It pains him deeply, and he blames himself entirely. He tried to explain to me what happened, but if you haven't lived it, it doesn't seem to make much sense. I still shudder at that awful scene at Christmas when Michael nearly wrecked the holiday."

"It's why I stayed on Broughby this past Christmas. I didn't want a repetition."

"The entire family, including your father, suspected as much. Ma spent a considerable amount of time glaring at him over your absence."

"It has to do with Mummy. It goes back to when I was four, and she let me watch her paint in the studio. I think they were in a period when the marriage was strained; he was gone a lot of the time because of being Government. He wasn't happy when he discovered that I was the only person she allowed to see her paint. I think in some strange, weird way, he thought I'd taken his place in her affections.

Even stranger, he may've been right. But you can't place the blame for all that on a four-year-old."

"That fits with what I understand. You've explained it more clearly than Michael, but it was something very similar he tried to tell me. He said that, when you were 13, you told him that it might be best to accept there was this issue between you that couldn't be resolved."

"I remember. He didn't say anything at all. Which I took as agreement."

They sat on a bench by the lake.

"Hank has taken Hannah to the Cayman Islands for a holiday. They both needed time to process what's happened and what it means. She suggested a divorce, but Hank said absolutely not."

"I'd be shocked if he accepted something like that. He loves Hannah dearly, more than himself, more than the throne. That option is off the table, if I know my brother."

"And you're right. Divorce would also be problematic from the Church of England's perspective. And there are options. One option is that nothing changes. He continues being the Prince of Wales, becomes king one day, and then the throne would pass to you as next in line or your children, or to you and then David if you had no children. And David's only 7. Speaking of David, he knew you were coming, and he's desperate to see you."

"We talk on Facetime once a week. He keeps me up to date on the family."

"He was the one who showed your dancing video to Michael. He was so proud he had such a cool brother." She laughed. "He didn't realize what the video had set into motion. You said in the interview that the girl was a member of the team. Is there more about her that you didn't say?"

"Yes, a lot more. But the relationship blew up this morning when she saw the video and the news stories. Dad's insistence on my alias caused a train wreck for us. Well, that's not quite fair. It's more honest to say she believed I'd been lying about who I was, and she'd been through a relationship that ended abruptly because of lying. And she's something of an anti-monarchist, so my title didn't help." He paused. "And it's likely to help even less now."

"I mentioned one option Hank is considering. There's a second one, and it's the one he considers best. He would publicly explain what's happened, resign his position as Prince of Wales, and sign away his succession rights, clearing the way immediately for you. He thinks anything else would be grossly unfair to you." She paused. "After a lot of discussion and prayer, Michael agrees with him, and Hannah supports him on this. To be frank, Tommy, I think this is the best option as well."

"Dad had you tell me because he knew I wouldn't yell at you?"

Mary laughed. "Perhaps. But seriously, one thing that does need to happen soon, regardless of what the decision is, is your investiture as Duke of York. Michael wants to do it after you submit your thesis, so it'd be early October."

Tommy sat in silence, seemingly lost in thought. "All right. We can go forward with the investiture. That would happen anyway. As for the other, I want to talk with Hank and Hannah, and I need to talk with Uncle David."

"Michael thought you might seek advice from David."

"I've been doing that most of my life, because he was there. That's not a commentary; it's just a fact. All right, I'll tell Dad at dinner I need to talk with Hank and Uncle David, that I'll go forward with the investiture as Duke of York, and that I'm open to what all this might mean. But I can't get my head around this yet. I always believed my future would be in teaching and research, and this is a lot to digest. I'll also tell him that Noah Bennington remains my security officer." He smiled. "I thought I was being brought to the palace to have my knuckles rapped for the media feeding frenzy or embarrassing the monarchy with my dancing. I'd no idea I was walking into this." He looked up at the dying rays of the sun in the sky. "Mum, I'm feeling a bit overwhelmed at the moment. I didn't expect to find this in my script. This was never the plan." And then he remembered what seemed like a call to the priesthood, years before.

"Perhaps it's God's plan, Tommy. It was my plan to never marry again, but God obviously had other ideas."

He took her hand. "What I'd like to do right now, is sit on the floor with my little brother David and play one of his card games."

Which is exactly what he did. Tommy was overwhelmed with the welcome from his half-brother, who looked extraordinarily like both Hank and Michael. David had been born a year after Michael and Mary had married. In one of those strange things that happen in families, he'd latched onto Tommy as his favorite sibling.

Sitting in the living area of the loft, they'd just finished a round of the card game "War" when Michael arrived after his staff meeting. Tommy looked up at his father, and he saw the worry lines on

Michael's face and the almost completely silver-gray hair. He realized that, on top of everything else his father dealt with, he now had a dynastic succession crisis. And the solution to the crisis was sitting on the floor playing a card game.

"Mr. Malone is bringing supper," Mary said, referring to the palace chef. "David, time to wash up." David scampered off with his mother.

"You and Mary talked?"

"We did. We should schedule the investiture for York. I know we can do the ceremony anywhere, but I suggest we do it at York Cathedral."

"A good plan. As for what you and Mary discussed, Trevor Barry is my key advisor on this, and he suggested two things. First, that we need to give you time to consider everything. Second, a meeting, perhaps when we're in York, you, me, and Hank, perhaps with Trevor, Josh, and Jay sitting in, to see what we do going forward. Tommy, I'm not trying to pressure you into making the decision I want. I want you to do what you think is best."

"What do you think is best, Dad? It's important for me to know."

Michael didn't answer immediately. Before he did, Tommy could see his father was fighting some internal battle, and he assumed it was because of the succession falling to him, Tommy, the child his father felt the least close to and the heir he didn't really want.

"I think Hank is right, Tommy. It would be best all-around if he publicly stepped away from the succession."

"But do you think it would be best for me to step up to it? You see what I'm asking here, Dad. I'm asking for your blessing. I feel like I've never had it. I'm not asking what you think because you have no other choice, and because Hank decided to step down, so let's go with the least bad alternative, the spare heir. I'm asking you if you can see me, Tommy, in your place one day, and that you see it as a good thing."

Neither Tommy nor Michael noticed that Mary and David had returned and were both listening.

"I'll answer you honestly, Tommy. My expectation has always been that Hank would succeed me. He was the first-born, and that's what happens, even with my own irregular succession to the throne. I didn't expect anything else. I've come to grips with the reality that my expectation had to change. That was the first step, and it was hard, but it was about me and your brother. The second has been actually easier. You'd have my full blessing, support, and approval to be king after me."

Tommy stood there, saying nothing, tears in his eyes.

"And I was wrong about Noah, Tommy. I've told Mr. Mitchell to cancel what I asked."

"Thank you, Dad. For all of it."

Returning to Edinburgh, Tommy engaged in a flurry of work related to Broughby. Ads were placed for staff; when Gavin arrived home, looking healthy and rested, Tommy talked with him at the Hughes' house in St. Andrews, and then with him and Emily, about considering the site manager position for the manor and excavation site. It took them all of a day to decide; Gavin accepted the offer and took over coordinating the staff applicant interviews.

Tommy stayed with the Hughes for two days, and he spent one long afternoon with his uncle walking the beach.

"It's easy for me to give advice," David said. "But you asked, and what I think is this. As much as my nephew has pushed and strained against the royal ropes that bind him, he knows he's bound. He knows he's a Kent-Hughes, and he knows what responsibilities he has because of that. That's what I think, Tommy, and I think you know it, too." He smiled. "And I think we now know what it was you were being called to six years ago."

From St. Andrews, Tommy met Noah at Aberdeen, and they took the ferry to Bergen. Meeting with a professor at the University of Bergen, they were able to confirm the Norse variant on the runes and complete a translation. Tommy emailed the news and the translation to the two professors, who'd returned from Broughby to their universities.

A week later, Tommy, accompanied by Noah, took the train from Edinburgh to London. At King's Cross Station, a palace car was waiting, and they were driven to the family home in Kent where Michael's birth parents had lived. Hank and Hannah had taken on the place as their weekend home.

Alerted by the driver, his brother and sister-in-law were waiting on the front porch as the car pulled into the drive. They escorted Tommy to the terrace, where a table was set for dinner. Noah went to the security office.

"Something to drink?" said Hank.

"White wine, if it's really dry."

"We've a Sauvignon Blanc from New Zealand that should do the trick."

Tommy looked at his brother. Hank seemed every inch the successor to their father. Not quite as tall as Tommy, he had the Kent-Hughes build, and moved with both grace and strength. Tommy knew his brother's charm; he also knew the charm opened into deep sincerity. And Hank, like Michael, was an Olympian, having led Britain's football team to a string of upset victories at the Olympic Games in Chicago and captured the gold medal. That summer, Tommy had just graduated ICS and was preparing to enter St. Andrews, and he and Mark had cheered Hank on. The British public had gone wild.

"So," Hank said, "have you thought much about all this?"

"I'm thankful I have my Ph.D. thesis to worry over. Otherwise, I'd be going crazy. And yes, I thought about it. Almost every waking moment. Hank, I never expected this. I never even considered it. You didn't just look and act the part. You were the part."

Hannah remained quiet, while Hank sipped his wine before he spoke. "Do you remember the story of Samuel anointing David in the Old Testament?"

Tommy nodded. "Saul had lost God's favor, and Samuel was told to anoint a new king."

"God sends him to Jesse's family in Bethlehem. And Samuel has Jesse put the sons through an inspection. And he sees one after the other, and he thinks, 'Surely, this one, Lord?' But the Lord tells him not to look at outward appearance, because God looks at the heart. I may have looked and acted the role, Tommy, but I don't think I ever really had the heart for it. I was having serious doubts well before Hannah and I married. Even after going through the investiture in Wales, I felt like I was kidding myself. I was going through the motions; this wasn't me. I wasn't comfortable in this Prince of Wales skin. My head and my heart were in the City; what set me on fire was how to harness investment and wealth to help people flourish." He paused. "But you do have the heart for it. Even when you were just a boy, you seemed like you'd been called to it. You were always the serious one, the wise one. You understood things long before the rest of us did. You never said a word, but I have the sense that you know what I'm talking about."

"Hank's speaking the truth, Tommy," Hannah said. "Ever since the ceremony in Wales, Hank's been growing more and more quiet, almost withdrawn. I thought it was concern over the miscarriages, but that wasn't it at all. Right before the last one, he told me that being the heir didn't sit right, that something was wrong. He'd do it if he had to, but it wasn't something he wanted or felt called to. When we were in the Cayman Islands, he told me that as hard as it might sound, perhaps what had happened was actually a blessing, almost a confirmation that he'd been right."

"Of course," Hank said, "it all falls on you. It's easy for me to run around feeling free and liberated, getting to do what I want, when I've simply passed the ball and chain on to you."

"I understand what you're telling me. I don't think I consider it a ball and chain."

"How do you look at it, Tommy?"

"Something happened about the time I graduated from ICS. I'd a distinct impression that I was being called to do something. I thought I was being called to the priesthood, but that seemed off."

"The priesthood?"

"It's a long story, but I believed I was being called to something I was born to do. But I didn't understand what that was. Uncle David told me to bide my time, that if God was calling me, I'd be tracked down in God's time, not my own."

Hank smiled. "You were being called, but it wasn't to the priesthood."

Tommy turned in his thesis in early September, two weeks before deadline, but continued his readings and study to prepare for his thesis defense in November. He was invested as Duke of York the first week of October, the ceremony including a carriage parade to York Cathedral, with Michael and Mary in the lead carriage, followed by Hank and Hannah, and then Tommy, who had the beaming seven-year-old David ride with him. Sophie and Helen rode with Sophie's husband, Crown Prince Juan Carlos of Spain. Jason, Jim, and Mark had been invited to ride but all decided to wait, along with David and Betsy Hughes, their daughter Eleanor, Angus, and Mark, at the cathedral. Gavin and Emily were in Edinburgh, having just had their second son, whom they named Thomas David Hughes.

Tommy's decision to have the ceremony in York was a good one; Yorkshire turned out, and the streets were packed with cheering citizens waving British flags. After the ceremony and before heading to the reception, Tommy, with Noah at his side, plunged into the crowd in front of the cathedral, shaking hands, thanking people for coming, and posing for numerous selfies and photos of him holding babies.

Hank, standing next to Michael on the cathedral steps, leaned and whispered, "My decision is the right one. I'd never have thought of wading into the crowd. It's like something you'd do, or should I say, like something you actually did in front of the palace years before he was born? Is it possible to imprint experience on DNA?" He smiled. "I never realized this before, Dad, but of all of us, Tommy's the most like you."

Michael nodded. His mind was on the meeting after the reception, but watching Tommy in the crowd, Michael felt close to tears. He was remembering the words spoken in a hospital.

The post-reception meeting involved the entire family, including David and Betsy, along with Josh, Trevor, and Jay. Michael turned the meeting over to Hank.

"Not all of you know that Hannah and I are in the process of adopting a child. The fact is that we're unable to have natural-born children. There's been considerable personal heartbreak, but there are also serious implications for the succession. We've considered a number of options, and Hannah and I, in consultation with Dad and a long weekend talk with Tommy, have decided that, at some point in the near future, I'll resign my position as Prince of Wales and renounce my succession rights."

The group looked shocked. Even Tommy felt the shock of hearing Hank say the actual words.

"I could remain as Prince of Wales, and then Tommy would follow me on my death. Hannah and I both believe doing that would be terribly unfair, not only to the monarchy and Dad, but especially to Tommy. He and his eventual future family would be locked into limbo, possibly for decades. We feel profoundly that doing that to him would be wrong, and it would be wrong for Britain. We decided, I decided, that something better was needed.

"We're not sure when or how we will make the public announcement. Tommy, in fact, has asked that we consider delaying it at least a year, if possible, and preferably two or more. We'll just have to see. For the time being, we're proceeding as if nothing's changed. We're aware of published reports, mostly gossip columns, wondering when the Prince and Princess of Wales will have children. We expect that to continue, and Mr. Lanham here will help us deal with that."

Hannah spoke. "What Hank isn't saying, out of kindness to his wife, is that, after my last miscarriage a few months ago, complications arose, and the doctors had to perform a hysterectomy. If they hadn't, I likely would've died, and Hank made the decision while I was in surgery."

Helen, sitting next to Hannah with tears in her eyes, reached for her sister-in-law's hand. David, sitting next to Tommy, put his hand on top of his nephew's.

"So, there we are," said Hank.

All eyes in the room turned to Tommy.

"I never thought I'd be in this position. I always thought I'd end up teaching at university. As much as that might be my personal preference, I realized I've a larger responsibility to the family and the monarchy, and to the country. I've spent so long trying not to be a royal that it's completely disorienting to find myself in this position. And unless and until I marry and have children, this puts my little brother David in a completely unexpected position as well.

"I need your prayers. I know I'm supposed to act regal, but I find all of this to be rather terrifying. I'll rely on Hank and Dad, and God, to help me, but I truly need your prayers."

Tommy and Erica

In early November, two weeks before Tommy's scheduled thesis defense, word began to leak about a major archaeological find on Broughby in the Orkneys. The initial news reports had pieces of correct details – a tomb, some Viking artifacts – but missed the larger story and context. Eventually, reporters from various archaeology and historical journals pursued the story with Professors Elliott and McNeill. After a telephone call with Tommy, the two professors referred reporters to the new Duke of York.

Tommy responded to the queries and a few more generated in general news media. He confirmed the discovery of what appeared to be a tomb and what looked to be 9th century Viking runes. He said work was continuing, but it would be some time before investigations were conclusive enough to publish a full study.

The editor of *The British Archaeology Quarterly* contacted Tommy and asked for an interim report on the work at Broughby. Tommy contacted the professors and the team; he wrote an abbreviated paper that would be published in January, some six weeks after his Ph.D. defense and assuming his thesis was accepted and approved. He and Noah traveled to Broughby to meet with the community there, explaining what was likely to come. They also allowed anyone interested to come to the tomb site and view what the team had discovered. The entire village accepted.

The stories heightened interest in Tommy's thesis and the meeting for his defense. Normally, these meetings were held in conference rooms or small classrooms. The History Department at

Edinburgh sensed a publicity opportunity and announced the defense would be held in one of the university's large lecture halls and open to the public. Tommy was put out at first but realized there was little he could do. He worked with Jay Lanham on public and media considerations, and he spent considerable time being coached by his uncle, who'd read Tommy's thesis.

"Remember most of all," David said, "that your panel is three professors with vast knowledge of your subject. Your thesis not only challenges what they know, it also challenges a large amount of their own work. Make every effort to note how the clues and signposts in their research and books pointed you in the direction you took."

"But that's true. That's exactly what happened. It happened with the work by Dr McNeill and Dr. Elliot as well. I even cite their works in the text, footnotes, and bibliography."

"That's excellent. Don't make it obvious but communicate that clearly. It'll give them a reason for having some ownership in your thesis. And remember they're likely as upset as you are with the decision to make this a public event."

The lecture hall, in descending theater style, seated 400, and it was packed. A roped-off area was reserved for the Broughby team, including Mrs. Bixby and Angus. Angus had joined the permanent staff at Broughby, responsible for site infrastructure and working under Gavin. Directly behind the team's seating was another reserved section for news media. A BBC crew set up to film.

Tommy entered the hall and made his way to the raised platform. He'd sit at a small table facing the three professors. They'd enter last, quiet the crowd, explain how the defense worked, and remind them that it was not an entertainment but a serious discussion. Applause and noise were not allowed.

As he waited for the professors to arrive, he smiled at the team, all of whom were grinning, giving him a thumbs up. Dr. McCrae had joined them; Noah must have slipped him in, Tommy thought.

One seat was empty.

He hadn't heard from Erica since the day of the media on the ferry. He also hadn't tried to contact her. He felt an ache, but he knew if she was angry about his royal connection then, the investiture as Duke of York would have only made it worse. And then there was the other news to eventually come. But she'd been invited as a member of the team, and he felt deeply disappointed she wasn't there.

With less than a minute before the start, amidst all of the movement of people taking seats, he didn't notice four palace security agents rise from seats on the end of a row near the back and four people take their place. King Michael, Henry, Prince of Wales, Prince David, and Jay Lanham sat down. The young prince was nearly beside himself with excitement to see his brother, although he figured he'd be bored to tears with what sounded a lot like school.

Right on time, at 10 a.m. sharp, the three professors in their academic robes entered from the rear of the hall. Tommy's thesis defense started.

At 11:35, the professor chairing the session announced a break and said they would return within the half hour.

David spotted Michael and the others in the royal party and walked up the steps to where they sat.

"Well?" Michael said. "What do you think?" Hank and Jay leaned forward to hear David's response.

"Tommy was magnificent, Michael. I've never seen a better defense. He was polite and confident. He knew his subject cold. He anticipated every one of their questions and possible objections. He was kind; he could've demolished them, but he held back. That professor on the right, and I know him well, was being snarky for a time, but Tommy handled him perfectly. I don't expect a continuation. And it was more than clear that all three had closely read his thesis."

At that point, the rear hall door opened, and the three professors filed in. Everyone hurried back to their seats.

The lead professor switched on the microphone at the table.

"What we have witnessed here today, is the most remarkable thesis defense I've known. What you may not realize, unless you read this young man's work, is that our understanding of early British history is now deeply and profoundly changed. Dr. Kent-Hughes, and it is my honor to be the first to call him that, grasped what none of the rest of us, nor any of our predecessors, had seen, about the early Viking invasion period. What he's accomplished here is the beginning of a fundamental reassessment of our understanding of Britain's history. Congratulations, Dr. Kent-Hughes. Your thesis is unanimously approved."

Despite the earlier admonition, the hall broke into cheers and applause. Tommy looked up and saw his father standing and applauding. After shaking hands with his review panel, he made his way through the congratulations of the Broughby team, answered a few questions from reporters ("See me at the reception at 2"), and then made his way to his family.

Hank was beaming. "Bravo, little brother!"

Little David was doing a happy dance. "My brother is brilliant!"

His uncle appeared behind him and put his hand on Tommy's shoulder. "Well done, indeed, Dr. Kent-Hughes."

Tommy looked at his father and saw the pride in Michael's eyes. He grasped Tommy's arm and shook his hand. "You were brilliant, son."

They walked up the stairs to the back of the lecture hall and exited to the entrance hallway.

Erica was standing by the windows.

"My train from Cambridge was late. They let me stand at the back."

Tommy couldn't speak. He just stared. Suddenly Erica paled and curtsied.

"Your majesty," she said.

Michael appeared next to Tommy. "Son, might you introduce us?"

"I'm sorry. Dad, this is Erica Larsson. She was part of our team on Broughby this summer. Erica, this is my father, King Michael."

Erica curtsied again.

"Miss Larsson, it is a pleasure to meet you. I've been hoping that one day I might meet the other half of the famous viral video."

She smiled. "Your majesty, I can take credit for no more than 10 percent of that video."

Michael laughed, Tommy reddened, and then they all laughed together.

"She's wonderful, Tommy," Michael said.

Tommy continued the introductions. "Erica, this is my brother Henry, Prince of Wales."

She curtsied again and Hank took her hand. "It's a pleasure, Miss Larsson."

"And this is my brother, Prince David."

She curtsied yet again, and little David just grinned and nodded his head.

"You remember my uncle, David Hughes, from his visit to Broughby." David leaned over and shook her hand. "Just normal here," he said. "No curtsy required."

"And this is Mr. Lanham, the communications director for the palace. He saved me when I rode the ferry with the media."

"Miss Larsson," Jay said, shaking her hand.

Angus poked his head around Tommy. "And I'm Angus. Do you remember me, Erica?"

Erica grinned. "Of course, I do. Angus, may I give you a hug?"

He nodded, and she hugged him.

"We're going to have a quick lunch before the reception," Michael said. "Would you join us, Miss Larsson?"

"I'd love to, your majesty, but I have to catch the train for Cambridge." She looked at Tommy. "I have an oral exam on Chaucer tomorrow."

Michael touched Tommy on his arm. "Tommy, why don't you escort Miss Larsson to Waverly Station, and then catch up with us at the reception?"

Tommy turned to Erica.

"I'd like that, Tommy," she said.

Followed by Noah Bennington, they stopped at a coffee shop near the university and not far from the station. Tommy placed their order with the barista. Noah sat at the bar near the coffee machines.

Tommy returned to the booth, carrying a tray with two cups of tea and a piece of dark chocolate cake. Two forks.

Erica cradled the teacup in her cold hands. "Do you come here often?"

"Often enough. I put honey in your tea. You still use honey?"

She nodded. "You remembered. And you remembered I like chocolate cake."

"It's only been three months." Tommy looked around. "This place has been a coffee shop as far back as anyone can remember, but Keir over there" – he pointed to the barista – "Keir will fix tea if you ask. And properly, with leaves in the strainer." He smiled. "This was the place my parents came when they were at university here."

"Really? Here?"

"This very table. I come here to study and write. Sometimes I sit and imagine the conversation they had with their friends, like Dad bringing Mummy and Uncle David home for Christmas and planning an end-of-term fling. I even have copies of a few of their pictures taken right here." He grinned. "And I've worked out more problems that you might imagine with the Viking invasions of the 9th century with a pot of tea right at this table."

"Your Ph.D. defense today was brilliant. I wouldn't have had the nerve. That array of establishment dons and an audience of – what, hundreds of people, including the press? And you're there with your thesis to turn the establishment upside down?"

"I was petrified."

She laughed. "Then you fooled all of us. You looked calm and collected. And well prepared. You took every barb and challenge and turned it back on them so adroitly and kindly they almost thanked you for it. Tommy, you were upending three gigantic academic egos, not to mention what they'd built their careers upon, and you did it brilliantly. You were absolutely brilliant."

"The team was brilliant, Rikki."

She sipped her tea. "The team was brilliant because our leader was brilliant. Spending three months on a remote island like Broughby could've ended in acrimony and something out of an Agatha Christie story. Instead, we proved your theory and came away feeling we each had accomplished something incredibly wonderful and important. And we had. We changed the understanding of the pre-Norman history of Britain." Her voice softened. "And our team leader inspired each of us. Don't denigrate that."

He smiled. "I'd inspiration of my own."

She forked a piece of the cake to cover the sudden silence.

"I hurt you. And don't argue. I know I hurt you. And it killed me. I kept hoping you'd call."

"I hurt you as well, Rikki. I thought about calling every day, almost every hour. But I thought you never wanted to see me again. Why did you come today?"

"I received my team invitation. I wanted to see the defense." She looked down. "That's only partially true. I wanted to see you. I wanted to see how you were. And if you looked the same and sounded the same. I wanted to hear your voice."

He reached across the table and touched her hand, still holding the fork. "So, do I look the same?"

She nodded. "You still have the beard."

He laughed.

She smiled back at him. "Although one thing's different. I've never seen you in a suit and tie before. You look like an adult. Well, I did see you all dressed up in the news reports about York, but it's not the same as in person."

"I'm feeling a lot like a little boy right now."

She glanced at the big clock on the wall. "I have to catch my train for Cambridge. My oral exam tomorrow."

"I'll go with you to the station."

"You don't have to do that."

"Yes, I do."

He paid for their cake and tea, and they walked into the early Edinburgh afternoon. She took his arm. Noah followed as discreetly as he could, speaking into the radio behind his lapel to let the security office know what was happening.

"What is it like?" she said as they walked.

"What is what like?"

"The palace. The royal family. Everything. What is your staff like?"

"My staff?" He thought for a minute. "Well, actually, it can get quite crowded in my flat here in Edinburgh. There's the butler and the cook for starters. My personal valets. The two maids. The secretarial staff. And then the liaison staff with the palace." He laughed when he saw the look of consternation on her face. "Rikki, I don't have a staff. It's only Noah here. He's my security officer, and he's more my friend than what the word 'security' implies. We weren't raised with servants. We made our beds, we washed and ironed our clothes, we helped in the kitchen. Dad wouldn't have it any other way; he wanted us to learn how to take care of ourselves. We were raised like my father was raised, with solid middle-class values. Adulthood brought complications, for lots of reasons. But I don't have a staff of servants in formal dress to take care of me."

She bit her lip. "I didn't know. I think not knowing scared me. I had this image of what I thought it was all like, people with titles waiting on you hand and foot. What you're telling me is that I've been vastly wrong."

"There's staff, of course, but no one waits on us hand and foot. People work hard, and I know that no one works harder in the monarchy than my father."

"The one you said was in government service."

"And I believe you said yours was something in manufacturing, about as honest as my own answer."

She started to respond but he stopped her.

"We both had good reasons. I suspect it was what we both had been told to say."

Erica nodded.

They had reached Waverly Station.

"Can I see you?"

"When?"

"This weekend? I'll take the train Friday."

"Don't you have plans? You don't have to go to London?"

"I don't have to be there until Saturday night," Tommy said. "I'll come down Friday."

She leaned closer to him. "I'm glad. I want to see you, too."

"This time, I'll let you buy the tea and cake." He touched her face with his hand.

She laughed. "Done." As she looked up into his eyes, he leaned toward her and kissed her.

Late Friday afternoon, Erica's mobile buzzed. It was Tommy. "I'm here. Noah's here, too, just so you won't be surprised. When can I see you?"

"Anytime," she said.

"Good. I'm at your front door. Might I meet your grandmother?"

Tommy surprised Erica and her grandmother when he invited both of them to dinner; he also insisted Noah sit with them. They talked and laughed, and Erica could see Tommy had completely charmed Nan.

Back at the house, Noah joined Nan in the kitchen to make tea while Tommy and Erica talked in what was an almost stereotyped Victorian parlour. On the most prominent wall hung the portrait of Erica painted by Tommy.

"Nan thinks you're wonderful."

"She's lovely. Rikki, I need to talk to you about something."

She smiled. "This sounds serious."

"It is serious." He took her hands in his. "I don't want us to get caught, or me to get caught again, in not being completely up front with you. What I have to tell you is known only among a tiny handful of people. Even Noah and Angus don't know."

Erica had no idea where the conversation was headed, so she waited, saying nothing.

"My brother Hank and his wife Hannah can't have children, and this is what's going to happen because of that." And he told her.

Erica sat stunned.

"Of all the things I thought you might say," she said, "this wasn't one of them."

"I've told you this because I want you to be part of my life forever, Erica. I love you, and I want to marry you. I want to be your husband and your helpmate and your lover and the father of your children. And I know this is a huge thing, and I'd also be asking a huge thing of you. But I'm asking you if you'd marry me. I know you need time to consider everything, and I'm giving you that time, however long it takes.

"But the one thing I can't do is turn my back on my family and what I'm being called to do. I want you to be part of that, too. I can't imagine doing it without you."

For a moment, Erica said nothing. She reached to touch Tommy's face. "You just asked an anti-monarchist to marry you. Are you sure?"

"Of course, I'm sure. I'd have the added advantage of having an anti-monarchist close at hand to keep me honest."

She laughed. "You're irresistible, you know. And it's worse when I don't want to resist. I don't need time to think about this, Tommy. I want our lives to be together, always. And I don't care if it's London or the palace or Broughby. I want to be with you. I'm terrified at the idea of what will happen one day, but there's no place else I want to be unless it's with you."

They spent Saturday together, trailed by Noah. They wandered the streets and alleyways around Cambridge's colleges, spending an inordinate amount of time in the antiquarian bookshops. They spent their last hour in King's College Chapel, talking quietly, before Tommy had to leave for the train station.

"Dinner tonight with Dad and Hank. And I'll tell them about us. Tomorrow I have a meeting with Dad's staff. I go back to Edinburgh on Monday but I'm going to Birmingham first."

"Birmingham?"

"An appointment with your father. I'm asking him for his permission to marry his daughter and for his blessing."

"My mother."

"Your mother?"

"She's going to completely freak. Do you how long and hard she's worked to find a way to meet your father?" Erica closed her eyes. "I didn't even think about my royal-addicted mother."

Tommy chuckled and kissed her.

At dinner that night, when Tommy told his father, Mary, Hannah, and Hank about the engagement, Michael excused himself for a moment. When he returned, he handed Tommy a small velvet box. Tommy opened it and saw a sapphire-and-diamond ring.

"It was Sarah's. She had several different rings, and Hank gave Hannah one as an engagement ring. Do you think it might work for Erica? The sapphire might complement her eyes."

Tommy nodded. "It's perfect. Thank you, Dad."

In early February, Buckingham Palace announced the engagement of HRH the Duke of York and Miss Erica Elizabeth Larsson of Cambridge, daughter of Jenner Larsson of Birmingham and Billie Larsson of Cambridge. A June wedding was planned, and afterward the royal couple would reside in Oxford, where the duke had accepted an appointment at Merton College as a lecturer in early medieval history.

The article was published in *The British Archaeology Quarterly*, creating a huge wave of news coverage for the Broughby project. Supervised by Gavin, the *Journal's* photographer had taken dozens of photographs to illustrate the report. The runes on the tomb, translated with the help of researchers at the University of Bergen in

Norway, identified a male by the Norse name Ulf and a female by the Celtic name of Aoife. DNA and forensic analyses showed the male to be Scandinavian and the female to be Celtic and Scandinavian.

Two weeks later, Erika's family arrived at Buckingham Palace to meet Tommy's family. Michael and Mary had been warned of Billie Larsson's royal infatuation, and Michael decided to go with the flow, making himself Billie's escort the entire evening.

Erica could see that her mother was starstruck and barely able to contain her excitement. Briefly, she considered slipping a sleeping pill in her mother's pre-dinner cocktail, but she figured it would have no effect. The entire Kent-Hughes clan was there, including the children. Dinner was formal in the palace dining room; the men wore dinner jackets and the women evening dresses.

They were in the middle of the main course when Billie looked across the table at Tommy and Erica and asked if they'd selected their wedding attendants. Erica's eyes narrowed. She knew her mother knew who the attendants were; it had already prompted an argument in Cambridge. Erica thought it was settled, and suspected her mother was going to try an end run.

"Julia Heaton is maid of honor," Tommy said, "and several family members are joining the party as well."

Billie took a sip of her wine and smiled. "And your best man?"

"Angus McLin is my best man."

"Really? Not your brother, the Prince of Wales?"

"Actually, Mrs. Larsson," Hank said, from a little farther down the table, "I think Angus is a stellar choice. I'm one of the groomsmen, along with Jason, Jim, Gavin, and Mark."

She glanced at Michael and looked at Tommy again. "But aren't you concerned about the possibility of mishaps? Doesn't Angus have some developmental disabilities?"

The table went completely silent. Michael was considering intervening when Tommy spoke.

"No, I'm not concerned at all, Mrs. Larsson. Angus has been my best friend since we were 10 years old, and I consider him the perfect choice as my best man."

"But this will be on television, Tommy, and he could drop the ring or do something that might disrupt the ceremony."

Erica had had enough. "Mother!"

"I'm just trying to consider the best interests of all concerned. And I'm sure Angus would be mortified if he made a mistake." Billie Larsson sipped her wine again and signaled to the server for a refill. "This will be a televised wedding, with millions of people watching, and you want it to be perfect."

Tommy's jaw was set. "And it will be perfect, Mrs. Larsson, including Angus as best man."

"But have you considered—"

Tommy cut her off. "We've considered everything, and it's time for us to change the subject."

"I simply think you're making a terrible mistake—"

Tommy turned his attention to Jenner Larsson's wife, Ann, "Mrs. Larsson, Erica tells me you operate an interior design firm. Do you do both residential and commercial?"

Billie Larsson's cheeks turned bright red, but she said nothing. Instead, she focused on her plate and began cutting her salmon. She looked up, and then turned her attention to Michael. "Can you explain to them that they're making a mistake, your majesty?"

Utter silence reigned at the table. Erica lowered her head. Tommy's eyes flashed anger.

The king leaned forward. "Mrs. Larsson, I've known Angus almost as long as Tommy has. I've hiked with him twice. From what Gavin has told me, Angus was an outstanding contributor to the work on Broughby, including being the one who uncovered the start of a significant archaeological find. But more than all that, he is my son's best friend, and he'll do an outstanding job as best man. If you can't accept that, I suggest you rethink what it is you truly want here, to celebrate your daughter's wedding or to design a ceremony that you'll find to be acceptable. And then realize what's most important." He looked down the table at Ann Larsson.

"Now, I'm interested as well, Mrs. Larsson. Do you design both residential and commercial?"

"I'm sorry." Erica was near tears, when she and Tommy had a brief private moment together after dinner.

"It's a poor way to begin a relationship with my mother-in-law, but I think she was a bit out of bounds."

"A bit? Mother was so far out of bounds she could've been playing in France."

Tommy laughed and took her hand. "I was rather rude at the end, when she showed no inclination to stop. I didn't expect Dad to step in, but I'm glad he did."

They walked into the post-dinner reception room. Billie Larsson was sitting on a sofa by herself, drinking. They saw Erica's grandmother walk over to her and sit beside her. They talked briefly, and then Nan rose, helping her daughter up. Billie stood unsteadily.

"Oh, Tommy, I could die. She's had too much to drink."

Tommy quickly moved to where the two women were standing.

"Nan, would you like me to call the driver?"

"That would be most appreciated, Tommy. My daughter is feeling unwell."

Tommy signaled to the bartender and mouthed "car," and the bartender nodded, picking up her mobile. He stayed with Billie while Nan walked to Michael and Mary, apologized, and said they'd be returning to the hotel. She returned to Tommy and Billie, and the three left the room.

Erica walked to Michael and Mary. "I'm sorry, your majesty. I don't know what to say to make this any better."

Michael smiled. "It's all right, Erica. I hope your mother feels better, and I loved meeting your grandmother. She's a lovely person. Tommy tells me that she was the one who brought you up?"

She nodded. Jenner and Ann Larsson walked up, and Jenner put his arm around Erica. "I am sorry, too, your majesty. We'd hoped for a better evening."

They continued talking. Tommy rejoined the group and took Erica's hand. "I've alerted Mr. Mitchell that I'm going to walk Rikki back to the hotel. It's only four blocks, and two security officers will be with us." Michael invited Jenner and Ann Larsson to join them for a glass of wine in the family loft.

The March night was clear but cold; Erica and Tommy wore coats over their evening clothes as they walked along Buckingham Gate Road to the hotel.

"Tommy, does this ruin everything?"

"Not at all. Dad knows I'm marrying you, not your mother." He paused. "He's told me about his own mother-in-law, whom he didn't meet until two years after he and Mummy were married. They met here in London. Unbeknownst to everyone, including her husband, she'd made all kinds of promises to friends about royal endorsements, even promising a royal warrant for an art gallery. My mother had an ugly scene with her, and they never spoke again. I don't think that what happened tonight is anywhere close to that league. And he thinks very highly of you. That won't change because of your mother."

They'd reached the hotel's arched entrance, and he walked her through to the interior courtyard and the small lobby entrance.

"I'll see you tomorrow at lunch."

"I'd forgotten we're going back for lunch. Tommy, what can I do with Mother?"

"Bear it with grace. It'll be fine." He kissed her good night.

The wedding in June went exactly as planned. It was a spectacular Saturday, with cloudless blue skies and abundant sunshine. From the palace, Tommy rode with Angus and Noah in a carriage to Westminster Abbey. It had been six years since Hank and Hannah's wedding. Sophie had been married in Madrid and Helen in Amsterdam, and London was ready for another royal wedding. Tommy smiled and waved at the dense crowds along The Mall and Whitehall, while Angus stared straight ahead, occasionally looking to the side and nodding.

Tommy leaned toward Angus. "You can wave, you know."

Angus scrunched up his face. "They're very loud. Not storm-loud, but almost."

Tommy continued to wave. "They're expressing their support for the family."

"It's very loud support."

Both Tommy and Noah laughed.

Erica and her father rode in what was known as the "wedding coach," leaving the hotel on Buckingham Gate and making their way to The Mall and Whitehall. She had seen the reports of Hank and Hannah's marriage and the procession to the Abbey, but it was an entirely different experience to be in the procession itself.

After the wedding, where Angus handled his duties perfectly, and the return to Buckingham Palace, the new couple and the royal family appeared on the balcony, to the roar of thousands. It was a full afternoon, with official wedding photographs, two receptions, and then the wedding dinner.

When Angus stood to give the best man's speech at dinner, Erica felt a momentary flutter of anxiety, not for herself or Tommy, or worry from being embarrassed. Instead, her anxiety was for Angus, because she knew he wanted to do well. She watched him approach the microphone. She avoided looking at her mother.

"I've never made a speech before," Angus said, looking around and down. "Which you probably couldn't tell."

There was a small ripple of laughter, and Angus grinned.

Tommy leaned and whispered to Erica. "He made a joke and carried it off."

Angus cleared his throat. "When I was little, doctors said I couldn't talk. They sent me to a home, and it was bad. The doctors said I was—" here he stuttered – "unreachable. But I heard the music on the radio, and my mum took me to the church that made the music. Tommy helped play the music, and he let me play his guitar." Angus was slightly rocking back and forth; Tommy knew it was caused by anxiety.

"He became my friend. He became my best friend. And he said I was his best friend."

Erica looked at her new husband; she could see the tears in his eyes.

"He wouldn't let me slack off. I called him 'no excuses man' because he always said," and here he perfectly imitated Tommy, "'Angus, no excuses. You can do this. You're not going to let autism stop you.' Sometimes I told him he was mean. But he wouldn't let me slack off.

"I got to work at Broughby. It's the best place ever. Tommy met Erica there, on the dig. I told everyone they liked each other. A lot." That evoked laughter and some applause. Angus smiled and seemed to stand straighter.

"When I talk, my brain talks faster than my mouth, and it can jumble. But it all works right with music. I wrote a song. For Tommy and Erica."

Angus walked back toward the wall and returned to the microphone, carrying a guitar. He sounded the strings, and then began to play and sing. He sang with a clear if not strong voice, and it had none of the halting and choppy flow of his speech. He sang and played a love song, a love song for his friend Tommy which became a love song for Tommy and Erica.

When he finished, the wedding guests were on their feet, cheering. Even Erica's mother.

They spent the first week of their honeymoon in Brittany, in a large house facing the sea owned by a friend of Michael's. It included a private beach. Their third day there, they ventured down to the nearby village and enjoyed the annual village fete. They were recognized and welcomed but treated like any other visitors.

At the end of the week, they boarded the royal plane and flew to Kirkwall, where they transferred to a high-speed boat for Broughby. After a late lunch with Gavin, Emily, their two boys, and Angus, Tommy and Erica began the hike to the cottage. Two security officers followed with their bags.

Erica's eyebrows had gone up when Tommy told her they'd be spending the next week at the cottage. Wondering if they'd be sharing the sleeping bag again, she knew something was different when she saw a new, small building about 50 yards down the hill from the cottage.

"It's the security station," he said. "We'll get used to it."
Security officers had accompanied them to Brittany and then Kirkwall.
As they reached the new security house, Noah Bennington opened the
door and came outside, welcoming them and again offering his
congratulations.

The cottage looked the same from the outside but was
transformed on the inside. The walls had been whitewashed. The
kitchen was new; the bathroom had been modernized, with a new tub
and shower installed. The furnishings were all new, including the large
king-sized bed.

The bed had a comforter, sheets, and numerous pillows, but,
following the Duke of York's instructions, lying atop it was the
oversized sleeping bag.

Afterward

Ten months after the wedding, Buckingham Palace announced that the Duke and Duchess of York were expecting their first child, due in late August. The announcement prompted the Prince of Wales to talk with his father and brother and tell them it was time to begin planning the change in succession.

On August 25, his grandfather Michael's 54th birthday, Michael David McLaren Kent-Hughes was born at University Hospital, Oxford, weighing 9 pounds, 5 ounces and measuring 21 inches in length. Mother and son were reported in excellent health. Father was reported ecstatic.

Over the next seven years, Michael would be followed by Henry Ian McLaren Kent-Hughes, known as Little Hank inside the family; Sarah Elizabeth McLaren Kent-Hughes, called "Suds" by Little Hank who, at two years old, had trouble pronouncing his new baby sister's name (the nickname would stick); and identical twins Angus Jenner McLaren Kent-Hughes and Noah Thomas McLaren Kent-Hughes, whose namesakes and godfathers would become the royal children's dearest loved family friends.

Two weeks after the birth of Michael, the Duke and Duchess of York and their new son traveled to London, for a special television broadcast by the Prince of Wales, to be followed by a press conference with King Michael.

While the BBC crew prepared Hank for the broadcast, Michael and Tommy waited in the king's office, where they'd watch the broadcast together. They'd already been briefed and prepared by Jay Lanham. The Queen, the Princess of Wales, the Duchess of York, the Duke and Duchess of Norfolk (also known as Jason and Jane Kent-Hughes), the Duke and Duchess of Sussex (Jim and Laura Kent-Hughes), Prince David, and Lt. Mark Penniman of the Royal Army Engineers were all gathered in the family loft, to watch the broadcast on the large-screen television.

The news media had gathered in the palace ballroom, with television jumbo-screens set up for the broadcast. The press conference would be held here after the broadcast ended. The Duchess of York would join the king and her husband. The media had been given no pre-conference briefing, but the unusual combination of a broadcast by the Prince of Wales and a press conference by the king had brought more than 300 national and international journalists and camera crews pouring into the palace. Speculation abounded.

"How is Rikki doing, Tommy, after the birth?" Michael said.

"She's doing well, Dad. We're both a bit sleep-deprived, but it comes with the territory, as you well know."

Michael smiled. "The little bundle upstairs can keep two adults in constant motion and completely exhausted. Have you considered help?"

"We have a cleaning service," Tommy said, "and I've already ordered food for takeaway more times than I can count. But we both wanted to do this on our own, at least as long as we could. Most people manage to survive. But a long sleep-in would be nice."

Michael cleared his throat. "I need to tell you a story, Tommy. Actually, it's several stories. They're stories I should've told you long before now."

Tommy tensed at his father's words, unsure as to what was coming.

"Less than an hour before your mother died, she was giving me instructions about the four of you children, along with Jason and Jim. It was generally the same as she'd told each of you, perhaps with a bit different emphasis or detail. None of it was a surprise, really, with one exception. It had to do with you and Hank.

"Sarah said she was unable to see Hank as king. She saw him as representing Britain's future, but not as king. She said she knew it would make me angry, but the person she saw as king after me was you. The 'angry' reference was because of what had happened that day in her studio.

"It was as if she knew we'd come to this day. She couldn't have known why or how, but it was one of the last things she said to me. I don't know, Tommy, if this explains or helps explain the rock you and I've had between us, but it certainly added to it. There was no way you could've known; I was the one who put the rock there.

"The studio blowup was never your fault, but I've behaved like it was. I was hurt, I felt guilty about being away so much, I was upset, and our marriage was falling apart. We'd started to make plans to try to restore what we once had, but she got sick. By the time she died, we'd restored nothing. There'd been no time. The person I loved most in the world was gone, believing we'd never salvaged our marriage. It was the worst part of losing her.

"I transferred all of that to you. It was a mistake, the worst mistake I've made as a father and as king. I'm still ashamed of my actions and behavior, and I hope that one day you'll forgive me.

"When I asked your mother why she saw you instead of Hank on the throne, she said it was because you were the most like me, and that's what Britain needed. She told your Uncle David that you and I had the same capacity for faith and love, but that we likely wouldn't see it in each other."

Michael paused before going on.

"A second story concerns your grandfather, my Da. You were there when he died, him holding on to your hand. Ma told me that, right before he let go of your hand and passed away, he motioned her to him and whispered. What he said mystified her; she thought he was rambling or perhaps she misheard. What he said was, 'Tell Michael it's Tommy. It's Tommy.' Those were the last words he spoke. Your name was the last word on his lips. She told me when I was explaining what Hank was planning and why. She'd no idea how Da knew it, or what prompted him to say it."

Tommy sat in silence, stunned by his father's words.

"That painting," Michael said, "that last one Sarah did, the portrait of you."

"It's in Oxford, on our living room wall."

Michael nodded. "Jason did a phenomenal job on the exhibition, but he didn't tell the story of that painting publicly. He'd figured it out, because he asked me about it, as did Trevor Barry when he saw it. That painting was the best thing she'd ever done; we all saw that, as soon as Jason pulled the wrapping off. But it wasn't only a painting of you. It was and still is the portrait of a boy who'd one day be king. As soon as I saw it, I knew it. You're not holding a ball in that painting; she slightly blurred it. You're holding the orb, the symbol of God's power, the orb I held when I was crowned. And you're sitting with a clear view of the throne room behind you. She'd sent me a message, and it shook me to my core." Michael went silent.

Tommy finally spoke. "Thank you for telling me. Knowing this means a lot, more than you know. I need to tell you a story as well. Perhaps several stories.

"The night before she went to the hospital, Mummy came to my room and woke me, asking me to help her. We went to her studio, and she showed me the painting. She asked me to help her to hide it for a time, and I helped her carry it to the toy room. She told me it was about the future, and specifically my future, but it would also be about everyone else's future. And because of that, it needed to be hidden for a short time."

"She knew I'd be upset."

"Most likely." Tommy paused. "When I was 15, and getting ready to start St. Andrews, I knew I was being called to something."

Michael looked directly at Tommy. "Called?"

"Called. I wasn't quite sure what it was about. But there was a certainty about it. I knew something was happening that I didn't understand. I asked Uncle David about it; I told him it felt like I was being called into ministry, but it wasn't that, exactly. Before I decided on St. Andrews, I seriously considered entering the theology program at Edinburgh. But it seemed too much of a period piece. 'Younger son goes into the church, following in father's footsteps.' But I had to set it aside. It made no sense. I didn't even know how to talk with you about it. Uncle David advised waiting and pursuing the course of study I ended up doing. He said that if it was a genuine calling from God, God would eventually track me down.

"I didn't understand it. It didn't feel like a ministry call. And then that night in the palace woods, when Mum told me about Hank and Hannah, I knew. I was overwhelmed, but I knew. I took soundings, of course, from you, and Uncle David, and Hank. And I prayed. But I realized what the call had been about.

"And, yes, Dad, there's been this rock between us, and perhaps it will always be there. But what I know is that I desperately need you now, and I'll continue to desperately need you in the years ahead. Of course, I forgive you. And more than that, Dad, I love you."

There was a knock at the door, and Jay Lanham stuck his head in. "They'll be starting any moment now, sir. I'm watching from the control booth." And then Lanham withdrew, closing the door.

For a moment, Michael said nothing, as he fought back tears. "I love you, too, son, and you've blessed me in ways I never deserved, including my beautiful new grandson."

"We're already calling him Little Mike."

"Little Mike." Michael smiled. "There's a lot packed into that name."

"I know. It's what Mummy called you. Dad, in my last conversation with Mummy, she told me that one day I would need to tell you something. Today may be that day. She said to tell you that she always knew, and would always know, how much you loved her."

Michael looked down, feeling a sob in his throat. He then looked at his son. "I'm grateful to God for the blessing you are to me, Tommy. Perhaps this is what your mother meant when she told David we wouldn't see what we had in common, and that could become a tragedy. I'm glad it hasn't. And I owe your Uncle David a debt I can never repay, for being there for you when I wasn't. And I thank you for that message from your mother." He reached over and put his hand on top of Tommy's. "I'd like to ask a huge favor of you. I was wondering if you and I might start over."

Tommy, tears welling in his eyes, looked at his father and nodded. "I would like that, Dad. Very much."

The television screen went live. Henry, Prince of Wales, announced to the British nation that he'd resigned, with immediate effect, and relinquished his rights of succession to the throne. He explained why he'd made this decision, and said his brother Thomas, Duke of York, would become the new Prince of Wales and next-in-line to the throne. Henry was being given the title of Duke of Kent, and he and Hannah would remain active in royal family activities.

The father and son watched quietly, without speaking. When the broadcast ended, Michael stood, as did Tommy.

Michael put his hand on Tommy's shoulder. "I think it's time for our press conference."

Together, they walked down the hallway to the ballroom. When they reached it, Erica and Jay Lanham were waiting for them. Tommy took Erica's hand.

Lanham nodded at them both and smiled, and then he opened the door.

Glynn Young

Epilogue

Island

By Erika Larsson Kent-Hughes

with Glynn Young

Foreword by Farley McNeill, Ph.D.

I had the good fortune to spend five months as part of an extraordinary team on the island of Broughby in the Orkneys. We were there to investigate a hypothesis that Norsemen had not only been present in the British Isles far earlier than previously shown but also that they brought their religions, plural, with them, including Christianity.

The hypothesis, since published as the doctrinal thesis of His Royal Highness Thomas Kent-Hughes, Duke of York, was developed by the duke during studies at St. Andrew's, University of Edinburgh, and universities, libraries, and archives in Norway, Denmark, Iceland, Sweden, and the United States. Tantalizing hints of a structure on the island we call Broughby suggested a settlement by Norsemen, among whom were likely some Christians.

As recently announced in the British Archaeology Quarterly, a tomb was excavated on Broughby. The skeletal remains of a man and woman were found in the tomb, and forensic and DNA analysis suggested a man of Scandinavian heritage of between 45 and 55 years of age, and a woman of Celtic heritage of between 35 and 45 years of age. The condition of the skeletons suggested no evidence of violent deaths.

With the help of Old Norse experts in Bergen, the rune inscriptions on the tomb's exterior were eventually translated to read, "Ulf, son of Erik, and Aoife, daughter of Braden, one in life, one in death, one in Christ." The tomb and its contents date to late 9th or early 10th century A.D., the very earliest period of the Norsemen's invasions of the British Isles.

The Broughby excavation team was comprised of students in archaeology, Germanic languages, Anglo-Saxon literature, history, and other disciplines. Under the direction of Dr. Evan Elliott of the University of Cumbria and myself, the team excavated the site and documented all findings.

The work entailed addressing several mysteries, chief among them being how a Norseman, presumably part of a group, came to be a Christian far earlier than any previously published reports – at least a century earlier. While we have some hints that are already the subject of additional research, the reality is that, right now, we don't know.

Erika Larsson, then a student in Anglo-Saxon and early Norman Conquest literature at Christ's College, Cambridge University, undertook a creative writing project, envisioning how that might have happened. She wrote in story form and shared the story in readings to the team and the residents of the village of Broughby. It is fiction, but it is also fiction highly informed by her studies and the work she was directly involved in on Broughby. As a historian, I find her story to be eminently plausible. As a listener and reader, I find it to be enthralling.

Not long after she submitted her manuscript to the publisher, she became HRH the Duchess of York. I find she has told not only a plausible account of Aoife and Ulf, but also a bit of her own story. That is how it should be, for we are always part of a story larger and older than ourselves.

University of St. Andrews
St. Andrews, Scotland

Island

The sails change everything.

She likes the sameness of her days, the sameness of the seasons. She feels a slow rhythm in the change from winter to spring, and spring to summer. Winters are long and hard, summers short and glorious. Being here, on the far hillside, tending a few goats and sheep, is the late spring day she likes best, with its cool mornings, warm mid-days, and sharply cooler nights.

She fingers the shiny blue stone she wears on a leather strip around her neck. It is her mother's, saved by her father for Aoife when her mother dies.

The hut she shares with her father is near the village but still set apart and slightly up the hillside. He likes the separation, she knows. So does the village. People are kind and amiable but also slightly afraid. Whether it is fear of her father or fear of her, she doesn't know. It is something she always knows.

Her mother dies in the birthing and is buried near the large hut that serves their worship. The priest doesn't come every Sun Day, but he comes often in his boat, hears confession, says a mass, performs a baptism or burial if needed, and then leaves. The men, when they aren't fishing or tending to small farming plots, meet and talk about God on the Sun Days the priest doesn't come. The women listen.

For Aoife, God isn't in the hut or the men's gatherings. She finds him on the hillsides, and in the small forests that dot the island. She hears him, too, in the winter, his voice raspy with windblown snow, or strong and piercing in the icy waves pushing against the shore. They are more sheltered on this side of the island; no one lives on the setting sun side, with its jagged rocks, thin soil, and treacherous paths. The winds and snows come across the tops of the hills, are mostly tamed, and find the way down to the village and the shore.

She shivers in the winter; the cold seeps into her bones. Her father says it is because of her mother, who is from the south. He meets her on a fishing trip to the south island. He says little about her.

Aoife doesn't know what "south" means. She lives always on the island.

She asks him her mother's name. He says he can't remember. He might tell the truth; Braden is old now, and sometimes forgets. But she thinks he knows. He marries late and they are married only four turns of the seasons when she dies. Aoife sometimes sees him open a chest and finger a lock of fair hair when he has too much ale.

He still goes out with the boats, but he isn't much use in the fishing. No longer is he strong to control the sail or haul the nets. Maedoc does that for him. Maedoc has his eye on her since they are children. He is a strong, strapping boy becoming a man, with his black curly hair and dark eyes. He walks with her in the village, although his mother worries. Born with a cowl, Aoife carries a great blessing or a great curse. Maedoc's mother doesn't want to risk her oldest son on the girl she and the village see as strange, the fair-haired girl who moves like a spirit in the hills and charms the animals with her words.

The people of the village, including Braden, have dark hair and dark blue or brown eyes. They are a dark-skinned people, touched long by the sun. Aoife has dark blue eyes as well, but with the fair hair and fair skin of her mother.

Her father names her Aoife, saying she is his shining beauty. She sees the boys in the village look at her slyly, but none cross Maedoc, now that he speaks to her father. She has little say, but she isn't unhappy. Maedoc is kind, drinks little, and is a good provider. She knows this is her lot, even as her heart yearns for the hillsides and mountain ridges, and the clouds beyond.

God has put this yearning in her heart, she thinks.

When the boats return from the last fishing trip, her father tells her the wedding is when the priest comes next. She prefers her freedom to roam the hills with the birds and the winds. But she doesn't object. When they wed, soon Maedoc moves into the hut and cares for her and Braden.

She knows little about marriage. She understands what is involved; she sees the village boys laugh when dogs mate. But much she doesn't know. She works up courage to ask Maedoc's mother, who replies with a hard glare. "You find out soon enough."

From a chest in the corner of the hut, her father brings her a dress, finer than she knows, and a wooden circlet, carved with a symbol in the center. "Your mother's," he says. "She wears them on our marriage day. The circlet is decorated with flowers. The priest remembers." He pauses. "The women chatter about the dress, but your mother says the circlet is more important. She doesn't say why." He returns to the chest and brings a jeweled knife and scabbard to Aoife. "She gives this to me at the end of the ceremony. She says it is her family's. It means that the responsibility for her passes from her father to me. You give this to Maedoc on your wedding day." And then he leaves to look for ale.

Here on the hillside, Maedoc and her father and marriage seem far away. In the hut, she works on the dress; her mother is bigger and taller when she wears it. Aoife feels the fine material, and studies the intricate designs sewn on the cloth. Her father calls it linen.

Sitting on the hillside and staring at the sea, Aoife is the first to see the sails in the distance. She knows they are not fishing boats, but she's never seen anything like them. She isn't sure why, perhaps because there are so many, but surprise gives way to unease. And then to fear and panic. Leaving the grazing animals, she runs down the hillside toward the village.

As the boats draw nearer, she hears gasps and the beginning of wailing.

Her father grabs her by the shoulders. "Aoife! Run to the hills. Take what you can. Run, girl! Hide! It's the Norsemen!"

She dashes up to their hut. She grabs bread and her shawl, and then, seeing it hanging from the roof, her wedding dress, the circlet, and the knife. Then it is up the hill, turning her head once to see the first boats landing and men swinging swords and shouting. She runs high, higher than she usually goes, passing the grazing sheep and goats. She runs past trees and rock outcroppings to a place right before the ridge, where she knows of shelter. She is safe, for a time, but she can't see the village or hear what is happening.

She doesn't see Braden clutch his chest and fall before the ships land.

Aoife waits. At some point she sleeps.

It is dark when she wakes, but she can see by the moon's light. She quietly makes her way to where she might see. It is a distance, and it takes more time because of the need to keep hidden.

Part of the village glows, near where the fishing boats cluster. She feels a dark fear at the idea of boats burning; that is where work and food come from. Without the boats, the village starves.

She returns to her shelter and eats a small piece of the bread. She is hungry but doesn't know when she finds food again. It is a long time before sleep finds her.

The morning sun dazzles with a radiance that belies what Aoife fears she'll find in the village. She doesn't know what her father meant by "the Norsemen," but she hears the fear in his voice.

She eats another piece of bread, chewing slowly.

She decides to find out what happens to her father and the village. And Maedoc.

She moves slowly down from the hills, finding cover and hiding for a time. As she gets closer, she smells smoke. And something else, something raw and frightening, something she's not smelled before. It reminds her of a sheep, butchered to eat. Reaching and hiding behind her father's hut, she listens for a long time. The village is silent, except for an occasional cry. She can hear movement inside the hut, and she hopes it is her father. She gathers enough courage to enter the hut, and darts through the doorway. She catches her foot and stumbles but stops herself before she falls.

He stands there, looking at her. He is tall, broad-shouldered, and muscular. His fair hair is long to his broad shoulders and his face bearded but trimmed. He stares at her without speaking, his pale blue eyes looking her over.

Never has she felt such fear. Never has she felt such attraction. Not even with Maedoc.

He holds a loaf of bread, and he tosses it to her. He puts his finger to his lips, and motions with his head toward the hills.

She runs. She doesn't stop until she reaches the shelter. She falls on the ground, panting. Her folded wedding dress, circlet, and knife lie nearby, sheltered by the rock.

When night comes, it is cool. She wraps her shawl around her. She has a flint to make a fire, but she cannot risk it.

She eats a piece of bread. She thinks about the fair-haired stranger with the piercing blue eyes, blue the color of ice. Where is her father?

It is late, almost the setting of the sun, when she steals back to the village. No one seems to stir. She almost screams when she sees a body, a man she knows from the fishing boats. The back of his head is sliced open. Nearby lies a woman's body, blood across her blouse and her skirt pulled up. Her body is bruised. Aoife can see she, too, is dead. She looks closer, and sees it is Maedoc's mother. Aoife pulls the dress down and looks toward the shore. The strange boats are still there, clustered. She hears voices, singing.

She senses someone is nearby, watching her. She peers through the dark but sees no one. She wants to find her father, or Maedoc, but she senses danger. She begins to move quietly back toward the hill.

A rough hand seizes her and shoves her to the ground. A large man, smelling of drink and foulness, straddles her as he rips her blouse.

Suddenly he is pushed away. An angry voice shouts. The man at first moves to fight, until he sees it is the fair-haired stranger who shoves him. She sees the first man's anger, but he checks it, and staggers away, muttering. Other men come and watch the man with the long, fair hair. A new man comes up from the village, larger than the fair-haired stranger, and stands by him.

The fair-haired stranger pulls her to her feet, and signals for her to follow. She hears laughter behind her.

Aoife follows him to her father's hut. She knows what is to happen, but it is no worse than what she leaves. She prays he does not hurt her too much.

The second man speaks words she doesn't understand and leaves them.

In the hut, the fair-haired man motions her to sit on a stool, her father's stool. He stares at her for a time.

She trembles in fear, but she does not look away from him.

He smiles. He points to himself. He says what sounds like a word and then repeats it when he sees her confusion.

"Ulf," he says, pointing to himself. "Ulf."

She stares for a moment, and then says "Ulf."

He nods and smiles, and then points to her.

"Aoife," she says. "Aoife."

"Aoife," he says. He smiles. "Aoife." And he speaks in words she doesn't understand. She doesn't know what he says, but she hears gentleness in his voice.

None of this makes sense.

He makes a motion to indicate eating. She nods. He points to the table. Once her table, but no longer. Food waits to be prepared. The fire is already lit. He wants her to prepare the food, she thinks; she is to be his servant. She walks to the table as he watches her.

A knife lies with the food. She realizes he does not forget it; he trusts her to use it only with the food. She begins to work.

When he sits to eat, he points to the stool by the table. She is to join him, she thinks. She sits, and begins to eat, watching him from the corner of her eye.

Later, as the fire is getting low, he points to the bedding on the packed earth of the hut. She lies down, fearful, waiting for what comes next. She asks God to spare her pain. She sees Ulf remove his tunic. His chest is muscled and strong. It is then that she sees the cross hanging around his neck. He lies next to her, and she closes her eyes, waiting. Soon she hears him breathing deeply. She opens her eyes to find him asleep.

And somewhere in her mind works the idea that he makes a pretense of taking her. He protects her from an evil fate with the other men.

In the dying firelight, she watches him sleep. She stares at the cross on his bare chest.

In the morning, he awakens her with a nudge. They walk outside to the privy, and he turns away to protect her modesty. She does the same for him. They return to the hut and eat.

He speaks with his strange words. She hears him say her name but doesn't understand. He has long bands of leather, and he ties one around her waist and the other end around his. He walks to the door and she follows him down the slope to the village, hurrying to match his long stride.

The other men are stirring. She sees how threatening they look and how sleepy they are. They greet Ulf with what sounds like deference, give her a quick look, and smile. But they also nod. She then understands the purpose of the leather bands. He lets them know she belongs to him and is under his protection. And his control.

Shouting comes from farther up the shore, and Ulf walks there, giving her no choice but to follow. She sees the prows of the boats decorated with what look like the heads of beasts.

A group approaches. She sees men and older boys from the village, their hands bound, being brought to one of the ships. She looks for her father but doesn't see him. But she sees Maedoc. His face is bruised like he's been beaten; his wrists are bound together.

"Aoife!" he cries out to her, and Ulf turns to see Maedoc.

"They take us for slaves," he says, as one of the Norsemen hits him.

"My father!" she cries out to him.

"Dead," he said. "He grabs his chest and dies before they land." The Norseman hits him again, and Maedoc says nothing more.

"God protect you, Maedoc!" she calls, but she's not sure he hears her.

She watched them step into the water and climb aboard the boat. They're positioned to row, until the wind catches the sail. The boat moves into the waves.

Unable to bear their leaving, overwhelmed by the news of her father, she turns away, tears in her eyes. She sees Ulf watching her closely. He says nothing.

But when he moves back to the village, she feels his anger through the yank and pull of the leather strips. She half runs to keep up with him, tears streaking her face.

Days pass, then weeks. Little changes. Her days, and his days, take on a sameness, a rhythm.

She knows some of the women and girls in the village are still alive, being kept by the Norsemen for amusement and for servants. The younger children are not harmed. She sees Maedoc's two young brothers near the shore, playing with sticks for swords. A Norseman teaches them.

Some days Ulf walks down to the village, leaving her alone in the hut. She considers running back into the hills, but she remains.

Ulf values one man above the rest, the man who joins him that first night. He calls him Sten, picking up a stone for Aoife to see, saying "Sten" and pointing to the man. Sten is tall, taller than Ulf, and larger, a big man. She sees the affection Ulf has for him, and the loyalty Sten has for Ulf. She says the man's name, "Sten," and she sees him smile.

Early one morning, she's awake, watching Ulf sleep, his chest rising and falling. He has not touched her, except to tie the leather bands when they go to the village. They teach each other their words. Stool. Cup. Hut. Fire. Bread. Eat. Sleep. His words sound harder, harsher.

Sten sticks his head in the doorway. He sees her awake next to Ulf, and he smiles. He nods toward Ulf.

She touches his chest, calling his name. "Ulf."

He awakens quickly, immediately alert, and sees her nod toward Sten. They talk in their strange words.

She's not sure what they say, but she hears her name and knows it's about her.

An hour later, tied to Ulf, she follows him to the shore. Sten and three of the Norsemen prepare to leave. He looks at Ulf, and he nods. Ulf turns to her and holds up his hand, ticks off each finger, then points to the sun.

Five. She thinks. Five turns of the sun. But for what?

Sten and the other Norsemen return on the sixth day.

With them are several older women. Even from a distance she sees them talking and gesturing. As they get closer, Aoife hears one in particular chattering loudly in the Norse words. Sten looks at Ulf, shaking his head. Ulf laughs. They are followed by a second boat, with more Norsemen.

On the second boat is the priest from the south island, Father Jaffrez. Aoife sees a bruise on the side of his face. He does not come willingly.

The woman, husky and ruddy-faced, her hair wound in a braid, jumps from the boat and runs to Ulf, throwing her arms around him. Ulf laughs and picks her up. When he puts her down, he turns to Aoife and points to the woman. "Gro," he says.

Aoife repeats the name. "Gro." She is too old to be Ulf's wife, too young to be his mother.

The woman walks around her, inspecting her closely. She looks at Ulf and speaks the Norse words. Ulf nods, smiling.

Sten roughly drags an unwilling Father Jaffrez to them.

Father Jaffrez speaks to her. "They bring me here to marry you to this barbarian," he says. He sees the shock on Aoife's face. "You don't know?"

She shakes her head.

"This is a sacrilege," he says.

Ulf speaks harshly to the priest, and Aoife is surprised to hear the priest answer in Ulf's words. Ulf nods, Gro throws up her arms, and Sten laughs.

"Are you ready for this?" the priest says to Aoife.

She nods. "I have no choice in this."

"What's happens to Maedoc?" he says. "Your father? You are to marry."

She nods. "They take Maedoc for a slave. My father is dead."

"God forgive these pagans. Does he violate you?" the priest says, nodding toward Ulf.

She shakes her head. "I sleep next to him, but he doesn't touch me. He protects me."

Ulf puts his hand on the priest's arm. "Maedoc?" he says, slightly mispronouncing the name.

Father Jaffrez answers in Ulf's tongue.

Ulf stares a moment at the priest, and then at Aoife. He unties the leather strap around his waist and hands it to Gro. He walks off.

"You have two weddings," the priest says. "Norse first, then Christian. This she-bear and the other women come to prepare you. She is the barbarian's nurse when he is a baby. I am to explain the words. It is in two days. The barbarian stays with the men here in the village until the wedding."

"Do you know why he marries me and does not take me, like the other women?"

The priest nods. "Your mother was Norse. Your Norse blood saves you, but who knows for what?"

Aoife, the priest, and Gro begin the walk to the hut. Sten follows.

"Do you know my mother?" Aoife says.

The priest nods. "I marry her and your father. She lives with us in the south from a child. She comes when a boat washes up on the shore. Her name is Astrid. In the Norse tongue it means beautiful. And you favor her closely."

"How do you speak their words?"

"I am one of their slaves when I am a boy, taken from my family. I learn to speak their words."

She stays at the hut, away from Ulf. She wonders where he is. And what he thinks. She wonders where Maedoc is.

When Gro opens a chest brought with her, she removes a plain linen dress and holds it against Aoife. Aoife turns to the priest, who sits at the table.

"You tell her I have a wedding dress. It's in the hills. I hide it when the Norsemen come."

The priest speaks to Gro, and Aoife sees the older woman frown before she speaks.

"She goes with you to retrieve it," Father Jaffrez says. He points to Sten. "And the ogre goes as well."

The three of them walk up into the hills. Aoife knows she takes them to her hiding place, but there's nothing to be done. If she is to marry, she wears her mother's dress.

The dress is where she left it, neatly folded and protected from the rain. The circlet and knife are underneath it. She wants to return to the hut immediately, but a panting Gro, out of breath from the walk, motions to her to unfold it.

Aoife unfolds it and holds it against her. She sees surprise on the faces of Gro and Sten. She looks at the dress but sees nothing different.

When she shows them the circlet and the knife, surprise gives way to shock.

They continue to stare, and then Sten speaks gruffly to Gro, motioning to return. Gro carries the dress, circlet, and knife.

The priest sleeps at the table but awakens when they enter the hut. He sees something changes in the demeanors of both Gro and Sten.

When Aoife unfolds the dress, the priest nods.

"Your mother's dress," he says. "And the circlet with its pagan symbol."

"Why do they show surprise?' she says.

The priest speaks to Gro. At first, she says nothing, only looks at Sten. Finally, she says something to the priest, and Aoife sees Father Jaffrez is surprised.

"The she-bear says this is the circlet of a princess," he says to Aoife. "I do not tell them, but it is with your mother when she is found as a child. The boat contains a chest." He pauses. "There are old stories told about your mother, that she is the daughter of a king. She tells me she waits for her family to come for her, but they never come. She is old when she marries your father, some 30 summers. She wears this dress and circlet. I do not tell them this, but they ask if you are more than a simple island girl. Does the barbarian say anything to you?"

She shakes her head. "Nothing. I only know a few of his words, and he a few of mine. "

The priest points to the knife. "I remember that. Your mother presents it to your father when they marry."

Sten pushes the priest and mutters in his words.

"He wants me to speak their language. I explain what I know." He begins speaking their words, and Aoife watches as Gro's eyes widen at the priest's tale. Then she speaks at length.

The priest turns to Aoife. "There are two ceremonies. Before the Norse wedding, pagan as it is, you sit in the bathhouse. First water is poured over heated stones, very warm, to sweat the dirt away. You are given small branches to strike yourself with. It is part of the cleansing. Then a bath of ice. Finally, a warm bath, and the she-bear finishes by scrubbing you. Your barbarian does the same, but in a different bath house. Then the ceremony comes, and we learn what it is when they do it. My child memories fail me. Then I marry you according to the faith. Do you know your barbarian says he is a Christian?"

"He wears a cross," Aoife says. "I see it on a leather strip around his neck."

"This is something odd," the priest says. "The she-bear says your barbarian is the youngest of three sons of a king named Erik. The oldest brother is sickly; the middle brother is king after his father, but he prefers to fight and pillage. But he is king when his father dies, and your barbarian loves him and supports him." He shakes his head. "I perform your wedding, or this ogre here kills me. And it is Friday, or what these pagans call Frigge's Day, their goddess of marriage."

Early Friday morning, before the sun rises, Gro pokes Aoife awake. She eats bread and cheese. Gro and the other women hurry her down to the village, where Aoife sees a new hut. They rush her inside, giggling, and quickly strip off her dress and under-garments. Then the cleansing begins. Steam from water poured over heated rocks makes her sweat. Gro hands her a small branch, and then holds her hand to show her how to strike herself. It's not a gentle strike, but neither is it hard. When she's done it enough to satisfy Gro and the women, they set her into a tub of freezing water, pushing her head under so that she surfaces choking and coughing. The women laugh and nudge each other, speaking their Norse words.

The women wrap her in coarse wool cloth, surround her, and take her back to the hut. They dry her hair, combing its length. Aoife wears it tied with a strap, but they leave it untied. They murmur and nod to each other. They lift the wedding dress over her head, and on to her body, tying it with a linen belt. One of the women brings the wooden circlet, decorated with flowers and vines. Gro fully inspects her and eventually nods approval. Then Gro walks to the door and shouts at a Norse guard, who sits with the priest many paces from the hut.

The guard yanks the priest to his feet, and Father Jaffrez comes grumbling to the hut. When he sees Aoife, he stares before he speaks. "Whatever else your barbarian thinks, he gets a beautiful wife today."

Gro barks something to the priest. She speaks for some time.

He glowers at her, then turns to Aoife. "At the end of the ceremony, your new husband presents you with his sword. It is a symbol of the sons you bear him. And you present him with your knife, that you accept his authority over you. The she-bear here asks if you have a present for your husband."

"A present?" Aoife says.

"Yes," the priest says. "You give him a marriage present. It does not have to be of great value."

She thinks, and then she nods. "I have something."

"I don't know what pagan does the Norse ceremony. The ogre says someone comes. We see. Maybe he won't come, and I marry you in the eyes of God alone. That is enough."

When they walk down to the village, Aoife sees two new boats on the shore. More people come, men and women.

She hears laughter and good-natured shouting. She sees the remaining villagers, mostly women and children, are there as well, standing to the side and staring at feast tables laden with food.

Villagers and Norsemen alike stare at her when she arrives. She hears the murmurs.

"Your barbarian says all are invited," the priest says, "even the villagers. The Norsemen are not pleased, but they accept it. This is the best food the villagers eat for weeks, so there is that blessing from God." He pauses. "It is unusual that your barbarian goes to this much trouble and effort. There is something here I do not understand. There is more to this wedding than only a wedding."

They approach the area for the ceremony. Ulf stands there, wearing a white linen tunic and both the cross and a small hammer hanging around his neck. His hair, like hers, is decorated with flowers. She sees the sword nearby. Ulf stares at her as though he never sees her before.

A Norseman steps between them and speaks words she does not understand. She repeats words when the man motions to her, with an occasional nudge from Father Jaffrez. And then Ulf kneels before her and presents the sword, which she accepts and then hands to Gro. Then she kneels before Ulf, removes the jeweled knife from the bag tied to her waist, and presents it to him.

She hears loud audible gasps from many of the Norsemen. At first, Aoife is not sure if everything suddenly goes wrong. And then

Ulf reaches to her and accepts the knife. She sees wonder, shock, and even mild alarm on his face. He speaks to the priest.

"Your barbarian asks if this belongs to your mother," the priest says.

She looks into Ulf's face and nods. She touches the dress and the wooden circlet, and she sees his eyes widen when he sees the symbol, which he gently touches.

The Norse priest speaks loudly, and the people erupt in cheers.

Ulf motions to Father Jaffrez, who begins the Christian ceremony. He says the words in Norse and repeats them in the words of the village.

At the end, the priest speaks to Ulf, who turns to Aoife. He takes her chin with his thumb and forefinger, leans toward her, and kisses her.

His lips taste sweet. She sees uncertainty in his eyes.

They sit at the wedding table. Everyone finds a seat. The villagers are set apart, but they have tables and the same food and drink. The priest sits next to Aoife.

"Can you tell my husband that I thank him for inviting the villagers?" she says to the priest. "And make sure he knows I call him my husband."

The priest raises his eyebrows and mutters. He speaks to Ulf, who looks at Aoife and kisses her again. He then speaks to the priest for several moments, nodding toward Aoife.

"He wants me to tell his beautiful wife," Father Jaffrez says, "that he tells his people not to expect the bride and groom to get drunk.

That is apparently a custom the pagans have, which surprises me not. He also says it is a Norse custom for your wedding night to be seen by six witnesses, God preserve us from these pagans, but that he decides they stay outside the hut, not inside. There is hope for your barbarian yet."

Aoife looks at Ulf and touches his face. "Thank you."

The feast continues for several hours, and there is dancing, storytelling, and much drinking. Finally, Ulf stands, speaks to the assembled people, and leads her away, towards the hut. The celebration continues behind them.

They are followed by Gro, two other Norse women, Sten, another Norseman, and Father Jaffrez. When they reach the hut, Ulf motions to them to sit several feet from the entrance. He leads Aoife inside.

They spend long moments looking at each other. He pulls from his tunic a small parcel wrapped in cloth and places it in her hand. She opens it to find a ring with a beautiful green stone.

When she looks at him, he speaks in her words. "My mother's."

She's not sure why the tears form in her eyes, but they do. She then pulls her blue stone necklace from round her neck, and places it over his head and on to his chest. He touches it. He stands there, staring at her almost in wonder, and then he loosens his belt. He reaches and unties hers.

Later, she sees him get up and go to the door. She's not sure what he's says but she knows he dismisses the six witnesses. He then comes back and lies next to her. He has been gentle with her. She traces his lips with her finger.

When she wakes, she can see by the fading darkness that the day has barely begun. Ulf is standing in the doorway, looking toward the village and the sea. She walks to him and reaches around him to place her hands on his bare chest, leaning her head against his back.

"Eat?" she says.

"Eat," he says. "Yes."

Her heart tells her she has fallen in love with this strange man, with his harsh-sounding words, the words she does not understand, and the tenderness he gives her. But she is not sure he loves her.

Three full moons come and go. Ulf, with Sten's help, enlarges the hut, with three more rooms. One room contains the new hearth, large for several cooking pots at once. Aoife gathers white carrots, cabbages, and peas. Gro teaches her to boil mutton for the mid-day stew, which Gro calls *skause*. They store grains from the south, and Ulf says next year the seeds are planted.

The village changes. The Norsemen rebuild what they burn and add new huts, some of stone but most of wood. A small hut is made for Father Jaffrez, who complains about the pagans and barbarians but is surprised to find more of them each Sun Day at worship. At first, they come because of Ulf, the one they look to as leader. Then it is more from their own interest. He marries some of the Norsemen to village women.

Ulf takes her out in a fishing boat. She's never been on the sea, and she finds it a wonder. She feels a different wind from the hillside, a wind smelling of sea salt. All the Norsemen fish, and Ulf laughs as they haul in laden nets. She watches him guide the sail in the wind, the same intent look on his face as when he lies next to her at night.

She and Ulf learn each other's words faster and faster. She now speaks in Ulf's tongue, at least like a Norse child. Gro laughs and encourages her, gently correcting her when she makes mistakes. She sees Ulf smiles when she speaks his words.

Everything changes the day the new boats arrive.

Aoife and Gro are harvesting carrots when she straightens her back. She feels something changing in her body. She suspects she's with child, but she says nothing, not even to Ulf. She misses her time twice, and the third time is now due. She also feels a slight thickening in her stomach, and her dress is tighter. Her appetite grows. So far, she hides it. She wants to be sure. She does not know if it pleases Ulf or not.

As she stands straight, she sees the sails of boats arriving near the shore. The Norsemen crowd at the water's edge. She can even make out Ulf's fair hair, because he is so tall.

"Boats," she says to Gro. "Strangers."

Gro stands quickly and looks. "Come. We clean up. It is the king, your husband's father. It is his sails."

They hurry to the hut and wash their hands and arms. Gro quickly winds Aoife's hair into a bun and secures it. She gives her a quick inspection and nods. "This is good. When Ulf presents you to his father, remember to do this," and Gro manages a small curtsy and bowed head.

Aoife nods, and the two women hurry to the village.

The king is tall, like Ulf, with the pale blue eyes, but with black hair and beard both turning gray. Aoife sees the man's strength. He embraces his son and Sten, and he greets the other Norsemen with laughter and great shouts. When he sees Aoife, he stands still and stares.

Aoife remembers to curtsy. But she stares at the king. He is wearing the mate of the jeweled knife she gave to Ulf on the wedding day. Ulf follows her stare, and he sees the knife as well.

"Who is this?' the king says to his son.

"This is my wife, Aoife." He pulls the matching knife from his tunic and shows his father. "I obey your words and marry her."

A younger man looking much like the king but shorter swaggers into the group. "Good work, little brother. You found her."

Aoife looks in confusion at Ulf. The king continues to stare. Then he speaks.

"What is your mother's name?"

She's aware that the priest now stands next to her.

"Her mother's name is Astrid," Father Jaffrez says. "She marries Aoife's father and presents him with the knife your son holds. Aoife presents it to Ulf on their wedding day."

The king staggers as if hit. He leans against Ulf, and Ulf puts his arm around his father to steady him.

"Were you married the Norse way?" the king says to Ulf.

"Yes, Father. The Norse way first, then the priest marries us the Christian way."

The king glares at Father Jaffrez. "Priests!" He spits on the ground.

Father Jaffrez smiles and shrugs.

The king looks again at Aoife and points at her stomach. "And when is my grandchild born?"

Ulf, startled, looks at Aoife, as do Gro and Sten.

Aoife looks directly at King Erik and speaks his words. "In six more passings of the moon."

The Norsemen break into cheers.

The king smiles and laughs, clapping Ulf on the back.

"We have a feast," he says, "a feast to celebrate. It is to be our farewell. My sons and I sail south." He laughs again.

It's Aoife's turn to be shocked.

Later, when his father goes to rest, Ulf and Aoife return to their hut. They walk in silence, followed by Gro and Sten.

At the hut's door, Ulf turns to them and says, "I speak with Aoife alone."

She sits at the table, and he joins her.

"Why do you not tell me about the child?" he says.

"Because I want to be sure," she says. "Many times, women lose their children before birth."

"If I know, I am gentler with you."

"You are always gentle with me, Ulf. It's how I come to love you. You are tender with me, even if you're not sure you love me. I see confusion in your eyes."

He is quiet for a time. And then he speaks.

"For years, I am to marry Revna. She is of a good family but not royal. She is a very beautiful woman. I have strong feelings for her, and I believe she has strong feelings for me."

"You do not marry her?"

"My father comes to me and says Revna marries Roar, my brother you meet today. Revna decides that marriage to me is not enough. She wants to be a queen. And so, behind my back, she plays up to my brother. He likes the attention and to best his younger brother. My father sends me away; there is much anger in my heart, at my brother and my father. He sends me to the Dane Land, where your mother is born, and I stay there two cycles of the seasons. They marry when I leave. When I return, we live in peace, but it is not friendly. Then my father tells me he sends me west to see if the tales are true."

"The tales?"

"When my father is a boy of 10 seasons, a treaty is made with the Danes. It is about trade and alliances, and to seal it a Dane princess is promised to my father, a binding of the two families. She is still very young, but she is sent to my home. The boats leave the Dane Land with her but are never seen again. It is thought a storm finds them, and all are lost. The treaty is never completed, and my father marries my mother, from our own homeland, when he is of age."

He pauses. He is not a man of many words. Aoife sees that speaking so much costs him great effort. She puts her hand on his on the table. He places his other hand on hers and gently caresses it.

"When the priests come from the west, with their stories of the Christ, my mother believes. As do I. My father and my brothers do not. But the priests also bring a story, of a young girl who shipwrecks on a shore. She says she is a princess." He looks at her. "The Dane princess who is to marry my father is named Astrid. The priests say she grows, marries, and has a child, a girl."

Aoife gasps.

"My oldest brother is named Arne, which means eagle. He is always a wounded eagle. He breathes hard, with great effort. He is a kind man, but he cannot fight, and he cannot rule. Roar is the next son, and like his name he loves fame and he loves to fight, but he does not make a good ruler. He and Revna are married six cycle of seasons now and have no children. It causes my brother great pain, and the same for Revna. My father makes himself a thorn in the flesh on this. I love both my brothers. I see their failures, as they see mine, but I love them.

"When I come home from the Dane Land, Roar is full of anger and disappointment because Revna has no children. They blame each other and they fight with words. Roar picks fights with me and others. Seasons pass, and my father loses patience. But he sends me away, not Roar. I am to look for Astrid and her daughter, much to my mother's sorrow. He wants to find out if the priests' stories are true.

"We go to many places where shipwrecks happen, but we learn nothing, until we come to Father Jaffrez's island. He knows, and he says there is a child. While we talk, men sent by my brother come to invade, and we are busy to stop the attack. Some of his men hear of what the priest says and leave at night to come here to your island. We give chase but arrive almost too late. Men of your island die, and your father with them.

"When you return to the hut that day, the day we first see each other, I know that you are Astrid's daughter. You are fair-skinned and fair-haired, like no one on this island. My father tells me if I find the daughter, I am to marry her, to fulfill the old treaty. To obey my father, I cannot give you a choice. When the priest tells me about Maedoc that day on the shore, I am angry. Not with you or Maedoc, but with my father and brother. We rob you of your happiness. Your father dies and Norsemen enslave the man you are to marry." He pauses. "I ask you to forgive me."

Aoife sits, trembling. Ulf's words stun her. They tell her there is a larger story she doesn't know she is a part of. She feels the tears in her eyes.

"You say you love me," Ulf says. "What I do not expect, when I obey my father, is I come to love you. I love your wildness, when you run into the hills and laugh at the waves on the sea. I love you learning my words. I love you planting seeds in the garden. I love the light I see in your eyes. I love how you touch me when we lie together at night. I do not expect this to happen, but it does. And I am grateful."

She rises and sits in his lap, resting her head on his shoulder with her arms around his neck. "What is your mother's name?" she says.

"It is Liv, which means life."

She strokes his chest. "If we have a daughter, we name her Liv. If a son, we name him Erik, after your father. Must you go with your father and brother?"

"Yes. It is a command."

"How long?"

"A full turn of the seasons. Perhaps two."

She clung closer to him. "You are in danger. Your father and brother go to fight, and to attack."

"I promise you I come back to you. And to our child. And to make more children. I promise you."

She can't stop the sob that rises in her throat.

"Aoife, my father says you go to our homeland, to protect you and the child who is his heir. You leave here and go to my mother. Gro goes with you, and I tell Sten he comes not with me but with you. He is not happy, but he accepts it."

"Do I need his protection in your homeland?"

"No. But I rest easier, knowing Sten watches over you. And the child."

She places his hand on her stomach.

The next night is the feast. The king brings much food with his ships for the journey. His men use some now for the feast; some goes with the boats carrying Aoife to the homeland. The king and his boats first return to the south island for more.

Music and dancing fill the night, but Aoife is in no mood, and she knows Ulf will not let her dance, not now when she carries his child. They sit together and watch the others, his arm around her as she leans on his shoulder.

The night is cool, and in the hut they lie together under a wool blanket. He places his hand on her stomach.

"Gro will help you when the time comes," he says. "She is there with you. And you see me there as well, holding your hand and letting you hit me and shout at me for causing this to happen."

She smiles. "Do Norse women allow the men at the birthing?"

He laughs. "No. Men are banished from the birthing. But I force my way in and make Gro drag me out."

"Ulf. My heart aches. You are gone a long time."

"It comes right. I stay safe, and I promise you I return to make more babies."

She snuggles close and clings to him.

"Gro makes clothes for you to wear. When you arrive, you come as my wife and a princess. You know I love you. You are calm and have a steady heart. My mother welcomes you with joy, and she sees you carry a child. She loves you, Aoife. Gro helps you. And Sten watches over you."

"And God watches over you, my husband. He keeps you safe."

They eat the morning meal quickly, and Ulf walks with Aoife, Gro and Sten to the waiting boats. Gro uses one of her own traveling capes and fits it to Aoife. Sten carries the trunk, with her clothes, wedding dress, and circlet.

Standing in the surf, Ulf lifts her into the boat. "When you arrive," he says, "wear the circlet. Let them know that a princess comes, my beautiful princess."

She sees the tears in his eyes, and she kisses him with passion.

Sten comes to the boat, dragging Father Jaffrez, lifting him up and seating him behind Aoife. Then he climbs in next to him.

"It appears," the priest says, "I come with you, the she-bear, and the ogre."

The Norsemen row the boat toward the sea. They row until they find the wind for the sail. Aoife watches Ulf on the beach until he becomes a speck and disappears.

The journey requires ten risings and settings of the sun. Gro is sometimes sick with the rolling of the waves, as is Father Jaffrez, but Aoife is untouched. She tends to both. A small storm brings rain, but it quickly passes.

On the eleventh day, Aoife hears a shout from the boat on their right. She looks ahead, and sees a dim shape, one that grows larger. It gradually becomes brown and green and white. Aoife sees mountains, cliffs, and huge forests of trees.

The boats turn north. Aoife sees anticipation on the faces of Gro, Sten, and the Norsemen. They know they are nearing home. The Norsemen chatter with excitement. Aoife feels only tension. She hears Ulf's words in her head, but she worries about his mother, the people, Revna, and this new place she doesn't know, this place with its hard, harsh words. She thinks of the hillsides on her island and chasing the goats and sheep. She thinks of her father.

They sail for a day, passing many inlets, until they reach a wide opening. She never sees so many trees. The wind pushes the sails, until they turn into the inlet. Now the men row, even Father Jaffrez.

They reach a landing place among the trees by the shore, and Sten signals the boats to pull in. "We rest here tonight," he says. "Tomorrow, we see Trondelag."

Aoife looks at Gro. "Trondelag?"

Gro is smiling. "Yes. Home. Your home now. Where we live. The name means 'throne of law.' It is the place first made by King Erik's grandfather. You see it is a fine place."

Sten helps Aoife from the boat. They step on land for the first time since leaving her island. Gro jumps up and down in joy. Even Father Jaffrez seems pleased. The men build a fire, and they eat fish they catch in the shallows. There is singing and some stories told. Then they sleep; Aoife is surprised to fall asleep so quickly.

Gro is shaking her awake. "Up, girl! Today is the day. We get you ready."

Woolen blankets are hung between small trees. Two Norseman bring a small pot of water warmed over the fire. Gro washes her and her hair, fluffing it dry and then combing it. She pulls a dress of light and dark blue from the chest and drops it over Aoife. It fits tight at her stomach. She finds the wooden circlet and places it on Aoife's head. Gro nods, smiling.

Sten lifts her into the boat, and they push off into the water, heading deeper into the inlet. Aoife watches the water change from the green of the sea to the blue of fresh water. She sees some of the men dip their hands over the side and scoop the water to drink.

"It is the river," Sten tells her.

"What is a river?"

"It's a very big stream. You see."

The boats make a turn, and Aoife sees what she has never seen before.

"Trondelag!" Sten says with a shout. "Trondelag!"

The Norsemen cheer.

403

It is bigger than any village Aoife imagines. Hundreds of houses and buildings, with steep carved roofs, line the shore and go up into the hills.

And at the top sits the largest house of all. Aoife has no words to describe it.

Gro sees where she's looking. "Home," she says. "You live there. The king's house."

People see them hundreds of yards from the shore. They run down the hill to greet the boats. Aoife sees many boats, of many sizes and with many kinds of sails. She is struck with wonder at all she sees.

Then she remembers Ulf's words, that she arrives as a princess. She sits very straight, her hands folded in her lap.

Behind her serious smile, she worries. She is Ulf's wife, yes, and carrying his child. But she is also the daughter of the woman picked for King Erik, the woman he sends his son to search for. What does Ulf's mother think?

The boats reach the riverbank. Voices of welcome call out to Sten and the other Norsemen, and the growing crowd cheers. Women call out Gro's name when they see her.

Father Jaffrez touches Aoife's arm from behind. "It is best I walk behind you, not with you."

Aoife nods. She understands. As she looks around, she sees intense interest and curiosity on the faces of the people. People are craning their necks to see her and Father Jaffrez. They point at her circlet.

Sten speaks. "I escort the Princess Aoife, wife of Prince Ulf, to the queen." The people clap their hands and break into cheers. She sees a few boys dash ahead up the street leading to the tall building at the top, running to tell the news.

They walk as a group. Sten leads; the Norsemen from the boats form a guard in front and back. Sten walks ahead of Aoife; Gro and Father Jaffrez follow her.

As the street leads upward, they pass houses and shops. The smells are wildly different from what she has known – animals, yes, and people, but also strange, exotic smells, like spices. They pass vendors cooking food in pots and offering bowls to taste. She manages to control her fear when she sees what Gro tells her later is a horse; Aoife never sees one before.

They reach the gate of the large house, with people crowding around them. The guards nod at Sten, and they pass into a courtyard. Waiting near a large door is an older woman wearing a crown, attended by a beautiful, raven-haired woman. Sten bows, as Aoife and Gro both curtsy.

"What have you brought me, Sten?" the queen says.

"This is Princess Aoife, the wife of Prince Ulf."

The queen walks forward and quickly looks Aoife up and down. She eyes the priest behind her.

"Is this your priest?" the queen asks.

"Yes, ma'am," Aoife says in her soft voice. "He serves our island, and others."

"Your father's name?"

"It is Braden."

"And your mother's?"

"My mother's name is Astrid, ma'am. She dies giving me birth. My father is a fisherman, and he raises me."

The queen suddenly smiles. "Welcome to Trondelag, my daughter. Sten, tell your men we eat in the great hall. It is being prepared. Aoife, this is your sister Revna, the wife of my son Roar."

Equals, Revna and Aoife both nod their heads to each other. Revna looks her over and speaks. "You carry Ulf's child."

The queen peers closely at Aoife's stomach and laughs. "Sten, you bring more than a daughter to me! Come, let us celebrate."

The queen seats Aoife between herself and Revna. Servants hurry with food and drink.

They talk as they eat. Aoife wants nothing more than to sleep, but she sees this meal is important. She prays she remembers everything Gro tells her. Gro sits nearby but not close enough to help if Aoife makes a mistake.

"I tell you, daughter," the Queen says, "that my heart aches when my husband sends my son on his journey. My husband thinks of his youth and what he loses, the princess he is to marry to seal the treaty. He settles for a village girl he finds in a wheat field at harvest." She sees the surprise on Aoife's face. "No, I am not of royal blood. He wants his way with me, but I refuse, so he marries me. His family is not happy, but so be it. They are gone now. How does Ulf find you?"

"I tend the sheep and goats on the hillside when the Norsemen come. My father makes me hide. Ulf finds me when I return to find my father. Father Jaffrez tells him my mother's story."

"Your father stays on the island?"

"My father dies on the shore, ma'am."

The queen is quiet for a time. She drinks the mead in her cup.

"The path of a woman is hard, Aoife," she says. "Our husbands put children in our bellies and go off to fight their wars, to gain fame and glory. We sit and pray they return to us unharmed. And they think we are grateful when they do. Tell me, do you love my son?"

"I love him, yes, ma'am. More than my words speak."

Servants bring her to her room, which is Ulf's room. The bed is large, with fur covers. From the window she sees down to the boats. The bigness of Trondelag overwhelms her, but she determines to learn it.

Days pass. She spends much time each day with the Queen and Revna. They talk, they sew, they weave, they walk through Trondelag. Gro is always with them, and Sten follows when they walk. The queen teaches her the story of the family, how they come to this place, and what they build and do. It is a story that fills the queen with pride.

She meets Arne. She sees his illness grows worse, and he never leaves his bed. He asks his mother to send Aoife every day, to tell him stories of her life, her island, and Ulf.

Aoife sees how much Ulf looks like Arne.

"Ulf is the best of us," Arne says. "He is strong and honest, and he is brave. He does not need to show his courage like Roar, because it is in his bones."

"He is gentle with me," Aoife says.

Arne smiles. "It is his way, from when he was a boy. My father mistakes gentleness for weakness. It is Ulf's strength."

As Arne grows weaker, he asks her to retell her stories of the rocks and hillsides, and the sounds of the sea.

"Why do you believe in this Christ?" he says.

"Because it is true."

He is silent, thinking. "Can you send your priest to me?"

A few days pass. Arne is too weak for their talks, but Father Jaffrez stays with him.

It is three moons before the birth when Arne dies. The queen says little; she does not weep. The Council of Elders sets the funeral; Arne's body is taken down to the boats. Aoife stands with Liv, Revna, and Father Jaffrez as they watch the boats sail toward the sea.

They walk back to the king's house, Liv and Revna walking ahead.

"They place his body in a boat and set it afire in the sea, according to the pagan custom," Father Jaffrez says to Aoife. "But it is too late. Prince Arne is already in the arms of Jesus."

"What?" Aoife says, clutching the priest's arm.

"He asks me to baptize him, and I do. He waits until the end, but he believes. The queen knows, but no one else. It is better to keep this between us."

Even when snows begin, Aoife walks in the town, always with Sten, as long as she can, learning streets and neighborhoods and the people. She learns that Trondelag has different sections, one for merchants, one for the foreign traders who crowd the shore, one for the food markets, one for the craftsmen and tradesmen, one for the rich, and one for the poor. Trondelag is a noisy place, she thinks, but it is a good noise, a busy noise, filled with purpose and work.

But she also sees what many do not wish her to see. She sees slaves beaten. She sees drunkenness. She sees women pulling men into sheds and doorways.

"They sell their bodies," Sten says, when she asks.

They walk on. "Sten, Ulf grows up with you from a child."

"Yes."

"How does he live with your family, and not the king's house?"

Sten is quiet for a time. He looks over his shoulder before he answers. "After his birth, Queen Liv pushes him away. She does not bind herself to him. She lives a dark time. King Erik blames the baby and sends him to my house. Gro is his nursemaid, and he lives in our house. He grows with me, my brothers, and Revna."

"Revna?" Aoife says.

"Revna is my sister. Ulf loves her, but she wants a crown. She chooses Roar." He pauses. "We all grow together, and he calls my papa his papa and my mama his mama. He learns later who he is. When the king sends Ulf to the Dane Land because of Roar and Revna, I go with him."

"The king and queen love their son Ulf?" she says.

"Yes," he says, "but it is a far love. It changes when they see you carry his child. The child they did not want, the baby they cast away, is the child who honors them with an heir."

Sten is with Aoife and Revna when they ride in a horse-drawn cart into the countryside. They stop often so Aoife can talk with the workers in the fields. She listens to their stories. She often tells the queen what she hears.

"Why do you spend so much time talking to the people?" Sten says.

"I am Ulf's eyes and ears while he is gone," she says. "And sometimes his heart."

"I think you are always his heart," Sten says. "You worry for his return, but Ulf will come back for you."

Disputes about law and property come to the Council of Elders, the older nobles and landowners who serve the king. At their table, she sees some empty seats; Revna says those elders are with the king and his sons on the journey. The queen presides but she rarely speaks or takes part in the council's talk.

One morning, she and Sten walk from the king's house to the tradesmen's quarters; she asks to see how a forge works to make weapons and tools. The owner walks them through the large hut; she sees the fires and hears the pounding of the hammer on the metal. Dirt and grime cover the men working.

One man, a young one, looks up and stares. His face is so filled with soot and smoke that Aoife can only see his eyes. She stiffens; she sees the eyes of Maedoc. Sten sees her looking but does not recognize him.

Maedoc gives her a slight shake of his head and returns to pounding a piece of metal with a hammer.

"He is one of the slaves," the forge owner says, following her gaze. "One of the better ones, but they're mostly useless."

"Do they work harder if they are free men?" she says.

"All of them, slave or free, dream only of riding the boats to find gold."

She thanks the owner, and they leave. As they walk back to the king's house, Sten speaks.

"You know that slave in the forge."

Aoife nods. "He is from my village on the island. If your boats come a few suns later, he is my husband."

Her words startle Sten into quiet.

The last weeks before the birthing are hard. She sleeps little: she finds no easy place to sit or lie down. The baby is large, which worries Gro and the midwife. The child now moves almost constantly, kicking her ribs.

Aoife is working at the loom when she feels a pain. Gro, always at her side now, sees Aoife scowl and press her hand to her back.

"Do you feel a pain?"

"I feel pain every day for weeks," Aoife says. "This is no different."

She stands to stretch, and water splashes at her feet. In an instant, Gro is up and shouting. Servants come running.

They bring her to her room, Ulf's room. Gro and the midwife insist she lie down on the bed. But Aoife shakes her head. "I walk."

She walks around the room, pausing only to breathe deeply as the midwife tells her when the pains come. The queen arrives and walks with her. They walk in the room and the hallways.

At times, the midwife tells her to lie down and part her legs. The midwife looks, and for several times shakes her head. "Not yet."

Aoife loses track of time. She keeps walking. The pains are more frequent, coming closer together. When the midwife looks again, she nods. "Soon. Time to push."

The queen leaves; she attends a meeting of the Council of Elders. In between pushes, Gro wipes Aoife's forehead with a cold cloth.

In her mind, Aoife talks to Ulf. She imagines he's in the room with her, and it is him, not Gro, who wipes her forehead. She hears him praying for her and the child.

"The head shows," the midwife says. "One last push. A big one."

She pushes with a loud moan and feels the child slide between her legs. She gasps for breath and hears the baby cry.

"A son," says the midwife. "You give your husband a son."

Aoife cries and laughs. Gro places the baby in Aoife's arms.

"It is better now," Gro says. "The pain is gone. The child sac comes soon."

Suddenly, another pain wracks Aoife's body. She cries out. Frightened, Gro takes the baby; Aoife grips the back of the bed. She breathes and pants, and then pushes hard with a huge groan.

The midwife's eyes grow huge, and she quickly grasps the second baby sliding between Aoife's legs.

There is a second cry, and the midwife laughs. "A daughter! You bear your husband a double yolk! The boy first and then the girl!"

Aoife falls back on the bed, panting. The sac is expelled. The wracking pains are gone, leaving her exhausted but calm.

"Ulf and I have the names," Aoife says. "The boy is Erik, after his grandfather. The girl is Liv, after her grandmother."

The midwife places the babies in Aoife's arms, guiding their mouths to her breasts. The boy sucks greedily. After a few moments, the girl does as well.

Gro sends a servant running to the great hall. The girl tells the master of the guard standing at the door. He enters the hall and pounds his staff.

"The Princess Aoife has borne a son, named Erik. And she has borne a daughter, named Liv." The Elders stand and cheer. The queen and Revna hurry from the Great Hall. They find Aoife feeding the babies.

She smiles at her mother-in-law and her sister. "They are beautiful," Aoife says. "My heart bursts with love."

The queen declares a celebration for Trondelag.

The children both thrive. The queen overflows with delight with her grandchildren. Aoife sees love for the children mingled with sadness on Revna's face. To her surprise, she and Revna become close friends, and Revna often accompanies Aoife and Sten into shops and quarters of the town.

"I am foolish, Aoife," Revna says as they walk. "I want to be a queen, so I leave Ulf and seek Roar. Now I have sadness. I have no children, and no love from Roar or my brothers, Sten most of all."

They are royal family, but they also work. When planting season comes, they join the people in the fields to work the soil, remove weeds and grasses, and plant seeds. The queen works with them; the babies are tended nearby by a nursemaid. Father Jaffrez works the fields as well. His duties are light; he leads worship on Sundays, hears confession, and performs two marriages. He baptizes the twins.

Sten surprises as well. Erik and Liv capture the big, gruff Norseman's heart. He likes nothing better than to hold them on his lap, tell them stories they don't understand, and sing songs that make them laugh.

"Who knows the ogre has a heart?" Father Jaffrez says.

Gro takes charge of the nursery. She instructs the nursemaids each day, watches their work closely, and sees the children are fed well and their cloths changed.

When they have free time, Aoife and Revna walk down to the shore to watch the fishermen and the trading boats arrive. They ask visitors for news. No word of the king, Roar, or Ulf reaches them.

It is at a dinner for new traders in the Great Hall that Aoife sees what she has not seen before. Skarde, a member of the Council of Elders, talks with Revna. Aoife sees Revna smile and blush. Skarde is a noble, with a large farm and house just north of Trondelag. He is also many turns of seasons older than Revna, with two grown sons sailing with the king and Roar. His wife is dead many seasons now. Aoife sees Revna glow with Skarde's words.

After the dinner, they walk to their rooms. Aoife tells Revna to take care. The woman first bristles, then calms herself. "You're right, Aoife, and you tell me what is best. But it is nice to hear a man say something other than how barren I am."

"Do you miss Roar?" Aoife says.

"I wish to. But my life is calm when he goes. When he returns, he puts me aside. He needs an heir."

"Surely, he does not, Revna," Aoife says.

"Surely, he does, Aoife. I know my husband. He seeks a new wife."

"What happens if he does that?"

"I go back to my family with shame; it is my oldest brother since my father is dead. Roar chooses to provide for me or not. I think not, but then he sends back my dowry. And I know what your kind heart tells you, that you try to stop him. For your own good, do not do that. It is bad enough when he returns and finds your children. They make Ulf a rival to his brother."

Time passes. They hear nothing.

The owner of the forge comes to the Council of Elders to seek an approval. Aoife and Revna are sitting with the other women, listening to the meeting.

"One of my slaves," he says, "wishes to marry. I come to the council for permission."

Revna leans and whispers to Aoife. "The Council decides if a slave marries. They worry about too many slaves in Trondelag."

"If they are concerned," Aoife whispers back, "why not free them and pay then a wage?"

"Shhh," Revna says.

The forge owner is questioned, and Aoife can see that the council is not inclined to grant permission.

"Who is this slave?" the queen says.

"His name is Maedoc," the forge owner says, "and he is my best worker. It is a boon to allow him to wed."

The elders talk and still seem against the idea. Aoife stands up.

The queen sees her and smiles. "Yes, my daughter, do you wish to say something?"

"I know this man," she says. "He is from my island. Because the Norsemen look for me there, the people suffer, and he and others are taken for slaves. I don't want to ask a favor. But can the council help this man? May I ask the elders that they grant permission for him to marry?"

It is at this moment the queen learns the great regard the elders and the rest of Trondelag have for Princess Aoife. The queen sees that the princess impresses the council with her words, their minds change, and soon the elders grant permission without dissent. When the meeting ends, the princess speaks to each elder and thanks them.

"It is because the people of Trondelag see you and know you," Revna tells her later. "The elders hear of the kind princess who cares for the city and its people." She smiles sadly. "The princess also has children, bringing order to the king's house."

A full moon later, Aoife is in the tradesmen quarter with Sten, buying pots for the royal kitchen, when Maedoc approaches her in the street. With him is a young woman.

They both bow their heads before her.

"I want to thank you, highness, for speaking to the elders.," Maedoc says. "This is Sif, my wife; we are wed."

Aoife takes Sif's hand. "I am happy for you both. I want you to love him, Sif, because he is a good man, and he provides for you and loves you." She looks at Maedoc and sees many emotions in his eyes. She smiles at them both, kisses Sif on the cheek, and returns to the king's house with Sten.

"He is the one you are to marry then," Sten says, "before we come."

"Yes. My father arranges it."

Sten is silent for a time as they walk, and then he speaks. "It is a kind thing you do."

"I have no regrets for me, Sten," Aoife says. "I am content with him, but I do not love him. It is my husband I love, with a passion that grows each day he's not with me. He grows in my heart, and it for his touch I hunger. I pray to God each day to keep him safe and bring him home to me and his children." She pauses. "Sten, how does Ulf come to believe in the Christ?"

"We are young men, barely 14 turns of the seasons, when the priests come," he says. "They come on a trading ship. And they speak to the people. Some are angry, but others listen. Ulf and I listen. Queen Liv hears the people talk, and she asks the priest to speak at the court.

417

She and King Erik listen, and the king wants to kill them. But the queen says no. She pays for their worship house to be built. It is when Ulf and I go to the worship house that she sees us and comes to love the son she sent away."

The seasons turn, and turn again. It is early spring, and the twins pass their second birthday. Revna and the queen no longer speak of the return of the king and his sons. But in good and bad weather, Aoife walks to the shore with Sten, asking for news among the traders and visitors. She refuses not to have hope. The queen says nothing, but Aoife hears rumors that she and the elders speak of a regency until Erik comes of age.

It is an unusually fair and warm day when a messenger arrives. The king's ships, or ships flying his sails, are rowing toward Trondelag.

Almost in one motion, the king's house empties of family and servants alike. All Trondelag races for the shore. Aoife, holding the hands of the children, must walk more slowly. Sten scoops them up, and they hurry to the harbor.

People throng the shore, all silent while they watch for the first sail to run the bend in the river toward the city. Aoife stands with the queen and Revna. She holds the hands of Erik and Liv, while Sten stands behind her. The two children hide in their mother's skirts.

The first sail is sighted, and the crowd cheers. Other boats are following but lagging behind the first, which lands. Norsemen jump off and begin shouting for wives and family.

The second boat lands. Aoife sees it is heavily laden with trunks and bags.

The third boat brings the king. Aoife hears a sob from the queen as she sees her husband. But he does not jump from the boat. Four Norsemen lift him in a chair. The queen rushes into the water to embrace her husband. As he comes to the shore, with the queen by his side, Aoife can see he does not look well. And his left leg is missing below the knee.

More laden boats arrive, and she sees no sign of Ulf or Roar. Revna is next to her, craning her neck.

"Where are they?" Revna says. "Why do they not sail with the king?"

The king sees the two princesses, and he turns his head. For the first time, Aoife feels fear.

The boats continue to land. Soon there are only two more coming. The shore contains great confusion, with masses of people and men from the ships shouting and laughing. Aoife hears wails from women hearing of dead husbands and fathers.

She contains herself, but she trembles in fear, praying to God for her husband.

And then a man steps in front of her. "Aoife?"

She looks into his ice-blue eyes. "Ulf?"

He takes her in his arms and kisses her with a passion that nearly knocks her down.

Tears on her face, she touches her hands to his face and his beard. "You are home."

She feels him peer over her shoulder. "What is this behind you?" Ulf says.

Aoife pulls Erik from her skirts. "This is Erik, your son."

Ulf kneels in front of the boy, who peers shyly at his father. Ulf suddenly scoops him up and kisses his head.

Aoife then pulls the girl from her skirts. "And this is your daughter, Liv."

Ulf's eyes widen. He lifts the girl with his other arm. "We have two?"

Aoife nods with smiles and tears. Tears in his own eyes, Ulf laughs.

"What do we say to this man, children?" Aoife says.

Together, the children speak. "Welcome, Papa."

Ulf can no longer control his tears. He pulls Aoife to him and holds his family.

"Ulf," says Revna, "where is Roar?"

"I'm sorry, Revna," he says, "Roar is dead. He dies in the fighting."

Flooded with her own happiness, Aoife reaches for Revna and holds her. Revna is silent but does not weep.

As she holds Revna, the meaning of Ulf's words strikes her.

Celebration mixes with sadness in the streets as the family makes its way to the king's house. Sten walks behind Ulf and Aoife. Ulf carries his children.

Ulf stops and turns to Sten.

"I owe you a debt I cannot repay," he says. "You watch over my Aoife and my children. I give you half of what I bring home."

Norsemen and slaves follow them into the great hall, bringing the trunks and bags. Servants are already bringing food to the tables. The king orders the women to sit with the men. The queen sits by the king. Aoife sits by Ulf, who has both the children on his lap.

"You spoil them," Aofie says, laughing.

"Good," Ulf says. "This is my plan." As food is brought, he feeds Erik and Liv.

Stories are told. But the telling of what happens to Roar waits for the king to tell it. When he speaks, the hall is silent.

"We sail on the sea many moons to the south," the king says. "We find gold and plunder, although my third son holds back, refusing to fight unless it is soldiers."

Aoife looks at Ulf, whose jaw is set as he listens to his father.

"We sail across the channel to the long coast, following it south. The days get warmer, even in the winter. At some towns we stop; others we pass by. Everywhere we bring Thor's hammer."

Aoife sees the king speaks with pride, but she does not see pride on her husband's face.

"We come to a land where the men wear robes, like women," the king says, causing laughter in the hall. "Their heads are wrapped in cloths, also like women." The laughter grows. "We think the fighting is simple and easy, but the men are fierce, stronger than we meet so far. We land at a place near a city called Lis-bo-ah, greater than Trondelag. They wait for us; they see us coming. They come on horses and with many men on foot. The fighting is fierce and close.

"Roar and his men are first, and I come behind him. But they are too many and surround us."

The hall is silent. The listeners know the king speaks of his son's death.

"Ulf does what he is told not to do. I tell him to hold his men back to protect the ships. He sees the fight, what happens, and he orders his men from the boats to come behind us. He leads the fight to break through the circle around us." The king's eyes glisten. "My son Roar is run through with a spear. I am on the ground, my leg sliced with a sword, my men fighting around me, when Ulf breaks through. He is a wolf, tearing and ripping his way through the robed men and their horses. They are finally driven back and away, and we return to the boats. Many of our men are dead, but Ulf has saved most. He saves his father and brings the body of his brother. He takes prisoners. One is a doctor. We leave on the boats and travel north to a deserted place. There we rest. My leg festers, and Ulf tells the doctor to cut it off before it kills me. The man closes the wound with a rod from the fire." He pauses. "We send Roar in a fireboat to the sea."

Listening to the king, Aoife can almost hear the sizzle of the burning flesh and feel the king's pain. And she can see the flames from Roar's boat as it slowly sinks. Ulf's face is unchanged as he listens.

"My leg heals but still suffers," the king says, "so we stay in the deserted place. I tell my son I want revenge for the death of his brother, something to tell the men in robes of what happens when they fight Thor. At night, Ulf and a few men steal into the harbor of Lis-bo-ah and set ships afire. The shops and the docks burn, and the fire spreads to the quarter of the city closest to the water. The city remembers Thor's hammer."

The hall buzzes with nods and murmurs of approval. Aoife bends to see Ulf's face, but it is expressionless. She knows the story is more than the king tells.

"They find our resting place and attack. Ulf holds them off and attacks. Five hundred of their men in robes die. My son shows one weakness. He allows their women to claim the bodies of the dead for burial. The doctor says it is an insult to their god unless bodies are buried in one turn of the sun. I want him to let them rot for the birds and animals, but he grants the women their request."

Aoife leans to Ulf and whispers, "It is not a weakness. It is a strength, and a kindness." He gives her a small smile.

"After that, they no longer come. We rest a few weeks. And then we leave." The king looks at his son. "Some want to come home, but I order us south, and farther. I will tell more stories later. Servant! Mead!"

It is night. Aoife lies in Ulf's arms.

"I dream of this, many times," Ulf says. "Sometimes it is all I have to hold on to. I dream of lying with my princess in the dark, only us."

"I listen to your father, and I think the story is more than he tells."

Ulf is quiet for a time. "Roar brings his death on himself. We have a council, and I say there is something wrong with this place. My father agrees. But Roar doesn't listen. He says that men who wear robes are weak. Secretly, without speaking to my father or me, he lands with his men, and they are surprised. The men in robes are fierce fighters waiting for them. My father leads his men to the shore to help. More men in robes come. Roar runs away from his men and a spear finds his back. Then I lead my men to the shore to save my father and Roar's men.

"My father is shamed by Roar's disobedience and then his cowardice. He says he orders Roar back and the spear finds him. We know it is untrue. But we do not speak of it." He pauses. "You tell me Arne died, and I find I am what is left of my brothers."

"Father Jaffez baptizes him before he dies," Aoife says. "Arne asks for it."

"That is good," Ulf says. "This the best of what I hear today about my brothers." He touches her arm. "I lie here with you, and I think this is all that matters."

"And Erik and Liv," she says.

"And my children. Is the birth hard?"

"Yes, but Gro is here, and the midwife, and time fades the pain. And in my heart, I talk to you through the birth. I think it's you wiping my forehead and holding my hand when I push. The surprise is Liv. No one expects a second child."

"They are beautiful, Aoife. I am a blessed man."

"A blessed man who keeps his promise to come back to his wife."

He laughs. "Yes, I keep my promise to come back and make more children."

They walk in the town. Ulf is pleased to see so many people smile when they see Aoife. He is surprised she knows people by name and asks after them and their families. He sees, too, how this helps his family. And himself.

"How do you know all these things about the people?" he says.

"When I come here, Ulf, I know no one. I look at the town and the people from the window and think I want to know this place and these people, as well as I know my island. This place is what shapes my husband, and to know the people is to know my husband better. I learn the streets you run down as a boy, and the mischief you do. And I hear the stories of you and Sten." She smiles.

He laughs. "I grow up with Sten. And we do plenty of mischief on these streets. Sten tells me you wear out his shoes twice with all the walking. He says you go to the farms and talk to the people there, too." He takes her hand and kisses it. "You learn my people because you love me."

"I think sometimes I can't love you more, and then I do." She leans her head against his arm as they walk. "Sten watches over me very well, Ulf. He never complains when he comes with me to town and to the farms. And he loves our children. Does he ever think to marry?"

"He courts a woman he meets on one of your farm journeys," Ulf says. "We see what happens."

"What about your father, Ulf? His stories tell of your courage and deeds, but he says nothing of the future."

Ulf is silent for a time. "Aoife, my father sees his first son become sick and not get well. He expects Roar to follow him as king. He trains Roar in the Norse ways, how to fight, how to be a king. Some teachings stick, especially fighting. Roar sees the glory but not what it means or needs. He has no patience for ruling and the Council of Elders.

"My father does not train me. He leaves me in the hands of Sten's father, who trains me and Sten the same. It is what I know, so I do not think it strange until I become a man. I still think Sten's papa is my papa.

"My father has a problem. The son that lives is the son who believes in the Christ. It is not the Norse way. The son who lives gives him grandchildren, his heirs. And my father is not well; the doctor who wears a robe saves his life, but it is too much for a man to bear. My father lives, but not long. Before much time passes, the Council of Elders presses him on who comes after. Some want a king who follows the Norse way. Some want the crown to stay with the family. My father decides first what he wants, and then he talks with the council."

"And if he decides on a man of the Norse way?"

"Then you and I and our children leave Trondelag to live in another place. I tell my father if that is what he decides, then he gives me two days to take you and the children away. We are a threat to whomever he chooses.

"Or I fight to take his place. If I fight, many people in Trondelag die. Fighting does not make sense to me, and I don't think it makes God happy." He smiles. "But I think the people here are happy to see their princess. They love you, and their love for you comes to me. My father sees this soon. It's a time to watch and take great care."

Months pass. Aoife tells Ulf she is with child. She thanks God for her husband, who is overjoyed at the news and loves their children. The news spreads throughout the king's house, and the queen cannot stop smiling. King Erik says little, but Aoife sees him with his grandchildren, singing and crawling on the floor, and she knows he loves them.

She is two full moons from the birth when Ulf goes with Sten and others to hunt. A servant says King Erik asks to see her. She is surprised. He is always polite with her, but they never talk alone.

She is big again, and she thinks it might again be two. The kicking of her ribs is like the first time.

She enters the king's room. He sits at a table near the window.

"Come, Aoife," he says. "Come join me." She moves to curtsy, but he stops her. "It's hard enough to walk, I know, so just sit."

She never sees him so warm.

"I ask you here with a reason," the king says. "But I should have no reason than just to talk. I do not think I am a good father to you."

"You provide a roof over our heads and food on our table," she says, "and a good life. Few have what we have. And I have my husband, and you provide him as well."

He smiles. "You are a grateful daughter, and Thor blesses me." He watches to see how she takes his words.

Aoife doesn't speak. She smiles and nods.

"They tell me the people love their Princess Aoife," he says. "She walks in the town in all weathers and sees what good she can do."

"I like talking with the people," she says, "and to help them. They are kind and friendly, and they love your family."

"You help even slaves, I hear," the king says.

She nods. "Slaves are people, your highness."

"Indeed. Well, it is your thought. It pleases me you are known for your kindness. Other princesses are known for arrogance or even cruelty." He looks out the window. "I ask you here to talk about my son."

"Should you talk about your son with your son?" she says.

"We are strangers," King Erik says. "It is my blame. I spend too much time on his sick brother and the brother who is too much like me. Both are dead now. Many things worry me. Ulf is brave but must be urged to fight. He seems soft when he should be hard."

"And most of all," Aoife says, "he follows the Christ way and not the Norse way."

"I see you are both kind and perceptive."

"He tells me of your problem," Aoife says. "He knows. But Father, he cannot believe another way. It's in his heart."

"Our people do not follow the Christ, or most of them."

"Who would your people want as king, a man who likes to raid and plunder and make widows and orphans, or a man who is brave and wise? In the battle with the men who wear robes, if he and his men remain in the boats, what happens to his father and brother and their men? He watches and then sails home to take the throne. But he loves his father and honors his brother. That is part of the Norse way, and it is part of the Christian way. He is shaped by both. The man he is believes in the Christ but honors what he is taught. And he honors his father. He tells you he takes us away and not make people suffer in a war if you decide someone else. He accepts your decision even if it is not him."

Aoife stops, thinking she says too much and angers the king. But he doesn't speak. Instead he stares outside the window and is silent. She sits quietly, waiting for him to speak or dismiss her. King Erik finally turns back to her.

"When my son returns from the hunt, send him to me. Do not tell him or the queen what I now tell you. My body tells me I will not see another harvest. Send my son to me when he comes."

Days pass. When the Council of Elders meets, Ulf is seated at his father's side. No one speaks of the change, but each elder understands. Sitting with the women, Aoife and Revna understand as well.

When her time for birthing comes, she finds it easier than the first. She births two sons who look the same, and she and Ulf name them Asger and Gorm. King Erik orders a celebration for all Trondelag.

In the late spring, as the seeds are planted, King Erik rests with his fathers. His son Ulf wears his father's crown. He carries his father's body to the boats. The family, Council of Elders, and many people sail down the river to the sea. Ulf lights the torch in the fireboat, and they watch it float away until it sinks.

At the feast for his crowning, Ulf announces that Revna marries the elder Skarde. He says that as a crowning present for Queen Aoife, he buys the freedom of the slaves from her island and what families they have, and they may stay in Trondelag as free people or return to their home. He says that Sten joins the Council of Elders. Sten and the woman Frida are to marry as well, Ulf says.

That night, alone in the room, Aoife holds up her hair as Ulf works to loosen the ties of her crowning dress.

"You have four children," he says, "and you still have the body of my girl from the island."

"You always say the right things, my husband, but I think you tell a story, one that is not true but one that I like."

He runs his hands along her sides and kisses her neck. "Think what you want, but I tell you no untrue story."

Aoife still trembles when he touches her.

Two full moons pass. Ulf and Aoife walk down to the harbor. Most of the people from Aoife's island freed by the king are leaving. Only a few remain in Trondelag. Sten is in charge of the five ships, and Frida decides to sail with him. They return when the people settle on the island.

Aoife sees Maedoc and Sif, who is fair skinned like the Norse. She holds a child in her arms. Maedoc carries a young boy. They bow as Aoife and Ulf approach.

"We thank you, highnesses," Maedoc says. "We return to the island."

"Maedoc," Aoife says, "you and Sig have children. What are their names?"

"My son is Ulf, and my daughter is Aoife. We name them to remember."

Aoife clutches her husband's hand.

"Good voyage, Maedoc," Ulf says, "for you and your family. You honor us with the names, and we thank you."

They watch and wave until the boats disappear from sight.

Aoife and Ulf have two more children. Two years after Gorm and Asger, a daughter is born, and they name her Astrid. The last child is a son, and Aoife insists until her husband relents to name him Ulf. They call him Little Ulf, and as he grows, Aoife sees that, of all their children, he most resembles his father in looks and deeds. All of their children share their father's ice-blue eyes.

Time passes. In Trondelag, Ulf is called Ulf the Wise. He follows the way of the Christ but does not force his people to do so. Many do, and many continue to follow the Norse way. Ulf leads no raiding or plundering parties. Trade grows. Two times, enemies from the south attack Trondelag, and Ulf leads his men to fight and defeat them. The kingdom grows larger. The king's mother is called home, and she is buried next to the large worship house her son builds in Trondelag.

Aoife is called Aoife the Beloved.

Father Jaffrez grows old. He talks with Ulf and Aoife, telling them to send to the south island for a new priest. Ulf sends Sten and two elders who believe in the Christ. They return with young Father Brennus, who tells Ulf and Aoife he thinks Sten means to kidnap him. "He's an ogre!" the priest says. Ulf and Aoife smile; know they have the right priest to follow Father Jaffrez. Six full moons later, Father Jaffrez is called home, and Ulf buries him near Queen Liv. No one mourns like Gro and Sten.

Ulf spends much time with his children. He trains all of his sons in the ways of ruling; he and Sten together teach them to fight. As they come of age, he and Aoife make sure the children marry well. Princess Liv is the first to marry, to the first son of the king of the Dane Land. Prince Erik marries a granddaughter of Skarde known for her kindness. Gorm and Asger are Ulf's mischievous sons, full of pranks and jokes, but they, too, marry girls who please Ulf and Aoife. Astrid marries the oldest son of Sten. Little Ulf, at 15 turns of the seasons, is still too young to marry.

Ulf has Prince Erik sit next to him at the Council of Elders. He is pleased with his oldest son's mind and his heart and knows he rules well. Prince Erik and his wife bless his parents with one, then a second, grandson.

Aoife asks her husband to walk with her to the harbor. Many more ships come now, with many kinds of people. The king and queen hold hands as they walk in the city.

The queen's hair is still fair, but it dulls with time. The king grays in both hair and beard. He still walks and even runs without trouble, especially with his Erik's two young sons.

They find a bench away from the bustle of the harbor and sit contentedly in silence.

"My husband," she says, "my body tells me I have not long to live."

Ulf, startled, turns to her. "Aoife?"

"It's a part of life, Ulf," she says. "Things don't work as well, and there are pains. And I see a little blood in my spittle. We have many good years; God fills us with blessings. But we grow old. Some time, he calls us home." She pauses. "I ask a favor from you."

"You know I never withhold anything you ask."

"I know, but you need to think about this. I want to go to the island of my birth. I want to live in our house there. I want to walk those hillsides while I can. And when my time comes, I want to be buried there. I love Trondelag, but I want to be buried where I am born. Am I selfish?"

Ulf puts his arm around her. "No, my beautiful wife, you are never selfish. How long does your body say?"

"A turn of the seasons, perhaps two."

He is quiet. She knows he is thinking. She rubs his hand, the hand that still makes her body warm and tremble.

"I grant us both the favor, Aoife. I do not let you go alone. Erik is ready to be king, and I place the crown on his head. We leave the next day for the island, and it is our home."

"But, Ulf, Trondelag is your home."

"No, Aoife. I learn long ago, when that girl stumbles into the hut, that my home is with you. We both go to the island."

Ulf calls a council of the family. He includes Sten. All attend, even Liv and her husband from the Dane Land. He tells them his decision, that Erik is to be king, and that he and Aoife sail to the island. Ulf allows the tears and sorrow but tells them it gives way to joy for the new king.

"I come with you," Sten says.

"No, my friend, you stay," Ulf says. "Erik needs your strength and wisdom, and your family needs you here. It is my decision, although my heart breaks." Sten surprises everyone when he weeps.

Ulf's oldest son and heir pulls him aside. "Father," Erik says, "my youngest brother Little Ulf says he comes with you. He takes care of you and Mother, and then he comes back to Trondelag. It is also my wish for this."

Ulf, tears in his eyes, nods. "I close your mother's eyes, and Little Ulf closes mine."

Erik looks at his father in alarm. "Are you sick?"

"Your mother dies first, Erik, and I after. She is sick, and she does not know that I am. I don't live much after her. This is between you and me. No one knows until three full moons after we leave. I tell Little Ulf after we arrive at the island."

Erik embraces his father.

The Council of Elders is told, and the news spreads quickly in Trondelag. The city is stunned but not worried; Erik is seen as one with his father.

Ulf sends men to the island ahead of them – a stonecutter, a wood master, helpers, and their families. They are to repair the house where Aoife and Ulf meet and where they live. He tells them to hire a young girl or woman to help Aoife.

It is late spring when Ulf crowns Erik and his wife Solveig. The city celebrates the crowning.

The next day, family, friends, and people gather at the harbor. Ulf and Aoife say goodbye to each. Ulf cries when he hugs Sten, his oldest friend, when he hugs his grandsons, and when he hugs Gro, among the oldest of Trondelag, carried down to the harbor in a chair. And then he speaks, to give his blessing.

"You do not lose us," he says, "and we do not lose you. We are in each other's hearts, and you see me and Aoife in your eyes and your hands and in the mischief of your children. My son Erik rules in wisdom and justice, and he is a loved king. Trondelag prospers now and after. Be kind. Show mercy. Show love. Serve the Christ."

Ulf helps Aoife into the boat; they cast off. Little Ulf sits next to his mother and Ulf himself stands to guide the sail, as the rowers move as one. With them are two boats of Norsemen, sent to ensure safety, and a boat carrying trunks and food.

The four boats follow the path of the river, until they are seen no more.

It is the sea air or knowing she soon sees the island, but Aoife gathers strength. All see she ails; dark circles under her eyes and her pale skin tell a story. They reach the sea, and she tells stories of her childhood to Little Ulf.

Ulf calls his son to the sail. Little Ulf sails on the sea once before now, when he goes with his parents to the Dane Land for the marriage of Liv. His father guides his hands, and then steps back.

Aoife smiles. Ulf has the same face she remembers from their sailing near the island, the same set jaw and focused eyes. Little Ulf shares that face; she is startled to see how much he looks like his father. He is now almost as tall.

They sail for 14 suns, many against a strong wind. They have much time to talk and tell stories. They celebrate Little Ulf's 16th turn of the seasons.

"Is there a girl in Trondelag, my son?" Aoife says.

Little Ulf shakes his head. "There are many girls, Mama, but none who speak to my heart. They like fine things to wear and ceremonies and jewels, and the excitement of the king's house. They're not for me." He smiles. "I know when it happens."

"Do you miss young Sten?" Ulf says. Sten's youngest child, also called Sten is the same age as Young Ulf. Close friends like their fathers, the two are called two bodies with one soul.

"No, Papa, I do not miss young Sten."

"A surprise. You two are everywhere together."

Little Ulf grins. "We still are." He points to the boat on their left, and they see young Sten, laughing and waving.

"Son," says Ulf, "does Sten know his boy is with us?"

"He hides him on the boat, Papa. He said that if you leave without your best friend, it is no reason why I do, too. And he tells young Sten to keep an eye on me and you and Mama."

Aoife laughs. "Our friend Sten still keeps his watch over us."

The four ships arrive at the island. Aoife sees the village grows into a small town, not as big as Trondelag but bigger than her days before. People see the sails and wait at the shore to pull the boats in.

"Highnesses," says a priest, "I am Father Timan, the priest here. Welcome to our home."

The artisans sent by Ulf all bow; Aoife recognizes Maedoc and Sif, even with gray hair.

"Father Timan," says Ulf, "thank you. We are Ulf and Aoife, no more highnesses. We come to live out our days in Aoife's home." He nods at Little Ulf and young Sten. "This is my youngest son, Prince Ulf, and his good friend Sten. They are here for the time they are needed."

Aoife walks to Maedoc and Sif, touching their hands. "It is good to see my friends again."

Maedoc bows his head and introduces his children, standing with them. They are grown with their own children. The young boy Maedoc carries in his arms at Trondelag is a grown man, looking much like his father. Maedoc places his hand on the shoulder of a young woman. "And this is Ailidh, my youngest child of 14 turns of the seasons. Your husband asks for a young woman to help you, and she is with your house."

Ailidh is fair like her mother, with fair hair and her father's dark blue eyes. Aoife sees the shyness and modesty in her eyes, and the beauty of the young woman's face. "I am pleased, Maedoc, to have your daughter to help. Can she show us the way to our house?"

Ailidh leads them through the village. Aoife sees many houses not from before, larger than the huts she remembers. They walk a short way up the hill; the hut of Braden and Aoife still sits apart, but Ulf's carpenters and stone mason build more and strengthen what is there. Ailidh shows them the large gathering room, the sleeping room for Ulf and Aoife, another sleeping room for Little Ulf and young Sten, and a room for making food and eating. Ailidh has a small sleeping room off the food room. The floors are swept, chairs, tables and bedding are newly made.

"I am pleased," Ulf says to the artisans and Ailidh. "It is good, more than I expect."

Aoife and Ailidh soon work with the trunks and bags, brought by the Norsemen from the boats. The men stay on the island a week to rest before the return to Trondelag. One boat is left for Ulf and his family.

Ailidh prepares the meal; Aoife sees the girl does well and knows her way with food.

Aoife and Ulf prepare to sleep. Ulf sees his wife's thinness, part from the voyage but part from her sickness. He hopes they have one or two turns of the seasons left to them, but he knows he is grateful for any time. He sees what he doesn't see for a long time: Aoife's face glows with being in her home on her island.

They have a sound sleep. They awake and eat, and Aoife says she will walk up the hill to where she tends the sheep and goats as a girl. Ulf and the two young men walk with her. The place is what she remembers. They sit in the grass.

She points to the sea. "I am here when I see the sails of the Norsemen and run to the village. My father says to hide, and I run to the hut. I take my wedding dress and circlet and run to the rocks above." She points to the rocks farther on.

"Your wedding dress, Mama?" says Little Ulf.

She nods. "I was to be married to Maedoc, the father of Ailidh. But the Norsemen come. One of the Norsemen looks for the daughter of a Dane Land princess. Her mother is to wed his father, but the ship from the Dane Land is lost in a storm. She comes to the south island. She marries a fisherman named Braden, my father, but dies giving me birth. The Norseman's father looks to his youth, and to see if the princess or her daughter are found. He sends his youngest son named Ulf, who protects the daughter and weds her. We do not tell much of this story before."

"Papa!" says Little Ulf.

"Son," says Ulf, "I see this girl and I know she is my life."

"It is hard," Little Ulf says, "to see my Papa as a young man and my Mama as a girl."

"Look in a glass," Aoife says, "or a pool of water. When you see yourself, you see your Papa as I first see him. He is tall and fair and handsome, with strong arms and shoulders. And this man honors and protects me all the days of my life."

"And this woman," Ulf says, "gives me sons and daughters, and she gives me love, all the days of our life."

Little Ulf and young Sten plow the ground by the house, and Ulf plants the seed they bring. Aoife gives coins each day to Ailidh to buy food in the village, and she's pleased to see the girl is frugal.

Ulf talks with the stone mason. He explains the job the mason is to do, using the small plot of land Ulf buys in the village not far from the church.

He talks with Father Timan, and he sometimes sails with the men when they fish. He sails in Maedoc's boat, and the two are good friends. Little Ulf and young Sten fish with the men as well. Maedoc tells Ulf that his youngest son Eogan fishes but also carves stone. Ulf talks with Eogan to carve runes when the stone mason's work is done.

Their days take on a sameness. Ulf and Aoife walk up the hill each day and sit in the grass, sometimes with the boys and sometimes alone. Ulf walks the shore with Father Timan and Maedoc, but he spends much time each day with Little Ulf and young Sten, talking and teaching, and hearing their talk. He sees Aoife is right; Little Ulf has his father's serious demeanor. He sometimes sees himself as a young man.

Ulf writes letters to his children in Trondelag and the Dane Land. The letters are taken to the south island and go when a boat sails to Trondelag.

Four moons pass, and Ulf harvests the garden. He and the boys work with the village to harvest the commons. He never knows a life so simple, a time when each sun is welcomed as a friend.

Aoife and Ailidh work to store food for the winter.

It is a winter day without snow when Little Ulf asks his father to walk with him along the shore. Ulf walks with patience. He speaks of the island and the house, some repairs for the church, and other things. He knows his son has something to say but finds the words hard. He waits.

"Papa," Little Ulf says, "I find the girl my heart aches for."

"Yes?"

"It is Ailidh, Papa."

"And what does Ailidh think?"

Little Ulf pulls his furs closer to ward off the chill. Ulf sees he is as tall as his father.

"She aches in her heart for me, too, Papa, but she is afraid. She is there to help Mama, and she thinks I am too highborn for her. I tell her that with Christ it is no matter who is highborn and who is not. I say I am not to be a king, so no councils or nobles have a say. And if they did, it still does not matter."

"You love this girl, Little Ulf?"

"With all my heart, Papa. I want my life with her."

"You have my blessing, son, and I think you have your mother's blessing as well. You talk with Maedoc and get his blessing as well."

"Yes, Papa, I talk with Maedoc. But I have your blessing first."

Little Ulf embraces his father.

That night, Aoife and Ulf lie together to sleep, warmed by the furs and the fire. The wind howls and the snow falls.

"Tomorrow, Aoife," Ulf says, "Little Ulf will ask Maedoc's blessing to wed Ailidh. I give him my blessing."

"I see the looks he gives her and the gentleness he shows her," she says, "and I wonder. She is not highborn, but she is highborn in spirit. She is one to give him love and many sons and daughters."

Ulf chuckles. "And after the sons and daughters, she still gives him love." He pulls her to him.

"You, my husband, never change. I like that."

Ulf and his son walk down to the village to see Maedoc. They find him on the shore, mending a net.

"A cold day to mend a net, Maedoc," Ulf says.

Maedoc grins. "Yes, Ulf, but when a wife is angry, it is not so cold on the shore."

Ulf laughs with him. "My son wants to speak to you."

"Maedoc," Little Ulf says, "I ask your blessing to wed Ailidh, to ask her if she marries me. I will provide for her and care for her all of her life. It is my promise to you."

Maedoc, mouth agape, stares from son to father.

"This has my blessing, Maedoc," Ulf says, "and Aoife's."

"It has my blessing as well," Maedoc says. "You honor us. You honor my family."

"It speaks much of your family, Maedoc," Ulf says, "that this son of mine loves your Ailidh. Now, I bring a jar of mead. And three cups."

The wedding of Ailidh and Little Ulf is in the spring. Father Timan says the rites. The people of the village are witnesses and celebrate.

Young Sten moves into the small room by the kitchen. Little Ulf brings Ailidh to his room in his father's house.

Weeks later, on a cool night, Ulf is almost asleep when Aoife nudges him.

"What?"

"They are noisy," she says.

"And we are not noisy when we are young?" Ulf says.

"Ulf!"

"Aoife, it takes children for a man and his wife to learn silence when they lie together."

She giggles. "You never change."

In mid-summer, Little Ulf and Ailidh tell their parents she is with child. The birth is in the spring.

"Ulf," Aoife says, "I see the birth of my youngest's first child, but I do not think I see much beyond."

Through the fall and winter, Ulf watches Aoife fade. The walks up the hillside stop, and she stays close to the hut. Now she sits by the fire, talking with Ailidh about babies and family and stories of Little Ulf as a boy.

Ulf feels his own decline. He lives longer than Aoife, but he knows by not much. They both determine to see the baby born.

In early spring, young Sten runs for the midwife and Ailidh's mother Sif. Aoife sits with Ailidh, placing cool cloths on her head and helping her to breathe with the pain. Ulf, Maedoc, and young Sten sit by the fire, while Little Ulf paces with the moans and cries of his wife. Ulf watches his son's lips move in prayer.

They hear the baby's cry. Little Ulf rushes to the room. Ailidh is tired but well, Sif weeps, his mother holds the baby.

"Little Ulf," Aoife says, "come hold your son. What is his name?"

Little Ulf looks at Ailidh, and she answers. "Papa is Ulf, my husband is Ulf, and no one else in my husband's family. Our son is also Ulf."

Aoife smiles. "Little Ulf, tell your Papa to come see his new grandson."

Aoife grows weaker through the spring. Now she stays in their bed. Ulf hires another village girl to help Ailidh with his grandson and Aoife with her illness.

"Does young Sten think of marriage?" Ulf says to his son. "He takes no interest in the girls here."

"He has a girl in Trondelag, Papa," Little Ulf says. "She lives on a farm. They meet when he visits with his mother. She pledges to wait for him, and he pledges to wait for her."

"Perhaps we tell him he returns now?"

"Papa, he does not return until his work is done here. It is his promise to his father."

Aoife mostly sleeps now. She wakes for Ulf to spoon soup in her mouth. Ulf's body weakens. He still walks to the village, but he moves slowly.

Walking with Little Ulf, he tells his son that his mother's time is soon, and his will be right after.

"But Papa, you are strong today."

"I am strong today for your Mama. I pass blood, son. It is not good. "

That night, Ulf lies by his wife, listening to her hard breaths. Suddenly, she sits up. "Ulf," she says, "remember always I love you. I cannot ask for better than you. God blesses me to be your wife." She looks at him closely. "You are not well, my husband."

"I follow not long after you, my wife. When you see the Christ, you say that He blesses Ulf, son of Erik, when He brings him Aoife."

She touches his face, and she falls back on the bed. Ulf knows she is gone. He kisses her and closes her eyes.

In the morning, Little Ulf finds his father in bed, holding the body of his mother.

"She is gone, Little Ulf,' he says. "The Christ calls her home."

The young man kneels by his father and weeps.

"I can go now in peace, Little Ulf," he says. "I see her through to the end. It is a promise I make to me, and a prayer I make to God. And He answers my prayer."

The women come to wash and prepare Aoife's body. It is dressed and taken to the stone tomb Ulf has the stone mason prepare. Eogan carves the runes on the tomb. The heavy stone is in place, with an opening for the bodies. Ulf tells Little Ulf how they are to be adorned when both are in the tomb. The young man weeps but nods. "Make sure to bury this blue stone around my neck with me," Ulf says. "I wear it all the days I marry, the gift from your mother."

That night, Ulf refuses his meal and takes to his bed. He asks to hold the baby Ulf a last time. "Little Ulf, you tell this boy that his grandparents live to see him, that he gives them life and they live through him. Tell him to honor his name and his parents, and to love the Christ."

"Yes, Papa."

"Young Sten, when you return to Trondelag, you tell your father he is always my true friend, and we always share one heart."

Young Sten nods, tears in his eyes.

445

"Little Ulf," Ulf says, "you are no longer Little Ulf. You are now my son Ulf, a man with a wife and son. May your Ailidh bless you with more sons and daughters. Ailidh, Ulf loves and honors you all the days of your life, because that is how he is made. And I know you love and honor him all the days of his life."

Ulf coughs. "And now, my son Ulf will sit with me while I sleep." Ailidh takes the baby from him, and she and young Sten leave the room.

Ulf sits by his father's bedside, his young hand on his father's old one. Hours pass, and he hears his father's breathing gradually slow.

Suddenly, his father opens his eyes, grips his son's hand, and speaks.

"Serve the Christ, Ulf. Serve the Christ." And then he passes. The son closes the father's eyes.

In the morning at the tomb, Father Timan speaks the rites for Ulf and Aoife. The people of the village gather alongside. When the priest finishes, the villagers walk quietly back to their homes, followed by the priest. Young Sten lowers Ulf into the grave, and Ulf adorns the bodies of his mother and father as his father says. Young Sten helps him up from the grave, and then the carpenters, the stone mason, and Eogan, two bulls tied with ropes all pull the top stone in place over the tomb.

As they leave, Ulf runs his fingers over the runes carved by Eogan.

Ulf, Son of Erik, and Aoife, daughter of Braden, One in Life, One in Death, One in Christ.

The End

Acknowledgements

Dancing Prince, the last in the *Dancing Priest* series, is the story that wasn't supposed to be written. It began as something completely different, but one character, Thomas Kent-Hughes, kept sticking his head in the story. I finally gave him a small part as something of a sop, to get him out of my head. It was all he needed. From there he took over, making the novel his story.

Events in the year 2002 were the inspiration for this series of stories about Michael Kent-Hughes. In early May of that year, I found myself in Eastern Europe for a week, part of a three-person mission team with an unusual purpose. Our job was to visit missionaries in Budapest, Prague, Brno, Dresden, and the Dresden suburb of Pirna and interview them. We would then create a series of stories and videos to help illustrate our denomination's overall mission in the region and provide tools for the missionaries to use in raising support.

Our itinerary was packed. Before we left, our church missions coordinator told us to be prepared for God to change the itinerary, even as planned and packed as it was. The day we left St. Louis, we saw on TV monitors at the airport that a shooting had occurred at a high school in Erfurt, Germany; 13 students and staff had died. For us, at that moment, it was simply a tragic news story.

When we arrived in Budapest, we were told that "it had been decided" that we would also be going to Erfurt. We found a way to work it into our travel plans. When we arrived in the Erfurt area and left the autobahn, we were met by a young pastor, waiting on the side of the road. I rode in his car, and the team car followed. He took us to his church, a small building that had once been a Communist Party social hall (yes, we liked the irony of it).

The pastor had been ministering almost without rest to grieving parents, students, and staff for three days. People higher than him or us had decided he needed to be interviewed. And so we set up the camera, and I began to ask questions. We weren't far into the discussion when I realized that he needed more than an interview; he needed to be ministered to. Something completely unexpected happened; before any of us realized what was going on, we found ourselves overwhelmed, with tears on our cheeks. The minister, the cameraman, and I were all affected the same way; we had clearly experienced a presence.

In October, I flew to San Francisco for an industry conference, and during the flight I heard a song in Italian that wouldn't leave my head. It evoked an image of a priest dancing barefoot on a beach. That was the beginning of what would eventually becoming *Dancing Priest*, the first novel, almost a decade later. What I didn't realize until very recently was that the young minister in Erfurt, dealing with a tragedy, would be the inspiration for Michael Kent-Hughes. Like a young minister dealing with a tragedy, Michael Kent-Hughes would be a young theology student, dealing with tragedy at the Olympics.

I didn't make the connection between the two until the late winter of 2020, some 18 years later. Writing can be a strange endeavor.

I have many people to thank, too many to list. At the top would be the people involved in the publication – Mark Sutherland of Dunrobin Publishing, (Carrie Sutherland and Jodi Richardson for proofreading and general reader responses), and Ryan Stiles, the cover designer for *Dancing King*, *Dancing Prophet*, and now *Dancing Prince*.

Many people have been faithful readers of the entire series, offering encouragement and support. You know who you are. And my family as well – son Travis and daughter-in-law Stephanie, with the three grandsons; and son Andrew, with Lucy and Petey, his Boston terriers. And Janet, my wife, who's lived this story as much as I have, and put up with a totally focused husband working at the manuscript, including his grumpy moods.

The end of a series of novels is always a time to take stock, consider the past and plan for the future. The story of Michael Kent-Hughes could have gone on, but I sensed the need to bring it all to a close. Other stories, and other books, are in my head, and it's time to give Michael a well-earned rest, even if the parting is a bit bittersweet.

Most of all: Soli Deo Gloria.

About the Author

Glynn Young is the author of the five *Dancing Priest* novels: *Dancing Priest*, *A Light Shining*, *Dancing King*, *Dancing Prophet*, and now *Dancing Prince*. He's also the author of the non-fiction book Poetry at Work. An award-winning speechwriter and public relations executive, he was named a Fellow of the Public Relations Society of America in 2005 and a member of the St. Louis Media Hall of Fame in 2009.

A native of New Orleans, Glynn received his B.A. degree in journalism from Louisiana State University in Baton Rouge (home, he is quick to note, of the 2020 national football collegiate champions, the LSU Tigers). He received a Masters in Liberal Arts degree from Washington University in St. Louis.

He is a contributing editor to the online poetry journal Tweetspeak Poetry (tweetspeakpoetry.com) and has blogged at Faith, Fiction, Friends (faithfictionfriends.blogpost.com) since 2009. You can learn more information about his books at dancingpriest.com.

Glynn and his wife Janet live in suburban St. Louis. They have two adult sons, Travis and Andrew; a daughter-in-law, Stephanie; and three grandsons, Cameron, Caden, and Jacob.

CPSIA information can be obtained
at www.ICGtesting.com
Printed in the USA
BVHW080915220620
582039BV00001B/13